U0469501

SHANGHAI
THROUGH
OUR EYES

百年大党：
老外讲故事

上海市人民政府新闻办公室 编

上海文艺出版社

content　目 录

▼

Preface	8	序	
Using the camera to show the world a real China : Malcolm Clarke	17	柯文思：用镜头向世界展现一个真实的中国	
Shanghai is one of the most innovative cities in the world : Sylvain Laurent	21	罗熙文：上海是全球最具创新力城市之一	
I think Shanghai is the best place to live in the world : Julian Blissett	25	柏历：我觉得上海是世界上最宜居的城市	
I truly respect those Party members in our team : Oscar	29	奥斯卡：我们队里的一些球员是党员，我特别尊重他们	
Without a powerful government, China wouldn't be able to truly develop : Simon Lichtenberg	33	李曦萌：没有一个很强的政府，没办法让中国真正发展起来	
Ordinary Chinese people all have smiles on their faces : Nusrat Marat	37	白马克：中国的老百姓脸上都挂着笑容	
I'm willing to root in Shanghai and commit myself to smart manufacturing : HIROSHI INUI	41	乾浩史：我愿扎根上海，深耕"上海智造"	
China is full of vigor and vitality : Javier Gimeno	45	孟昊文：中国社会释放出一股强大的活力	
Shanghai has a superb business environment : Allan Gabor	49	安高博：上海有着超一流的营商环境	
China is most active and successful in energy saving and emission reduction : Caspar Chiquet	53	西克：节能减排，中国非常积极与成功	
The security in Shanghai makes me feel safe : Roman Kupper	57	罗曼：上海的治安让我很有安全感	
Fast-growing Internet industry makes life easy and fun : Magand Lucine	61	李希：互联网的发展让现在的生活新鲜有趣又便捷	
I'm not only exploring the city of Shanghai, but also the world as a whole : Evangelos Tatsis	65	艾维他：我不仅是在探索上海这座城市，更是在探索世界	
Staying true to her original aspiration as a doctor in her second hometown : Wonsook Hong	69	洪原淑：在第二故乡，守护"大长今"的初心	
Shanghai is a welcoming smart city : Rajnish Sharma	73	沙睿杰："智慧城市"上海是热情的	
I love to measure every inch of Shanghai with my steps : Francois Tardif	77	唐德福：我喜欢用脚步去丈量上海的点滴	
With the film industry going strong, Shanghai is driving forward like a high-speed train : Miodrag Colombo	81	Mio：发展电影工业，上海像一辆高速列车	
Shanghai oozes warmth; it will continue to thrive : Chen-Jiang PHUA	87	潘正锵：上海迸发着热情，一定会继续腾飞！	
We give off the "warmth" of Shanghai with our service : Tarik Temucin	91	塔里克·铁穆青：我们用服务传递上海的"温度"	
Both my father and I witnessed Shanghai's transformation over the past 30 years : Upadhyaya Nagendra Rijal	95	那哲：我们父子两代人见证上海三十年变迁	
My love for Shanghai grows stronger as time passes : Gordon Boo	99	巫国端：时光经年，对上海的爱正浓	

In Shanghai, I'm enveloped in warmth	Akiko Tomonari	103	友成晓子：我在上海，被暖意包围
Shanghai people are open-minded	Martin Wawra	107	华伟廷：上海人的思想非常开放
I always feel refreshed by the bright sky and the clean air	Nicolas Poirot	111	柏昊天：明亮的蓝天和优质的空气总是令我神清气爽
A Love for Shanghai starts with food	Takumi Kato	115	加藤巧：爱上海从美食开始
Shanghai will take center stage in the global shipping industry	Claude Maillot	119	马优：未来航运业的主要舞台将是上海
Shanghai's scientific research is already among the best in the world	Jeremy Murray	123	杰睿：上海的科研水平已跻身国际一流
Shanghai is a sea of opportunities, brimming with life and hope	Lutz Frankholz	127	陆勋海：上海仿佛机遇之海，触目所及满是生机与希望
Carrying my ancestors' love for China to the next generation	Krupikova Oksana	131	奥克萨娜：将祖辈对中国的爱延续到下一代
I'm very glad to get the Foreign Permanent Resident ID Card and my dream of living in China for a long time has come true	Cameron Hume	135	何穆凯：很高兴拿到了永居证，长期在中国生活的梦想成真
China has made great progress in IP protection	Philippe Snel	139	施菲利：中国在保护知识产权方面取得了巨大进步
Shanghai embodies the spirit of the contract	Shin Hyungkwan	143	辛炯官：上海是一座很有契约精神的城市
I felt the considerate business-friendly service in Shanghai	DAIMON KAZUTO	149	大门和人：我感受到了上海贴心的营商服务
I think the achievement of Shanghai is just a beginning	Julie Laulusa	153	刘钰涓：我认为上海的成就还仅仅是一个开始
Permanent residence status gives me a sense of belonging in China	Owen K Messick	157	麦欧文：永久居留身份让我对中国更有归属感
My job every day was to serve well consumers in Shanghai	Jung Hwanuk	161	郑桓旭：我每天的工作就是服务好上海的消费者
I require that my child learn Chinese culture, because it will help his future development	Werner Gottschalk	165	高查克：我让孩子学习中国文化，这对他的未来会有很大帮助
I am very lucky to have achieved career development and met my love in Shanghai	Carsten Arntz	169	安克诚：非常幸运，我在上海事业进步，还收获了爱情
Many important events of my family took place in China	Richard Martin Saul	173	肖瑞强：我们家有不少人生重要时刻都是在中国发生
Shanghai is a kaleidoscope of the times, a century of silhouettes at a glance	Pilar Mejía Buenfil	177	逸馨：上海像支时代万花筒，一眼看尽百年剪影
I have a dream of training more brass talents for China	Alexander Filippov	181	萨沙：我有一个梦想，为中国培养更多的铜管乐人才
I love dumplings. Every Wednesday is "dumpling day" at my home	Alex Kopitsas	185	孔文卓：我喜欢饺子，每周三是我们家的"饺子日"

English	Name	Page	Chinese
I like Shanghai because it is a city with a soul	Jean-Etienne Gourgues	189	高晟天：喜欢上海，因为这是一座有灵魂的城市
I'm a pilot who looks forward to flying China-made planes around the world	Diego Benedetto	193	Diego：身为机长，我期待驾驶中国制造的飞机飞往世界各地
French Chef in love with Chinese Cuisine	Corentin Delcroix	197	戴广坦：爱上中餐的法国厨师
I hope more foreign friends come to Shanghai and experience China's social development	Adachi Ken	201	安达谦：希望更多外国朋友来上海，感受中国社会发展的成果
I became a veteran online shopper in Shanghai	Divine TUNUNGINI Kiese	205	刘迪心：我在上海成了名副其实的"网购达人"
I'm a fan of China	Doruk Keser	209	天山：我是一个中国迷
I have a yearning for the future of Shanghai sports and hope to work miracles of my own	Jimmer Fredette	213	吉默·弗雷戴特：我憧憬上海体育的未来，希望创造属于自己的奇迹
When I was 16 years old, I witnessed the historical moment of Shanghai's liberation	Betty Barr	217	白丽诗：16岁那年，我见证了上海解放的历史瞬间
I am a "dream promoter" in Shanghai	Luuk Eliens	225	陆可：我在上海当"梦想推手"
Quality is always the most important concern for doing a good job in the Chinese market	Nishimura Takashi	229	西村隆：做好中国市场，品质永远是最重要的
I hope to make my Chinese students more creative and responsible	Naomie Fortin	233	Naomie：我希望让我的中国学生们更富创造力，更具责任感
In Shanghai, I feel closer to my dream	A.A.M. Muzahid	237	安东尼：在上海，我感觉自己离梦想更近了
Shanghai's vibrant research environment attracts talents from all over the world	Laurent Kneip	241	康智文：上海蓬勃的科研环境吸引着全球的优秀人才
We hope to foster the children's sense of identity and make them aware that they are Chinese and shall cherish their country	Abbigael Clarissa Ford	245	小艾：我们培养孩子们的身份认同感，让他们知道要爱护自己的国家
I am almost a Pudong native now, and I express my love for Shanghai with music	Michael Kruppe	249	迈克尔：我是半个浦东人，用音乐来表达对上海的爱
Shanghai people are very satisfied with and proud of the local medical system	Alaeddin Ahram	253	安明德：上海人对本地的医疗保健水平感到十分满意与自豪
I've made many discoveries since I chose China as my "research subject"	Tolza Simon	257	西蒙：把中国作为"研究对象"后，我有了很多发现
Shanghai has translated into reality its Expo vision "Better City, Better Life"	Peter Cuthbert	261	裴文德：上海实现了2010年世博会时的主题——城市，让生活更美好！
Sanofi located its China headquarters in Shanghai because of its top-notch business environment	Pius S. Hornstein	265	贺恩霆：基于一流的营商环境，赛诺菲将中国总部设在上海
I'm a witness to China-Hungary friendship, and I might stay here longer	Back István	269	贝思文：我是中匈两国友好情谊的见证者，我会在上海停留更久……
My pastries and ice cream are beloved in Shanghai	Anne-Catherine HACHET ep. GUILLOUX	273	Anne-Catherine：我研发的点心和冰激凌深受上海人喜爱

Developing amazingly, Shanghai is a city that never sleeps : Thomas Och	277	托马斯·奥赫：上海是一个不夜城，发展得让人难以置信
I am "Western Lei Feng" in Pudong and the neighborhood committee has set up the "Huhndorf Volunteers Studio" in my name : Ralph Huhndorf	281	亨多福：我是浦东"洋雷锋"，居委会以我的名义成立了志愿者工作室
My happy time with "Maradona" in Shanghai : Franka Gulin	285	古兰兰：我和"马拉多纳"在上海的快乐时光
Chinese contemporary art industry is developing rapidly : Enrico Polato	293	里柯：中国当代艺术行业的发展非常迅猛
We started a blood donation volunteer team of expats in Shanghai : Maskay	297	阿思势：我们在上海组建了一个外籍献血志愿者团队
Shanghai is already the world's biggest port and China is our future : Mario MORETTI	301	马里奥：上海已经是世界上最大的港口，中国就是我们的未来
It is enviable to work in Shanghai : Juergen Beck	305	耕贝克：到上海工作，是令人羡慕的
There are many reasons to love Shanghai, a city filled with warmth : Shimizu Yasumasa	309	清水泰雅：爱上海的理由有很多，这是一座有温度的城市
I expect that it's the Chinese who will leave a footprint on the Moon again : Adam Strzep	313	亚当斯：我期待是中国人再次在月球上留下足迹
My family and friends were lost for words when I showed them my photos of Shanghai : Andrea Calducci	317	杜安德：当我把拍摄的上海的景象发给亲友，他们都震惊到说不出话来
Telling Shanghai stories with animation : Shawn Patrick Tilling	321	尚希林：用动画短片讲好上海故事
Shanghai's garbage sorting is a success : Marie Harder	325	玛丽·哈德：上海垃圾分类的效果是成功的
Shanghai and China have become the driving force for the development of the world fashion industry : Yann Bozec	331	杨葆焱：上海乃至中国正成为世界时尚产业发展的驱动力量
The huge advantage of the current Chinese political system is that it allows long-term plans : Javier Nieto	335	聂威尔：中国政治制度巨大的优势是可以做很长远的规划
Education in Shanghai is getting more inclusive : Lisa Martel De Santis Chisholm	339	丽莎·奇泽姆：上海的教育正变得更加包容
Looking for suitable labs in the world, I set my sights on Shanghai : Andre Rosendo	343	Andre Rosendo：放眼全球寻找合适的实验室，我把目光锁定了上海
I can't just take, I have to do as much as I can to give back to Shanghai : Amir Khan	347	阿米尔·汗：我不能光索取，也要尽可能为上海做点什么
Shanghai is working hard to become "the capital of global eSports," and I want to bring my girlfriend to China to show her all this : Fred Moynan	351	莫磊：上海打造"全球电竞之都"，我想把女友带来中国向她展示这一切
I enjoyed cycling along Nanchang Road to learn more about China and the Communist Party of China : Harmen Dubbelaar	355	哈曼：我常常喜欢沿着南昌路一路骑行，了解中国、了解中国共产党
You can feel the happiness of Chinese people in my paintings that are full of scenes of everyday life : Lucie Guyard	359	Lucie：你可以从我那些充满烟火气的画里，感知到中国人当下的幸福生活
The wisdom and determination of the Communist Party of China are very impressive : Gerd Knaust	363	格德·克瑙斯特：中国共产党的智慧和决心让人印象深刻

I begin to understand today's China once I have understood the CPC	Benjamin Travis Wood	367	本杰明：读懂了中国共产党，我就读懂了今天的中国
My father-in-law has been a Party member for many years and I have a deep bond Communist Party of China	Kris Van Goethem	371	柯瑞斯：我的岳父是一名老党员，我和中国共产党之间有一份深厚的感情
China is the right role model in fighting against the pandemic	Alex Szilasi	375	Alex：中国在抗击疫情方面是正确的榜样
The lovely and warm people in Shanghai made me feel at home	Astrid Poghosyan	379	马星星：可爱又温暖的上海人，让我找到了家的感觉
The government has strongly supported the development of enterprises, and I have also become a "river chief" to participate in social governance	Harald Sturm	383	史东：政府有力支撑了企业发展，我也当起了"河长"参与社会治理
Shanghai has become a world-class art center and it is inspiring to see the arts thriving here	Geoffrey Alan Rhodes	387	陆高安：上海已成世界级艺术中心，艺术在这里繁荣发展，令人振奋
I feel Shanghai's life and history through the novels of local writers	Lena Scheen	391	沈雷娜：通过本土作家的小说来感受上海的生活和历史
For any global leading company that wants to keep its position, it must join the Chinese market	Denis Depoux	395	戴璞：如果一家公司想要保持全球巨头的地位，就要加入中国市场
In Shanghai, I'm always enveloped in a strong atmosphere of innovation	Marc Jaffré	399	马锦睿：身处上海，我总是被浓浓的创新氛围萦绕
I make online videos so that everybody will know more about China	Lila	403	星悦：我在互联网上通过视频让大家更了解中国
It is a miracle that China has developed to the level it has, but the Chinese have made it happen	Noyan Rona	407	诺扬：中国发展到现在这个水平是一个奇迹，但中国人把这个奇迹做出来了
My favorite place to play as a professional eSports player is Shanghai	SONG UIJIN	411	宋义进：作为一名职业电竞选手，我最爱在上海比赛
Leaning against the window of Shanghai Tower I designed, I have a panoramic view of the city	Marshall Strabala	415	马溯：我在自己设计的上海中心大厦倚窗而望，城市景象尽收眼底
I see a harmonious development between people and nature in Shanghai	Kamran Vossoughi	419	伟书杰：在上海我看到了人与自然之间的和谐发展
Seeing the future in Shanghai, the future of a dynamic modern metropolis	Paul Devlin	423	德林：在上海看见未来，一个充满活力的现代城市的未来
Over the past 20 years, L'Oréal has witnessed the gradual realization of a "better life" for Chinese people	Fabrice Megarbane	427	费博瑞：20多年来，欧莱雅见证中国人一步步实现"美好生活"

序

我很高兴讲一讲我对《百年大党——老外讲故事》的感受。

这个节目在网上播出后,我一有时间就会看。中国故事大家都在讲,但如何让听故事的人有收获,这并不容易。

这些老外为什么讲得好,能让中外人士都很喜欢?也许是因为他们和我们的文化背景不同。他们是外国人,但大多有长期在中国生活和工作的体验,他们很理解中外思维的差异。我们讲故事,外国人听起来可能会感到隔阂或感觉生硬,但老外讲故事能从比较的视角,发现更多外国人感兴趣的细节。

《老外讲故事》节目另一个成功点在于,讲故事的人是多样的。他们中有企业家、工程师、艺术家、普通旅行者,有刚来上海的年轻人,也有长期在上海生活几十年的老人……他们从不同视角描述自己喜欢的上海。这样的故事中国人看了也颇有收获,知道外国人喜欢我们什么,或不甚喜欢我们什么;外国人看了也觉得有启示:原来中国和某些媒体讲述的不一样,原来中国是这样地在进步。

这一百个故事,都是从上海看中国,这个角度也很有意思。上海是中国最大的经济中心城市,位于中国沿海经济发达地区和长江流域发达地区的交汇点上,她的发展代表了中国的发展进程。在这里,你可以用更短的时间读懂中国,看到中国的方向和未来。

我的老朋友基辛格博士曾经多次来到上海。当时我是浦东新区开发的主要执行者,我对他谈上海的规划、上海的前途。他很冷静,说要观察。不久之后,他说,浦东开发不像西方说的,只是一个口号,只是一种宣传。你们是行动,你们会成功。

经过 30 多年的建设，浦东已经由农村变成了一个现代化城市。黄浦江两岸的建筑在风格样式、建造年代等方面相距甚远，但都赫赫有名，都带着上海变迁的时代印记。认真观察的人，无论他有怎样的意识形态，都会有一个问题：中国为什么发展这么快？

　　大家的回答可能不一样。但是看了《老外讲故事》，我发现这些外国人的回答倾向于一致：这里有一个中国共产党，她的决策指明了方向，中国人民的理想，他们的追求和共产党的决策高度吻合，因此人民愿意去努力，愿意发挥他们的聪明才智，这种领导力量和公众意志的高度一致，是中国飞速发展的最重要原因。

　　显然《老外讲故事》还有很多潜力可以挖，希望策划者继续努力。目前讲故事的老外，都是来到中国、对中国有直接观察的人，更多的外国人并没来中国，他们是通过各自的媒体观察中国。这个节目怎么能更大范围传播到没来过中国的，但对中国有兴趣的人们那里？100 位老外也许能出点主意呢。今天的中国还有很多不足之处，也会有外国人还不赞成的地方，我们欢迎指出，也欢迎批评。

　　1999 年在上海开财富论坛时，我曾和 CNN 创始人特纳（Ted Turner）说过，如果你到上海来拍一个纪录片，用 7 分钟的时间拍它的垃圾，用 3 分钟的时间拍它街头的鲜花，人家会觉得上海是个垃圾太多的城市，这就是时间和空间的处理出了问题。他同意我这个比喻。我们不回避中国有的地方垃圾清理得不及时，但我们更希望被看到的是，我们正在克服这些缺点。

　　所以外国人如果只是通过媒体来了解中国，很容易片面，这也是为什么我们要通过更多的途径向世界讲述中国故事。我们并不是在做 Propoganda（其实这个英文词和中文的"宣传"在很大程度并不对应），也不愿意一味地说教、讲理论。理论背后如果没有故事，理论也是空洞的，尤其很难被外国人理解。唯有真实的故事，真实的感受，才能得出真实的结论。所以我们要把中国呈现给世界，Present China to the World，原来是怎么样就是怎么样。

　　中国共产党今年已经成立 100 周年了。大多数人的生命都没有 100 年，像我今年已经 81 岁了，也能回忆很长的一段了：新中国成立以后的道路是曲折的，曾长期受到过一些西方国家的威胁，但我们始终保持一种坚韧的意志，不仅战胜困难、赢得发展，也获得了很多外国朋友的理解和支持。

　　对于这些朋友的理解，我们觉得很温暖，也希望不断加深这种理解，找到更多朋友。所以，讲中国故事是个长期的事，不仅自己要讲，也希望更多外国人来讲。我会做这些故事最忠实的听众。

赵启正
中共十六届中央委员
上海市原副市长
国务院新闻办公室原主任
第十一届全国政协外委会主任
2021 年 7 月 1 日

Preface

I am very glad to say a few words about my feeling towards "Shanghai through Our Eyes."

Since its release online, I would try to watch the program clips whenever possible. China's stories are being told by many people, but it's not easy to make the listeners feel rewarding.

Why can these Laowai (a friendly reference to foreigners) tell good stories that have been well received among Chinese and international audiences? Perhaps it's because their cultural background is different from ours. They come from all over the world, but most of them have long experience of living and working in China, which helps them better understand the Chinese and foreign differences in thinking. When we tell stories, it may sound odd or feel blunt for foreigners. But when Laowai tell stories from a comparative perspective, they can discover more attractive details foreigners are interested in.

Another success factor of the series "Shanghai through Our Eyes" lies in the diversity of storytellers. They include entrepreneurs, engineers, artists, ordinary travelers, young people who have just arrived in Shanghai, as well as elderly people who have lived here for decades .... They describe the Shanghai city that they love from their different perspectives. Their stories are also rewarding for Chinese people when they watch, because we can learn what foreigners like and also what they don't like so much about us; foreign viewers also find these stories enlightening as China turns out to be different from what some media have described and the country is in fact making progress in such a way.

These one hundred stories all look at today's China from Shanghai, which is a fascinating perspective. As China's largest economic center, Shanghai is situated at the intersection of China's economically developed coastal region and the Yangtze River belt, and its growth epitomizes the course of China's development. Here you can better understand China in a shorter time and foresee the country's direction and future.

My old friend Dr. Kissinger has visited Shanghai many times. As the major executive official of Pudong New Area development, I talked to him about Shanghai's planning and future blueprint. He remained calm and said he needed observation.

Shortly afterwards, he said that the development of Pudong was not just a slogan, or a publicity stunt as claimed by the West. What you did was substantial actions, so you would succeed.

After more than 30 years of development, Pudong has been transformed from a rural area into a modern urban district. The buildings on both sides of the Huangpu River are remarkably unique in styles and historic periods, but they are all iconic and bear the marks of vicissitudes in the history of Shanghai. A serious observer, no matter what his ideological background is, cannot help asking one question: why is China developing so fast?

People may have different answers. But after watching "Shanghai through Our Eyes," I discover a convergence in the answers of these foreigners: there is a Communist Party in China, and her decisions point out the direction. The aspirations and pursuits of the Chinese people are highly consistent with the decisions of the Communist Party. Therefore, people are willing to work hard and unleash their creativity. The high degree of consistency between the leadership power and the public aspiration is the most important reason for China's exponential growth.

It is clear that there is still a lot of potential to be explored in "Shanghai through Our Eyes" and I hope the planners will continue to make efforts. At present, all the foreign storytellers have arrived in China and have direct observations of the country; but many more foreigners have not been to China and they can only see through their own media channels. How can this program be widely distributed to people who are interested in China but have never been here? These one hundred foreigners might contribute some ideas. In today's China, a number of places may still be unsatisfactory, and there may be things that foreigners do not yet agree with. We are open to suggestions as well as criticism.

During the Shanghai Fortune Global Forum in 1999, I said to Mr. Ted Turner, the founder of CNN, that if you came to Shanghai to make a documentary and spent seven minutes shooting rubbish and three minutes on the flowers on the streets, people would think that Shanghai was a city with too much rubbish. The misleading impression was created by the mishandling of time and space. He agreed with my analogy. We don't shy away from the fact that there are places in China where rubbish is not removed in a timely manner, but we prefer to be seen as a country taking measures to overcome these flaws.

So if foreigners only learn about China through media, it is easy for them to get an incomplete picture, which is why we have to tell China's stories to the world through more channels. We are not doing Propaganda (In fact, this English word does not correspond to the Chinese word "propaganda" to a considerable extent), nor do we want to be preachy and theoretical. Theories with no stories are hollow and especially difficult for foreigners to understand. Only true stories and true feelings can lead to true conclusions. That is why we want to present China to the world as it is.

The Communist Party of China has celebrated its 100th anniversary this year. Most people cannot live for 100 years, and for a person like me, who is 81 years old this year, I can recall a long memory: the road has been tortuous that the People's Republic of China went through since its founding, and the country has been threatened by some Western countries for a considerable period of time. But we have maintained a strong resilience these years, which helped us in overcoming difficulties and winning development opportunities, and gaining the understanding and support of many foreign friends.

The understanding of these friends gives us warmth and should be deepened. We should make more friends. So telling China's stories is a long-term task; not only do we need to tell them ourselves, but hopefully more foreigners will also join us. I will be the most faithful listener of these stories.

Zhao Qizheng

Member of the 16th CPC Central Committee
Former Vice Mayor of Shanghai
Former Director of the State Council Information Office
Chairman of Foreign Affairs Committee, the 11th CPPCC National Committee

July 1, 2021

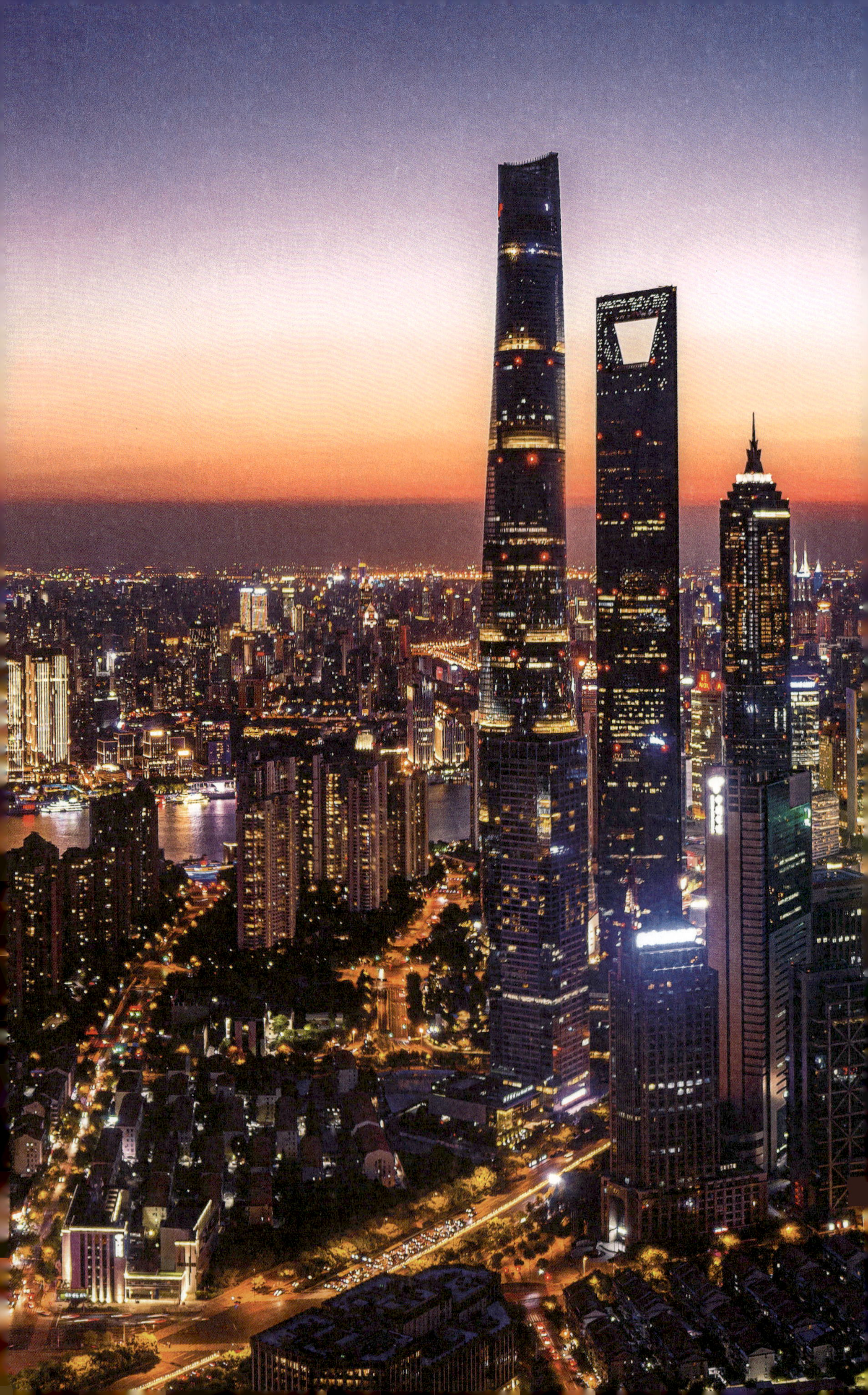

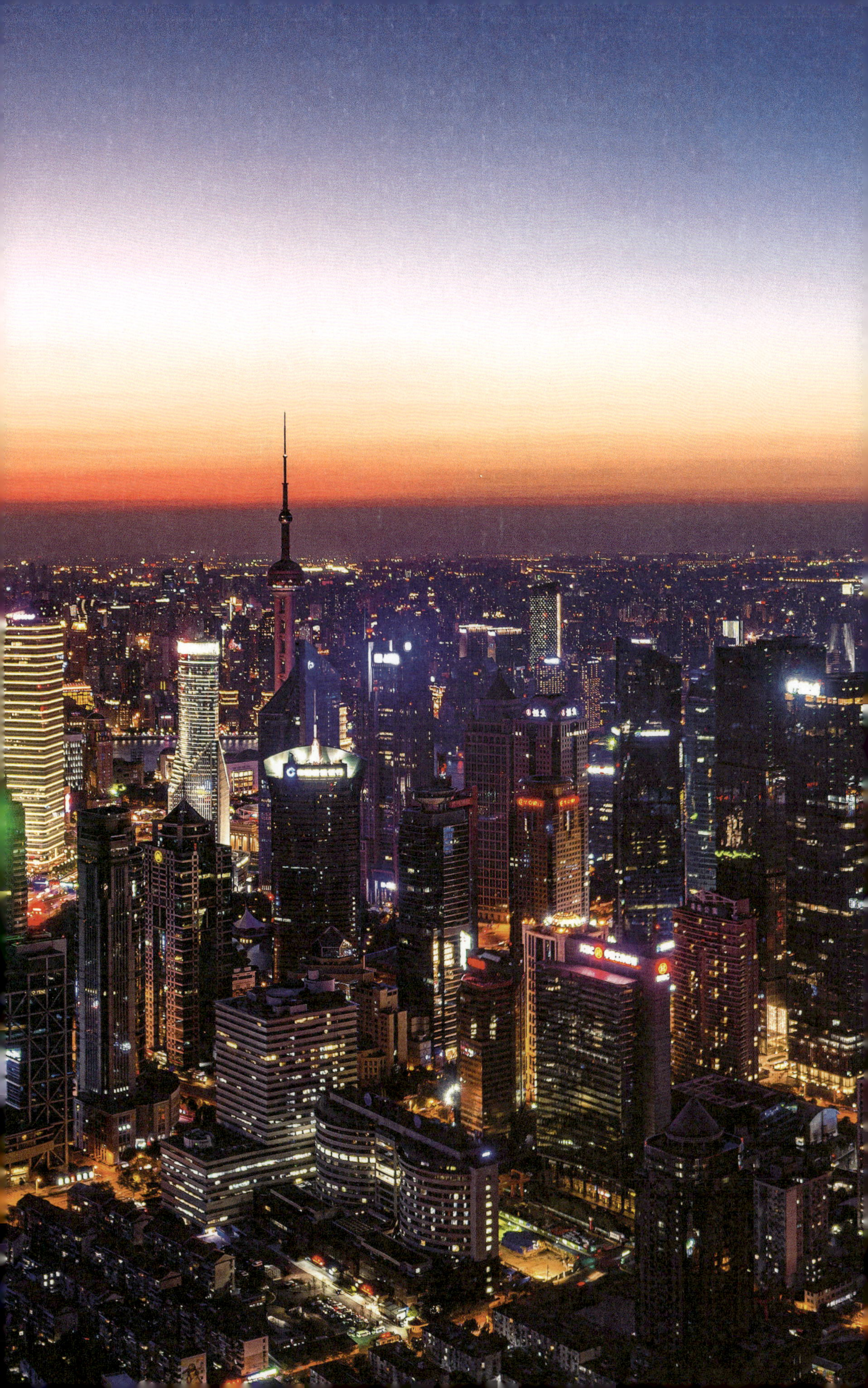

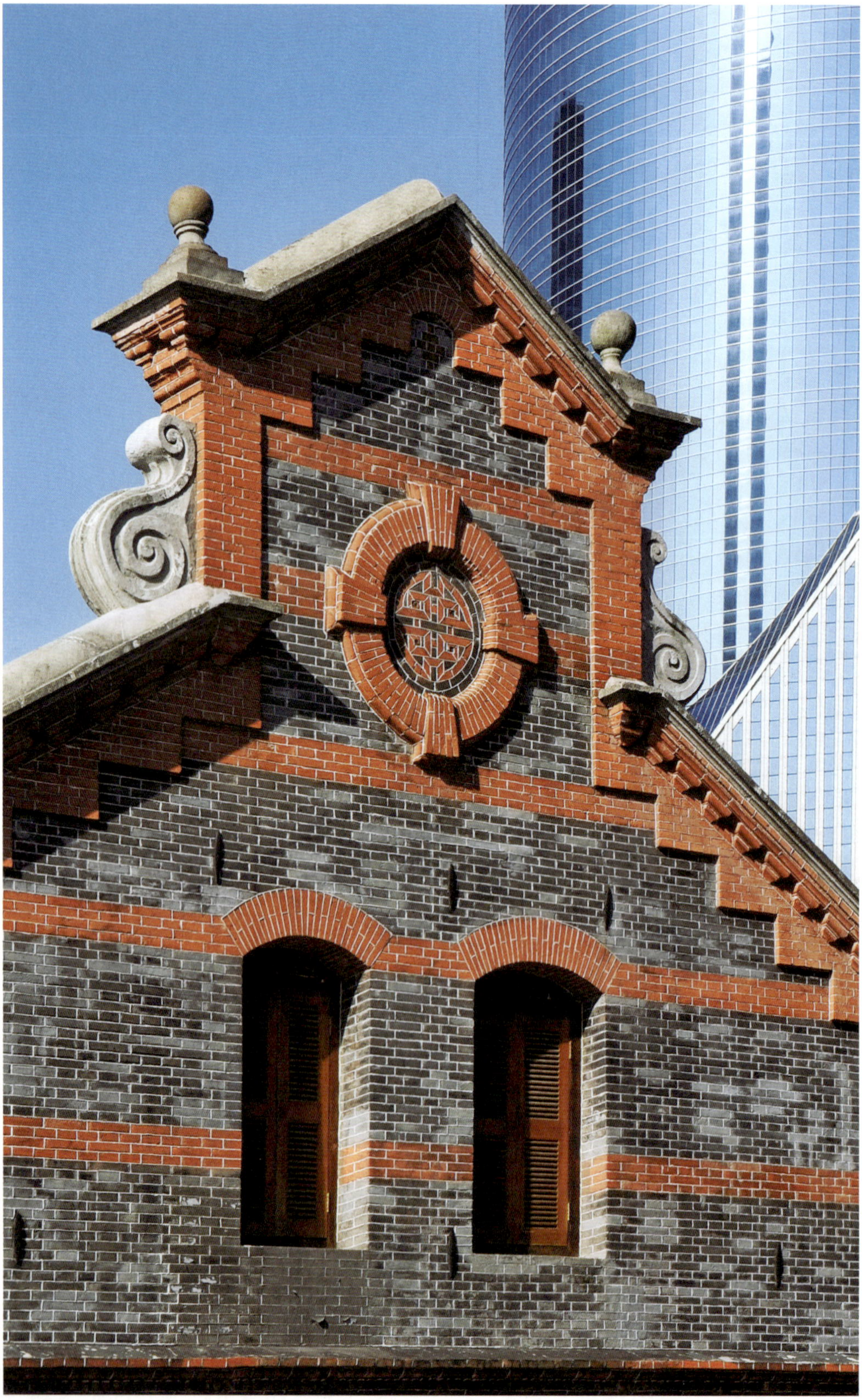

姓　名：Malcolm Clarke
中文名：柯文思
国　籍：英国
职　位：电影导演

柯文思：
用镜头向世界展现一个真实的中国

"中国的崛起"或者"中国的复兴"是21世纪最大且持续的新闻故事。

"那不是我看到的中国"

20世纪80年代，为了筹备一部纪录片，柯文思第一次来到中国，并在中国居住了九个月。因为接触到了真正的中国，自那时起，他就爱上了中国。柯文思能清晰地记得40年前的点滴，他回忆道："当时的外滩是一个非常特别的地方，它的一部分仍然是一个工作的码头，船只停泊在如今的和平饭店门口。"

此后，柯文思游历世界，在伦敦、纽约、洛杉矶等知名城市居住过，用镜头书写着他的电影人生，共获得4次奥斯卡提名，拿到过2座奥斯卡小金人、16座艾美奖奖杯。

看着西方媒体的报道，柯文思总觉得那不是他看到过的中国。慢慢地，他动了记录真实中国的念头。从2013年开始，柯文思将工作的重心放在了中国，并在中国拍摄电影。柯文思坦言对他来说，"中国的崛起"或者"中国的复兴"是二十一世纪最大且持续的新闻故事，"对于一个纪录片导演来说，这是一个绝佳的地方"。

"人们常说，如果一个人渴望看到未来，那么他应该去中国旅行。在很多方面，未来就是现在。没有任何一个国家能在如此短的时间内取得中国所取得的这些成就。"柯文思回忆道，自2013年起，他走遍了中国大多数省市，每到一处他都能看到巨大的挑战和发展的潜力。"所有人都在努力工作，他们都渴望建立一个更美好的未来。"

柯文思：

用镜头向世界展现
一个真实的中国

我在中国拍电影

历时五年打磨，2018年，柯文思导演的《善良的天使》在北京举办了国内的首映礼，这是一部以中美关系为题材的大型纪录电影。柯文思认为"需要一个从世界来观察中美关系背后普通人命运的视角"。

"然而该片在北美地区上映后，因为不符合美国一些人对中国的偏见认识，我们遭到了很多批评。"尽管如此，柯文思并不打算改变自己的目标——记录下真实的中国。

2019年，他又开始筹拍一部关于中国脱贫攻坚故事和小康生活的纪录片。众所周知，2020年是中国全面建成小康社会和"十三五"规划收官之年，也是脱贫攻坚决战决胜之年。"近6亿人摆脱了贫困，普及了识字率，中产人群迅速壮大，中国仅仅用了40年时间就实现了今天的成就，这确实令人震惊。"柯文思认为。

来沪四十年

"作为一个英国人，我对西方超级大国的兴衰比较了解。中国将塑造二十一世纪，这一点毫无疑问，我们只需要看看西方应对新冠肺炎疫情危机的方式就知道。西方一些国家的政府过于短视、傲慢，没有从中国的经验中学习。"柯文思感叹。

距第一次来沪已经40年过去了，如今定居在上海的柯文思仍旧最爱外滩，在他看来外滩是一个完美的地方，它静静述说着中国在过去100年间的进步和发展。从浦东看外滩和从外滩看浦东，有着不同的美景，诉说着不同的历史故事。

柯文思希望用他的镜头继续向世界展现一个真实的中国。

Name: Malcolm Clarke
Chinese name: 柯文思
Nationality: British
Position: Film director

Malcolm Clarke:
Using the camera to show the world a real China

> "The rise of China" or "the renaissance of China" is the biggest ongoing news story of the 21st century.

"That's not the China I've seen with my own eyes"

In the 1980s, Malcolm Clarke came to China for the first time for the preparation of a documentary film and lived here for nine months. As he got in touch with a real China, he fell in love with the country from then on. Clarke can clearly remember every moment 40 years ago. He recalls: "The Bund was a special place then. Part of it was a dock, with the boats berthing at the place which is now the entrance of Peace Hotel."

Since then, Clarke has traveled the whole world and lived in London, New York, Los Angeles and other famous cities, shooting films along the way. Altogether, he has won four Oscar nominations, two Oscar statuettes and 16 Emmy Awards statuettes.

When reading the Western media reports, Clarke felt that it was not the China he had seen, so he decided to document the real China. Since 2013, Clarke has focused his work on China and began to produce films in China. For him, "the rise of China" or "the renaissance of China" is the biggest ongoing news story of the 21st century. He says frankly: "For a documentary filmmaker, this is a perfect place."

He says: "It's often said that if someone is eager to glimpse the future, they should travel to China, where in so many ways, the future is now. No other country has achieved what China has achieved in such a short time." Since 2013, Clarke has traveled to most of the provinces and cities in China and seen great challenges and development potentials in each place he went. "Everyone worked very hard, eager to build a better future," he recalls.

Malcolm Clarke:

Using the camera to show the world a real China

"I'm making a film in China"

After five years of refinement, the domestic premiere of *Better Angels* directed by Clarke was held in Beijing in 2018. It is a large-scale documentary film focusing on Sino-US relations. Clarke believes that "a perspective from the world is needed to observe the fate of ordinary people behind the Sino-US relations."

"However, after the film was released in North America, we were criticized a lot for its nonconformity with the prejudice of some people in America towards China," says Clarke. Nevertheless, he doesn't intend to change his goal — to document the real China.

In 2019, he began to make preparations for another documentary film about China's poverty alleviation and its building of a moderately prosperous society. As everyone knows, the year 2020 was the year when China finished building a moderately prosperous society in all respects and it was also the final year for the 13th Five-Year Plan. Meanwhile, 2020 was also a year of a decisive victory for the elimination of poverty. Clarke says: "Nearly 600 million people have been lifted out of poverty with universal literacy and a burgeoning middle class, and all this was achieved in just 40 years. It's astonishing."

"I first came to Shanghai 40 years ago"

He says: "As an Englishman, I know well the ups and downs of the Western superpowers. There's little doubt that China will shape the 21st century. We need to look no further than the way we're dealing with the pandemic crisis in the West. The governments of some Western countries were too short-sighted and arrogant to learn from China's experience."

It has been 40 years since Clarke first came to Shanghai. He has settled here now and the Bund is still his favorite. For him, the Bund is the perfect place to illustrate China's progress and development during the past 100 years. Looking at Pudong from the Bund or the Bund from Pudong, people can catch different beautiful scenery and learn different historical stories.

Clarke hopes that, with his camera, he can continue to show the world a real China.

姓　名：Sylvain Laurent
中文名：罗熙文
国　籍：法国
职　位：达索系统全球执行副总裁、基础设施和城市委员会主席

罗熙文：
上海是全球最具创新力城市之一

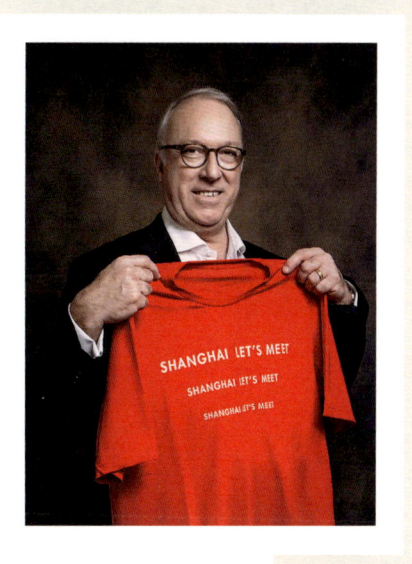

下班回家的路上，时常看到有人在跳广场舞或做瑜伽，每个人的脸上都洋溢着快乐和幸福。这在世界其他地方是见不到的，让人觉得时光特别美好。

"上海是全球最具有创新力的城市之一。" 2012 年刚来到上海，罗熙文便发现了这座城市的创意因子，开始着手将达索系统亚太总部从东京迁至上海，并于 2020 年正式完成了核心部门的迁移。

作为达索系统全球执行副总裁，罗熙文见证了上海对优化营商环境孜孜不倦的追求。他说在上海这座城市"让人感觉生活特别美好"。

创新力聚集地

在达索系统位于浦东陆家嘴的办公区域内，大屏幕上滚动播放着企业参与过的各种项目。作为世界最大的工业软件提供商，达索系统的身影早已出现在中国近年来许多家喻户晓的项目中，例如鸟巢体育馆、京雄高铁、大兴机场、C919 大飞机、海巡 160 号等，还曾为上海世博会提供过综合解决方案。

将亚太总部迁至上海的决定并非"一时冲动"。罗熙文说，来到中国后，他和达索系统董事长一起做出的第一个决策便是把亚太总部从日本迁到中国。活力、创新，是罗熙文眼中上海最大的"魅力"所在。

为了表示对中国市场的重视，达索系统不仅在此建立了地区总部，还制定了针对各省市的业务战略，确保可以覆盖各个行业和领域，并满足当下及未来对城市方面的创新需求。"不管是从战略角度，还是创新活力，又

罗熙文：

上海是全球最具
创新力城市之一

或是未来的发展需求和前景来看，我认为，中国都最有潜力成长为这一地区的中心，也有可能成为整个世界的中心。"

与中国共成长

上海对于外商投资的开放姿态，让达索系统进入中国的道路更加顺畅。罗熙文介绍，在总部迁移过程中，上海市人民政府在税务、人才等方面给予了达索系统诸多支持。

进入中国市场近二十年间，达索系统一直积极推动"In China, For China, With China"的战略。如何和中国共同成长，是达索系统不断探索的目标。

"中国将提高国家自主贡献力度，采取更加有力的政策和措施，二氧化碳排放力争于2030年前达到峰值，努力争取2060年前实现碳中和。"2020年9月22日，国家主席习近平在第七十五届联合国大会一般性辩论上郑重宣布。"碳中和"无疑将是"十四五"期间乃至更长时间维度的一大主题。

"达索系统的理念、目标和能力与'十四五'规划的内容非常契合，无论是有关创新的话题，还是安全、新制造、环保等。"罗熙文坦言。

城市充满乐趣

罗熙文早早融入了这座"充满乐趣"的城市，"下班回家的路上，时常看到有人在跳广场舞或做瑜伽，每个人的脸上都洋溢着快乐和幸福。我觉得很有趣，有时还会停下来围观一会儿，这在世界其他地方是见不到的，"罗熙文语气欢快地说道，"让人觉得时光特别美好。"

热爱烹饪的罗熙文，在闲暇时间会尝试将法国和中国的饮食文化相结合。因为喜爱这座城市，近年来，这位法国人积极推动中法在商业、科技等多领域的交流与合作。为了表彰和感谢他为上海对外交往和城市发展做出的积极贡献，上海市政府向罗熙文颁发了2019年"白玉兰荣誉奖"。

"我很喜欢白玉兰，因为这是上海的标志。"他颇为自豪，"荣获'白玉兰荣誉奖'，我深感荣幸，这也是全体达索系统人的荣誉。"

Name: Sylvain Laurent
Chinese name: 罗熙文
Nationality: French
Position: Executive Vice President, Chairman 3DS Infrastructure & City Board, Dassault Systèmes

Sylvain Laurent:
Shanghai is one of the most innovative cities in the world

On my way home from work, I often see people dancing or doing yoga in a square, and everyone's face is full of joy and happiness. This is something you don't see anywhere else in the world and makes for a particularly good time.

"Shanghai is one of the most innovative cities in the world," says Sylvain Laurent. When he first came to Shanghai in 2012, Laurent discovered that the city sparks creativity and set about moving the Asia-Pacific headquarters of Dassault Systèmes from Tokyo to Shanghai, officially completing the move of the core departments in 2020.

As Executive Vice President of Dassault Systèmes, Laurent has witnessed Shanghai's tireless pursuit of optimizing its business environment. He says that the city "makes life particularly good."

Innovation power center

As the world's largest industrial software provider, Dassault Systèmes has been featured in many of China's most famous projects in recent years, such as the Bird Nest National Stadium, the Beijing-Xiong'an Intercity Railway, the Beijing Daxing International Airport, the COMAC C919, and the Haixun 160, and has also provided integrated solutions for the 2010 Shanghai World Expo.

The decision of moving the Asia-Pacific headquarters to Shanghai is not an act of impulse. Laurent says it was one of the first decisions he made together with the Chairman of Dassault Systèmes. Vitality and innovation are what Laurent sees as the greatest charms of Shanghai.

He says: "Shanghai is a meeting point, a gathering place for innovative capabilities. Not only for Dassault Systèmes but also for me, the city is an engine and benchmark of new innovative capabilities and approaches in the future."

As a sign of its commitment to the Chinese market, Dassault Systèmes has not only established its regional headquarters here but has also developed a business strategy for each province and city to ensure that it can cover all

Sylvain Laurent:

Shanghai is one of the most innovative cities in the world

industries and sectors and meet the current and future demand for innovation in urban areas.

Laurent says: "I think China has the greatest potential to grow into the center of the region and potentially the world, both from a strategic point of view and in terms of innovation dynamism, as well as future development needs and prospects."

Growing with China

Shanghai's openness to foreign investment has smoothed the path for Dassault Systèmes to enter China. Laurent says that the Shanghai Municipal People's Government has given Dassault Systèmes a lot of support in terms of taxation and human resources during the relocation of its headquarters.

For nearly 20 years, Dassault Systèmes has been actively promoting its "In China, For China, With China" strategy in the Chinese market. How to grow with China is the goal of Dassault Systèmes.

On 22 September 2020, at the General Debate of the 75th Session of The United Nations General Assembly Chinese President Xi Jinping said: "China will scale up its Intended Nationally Determined Contributions by adopting more vigorous policies and measures. We aim to have CO2 emissions peak before 2030 and achieve carbon neutrality before 2060." Carbon neutrality will undoubtedly be a major theme during the 14th Five-Year Plan period and beyond.

Laurent says: "Dassault Systèmes's philosophy, objectives and capabilities fit well with the 14th Five-Year Plan, whether it's about innovation, safety, new manufacturing, or environmental protection."

A fun city

Laurent has got used to the lifestyle in Shanghai, a city filled with delight, early on. He says: "On my way home from work, I often see people dancing or doing yoga in a square, and everyone's face is full of joy and happiness. I find it very interesting and sometimes stop and watch for a while. This is something you don't see anywhere else in the world and makes for a particularly good time."

A keen cook, Laurent tries to combine French and Chinese cuisine in his free time. Because of his love for the city, in recent years the Frenchman has actively promoted Sino-French exchanges and cooperation in various fields such as business and technology. In recognition and appreciation of his positive contribution to Shanghai's foreign relations and urban development, the Shanghai Municipal Government has presented the 2019 Magnolia Gold Award to Laurent.

He says: "I like magnolias very much because they are the symbol of Shanghai. I feel deeply honored to receive a Magnolia Award. It is also an honor for all Dassault Systèmes employees."

Scan for videos

姓　　名：Julian Blissett
中 文 名：柏历
国　　籍：英国
职　　位：通用汽车全球执行副总裁、通用汽车中国公司总裁

柏历：
我觉得上海是世界上最宜居的城市

从我来中国的第一年起，我就体会到上海和中国政府对企业非常友好，并且十分支持我们的发展。

"我先后在很多国家生活过，英国、德国、日本、波兰，以及现在居住的中国。我觉得上海是世界上最宜居的城市。"2021年，是通用汽车全球执行副总裁、通用汽车中国公司总裁柏历在上海度过的第15个年头。"上海是全球汽车产业的领军城市，是打造未来出行，推动行业变革的前沿之地。我非常高兴能在上海生活和工作。"

柏历说，在他的人生经历中，没有哪一座城市如上海这般让他停留这么久，上海已经是他不折不扣的第二故乡了。

发展速度令人惊叹

柏历是个铁杆足球迷，喜欢看球赛之余，自己也会上场一展身手。"时间允许的情况下，我每周会踢两三回足球。"和柏历一起挥洒汗水的有来自世界各地的外国友人，也有不少上海人，场上阵容非常"国际化"。

相较于足球，柏历的夫人则更喜欢散步，于是，这对夫妇常常一起在上海街头漫步。2017年与2018年相交之际，黄浦江两岸从杨浦大桥至徐浦大桥45公里岸线公共空间贯通，上海最精华、最核心的黄浦江两岸开放给了所有人。柏历也切身体会到了这一变化。"在过去几年里，上海市政府大力投资，开发公园、滨江岸线等公共区域，那里环境优美，非常适合与家人散步、聊天。我很享受这样的生活。"

"上海在过去15年里发生了翻天覆地的变化。"柏历还记得2006年刚到上海时，浦东机场还只有一个航站楼，如今，浦东机场已启用卫星厅，

柏历：
我觉得上海是世界上
最宜居的城市

T3 航站楼也已列入规划。"上海的基础设施建设发展如此迅速，这种速度让人觉得不可思议。"

目标剑指"零排放"

"碳达峰、碳中和"是当下热议的焦点话题。2020 年召开的中央经济工作会议将"做好碳达峰、碳中和工作"作为 2021 年重点任务之一。这项任务对通用汽车与企业掌舵人柏历而言同样重要。

"最近，通用汽车宣布到 2040 年计划实现全球产品和运营碳中和，我们有信心也有能力达成这一目标。通用汽车不仅将在产品上实现零排放，还将在制造环节中实现零排放，这是我们面向未来的郑重宣言。"柏历还透露，未来 5 年内，通用汽车将对电动车项目投资超过 270 亿美元，在中国推出的新车型中，40% 将是纯电动车型。

好的产品也需要好的展示平台与窗口，在柏历眼中，进博会正是这样一个面向世界的大舞台。如今，参加进博会已经成为了通用汽车一项新的传统。提起第四届进博会，柏历笑着说，"去年我在进博会现场就签约了今年的参展。"

"店小二"不遗余力

"从我来中国的第一年起，我就体会到上海和中国政府对企业非常友好，并且十分支持我们的发展。"柏历提到，政府为企业提供了一系列的服务与政策上的支持，包括鼓励新能源汽车消费、保护知识产权等。

对于营商环境的重视，上海可谓一以贯之、不遗余力。上海市委、市政府表示，政府要当好服务企业的"店小二"，做到有求必应、无事不扰。

在"店小二"努力让营商环境做到"没有最好、只有更好"的过程中，有一件事令柏历印象深刻。在柏历去年履新之时，遇到了一个大问题：通用汽车有许多外籍员工在上海工作，但由于疫情原因，他们的家庭成员"被困"家乡，无法回沪团聚。

"于是我向上海市政府、上海外事办和上汽集团等方面求助，他们给予了很大的支持。"最后，250 多名员工家属，按规定程序办理签证，顺利抵达上海，严格隔离防疫后，最终阖家团聚。柏历感叹道："真是太了不起了！"

Name: Julian Blissett
Chinese name: 柏历
Nationality: British
Position: GM Executive Vice President, GM China President

Julian Blissett:
I think Shanghai is the best place to live in the world

Since I first came to China, I have felt that Shanghai and the Chinese government are very friendly to foreign business and very supportive of our development.

Julian Blissett says: "I have lived in many countries: England, Germany, Japan, Poland, and now China. I think Shanghai is the best place to live in the world." The year 2021 marks the 15th year he has spent in Shanghai as General Motors's Global Executive Vice President and President of GM China.

He says: "Shanghai is a leading city in the global automotive industry, and is at the forefront of building the future of mobility and driving change in the industry. I am very happy to live and work here."

Blissett says that in his life, no city can keep him so long as Shanghai does; the city has definitely become a home away from home.

The incredible speed of development

As a hardcore soccer fan, Blissett enjoys playing on the field to feel the fun besides watching soccer games. "I play soccer two or three times a week when time allows," he says. He finds himself in a highly "international" team, consisting of foreigners from all over the world and many Shanghainese as well.

As Mrs. Blissett prefers taking a walk to playing soccer, the couple often strolls through the streets of Shanghai together. At the end of 2017 turning 2018, Shanghai saw the opening of a 45-kilometer public space from Yangpu Bridge to Xupu Bridge, opening up the best and most central banks of the Huangpu River to the public. Blissett himself felt the benefit from the change.

He says: "In the past few years, the Shanghai government has invested heavily in developing public areas such as parks and waterfront promenades. Walking and talking with family in those beautiful areas are truly delightful. I am enjoying this life very much."

"Shanghai has changed dramatically in the past 15 years," says Blissett. He recalls that when he first arrived in Shanghai in 2006, Shanghai Pudong

Julian Blissett:

I think Shanghai is the best place to live in the world

International Airport had only one terminal; today, it has opened a satellite hall and a T3 terminal is in the planning. "Shanghai is developing its infrastructure so rapidly. The speed is incredible," he says.

To achieve "zero emissions"

"Emission peak and carbon neutrality" have become buzzwords in China after its Central Economic Work Conference in 2020 made preparing for bringing the country's emissions to its peak and achieving carbon neutrality one of the key tasks in 2021. This task is as important to GM as it is to Blissett, the man at the helm.

Blissett says: "GM just announced plans to achieve global product and operational carbon neutrality by 2040, and we are confident and capable of reaching that goal. GM will achieve zero emissions not only in our products but also in our manufacturing. That is our solemn declaration for the future." He also reveals that GM will invest more than US$27 billion in its electric vehicle program over the next five years and that 40 percent of the new models launched in China will be purely electric.

Good products also need a good platform. In Blissett's eyes, China International Import Expo (CIIE) is just such an international stage. It has become a routine for GM to participate in CIIE. Speaking of the fourth CIIE, Mr. Blissett says with a smile, "I signed up for this year's participation at last year's CIIE."

The hardworking "shop assistant"

Blissett says: "Since I first came to China, I have felt that Shanghai and the Chinese government are very friendly to foreign business and very supportive of our development." The government provides a series of services and policies to support foreign enterprises, like encouraging the consumption of new energy vehicles and protecting their intellectual property rights.

Shanghai has been consistent and hard-working in improving its business environment. The Shanghai Municipal Committee of the Communist Party of China and the Shanghai Municipal Government compare their role to that of an attentive "shop assistant" in serving the needs of foreign enterprises — quickly responding to requests yet keeping from interfering.

One thing deeply impressed Blissett as the municipal "shop assistant" spared no efforts to improve the business environment of Shanghai. When he took up his new position last year, he encountered a big problem: owing to the pandemic, many GM's foreign employees working in Shanghai found their family members "trapped" in their hometown and could not return to Shanghai for a reunion.

"I asked for help from the Shanghai Municipal Government, the Shanghai Foreign Affairs Office, and SAIC, and they gave me great support," he says. In the end, more than 250 employees' families, who had followed the prescribed procedures to obtain visas, finally arrived in Shanghai and joined their families after strict quarantine. Blissett says: "It was amazing!"

姓　名：Oscar
中文名：奥斯卡
国　籍：巴西
职　位：上海海港足球俱乐部球员

奥斯卡：
我们队里一些球员是党员，我特别尊重他们

今年是中国共产党建党 100 周年，我们队里的一些球员是党员，我特别尊重他们。

奥斯卡的上海生活

"因为特别喜欢上海这座城市，希望自己能够帮助到中国的小孩子成长进步，踢得越来越好。"奥斯卡计划今年在上海开一个小的足球培训学校，让小孩子们像他一样去踢球，感受足球的快乐。

2016 年 12 月 25 日，上海上港集团足球俱乐部（现上海海港足球俱乐部）给球迷们送上了一份大礼——国际知名球星奥斯卡加盟。从此，奥斯卡开启了他的"上海生活"。在上海的 5 年间，奥斯卡和他的队友夺得了 2018 年中超联赛冠军和 2019 年超级杯冠军，未来他和队友们还将继续为荣誉而战。

"现代化"是上海这座城市留给奥斯卡的第一印象，每当从外滩看向浦东，奥斯卡都会由衷赞叹。在上海居住的岁月里，奥斯卡感受到了在上海生活的便利和人们的友好，"对于外国人来说，在这里生活很便利，而且当地人对外国人也非常友爱。"奥斯卡告诉记者。

尽管网络已经十分发达，但外界对于中国并不了解。"我经常跟朋友们提起上海的点滴，他们都不敢相信，因为在巴西和欧洲的一些人不是很了解上海，所以当他们来到上海时也会被震惊到。"奥斯卡坦言。

据奥斯卡回忆，刚到上海时，女儿刚满 2 岁，儿子才 9 个月大。女儿

奥斯卡：

我们队里的一些球员是党员，我特别尊重他们

到上海的第一件大事就是读书，"上海的教育条件特别好，比圣保罗好很多，而且还在不断提升。"奥斯卡的家人们都很喜欢这里，如今孩子们能熟悉掌握葡萄牙语、中文和英文。

适合体育运动的上海

除了上海的生活环境和教育，奥斯卡还会向朋友们介绍上海的体育设施。奥斯卡觉得上海八万人体育场和虹口足球场都非常漂亮，管理水平也非常高。家人和朋友们常去观看他的比赛，从赛事保障到球迷服务都非常到位。

目前，上海正在为打造全球著名体育城市努力，2020年，新建成的浦东足球场是上海"十三五"期间体育基础设施建设的重要成果之一，这正是奥斯卡所在足球俱乐部的主场。"新的体育场我觉得会是中国最漂亮的体育场，特别现代。"奥斯卡告诉记者。

按照《上海全球著名体育城市建设纲要》，到2025年，上海要基本建成全球著名体育城市；到2035年，上海要迈向更高水平全球著名体育城市；到2050年，上海全面建成全球著名体育城市。

我的队员是党员

上海海港足球俱乐部有多名队员是党员，来到上海后，因为队友的关系，奥斯卡知道中国有一个强大的组织叫中国共产党，党员队员们需要定期开展学习。在他的眼中，共产党员是一群优秀的人，"我知道我的队友颜骏凌是一名共产党员，他很聪明、很优秀、有领导力，工作和生活中都非常关心大家。"奥斯卡告诉记者，每当有新的球员到来，颜骏凌都会主动去关心他们。"这样的品质对我们足球队很重要，对于一个刚到新城市的人来说，能够让我们很安心。所以队里的党员们我都特别尊重，也特别喜欢颜骏凌。"

奥斯卡希望能和队友一起取得更好的成绩，为上海赢得更多的冠军。此外，奥斯卡在体育产业上也有自己的规划。这段时间奥斯卡在寻找适合做足球培训的场地，今年他计划在上海开一个小的足球培训学校，让小孩子们像他一样去踢球，去感受足球带来的快乐。

奥斯卡表示，要为上海体育事业、上海足球贡献一份力量。

Name: Oscar
Chinese name: 奥斯卡
Nationality: Brazilian
Position: Player at Shanghai Port Football Club

Oscar:
I truly respect those Party members in our team

At the 100th anniversary of the founding of the Communist Party of China, I'd like to show special respect for those Party members in our team.

Oscar's life in Shanghai

"I like Shanghai very much, so I hope I can help Chinese kids get more progress at soccer," the Brazilian footballer says. Oscar plans to open a small soccer training school in Shanghai this year, teaching kids to play and feel the joy of soccer like he does.

On December 25, 2016, Shanghai SIPG Football Club (later renamed Shanghai Port Football Club) presented a nice surprise to its fans as Oscar, a world-famous footballer, joined the club. Oscar has started his "Shanghai life" since then. During his five-year stay in Shanghai, Oscar and his teammates won the 2018 Chinese Super League Championship and the 2019 Chinese Football Association Super Cup. He is still fighting for more glory with his teammates.

"Modernity" is the first impression Shanghai gave Oscar, who deeply admires the city whenever looking from the Bund to Pudong. "For foreigners, life here is very convenient and the local people are very friendly," he says.

Despite the quick development of the internet, the outside world knows little about China. "My friends can hardly believe what I constantly tell them about Shanghai. Some people in Brazil and Europe are blown away by Shanghai at first sight, since they knew so little about it."

When he first arrived in Shanghai, his daughter had just turned 2 and his son was only 9 months old, Oscar recalls. When his daughter arrived in Shanghai, the first thing Oscar did was to find a good school. "Shanghai boasts exceptional educational resources, which keeps improving, much better than that in São Paulo," he says. All his family members love it here. His children now are fluent in Portuguese, English and Chinese.

Oscar:

I truly respect those Party members in our team

Shanghai, a city for sports

Oscar would recommend to his friends the sports facilities in Shanghai, besides the living environment and education quality here. He thinks both the Shanghai Stadium and Hongkou Football Stadium look marvelous and are well-managed. His family and friends often go to watch him play. The event operation and service to football fans are very satisfactory.

Currently, Shanghai is striving to become a world-renowned sports city. Home of Oscar's soccer club, the newly built Pudong Football Stadium is one of the major achievements of the city's sports infrastructure construction during the 13th Five-Year Plan period. Oscar says, "I think the new stadium is super modern. It will be the most beautiful stadium in China."

According to the Outline of Building Shanghai into a World-renowned Sports City, Shanghai will basically achieve the goal of becoming a world-renowned sports city by 2025, move towards a higher level by 2035, and become a world-renowned sports city in all respects by 2050.

"My fellow players are members of the Communist Party of China"

After arriving in Shanghai, Oscar learned the existence of a powerful organization in China, the Communist Party of China, as many of his teammates in the soccer club are Party members and they conduct regular studies. In his eyes, Party members are a group of excellent people. "I know that my teammate Yan Junling is a Party member. He is smart and outstanding, full of leadership skills, and shows genuine concern for everyone during work and daily life," Oscar says, adding that Yan would actively take care of every newcomer to the club. "That means a lot to us, making newcomers to the city feel at ease. I highly respect all the Party members in our club, and I really like Yan Junling."

Oscar hopes to achieve better performance with his teammates and win more titles for Shanghai. He also has his own plans in the sports industry. Recently, he is looking for a suitable venue for soccer training, paving the way for his plan of opening a small soccer training school in Shanghai this year, so that kids can play and feel the joy of soccer like he does.

Oscar says he would like to contribute to the development of soccer and the whole sports industry as well in Shanghai.

姓　名：Simon Lichtenberg
中文名：李曦萌
国　籍：丹麦
职　位：特雷通集团创始人、董事会主席兼首席执行官

李曦萌：
没有一个很强的政府，没办法让中国真正发展起来

没有一个很强的政府，没办法让中国真正发展起来。

从丹麦来上海之前，李曦萌完全不知道他的祖先早在一百多年前已经与上海结下了不解之缘。祖先伟贺慕·马易尔于1906年创办了慎昌洋行（上海锅炉厂的前身）。如今在上海经商28年的李曦萌凭借优良的设计和品质，将产品销售到世界各地。

他也是浦东开发开放、工商税制改革、上海外高桥保税区、上海自由贸易试验区等系列政策的获益者和亲历者。

上海发生了翻天覆地的变化

1987年，读完中学的李曦萌幸运地成为复旦大学国际交流学院的首批外国留学生。刚到上海时，他能直观感受到上海人民生活水平亟待提高。那时中国还在实行计划经济，购买东西需要用饭票、粮票、自行车票等，路上也鲜有轿车。

进修中文一年后，李曦萌回丹麦完成了学业。1990年5月3日，上海市人民政府浦东开发办公室和浦东开发规划研究设计院挂牌。浦东开发办挂牌1个月后，1990年6月，国务院批准成立国内第一个保税区"上海外高桥保税区"。1993年，李曦萌重返上海创业时，就选在保税区注册企业。

李曦萌清晰地记得，那时自己的企业刚起步，并没有规模，但管理委员会的人还是很愿意和他交流，并给予他指导。

李曦萌：

没有一个很强的政府，没办法让中国真正发展起来

1994年，中国对工商税制进行了新中国成立以来规模最大、范围最广、内容最深刻的一次改革。新税制为企业公平竞争创造了条件。李曦萌感慨道："税收规则的建立，使我觉得做一个商人很安全。"

政府在做"店小二"

在上海，从2018年起，"店小二"理念频繁被提及，政府要当好服务企业的"店小二"。在中国经商近30年的李曦萌深有体会，他表示，最近四五年感觉政府部门的服务改变特别明显，"以前和政府部门开会，要去政府，但现在倒过来了，政府就是店小二，以服务为主，变化非常明显。"

李曦萌觉得中国经济社会的发展得益于中国共产党的领导，"没有一个很强的政府，没办法让中国真正发展起来。"

鉴于此，尽管他的一些竞争对手因为节约成本等因素将企业搬至其他国家，但李曦萌还是坚定选择在中国继续扎根和发展。

李曦萌感慨："中国梦，也是我的中国梦。"

Name: Simon Lichtenberg
Chinese Name: 李曦萌
Nationality: Danish
Position: CEO, Chairman of the Board, and Founder of Trayton Group

Simon Lichtenberg:
Without a powerful government, China wouldn't be able to truly develop

Without a powerful government, China wouldn't be able to truly develop.

Before coming to Shanghai from Denmark, Simon Lichtenberg had no idea that his ancestor had been closely tied to Shanghai more than one hundred years ago. In 1906, his ancestor Vilhelm Meyer founded Andersen Meyer & Co., Ltd., the predecessor of Shanghai Boiler Works Co., Ltd. Now Lichtenberg, who has been doing business in Shanghai for 28 years, sells well-designed and high-quality products all over the world.

He is the beneficiary and witness of a series of policies such as the Development and Opening Up of Pudong, the Reform of the Industrial and Commercial Tax System, the establishment of the Shanghai Waigaoqiao Free Trade Zone and the Shanghai Pilot Free Trade Zone.

Shanghai has undergone great changes

Having graduated from high school in 1987, Lichtenberg was admitted into the International Cultural Exchange School of Fudan University and became one of the first batch of international students. When he first arrived in Shanghai, he felt the living standard in Shanghai needed improvement badly. At that time, China was still under a planned economic system, where you had to use rice stamps, food stamps and bicycle tickets to buy things, and there were few cars on the roads.

After studying Chinese for a year, Lichtenberg went back to Denmark to complete school. On May 3, 1990, the Pudong Development Office of

Simon Lichtenberg:

Without a powerful government, China wouldn't be able to truly develop

the Shanghai Municipal People's Government and the Shanghai Pudong Development Planning Research and Design Institute were set up. One month later in June 1990, the State Council approved the establishment of Shanghai Waigaoqiao Free Trade Zone, the first free trade zone in China, where Lichtenberg registered his first enterprise when he returned to Shanghai to start a business in 1993.

Lichtenberg clearly remembers that when he started from nothing, the staff of the administrative committee of the government were very willing to brief him about related policies and offer guidance.

In 1994, the largest, most extensive, and most profound reform of the industrial and commercial tax system since the founding of the People's Republic of China was carried out. The new tax system created conditions for fair competition among enterprises. Lichtenberg says: "As a businessman, the establishment of these tax rules gives me a sense of security."

Government acting as attentive shop assistants

Since 2018, the Shanghai government has been frequently promoting the concept of "serving like an attentive shop assistant", which urges the government to help enterprises and become service-oriented. After doing business for nearly 30 years in China, Lichtenberg has been deeply impressed by the changes in government service.

He says: "In the past, when you had meetings with government departments, you had to go to their offices, but now it is reversed and the government is service-oriented and serves like a shopkeeper. The change is very obvious."

Lichtenberg attributes China's economic and social development to the leadership of the Communist Party of China. "Without a powerful government, China wouldn't be able to truly develop," he says.

With this in mind, Lichtenberg has firmly chosen to continue to lay down his roots and grow in China, despite the fact that some of his competitors have moved their businesses to other countries due to cost-saving and other factors.

"The Chinese dream is also my dream," says Lichtenberg.

姓　名：Nusrat Marat
中文名：白马克
国　籍：澳大利亚
职　位：上海市长宁区优秀志愿者

白马克：
中国的老百姓脸上都挂着笑容

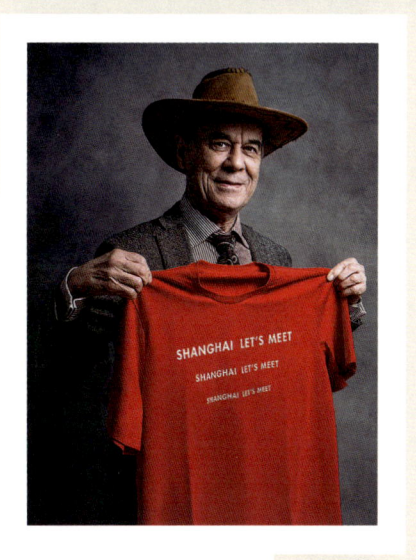

中国共产党带领中国不仅实现了脱贫，还做出了许多令世界惊叹的成绩。关键是中国的老百姓脸上都挂着笑容。

我想加入中国共产党

如果给他一个入党的机会，来自澳大利亚的白马克表示，他一定会义无反顾加入中国共产党，正如他选择留在中国一样。经过长时间的学习，白马克能说一口流利的普通话。在白马克的心中，在中国共产党的领导下，中国不仅实现了脱贫，还做出了许多令世界惊叹的成绩。"关键是，中国的老百姓脸上都挂着笑容。"白马克认为，中国的发展是一个令世界惊叹的奇迹，值得全世界学习。

据白马克回忆，1992 年，因为工作关系，他首次来到中国，在澳大利亚驻上海总领事馆工作，负责文化交流的项目。尽管那时的上海并不像现在这样国际化，但上海街头的烟火气和老百姓温暖的笑容很快让白马克找到了归属感。为了更好地融入上海，白马克开始学习中文。

完成工作后，1994 年，白马克回到了家乡澳大利亚，然而上海总令他魂牵梦萦，发生在上海的点滴时常浮现在他的脑海之中。于是，白马克开始寻找工作机会，希望能回到上海。"我去过新加坡、阿联酋、印度、瑞士等很多国家，但我觉得都不能和上海比，尽管瑞士像画一样，但我更喜欢上海。"

白马克：
中国的老百姓脸上
都挂着笑容

定居上海后的生活

2008年，白马克在上海找到了工作，从此定居在此。随着对上海这座城市的深入了解，白马克深深地爱上了这里。他在上海娶妻生子，将家安在了长宁区。

2020年疫情暴发前，白马克原本计划趁着假期带家人回澳大利亚。"武汉暴发疫情后，病毒的根源究竟来自世界的哪个地方始终没有确定，全球都显得有些紧张。"在街道工作人员的动员下，白马克和家人决定留在上海过年。

外出买菜时，白马克看到上海街头十分有序，食品、生活用品供应等一切正常。"世界各地的亲戚朋友打电话来问我，我都告诉他们上海很正常，让他们放心。"白马克说，他还告诉海外的亲友们中国有非常英明的政府在领导，有抗击SARS的经验。"中国经历过，没必要惊慌。"

疫情期间，街道工作人员和志愿者们不分昼夜的辛勤工作感动了白马克，于是他也加入了志愿者的队伍。据白马克回忆，那时他主要的工作是给进出小区的人测温和对楼道的扶手等消毒。有时见到不戴口罩的外国人，白马克会上前劝导，希望他们能遵守防疫要求。

2020年10月，第三届上海长宁愚园路历史风貌街区钢琴音乐节顺利举办。此情此景让白马克感慨道："中国人民在中国共产党的领导下，团结一心、抗击疫情、努力奋斗，全世界有目共睹。"愚园路本是上海市中心一条不起眼的马路，可许多近现代史上的风云人物和社会名流们曾在此居住生活过。如今，因为这些名人故居，愚园路已然成为了一条有名的红色旅游路线。闲暇时，白马克喜欢在愚园路漫步，《布尔什维克》编辑部旧址、中共中央上海局机关旧址、路易·艾黎故居、钱学森旧居等都令他着迷。在这里他一边给孩子讲解中国共产党的历史，一边惊叹于中国的发展。

"党的领导、政府的能力决定了一个国家的发展。"白马克赞赏中国共产党的执政能力，他认为中国的社会治理在世界上是一个奇迹。

白马克感慨中国的发展速度，并坚定地相信在中国共产党的领导下，中国将成为更加伟大的国家。

Name: Nusrat Marat
Chinese Name: 白马克
Nationality: Australian
Position: Volunteer of Changning District, Shanghai

Nusrat Marat:
Ordinary Chinese people all have smiles on their faces

Under the leadership of the Communist Party of China, China has not only eliminated poverty but also dazzled the world with her many achievements. More importantly, ordinary Chinese people all have smiles on their faces.

"I want to join the Communist Party of China"

Nusrat Marat, from Australia, is certain that if given an opportunity to join the Communist Party of China (CPC), he would apply for it immediately, with the same resolution when he chose to stay in China. After a considerable time of learning, now Marat can speak fluent Mandarin. He believes that under the leadership of the CPC, China has not only eliminated poverty but also made many achievements that have amazed the world. He says: "More importantly, ordinary Chinese people all have smiles on their faces." Marat sees China's development as an amazing miracle for the world, and also an example that other countries can learn from.

Marat's first visit to China, as he remembers, was in 1992 because of work. He was responsible for some cultural exchange projects at the Australian Consulate-General in Shanghai. Although the city at that time was not as international as it is today, soon Marat established a bond with Shanghai by seeing the daily lives of ordinary people on the streets and getting greeted by their warm smiles. To better merge into the local life, he began to learn Chinese.

In 1994, after finishing the job, Marat went back to his hometown in Australia. But Shanghai held a special place in his heart and he missed the little things in his life during his stay. Since then, he began to look for job opportunities that could bring him back to Shanghai. He says: "I've visited many countries such as Singapore, the UAE, India and Switzerland, but no place could compare with Shanghai. Switzerland has sceneries as beautiful as paintings, but I like Shanghai more."

Nusrat Marat:

Ordinary Chinese people all have smiles on their faces

Life after settling down in Shanghai

After securing a job in Shanghai in 2008, Marat has been living here ever since. With a deeper understanding of the city, he felt a stronger bond with this place. Later he became a husband and a father in Shanghai, and resided in Changning District.

Before the outbreak of COVID-19 in 2020, Marat was just about to bring his family to Australia over the holidays. "After the outbreak in Wuhan, which part of the world was the actual origin of the virus had remained a mystery and this unnerved the whole world," he recalls. As suggested by the people from his neighborhood committee, Marat decided to stay in Shanghai, together with his family for the Spring Festival.

While buying groceries outside, Marat could see that great order was kept in Shanghai's streets and the supply of food and daily necessities was completely normal. "When my relatives and friends from around the world called me, I always told them that everything was fine in Shanghai, and they shouldn't worry," he says. He also told them that China was led by a very capable government and the country had the experience of fighting SARS. He says: "China has dealt with this before. There is no need to panic."

To control the pandemic, the staff members and volunteers of the neighborhood committee worked very hard round the clock. Moved by their selfless contribution, Marat also joined the volunteers. He remembers that his main tasks were taking temperatures of everyone entering and leaving the community and sterilizing the handrails of stairs. Sometimes when he saw foreigners not wearing masks, he would persuade them to follow the pandemic control measures.

In October of 2020, the 3rd Piano Music Festival of the Yuyuan Road Historic Area was smoothly held. Marat says: "Under the leadership of the CPC, the Chinese people were strongly united and deeply engaged in the fight against the pandemic, which was witnessed by the whole world." Yuyuan Road is a quiet and inconspicuous street in Shanghai's city center. Actually, it is richly decorated with former residences of important figures and celebrities in China's modern history. Now, these residences are formed into a famous red tourism route. In his spare time, Marat would take a stroll along Yuyuan Road. He is fascinated by the buildings such as the former site of the Editorial Office of *Bolshevik*, the former site of Shanghai Bureau of the Central Committee of the CPC, the former residences of Alley Rewi and Qian Xuesen. In these places as he explains the history of the CPC to his child, he is also amazed by China's development.

Marat admires the governance capability of the CPC and regards the social administration of China as a miracle in the world. He says: "The leadership of the Party and the capability of the government determine the development of a country."

As he is amazed by China's development speed, Marat has a firm belief that under the leadership of the CPC, China will become an even greater country in the years ahead.

姓　名：HIROSHI INUI
中文名：乾浩史
国　籍：日本
职　位：大金空调（上海）有限公司总经理

乾浩史：
我愿扎根上海，深耕"上海智造"

> 我们的党员员工，我感觉更具智慧，对世界的关注和思考更为深刻。

大金空调的总经理乾浩史在上海的15年间，不仅见证了上海的高速发展，还对这片土地产生了浓厚的感情。乾浩史认为，尽管上海的人力成本相对国内一些地区较高，但"上海制造"却有着不一样的意义，大金空调在上海也将朝着"上海智造"方向发展。

鉴于中国政府的高效管理，乾浩史对中国的未来非常有信心。

坚守"上海制造"，中国潜力无限

2006年，乾浩史来到上海，初到上海时，他看到闵行区颛桥一带是一片郊区的景象。当时的莘庄工业区还有着大片的农田，乾浩史觉得与日本有很大差距。秉承"人的潜力无限"的理念，在乾浩史的带领下，大金空调一年内建起两条生产线。"这在日本是不可能的，但我们却实现了原先认为绝无可能的事情，我真正体会到了中国速度和无限潜力。"乾浩史回忆道。

莘庄工业区主动对接国家战略，成为上海首家国家级生态工业示范园。15年过去了，上海的发展速度令乾浩史惊叹，位于闵行区申富路的大金空调厂区周围也发生了巨大的变化，莘庄工业区从一片农田成长为世界五百强企业进入中国的"摇篮"。

近年来，上海产业结构不断调整，乾浩史表示，尽管上海生产要素成本相对较高、环保要求更严格，但"上海制造"的价值是无法用成本来衡量的，在这样的背景下，大金空调守护"上海制造"的同时，也将朝着"上海智造"

乾浩史：

我愿扎根上海，
深耕"上海智造"

方向发展。

目前，大金空调在中国制造基地生产的空调产品已经作为全球性产品出口至美国、加拿大、日本等多个国家和地区。而为了实现优势互补与资源共享，大金将长三角地区的优秀管理经验和制造经验复制到更多地区，借由上海生产基地，大金空调在中国成功孵化了18家生产基地。

身边的党员更具智慧，思考更为深入

和大多数外国人一样，乾浩史觉得上海的治安状况非常好，晚上在外面常常能看到小孩子出行玩耍。"有时候都觉得比日本的治安还好。"每逢节假日，乾浩史总会约着朋友去打高尔夫，这也成为他在上海社交的一部分。而最令他期待的是一年一度的大金纳凉节，乾浩史特别喜欢音乐，时常自己练习架子鼓，每年纳凉节他都要登台为大家演奏架子鼓。

大金空调的厂区内有这么一群人，他们胸口别着党员徽章在生产线上辛勤工作。在乾浩史的心中，这些胸前有党员徽章的员工们更具智慧，对世界的关注和思考更为深刻。

在乾浩史看来，在中国共产党的领导下，国家被管理得很好，对于中国的未来，有长期的规划和思考。乾浩史觉得中国人民会灵活运用科技的发展，并借助政府的力量，促使中国进一步发展。他坚信中国的国际竞争力会有进一步提升。

乾浩史在中国感受到了广阔的发展前景，这也坚定了他继续在中国深耕的决心。

Name: HIROSHI INUI
Chinese name: 乾浩史
Nationality: Japanese
Position: General Manager of Daikin Air Conditioning (Shanghai) Co., Ltd.

HIROSHI INUI:
I'm willing to root in Shanghai and commit myself to smart manufacturing

In my mind, our Communist Party staff are smarter, more thoughtful and insightful about the world.

During his 15-year stay in Shanghai, HIROSHI INUI, General Manager of Daikin Air Conditioning (Shanghai) Co., Ltd., has not only witnessed the rapid development of the city but also developed a strong affection for the land. He says that although the labor cost in Shanghai is higher than that of some other areas in China, "Made in Shanghai" means something different, and the Daikin business in Shanghai will move toward smart manufacturing.

Given the efficient management of the Chinese government, HIROSHI INUI is very confident in China's future.

Sticking to "Made in Shanghai", China enjoys the unlimited potential

HIROSHI INUI came to Shanghai in 2006 and when he first arrived, he saw that the area around Zhuanqiao in Minhang District was still a suburb. Xinzhuang Industry Park then was nothing but large farmland, which, in his eyes, showed a big gap with Japan in development. Believing in the notion of "nothing is impossible," he led the Daikin Air Conditioning business and built two production lines within a year. "It couldn't happen in Japan, but we made the mission possible, and that serves as evidence for the speed and unlimited potential of China," HIROSHI INUI recalls.

Xinzhuang Industry Park took the initiative to follow the national strategy and became the first national eco-industrial demonstration park in Shanghai. Over the past 15 years, HIROSHI INUI was indeed amazed at the rapid development of Shanghai. Huge changes have also taken place around the Daikin Air Conditioning plants, located on Shenfu Road, Minhang District. Xinzhuang

HIROSHI INUI:

I'm willing to root in Shanghai and commit myself to smart manufacturing

Industry Park has grown from farmland to a "cradle" for the development of the world's top 500 enterprises in China.

In recent years, Shanghai has been adjusting its industrial structure. HIROSHI INUI tells us that despite the relatively higher factor costs and stricter environmental protection regulations, the value of "Made in Shanghai" cannot be measured in cost alone. In such a context, while inheriting the spirit of Shanghai manufacturing, Daikin Air Conditioning will further advance itself in the direction of prominent smart manufacturing.

Nowadays, Daikin air conditioning products that are made in China have been globally popular and exported to the United States, Canada, Japan, and many other countries and regions. To achieve complementary advantages and resource sharing, it is duplicating the excellent experience of management and manufacturing in the Yangtze River Delta to a lot more regions and has successfully incubated 18 production bases in China.

Our staff members who are also CPC members are smarter and more thoughtful

Like most foreigners, HIROSHI INUI, often seeing children playing outside at night, pays a high compliment to the public security in Shanghai. "Sometimes I even feel it is safer here than in Japan," he says. During holidays, he always plays golf with his friends and it has become part of his social life in Shanghai. Among all, Daikin Summer Festival is what he anticipates the most. HIROSHI INUI is particularly fond of music and practices playing the drum kit frequently, and he goes on stage to play every year during the festival.

There are such a group of people in the plants of Daikin Air Conditioning, working hard on the production line with a badge of the Communist Party of China. In HIROSHI INUI's mind, these employees are smarter, more thoughtful and insightful about the world.

From Hiroshi's perspective, under the leadership of the Communist Party of China, the whole country is very well managed, due to the long-term planning for China's future. He believes that China will make flexible use of science and technology, and in addition, give full play to the role of the government to promote its further development. Never does he doubt the further enhancement of China's international competitiveness.

HIROSHI INUI is clearly aware of the broad prospect for China's development, which also strengthens his determination to continue to work and stay in China.

Scan for videos

姓　名：Javier Gimeno
中文名：孟昊文
国　籍：西班牙
职　位：圣戈班集团高级副总裁兼亚太区首席执行官

孟昊文：
中国社会释放出一股强大的活力

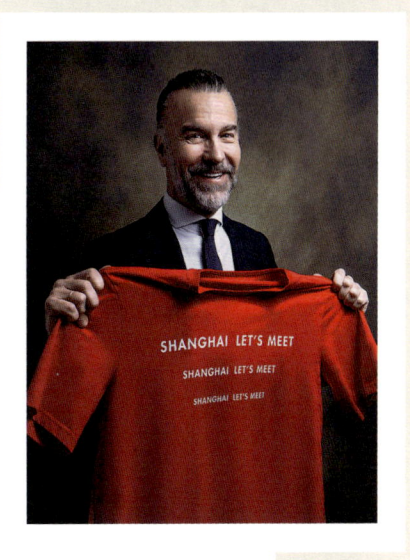

中国已为自己选择了一个适合的政治制度，应当得到所有人的尊重。

更多人愿意来这里工作

圣戈班是世界著名的"长寿企业"。在孟昊文的带领下，圣戈班在华已设立1家研发中心和40多家生产基地。

2010年，孟昊文来到上海，担任圣戈班集团亚太区首席执行官，回忆起刚到上海时的情景，孟昊文记忆犹新。"我刚来中国的时候，所面临最严重的难题之一是污染。"

2013年，中国政府出台被外界称为史上最严的《大气污染防治行动计划》。到了2017年，为了确保冬季空气更加洁净，无论是中央政府还是受污染最严重省份的地方政府都采取了新的预防性措施。环境的变化，孟昊文深有体会："在最近的4至5年，中国为此所作的努力是出色、显著且卓有成效的。今天，我们呼吸着更为清新的空气，同时也让更多人看到了中国的魅力，愿意来到这里工作。"

政府给企业许多帮助

令孟昊文感触颇深的还有政府给予企业的支持，圣戈班扎根中国已有近40年，最初在郊区选址建厂时，厂区周边还很荒凉，然而随着近年来的高速发展，圣戈班的厂区周围建起了诸多的居民小区，这就使得圣戈班需要考虑将厂房搬迁。"这是一个非常艰难的事情，因为从劳动力和资本支

孟昊文：
中国社会释放出一股
强大的活力

出角度来看，都是极其昂贵的。"孟昊文回忆道，上海给予了圣戈班极大的支持。"在其他国家，我曾有过类似的经历，我可以告诉你，他们比中国要复杂得多。"

十一年在中国的经历让孟昊文对中国乃至中国共产党有了更深入的了解，孟昊文认为，现有的体制对于中国最为适合，它也与中华民族的文化、历史和传统最为契合。

在孟昊文看来，中国共产党在过去的一百年中为中国历史作出了令世人惊讶的贡献，中国一跃成为世界第二大经济体，这一切归功于在中国共产党的领导下中国社会所释放的强大活力。

过去一年，新冠肺炎疫情肆虐全球，世界经济陷入深度衰退，人类经历了史上罕见的多重危机。习近平主席在世界经济论坛"达沃斯议程"对话会上发表特别致辞，提出要解决好这个时代面临的四大课题，强调解决问题的出路是维护和践行多边主义、推动构建人类命运共同体。

孟昊文深有感触。"尊重不同国家的思想、政治制度、文化和历史，这尤为重要。中国已为自己选择了一个适合的政治制度，应当得到所有人的尊重。"

孟昊文希望带领圣戈班在中国继续深耕，为地球的可持续发展和人们的美好生活作出贡献。

Name: Javier Gimeno
Chinese name: 孟昊文
Nationality: Spanish
Position: Senior Vice-President of Compagnie de Saint-Gobain; CEO of Saint-Gobain Asia-Pacific

Javier Gimeno:
China is full of vigor and vitality

> China has chosen a suitable political system for itself. It deserves to be respected.

Saint-Gobain is a world-renowned company with a long history. Under Javier Gimeno's leadership, the company has set up a research and development center and more than 40 manufacturing sites in China.

More people willing to come and work in Shanghai

"When I came here, one of the gravest problems we were facing was air pollution," Gimeno says. He arrived in Shanghai in 2010 to assume his position as CEO of Saint-Gobain Asia-Pacific.

In 2013, the Chinese government introduced the Action Plan for Prevention and Control of Air Pollution, the strictest air quality control measure in China's history. In the winter of 2017, the central government and local governments of the provinces most affected by air pollution adopted new precautionary measures to improve their air quality.

Gimeno says he has witnessed this improvement in China's air quality.

"Since four or five years ago, the efforts made by China have paid off," he says. "Today, we're breathing fresher air, which allows more people to experience China's charm so that they are willing to come and work here."

Generous support from the government

The extent of government support for Saint-Gobain also impressed Gimeno. The company has been in China for nearly 40 years. When it first built its factory in the outskirts of Shanghai, the surrounding area was mostly undeveloped. But as the city expands, residential communities emerged around the factory, making it necessary for the company to consider relocating it.

Gimeno says: "Relocation is usually tremendously difficult and expensive

Javier Gimeno:

China is full of vigor and vitality

because of the labor cost and other expenditures, but Shanghai provided the company with a lot of support. I've had similar experiences in other countries, and I can tell you that it's much more complicated there than in China."

11 years in China have deepened Gimeno's understanding of China and the Communist Party of China. He says he believes China's current system of governance is the most suitable system for the country given its culture, history and traditions.

Gimeno says: "The Communist Party of China has achieved remarkable accomplishments in the past 100 years. China has now become the world's second-largest economy thanks to the vigor and vitality of its economy under the leadership of the Party."

The COVID-19 pandemic swept across the world in the past year. The global economy has been in a deep recession, and mankind has faced multiple crises at the same time.

President Xi Jinping remarked in a special address at the World Economic Forum (WEF) Virtual Event of the Davos Agenda that it is important that countries properly address the major tasks facing the world today: jointly promoting strong, sustainable, balanced and inclusive growth of the world economy, jointly following a path of peaceful coexistence, mutual benefit and win-win cooperation, closing the divide between developed and developing countries, and coming together against global challenges. He emphasized the way out of challenges is through upholding multilateralism and building a community with a shared future for mankind.

"It is very important to respect different countries' ways of thinking, political systems, cultures and history," Gimeno says. "China has chosen a suitable political system for itself. It deserves to be respected."

Gimeno says he looks forward to continuing leading Saint-Gobain's growth in China and furthering the company's contribution to sustainable development and the betterment of people's lives.

姓　名：Allan Gabor
中文名：安高博
国　籍：美国
职　位：默克中国总裁、默克电子科技中国区董事总经理

安高博：
上海有着超一流的营商环境

今年是中国共产党建党 100 周年，这是一个值得纪念的时刻，无疑，中国取得了伟大成就！

安高博不止一次在公开场合表达过自己对上海的喜爱之情。作为一名企业家，他感叹上海有着超一流的营商环境；作为一名居住者，他流连于上海的高品质都市生活。距离安高博第一次来到上海已经过去 22 年，而他对这座城市的认知还在不断加深……

超一流的营商环境

去年 11 月，公共卫生防疫展区在第三届中国国际进口博览会首次"亮相"，默克集团作为一家深耕中国市场 88 年、全球领先的科技公司位列其中。

和许多前来参展的外国朋友一样，安高博把进博会看作一次千载难逢的机会。"进博会是创造沟通和合作的平台，我们很多重要的合作伙伴也都将参加，这个平台为众多的利益攸关方架起了沟通的桥梁。"安高博说。

近年来，越来越多的外国企业通过参加进博会走上了进入中国市场的"绿色通道"，上海作为进博会的"东道主"也在不断完善市场化、法治化、国际化的营商环境。2017 年年末，上海召开了优化营商环境推进大会。

上海的努力安高博看在眼里。"我们与政府在各个层面都有充分的沟通，包括政策和业务层面。上海市政府以服务为中心的理念非常具有国际化思维，这使得企业也从中受益。这也是默克把电子科技和生命科学业务的总部设在上海的原因之一。"谈及政府针对外国企业提供的一站式服务，安高博赞不绝口。

安高博：
上海有着超一流
的营商环境

高品质的都市生活

安高博眼中的上海处处都散发着浪漫的气息，最让他倍感惬意的地方就在他家附近。安高博住在苏州河沿岸，每天清晨或是傍晚，他都会和家人来到河畔漫步，他说："在家门口欣赏日出和日落，是每一天最奇妙、最治愈的时刻。"

去年年底，苏州河静安区段两岸贯通工程基本完成，安高博还目睹了改造的全过程。"我还记得这里原来的样子，这一次的改进非常成功，这里有自然美景也有人文风光，这是一条承载市民幸福生活的温情岸线。"安高博说。

除了家门口，安高博最喜欢的上海地标是新天地。安高博还去参观了位于新天地附近的中共一大会址，了解了中国共产党的历史。"今年是中国共产党建党100周年，这是一个值得纪念的时刻，无疑，中国取得了伟大成就！"安高博激动地说。

一座城市的生命力

安高博认为上海是一座有生命力的城市，这种生命力体现在创新和韧性上。在安高博看来，上海的创新生态系统发展非常强劲，"因为人才、学术和高科技产业以非常有效的方式结合在一起，从而使创新可以得到更快速、高效的发展。"

疫情期间，安高博还发现了上海充满韧性的另一面。"在新冠肺炎疫情流行初期，上海就能做到迅速响应，有效地控制住疫情并在第一时间复工复产，这给了我们企业很大的信心。"

此外，在全球疫情还具有不确定性的当下，进博会的如期举行发出了强烈的信号，给经济复苏带来了希望，也给全球企业提供了开放各国市场、探索新市场机遇的平台。

Name: Allan Gabor
Chinese name: 安高博
Nationality: American
Position: President of Merck China, Managing Director of Merck Electronics China

Allan Gabor:
Shanghai has a superb business environment

This year marks the 100th anniversary of the founding of the Communist Party of China (CPC), which is memorable, and undoubtedly China has made great achievements.

Gabor has expressed his love for Shanghai publicly many times. As an entrepreneur, he is impressed by Shanghai's superb business environment. As a resident, he is immersed in the high-quality urban life in Shanghai. Twenty-two years have passed since Gabor first came to Shanghai, and his knowledge of the city continues to grow.

Superb business environment

Last November, the public health and pandemic prevention zone made its debut at the 3rd China International Import Expo (CIIE), and Merck, a leading global technology company, with 88 years of experience in the Chinese market, was one of the exhibitors.

Like many foreign friends who came to the exhibition, Gabor saw it as a once-in-a-lifetime opportunity.

Gabor says: "The exhibition is a platform for building up communication and cooperation, and many of our important partners also came. The platform serves as a bridge of communication for many stakeholders."

In recent years, the CIIE has become a "green channel" for more and more foreign enterprises to enter the Chinese market, and Shanghai as the host city has been improving its business environment in marketization, law enforcement, and internationalization. At the end of 2017, Shanghai held a meeting to promote the improvement of its business environment.

Li Qiang, secretary of the CPC Shanghai Municipal Committee, requires the local government to offer meticulous service like an attentive "shop assistant" who is always there if needed.

Li says: "We must refer to the highest international standards and the best level, and strive to create a world-class business environment in terms of law

Allan Gabor:

Shanghai has a superb business environment

enforcement, internationalization and convenience so that Shanghai can become a city with the most convenient trade and investment, the highest administrative efficiency, the most standardized service management, and a perfect legal system."

Gabor has witnessed Shanghai's efforts, and he gives the local government's one-stop service lots of plaudits.

He says: "We have full communication with the government at all levels, both at policy and operational levels. The Shanghai government's service-oriented philosophy is very internationally minded, and this benefits the company as well. This is one of the reasons why Merck has based its electronic technology and life sciences business in Shanghai."

High-quality city life

In Gabor's opinion, every place in Shanghai is full of a romantic atmosphere. The most pleasant place for him is just near his home. He lives along Suzhou Creek, and every morning or evening, he and his family take a stroll along the river. "Watching the sunrise and sunset from my doorstep is the most amazing and healing moment for me every day," says Gabor.

At the end of last year, the project to connect the two banks of the Suzhou Creek in Jing'an District was completed, and Gabor witnessed the whole process of renovation.

Gabor says: "I still remember the original look of this place, and this improvement is very successful. There is a natural beauty as well as a humanistic touch, and it is a warm shoreline that carries the happy life of the citizens."

Besides his neighborhood, Gabor's favorite is Xintiandi. He has visited the Memorial of the First National Congress of the Communist Party of China, located near Xintiandi, to learn about the history of the CPC. "This year marks the 100th anniversary of the founding of the CPC, which is memorable, and undoubtedly China has made great achievements," he says.

A vibrant city

Gabor believes that Shanghai is a city with vitality reflected in innovation and resilience. In his eyes, the ecosystem for innovation in Shanghai is developing quite forcefully. "Talents, academics and high-tech industries come together in a very effective way here," he adds.

During the pandemic, Gabor also discovered Shanghai's resilient nature. "At the beginning of the COVID-19 pandemic, Shanghai responded quickly, and soon effectively contained the virus and resumed work and production, which gave our company lots of confidence," says Gabor.

In addition, at a time of global uncertainty about the COVID-19 pandemic, the CIIE held as scheduled, which has sent a strong signal of hope for economic recovery, and has provided a platform for global companies to open markets in various countries and to explore new market opportunities.

姓　名：Caspar Chiquet
中文名：西克
国　籍：瑞士
职　位：bp 中国环境产品负责人

西克：
节能减排，中国非常积极与成功

在国际上，中国是非常积极，也是最成功的践行节能减排的国家之一。

和中文结缘

会说中文的外国友人很多，但西克算是比较专业的那个。作为一名语言爱好者，1999 年，他高中毕业后，来到中国北京，把这里作为自己游学的首选地。在半年多的留学时光中，西克学会了用中文进行日常交流，也对这门博大精深的语言产生了浓厚的兴趣。回到瑞士后，他果断转换了专业，开始研究中国的"寻根文学"，其间大量阅读了莫言等作家的著作。西克说，换专业并非任性的选择，是不希望自己好不容易学会的中文因为太久不用而忘记了。"我和中文最先结缘，在慢慢掌握这门语言的过程中，逐渐加深了对中国文化的理解，也深深地爱上了中国。"

见证中国低碳环保之路

作为 bp 中国环境产品的负责人，西克见证了中国低碳环保的发展之路。2008 年，西克受朋友之邀，重返中国，加入了一家做环境产品的初创公司。"那时，中国的低碳发展刚刚起步，还处在将减排权出售给其他国家的阶段。但今时已不同往日。"西克告诉记者，十多年前，中国的工业高速发展，碳排放量较大。近年来，绿色发展的概念越来越频繁地被提及，能源、环境与气候等问题日益牵动着中国人民的心。"绿水青山就是金山银山。"习近平总书记这一重要论断体现出中国发展理念的转变，低碳环保的意识逐渐

西克：

节能减排，中国非常
积极与成功

在大家的心里扎下了深"根"。

对于这一变化，西克感到十分欣喜。在他看来，低碳发展不是挑战，更是一个机会。"当前中国已建立起了成熟的减排市场，依靠低碳发展理念，正逐渐减少使用过去低效高排放的技术，将目光投向了可再生能源，进一步提高了产业发展的速度与质量。"对未来，西克充满信心。他说："在国际上，中国是非常积极，也是最成功的践行节能减排的国家之一。节能减排代表着一种更长远的视野，也是减少飓风、台风等自然灾害的重要途径之一。"西克表示，希望有更多国家培养起环保意识，像中国一样积极行动起来。

上海的低碳生活方式

低碳环保的意识，也体现在西克的一言一行中。他说，生活在上海，这座城市最吸引人的特质就是开放与包容。"上海市民的文明素质很高，对新鲜事物、好的理念敞开怀抱，接受度也很高。"西克说，每天喝一杯咖啡提神醒脑已经成为了习惯。让他感到惊喜的是，如今走进上海的咖啡馆内，店员们总是优先向他推荐使用自带杯，会有优惠减免。"这可以减少塑料垃圾的使用。生活在这座城市里，有太多地方令人感慨了。"

西克认为，低碳环保应该成为一种生活方式，不只是口头谈谈而已，需要体现在点滴细节中，由大家共同实践。他分享了一个有趣的例子："很多人出差喜欢坐飞机，但其实，同等的距离下，飞机的碳排放量是高铁的十倍。所以我每次出差去北京，都会选择坐高铁，花费的时间其实差不多，但很便利，也不用担心延误，还做到了低碳环保，一举多得。中国的高铁很发达，举世闻名，其实对于低碳环保的发展也是很有益的。"

上海实行垃圾分类，这一举措也备受西克的好评。"其实，生活方式突然转变，人们是很难适应的。但是可以看到上海政府推行垃圾分类的决心，一经推行后，大家积极响应。在我的小区里，经常看到会有志愿者在旁边指导大家按时按类扔垃圾。上海做得很好。"

Name: Caspar Chiquet
Chinese name: 西克
Nationality: Swiss
Position: Environmental Products Originator, bp China

Caspar Chiquet:
China is most active and successful in energy saving and emission reduction

China is one of the most active and successful countries to implement energy saving and emission reduction in the international arena.

A relationship with the Chinese language

While many foreigners can speak Chinese, Caspar Chiquet excels in it. Keen on language learning, he came to Beijing, China, his first choice as the destination of his study tour, after graduating from high school in 1999. During his study here for over half a year, Chiquet learned to use Chinese for daily communication and developed a strong interest in the extensive and profound language. Returning to Switzerland, he changed his major decisively and began the study of Chinese "root-seeking literature", during which he read many works by Mo Yan and other writers.

Chiquet says changing his major was not an impulsive move, but a way to prevent him from forgetting the Chinese language he had managed to acquire if it were rarely used. "I first developed a liking for the Chinese language, and on the way to the mastery of it, I gradually deepened my understanding of Chinese culture and fell in love with China," he says.

Witnessing the development of China's low-carbon environmental protection

As the environmental products originator for bp China, Chiquet has witnessed the development of China's low-carbon environmental protection. In 2008, invited by a friend, he came to China again and joined a start-up company dealing with environmental products. "At that time, China's low-carbon development was just in its infancy, and it was still in the stage of selling emission reduction rights to other countries," he says. "But it's different now."

According to Chiquet, more than ten years ago, China's industry was developing rapidly with a relatively high level of carbon emissions. In recent years,

Caspar Chiquet:

China is most active and successful in energy saving and emission reduction

the concept of green development has been mentioned more and more frequently. Energy, environmental and climate issues have increasingly been the concern of the Chinese people. "Lucid water and lush mountains are invaluable assets." This important conclusion of Chinese President Xi Jinping reflects the transformation of the concept of China's development, and the awareness of low-carbon environmental protection has gradually been deeply "rooted" in everyone's mind.

Chiquet is happy to see the change. In his view, low-carbon development is not a challenge, but an opportunity. "At present, a mature emission reduction market has been established in China," he says. "Relying on the concept of low-carbon development, the country is gradually reducing the use of traditional technologies of low efficiency and high emission, focusing on renewable energy, and further improving the speed and quality of industrial development."

Chiquet is confident about the future. "China is one of the most active and successful countries to implement energy saving and emission reduction in the international arena," he says. "Energy saving and emission reduction represents a better vision in the long run, and is also one of the important ways to reduce natural disasters such as hurricanes and typhoons." Chiquet hopes that more countries will cultivate environmental awareness and take positive actions like China.

Shanghai's low-carbon way of life

The awareness of low-carbon environmental protection is also reflected in Chiquet's words and actions. He says for people living in Shanghai, the most attractive characteristics of the city are openness and inclusiveness. "Shanghai citizens are highly civilized, open and receptive to new things and good ideas," says Chiquet. He also says a coffee a day has become a habit for him to refresh his mind. To his surprise, these days whenever he walks into a cafe in Shanghai, self-brought cups are always recommended first, and he can get a discount if he uses them. "This can reduce plastic waste. There are so many things to marvel at in this city," he says.

Chiquet believes that low-carbon environmental protection should become a way of life instead of being merely talked about. It needs to be reflected in every detail of our actions and should be practiced by all of us.

He shared an interesting example: "Many people like to travel by plane, but actually, at the same distance, the carbon emission of the plane is ten times that of the high-speed train, so every time I go to Beijing on business, I choose to take a high-speed train. The time I spend is almost the same, but it's very convenient, and I don't have to worry about the delay. Meanwhile, I also achieve low-carbon environmental protection. Therefore, it is advantageous in multiple aspects. China's high-speed railway system is well-developed and world-famous, and it is also beneficial to the development of low-carbon environmental protection."

Chiquet also thinks highly of the implementation of garbage sorting in Shanghai. He says: "In fact, it is very difficult for people to adapt to the sudden change in lifestyle, but we can see the determination of the Shanghai government to implement garbage sorting. And people have responded positively since it was implemented. In my community, we often see volunteers guide us to throw classified garbage at a designated time. Shanghai has done a good job."

Scan for videos

姓　名：Roman Kupper
中文名：罗曼
国　籍：瑞士
职　位：德国德乐亚太区总裁

罗曼：
上海的治安让我很有安全感

> 上海的绿化、治安能给很多欧洲国家做榜样。

来自瑞士的 Roman 曾在 3 大洲工作，去过 50 多个国家。2013 年，Roman 来上海工作并很快爱上了这座城市。"虽然我是一个瑞士人，但我觉得上海更加安全，因为你永远不用为孩子们的安全担心，哪怕是半夜，他们都可以自己乘车或步行回家。"

城市更加安全

Roman 的妻子是法国人，他们有三个孩子，如今一大家子都住在上海。对于家长来说，孩子的教育非常重要。因为孩子们要在上海读书，所以夫妻俩开始研究上海的学校。令他惊讶的是，上海有非常好的国际学校，除了文化课，还有丰富的课外活动。

Roman 告诉记者，2 个儿子和 1 个女儿都非常喜欢足球，还参加了学校的足球队。"上海有许多操场，还有专业的足球俱乐部和足球比赛。"这让 Roman 很开心，在孩子们的影响下，Roman 也开始踢足球。随后，他和中国同事组建了一个公司足球队，还参加了上海的市民运动会。

作为父母，最令他欣慰的是上海的治安。Roman 表示，虽然他是一个瑞士人，但他觉得上海更加安全，作为家长，他完全不用为孩子们的安全担心。另一个让 Roman 觉得很有安全感的事情是，他一位外国朋友的钱包落在了出租车上，经过与出租车公司联系，钱包很快找到。"这在欧洲很多国家，是件不敢想象的事情。"

罗曼：

上海的治安让我
很有安全感

绿化堪称样本

工作之余，Roman 很喜欢运动，通常周末的早上他会和中国朋友们骑车去郊区，呼吸新鲜空气，欣赏美丽的风景。

他还经常和妻子在公园里散步，感受上海本地人的悠闲生活。2020 年底，苏州河上海中心城区段 42 公里岸线公共空间实现基本贯通开放。苏州河两岸，既有绿树成阴的自然景观，又有历经岁月沧桑的老建筑。"我们最喜欢的散步方式之一是沿着公园的小河一直往北走到苏州河，然后沿着苏州河散步。"Roman 告诉记者。

苏州河的贯通只是一个缩影，Roman 认为上海的绿化覆盖率非常高，一些公园因地制宜，巧妙地将中华文化融入其中。"上海的绿化能为欧洲很多国家做标杆。"

商务活动有保障

去年底，Roman 参加了上海市政协 2020 年情况通报会，政务服务"一网通办"和城市运行"一网统管"让他印象深刻。Roman 认为，政府做到了全心全意为人民服务。

因为新冠肺炎疫情，中国加强了进口食品新冠病毒检测。Roman 认为这非常好，尽管这些措施给政府带来了前所未有的挑战，但是却保护了正常的商务活动。

由于公司的部分员工需要在冷链环境下工作，接种疫苗能有效保护员工的安全，罗曼和妻子一起接种了中国研制生产的疫苗。"接种过程很专业，接种疫苗是非常重要的选择，当前情况下应该积极预防。我鼓励每一位有机会参与疫苗接种的人都来参加。"Roman 告诉记者。

对于上海，Roman 有着别样的感情，他说很高兴能有机会住在这里，并希望能为上海做出更大的贡献。

Name: Roman Kupper
Chinese name: 罗曼
Nationality: Swiss
Position: President of Doehler Group Asia-Pacific

Roman Kupper:
The security in Shanghai makes me feel safe

Shanghai's greenery and security can serve as an example for many European countries.

As a Swiss, Roman Kupper has worked on three continents and visited more than 50 countries. Kupper came to Shanghai in 2013, and quickly fell in love with the city. "Although I am Swiss, I feel safer in Shanghai because you never have to worry about children's safety, even in the middle of the night, because they can take the car or walk home by themselves," he says.

A safer city

Kupper's wife is French. The couple has three children and the family now lives in Shanghai. Education for children is very important for Mr. and Mrs. Kupper. As their children were to study in Shanghai, the couple started researching schools in the city. To their surprise, there are great international schools in Shanghai, which offer a variety of extracurricular activities in addition to cultural programs.

Kupper says that his two sons and daughter are very fond of soccer and joined the school's soccer team. Kupper is delighted to find that there are many playgrounds in Shanghai, as well as professional football clubs and tournaments. Under the influence of his children, he also started playing soccer. Subsequently, he and his Chinese colleagues formed a company soccer team and also participated in the Shanghai Citizens' Sports Meeting.

As a parent, he is most pleased with the security in Shanghai. Kupper says that although he's Swiss, he feels safer in Shanghai, where, as a parent, he doesn't have to worry about the safety of his children at all. Kupper feels more secure after another incident took place -- a friend of his once left a wallet on a taxi, but it was quickly found and returned after contacting the taxi company. "This

Roman Kupper:

The security in Shanghai makes me feel safe

is unthinkable in many European countries," he says.

Exemplary greenery

In his spare time, Kupper enjoys exercising a lot. He usually spends his weekend mornings with his Chinese friends and cycles to the countryside to smell the roses and enjoy the scenery.

He also takes regular walks in parks with his wife to experience the laid-back life of Shanghai. The 42-kilometer-long public space along the riverside of Suzhou Creek in the urban area of Shanghai had opened to the public by the end of 2020. The banks of Suzhou Creek are lined with trees and time-enduring old buildings. "One of our favorite is to follow the creek in a park all the way north to Suzhou Creek, and then walk along it," Kupper says.

The opening of the public space along Suzhou Creek is a microcosm of Shanghai's greenery coverage. Kupper says that Shanghai's greenery coverage is very high and that some of the parks are adapted to the local context, subtly incorporating Chinese culture. "Shanghai's greenery can be a benchmark for many European countries," he says.

Keeping the business running

At the end of last year, Kupper attended the 2020 Briefing of Shanghai Committee of the Chinese People's Political Consultative Conference and was deeply impressed by the unified online government service and the "one-network-wide" convenience the Shanghai citizens enjoy. Kupper believes that the government has done its best to serve the people's needs.

Owing to the COVID-19 pandemic, China has strengthened the SARS-CoV-2 detection of imported foods. Kupper thinks highly of such measures because they have kept the business running in spite of the unprecedented challenges the government had faced.

As some of the company's employees work in a cold-chain environment, vaccination is an effective way to protect them, and Kupper and his wife were vaccinated together with a vaccine developed and produced in China. He says: "The vaccination process is very professional. Vaccination is a key option to prevent the pandemic actively under the current circumstances. I encourage everyone who has access to vaccination to be vaccinated."

Kupper has a special feeling for Shanghai. He says that he is glad to have the opportunity to live here and hopes to make greater contributions to the city.

姓　名：Magand Lucine
中文名：李希
国　籍：法国
职　位：中国东方航空乘务员

李希：
互联网的发展让现在的生活新鲜有趣又便捷

> 上海人都很友好且开放，我在这里生活非常舒适！上海的地铁干净方便又便宜，很容易去很多地方。

今年是法国姑娘李希来上海的第七年，也是她成为东方航空乘务员的第四年，这些年，她总在上海和巴黎两座城市间往返。辗转之间，李希体会着两座城市不同的魅力。最让她欣喜的是，通过频繁的接触与交往，中法两国的距离正越来越近……

科技改变生活

"我的中国名字是李希，希望的希。"在上海交通大学学了三年中文，李希已经能说一口流利的汉语。

语言是融入一座城市最好的钥匙，李希也因此很快适应了新环境。在上海，她不仅结交了很多中国朋友，还找到了人生中的另一半。"我老公就是上海人，我对上海人有着很好的印象。"李希说，"上海人都很友好且开放，特别是对外国人和外国文化，作为一个外国人，我觉得在这里生活非常愉快、舒适！"

谈及上海生活，李希说，这些年，给她留下最深刻印象的是已经深入到衣食住行等人们日常生活方方面面的互联网科技。

党的十八大以来，以习近平同志为核心的党中央放眼未来、顺应大势，作出建设数字中国的战略决策。随着数字中国建设的深入实践，"推动信息化更好造福社会、造福人民"的美好愿景正成为现实。

李希：

互联网的发展让
现在的生活新鲜
有趣又便捷

"我飞过北京的大兴机场，你甚至可以直接扫脸登机，再也不需要携带或者打印登机牌。"大兴机场建成一周年之际，李希曾执飞过"进博号"彩绘机主题航班，并亲身体验了大兴机场酷炫的"黑科技"。

"你还可以通过扫描二维码添加微信好友、买东西、乘坐地铁，二维码已经成为生活必需品！"作为一个用惯了现金的欧洲人，李希正适应并惊叹于这样的变化。

互联网的发展让李希觉得现在的生活新鲜、有趣又便捷。

友谊拉近距离

因为新冠肺炎疫情，2020年成了极不平凡的一年。李希认为，在疫情防控方面，上海政府提供了非常好的服务。"疫情期间，城市管理者为居民普及防疫知识，提供自愿的疫苗接种预约服务。最棒的是，通过及时的流控调查，我们可以得知疫情发生在哪些区域，在做好防护的同时，还能走出去享受生活。"

也正是在百年未见的严重疫情面前，中法两国友谊谱写了新的篇章。过去一年里，中法两国积极开展抗疫合作，通过互赠防疫物资、分享防控经验、搭建"空中桥梁"等多种形式，共同书写了"千里同好，坚于金石"的中法友谊新佳话。东航保持中法主要运输航班不断航，"进博号"彩绘机的首班国际航班更是选择了巴黎，带着进博正能量激发法国人民的抗疫信心，共赴东方之约。

李希在关注中法两国疫情发展之时，也看到了两国政府和人民如何风雨同舟、守望相助。她为作为东航一员可以实实在在参与到抗疫中而感到自豪，东航既是第一家执飞国内援助抗疫航班，也是第一家执飞国际援助抗疫航班的航空公司，先后承运近2.3万名医护人员和近7万吨物资，执飞涉及防疫的各类运输航班2.4万架次。

"中法的航班越来越多，这是两国关系越来越好，两国距离越来越近的证明！"李希说，这也是她选择空姐这样一份工作的原因。

Name: Magand Lucine
Chinese name: 李希
Nationality: French
Position: Flight Attendant at China Eastern Airlines

Magand Lucine:
Fast-growing Internet industry makes life easy and fun

Shanghainese are very friendly and open-minded. My life here is very easy and comfortable. The subway in Shanghai is clean, convenient and inexpensive, making it easy to reach many places.

The year 2021 marks French young woman Magand Lucine's seventh year in Shanghai and fourth year as a cabin assistant of China Eastern Airlines. She has been travelling between Shanghai and Paris over the years and getting to know the different charms of the two cities. Through her trips, she is glad to see that the China-France relationship is getting closer and closer.

Technology changes life

"My Chinese name is Li Xi, and the word 'Xi' in Chinese means 'hope,'" says Lucine, who learned Chinese during her three years in Shanghai Jiao Tong University and now can speak fluent Mandarin.

Language is the key to getting along in a city, and Lucine quickly adapted to the new environment. She not only made a lot of Chinese friends, but also found her lifelong companion in Shanghai.

She says: "My husband is from Shanghai, and I really like Shanghai people in general. They are very friendly and open, especially when it comes to foreigners and foreign cultures. As a foreigner, I have a very chill and comfortable life here."

When talking about her life in Shanghai, Lucine says that over the years she is most impressed by the Internet technology that has connected every aspect of everyday lives such as food, clothing, living and transportation.

Since the 18th CPC National Congress, the Central Committee, with President Xi Jinping at its core, has taken a strategic decision to build a digital China with an eye to the future and in line with the general situation. With the construction of digital China well underway, the beautiful vision of "promoting

Magand Lucine:

Fast-growing Internet industry makes life easy and fun

information technology for the betterment of society and people" is becoming a reality.

"I once flew to Beijing Daxing International Airport and found that you don't need to bring or print your boarding pass. You can board the plane simply by scanning your face," Lucine says. On the first anniversary of Daxing Airport, Lucine worked in the "Jinbo Hao", a CIIE-themed (China International Import Expo) flight, and also experienced the amazing high-tech in Daxing Airport.

"You can friend each other on WeChat, buy things and take subways by scanning QR codes, which have become an indispensable part of everyone's lives (in China)," Lucine says. As a European who is used to paying in cash, Lucine is amazed by and trying to adapt to these mind-blowing changes. She thinks the fast-growing Internet industry is making life easier and more fun.

China-France friendship is looking up

The year 2020 was extraordinary due to the COVID-19 pandemic. Lucine points out that the Shanghai government has provided very good services in terms of prevention and control.

She says: "During the pandemic, the government educated residents on medical knowledge and provided voluntary vaccination services. The best part is that through timely epidemiological investigations, we can immediately know which areas are of risk, so we can protect ourselves while still enjoying our lives."

Through COVID-19, one of the biggest pandemics in history, the China-France friendship has reached a new stage. Over the past year, China and France cooperated in sharing medical supplies, experience and building "air routes" to fight against the pandemic. Despite their distances, the two nations forged a friendship stronger than metal and stone. China Eastern Airlines kept its major flights between China and France, and the first "Jinbo Hao" international flight was to Paris, pumping up French people's morale to fight against the pandemic with a shot of CIIE optimism.

While keeping up with the latest information on the pandemic in France and China, Lucine witnessed how the governments and people of the two countries supported each other amid the global crisis. She is proud to have contributed to the prevention and control of the pandemic as a member of China Eastern Airlines. It is the first airline to fly both domestic and international aid flights and has now reached a total of 24,000 times, transporting nearly 23,000 healthcare workers and nearly 70,000 tons of supplies.

"There are more and more flights between China and France, which is proof that the relationship between the two countries is going stronger and they are getting closer." says Lucine, adding that this is also why she chose to be a cabin assistant.

Scan for videos

姓　名：Evangelos Tatsis
中文名：艾维他
国　籍：希腊
职　位：中国科学院分子植物科学卓越创新中心研究组长

艾维他：
我不仅是在探索上海这座城市，更是在探索世界

上海可以找到一切，我感觉我不仅是在探索这座城市，更是在探索世界。

2014 年，中国科学院与英国约翰·英纳斯中心签署战略合作协议，5 年内共同投资 1200 万英镑建立中国科学院—英国约翰·英纳斯中心植物与微生物科学联合研究中心（CEPAMS）。随后，CEPAMS 向全球发布了一张"英雄帖"，希望能吸引全球顶尖科学家的到来。Evangelos Tatsis 看到"英雄帖"后，决定去上海试试。

开启在上海的城市探索

这也是 Evangelos Tatsis 第一次到上海，"大"是上海留给他的第一印象。"上海大到让我有些不知所措，这和我之前在欧洲的生活不一样。"Evangelos Tatsis 回忆，但令他意想不到的是，仅仅用了一个月的时间，自己就适应并喜欢上了这里，并开始了城市探索。

2016 年，CEPAMS 正式揭牌。"一个中心三个园区"的模式，分别在北京、上海、英国设立三个园区。Evangelos Tatsis 选择扎根上海。

"我认为上海最好的一点，就是你可以找到一切。可以找到全世界的进口商品，世界各地的料理等等，每周末都可以尝试新的事物。这让我感觉我不仅仅是在探索这座城市，更是在探索世界。"Evangelos Tatsis 告诉记者，每到周末，他喜欢去市中心走走，尤其是上海图书馆附近，尽管有

些建筑背后的历史他并不清楚,但他觉得这些建筑都非常漂亮。

"通过研究传统中国医学成果来完善药物分子的数据库"

Evangelos Tatsis 的研究组目前有两个不同的项目得到了上海市政府的资助,研究团队通过基因数据发现了植物中具有药用潜力分子的上游合成步骤,这为未来推广它们的药理性质和向合成生物学方面的发展延伸打下了基础。"在和英国约翰·英纳斯中心合作时,我们发现了一种具有抗癌作用的分子,它有可能在未来引领抗癌药物的研发新方向。"Evangelos Tatsis 告诉记者,这一类分子的应用在中国传统医药中是有迹可循的,但是直到目前为止都还没有人系统地研究过它的药用价值。通过与英国方面合作,Evangelos Tatsis 相信它有潜力成为新的抗癌药物。"这不仅可以造福中国,更将福泽世界。"

与很多外国人对中医的态度不同,Evangelos Tatsis 说:"我不太喜欢'传统中医'和'西医'的说法,这两者的区别与中国还是外国无关。实际上,我们在对比的是传统的、以经验为主的研究方法与现代的、更看重证据的科学研究。"中医的确是以经验为主的,但是如此长久的经验积累中一定有值得运用现代仪器和技术去研究的方面。相较于世界上其他国家,中国对于传统医学的记载最为详细,资源更加丰富,因此中医对于治疗疾病的手段也了解得更多。

Evangelos Tatsis 现在的工作就是通过研究传统中国医学成果来完善药物分子的数据库。"传统中医对现代药学和现代药物分子研发是一座隐藏的宝库,在未来 50 年中,一定还会有很多新药物来源于传统中国医学。"Evangelos Tatsis 非常有信心。

近年来,上海深入贯彻落实习近平总书记关于人才工作的重要论述,聚天下英才而用之,不断突破创新吸引集聚外国人才的政策举措,积极构建更具国际竞争力和吸引力的外国人才综合环境,围绕"五个中心"建设持续加大引进外国人才和智力工作力度。

Evangelos Tatsis 希望,未来通过加强国际交流和更多的国际合作项目,吸引更多的外国博士生和博士后加入到科研项目之中。

Name: Evangelos Tatsis
Chinese name: 艾维他
Nationality: Greek
Position: Research Group Leader, CAS Center for Excellence in Molecular Plant Sciences

Evangelos Tatsis:
I'm not only exploring the city of Shanghai, but also the world as a whole

Shanghai has everything to offer, and I feel that I am not only exploring the city, but also the world as a whole.

In 2014, the Chinese Academy of Sciences (CAS) and the John Innes Centre (JIC) from the UK signed a strategic cooperation agreement to jointly invest 12 million pounds over 5 years to establish the Centre of Excellence for Plant and Microbial Science (CEPAMS). Later the center released a global recruitment notice to attract top scientists. Evangelos Tatsis saw the notice and decided to come to Shanghai to have a try.

Embarking on the exploration of Shanghai

It was Tatsis's first time to Shanghai, and "big" was his first impression of the city. "Shanghai was so big that I was a bit overwhelmed, and my life here was quite different from that in Europe," Tatsis recalls. But to his surprise, it only took him a month to get used to and fall in love with the city, and he soon started his exploration of the city.

In 2016, the CEPAMS was officially inaugurated and it has three branches in Beijing, Shanghai, and the UK, respectively. Tatsis chose to stay in Shanghai.

Tatsis says: "I think the best thing about Shanghai is that it has everything to offer. You can find imported goods from all over the world, cuisines from all over the world and so on, and you can try something new every weekend. It makes me feel that I'm not only exploring the city, but also the world as a whole." Every weekend, he likes to walk to the city center, especially around Shanghai Library. Although he doesn't know much about the history of some of the buildings, he finds them all very beautiful.

Evangelos Tatsis:

I'm not only exploring the city of Shanghai, but also the world as a whole

"Improving the database of drug molecules by studying the TCM"

His research team currently has two different projects funded by the Shanghai Municipal People's Government. The team has discovered the upstream synthesis steps of molecules with medicinal potential in plants through genetic data, which lays solid groundwork for future promotion of their pharmacological properties and synthetic biology development. "In collaboration with the JIC, we have discovered a molecule with anti-cancer effects that has the potential to lead to new directions in developing anti-cancer drugs in the future," says Tatsis.

According to Tatsis, the application of this type of molecule is well documented in traditional Chinese medicine (TCM), but no one has ever systematically studied its medicinal value. By working with the British side, Tatsis believes it has the potential to become a new anti-cancer drug. "It will benefit not only China but the world as a whole," says Tatsis.

Holding a different opinion of TCM from many foreigners, Tatsis says, "I don't really like the term 'traditional Chinese medicine' and 'Western medicine'; the difference has nothing to do with whether it's Chinese or foreign. In fact, what we are comparing is the traditional, experience-based research versus modern, more evidence-based scientific research." It is true that TCM is mainly based on experience, but there must be something in such a long-term accumulation of experience that is worth studying with modern instruments and techniques. Compared with other countries, China has the most detailed documentation of traditional medicine as well as a richer stock of resources. Therefore, TCM boasts more knowledge about the methods for treating diseases.

Tatsis's current work is to improve the database of drug molecules by studying TCM. He says: "TCM is a hidden treasure trove for modern pharmacology and modern drug molecule development. I am sure that there will be many more new drugs derived from TCM in the next 50 years."

In recent years, Shanghai has been thoroughly implementing the important remarks of Chinese President Xi Jinping on talent development, by gathering talents from all over the world, constantly adopting innovative policies to attract foreign talents, actively building a comprehensive environment that is more competitive internationally and more attractive for foreign talents, and continuously intensifying its efforts to recruit foreign talents around the city's "Five Centers" -- global centers of economy, finance, trade, shipping and technology and innovation.

Tatsis hopes to attract more foreign Ph.D. students and post-docs to join the research projects through enhancing international exchange and initiating more international cooperation projects in the future.

Scan for videos

姓　名：Wonsook Hong
中文名：洪原淑
国　籍：韩国
职　位：上海市闵行区中医医院韩国籍医师、上海中医药大学副教授、医学博士

洪原淑：
在第二故乡，守护"大长今"的初心

上海的医疗水平变化中，我觉得最大的变化就是医疗服务的改善。

身穿白大褂，说着一口流利的中文，为患者望闻问切、对症下药开出处方……在闵行区中医医院里，有这么一位看似普通却又十分特别的中医师——中国首批通过中医执业医师资格认证的外籍医师、上海首位外籍中医师、首位注册任职于中国三级甲等公立医院的外籍中医师、上海市白玉兰荣誉奖获得者，她就是来自韩国的洪原淑。

"我在上海生活了29年，在这里的时间比在韩国生活的时间还长，上海是我的第二故乡。"洪原淑动情地说道。这些年间，她亲历了上海医疗卫生服务整体水平的不断提升，也见证了这座城市的迅速发展。

因为中医扎根中国

1992年，洪原淑从韩国东国大学毕业。彼时，她的父亲因癌症去世，哥哥被诊断出肺癌，姐姐身患系统性红斑狼疮（SLE），西医诊断结果显示无法治愈。为了治好家人的病，洪原淑放弃了去学校当老师的机会，来中国研习中医。

洪原淑还深深记得，当时就读的上海中医药大学零陵路校区较小，交通也不甚方便。当时，上海韩国料理店非常少，若想品尝韩国料理以解思乡之情，只能和其他留学生相约坐车前往。"因为距离太远，一年只能去一次。"洪原淑回忆。而如今，环球美食的多元性满足了各国人才在上海的餐饮消费需求。

"取得文凭并不代表我真正学会了中医，中国的中医环境优于韩国，所以我选择留在这里，不断提高临床医疗水平。"加上求学期间，家人的疾病

洪原淑：

在第二故乡，守护
"大长今"的初心

经过中医的治疗得到了有效控制，这更坚定了洪原淑毕业后继续留在中国钻研中医的决心。

因为热爱架起"桥梁"

作为一名医生，无论是遇到"非典"、H7N9禽流感，还是新冠肺炎疫情，洪原淑始终选择与上海"战"在"疫"起。2019年9月，洪原淑拿到了期盼许久的"中国绿卡"，她笑说当时的感受就和获得"白玉兰纪念奖"时一样兴奋。

鼠年春节前，洪原淑回韩国釜山看望母亲，此时新冠肺炎疫情刚刚暴发。了解到口罩在中国稀缺后，身为医生却没能在前线战斗的洪原淑内心十分焦急："上海是我的第二故乡，她遇到困难了，我心里很着急。"通过多方联系，洪原淑捐赠了6000只韩国医用口罩给上海中医药大学和医院，缓解燃眉之急。

29年间，洪原淑为中医学和韩医学架起了一座沟通的桥梁。去年9月，洪原淑在韩国韩医学研究院主办的"2020年度韩国东医宝鉴国际学术论坛"上发表视频演讲，将中国新冠肺炎中医诊疗方案和上海新冠肺炎中医诊疗方案传播到了韩国及世界。

因为融合心生羡慕

在上海的近30年间，洪原淑作为一名医生，亲历了这座城市医疗条件的飞速发展。"上海的医疗水平变化中，我觉得最大的变化就是医疗服务的改善。"洪原淑说道，20多年前，医院门口常常会有非常多的患者排队，这让她深感惊讶，因为在韩国的医院从未见过这种情况。但是20多年后，有了网上预约等制度，患者不用在门诊大厅等那么长时间了。"这就是一种贴心的进步。"

中医药是中华瑰宝，中国坚持中西医并重，实施中医药振兴发展重大工程。中医药的"中西结合"是让洪原淑心生"羡慕"的一点。"这不仅让我，更让韩医界感叹和羡慕，在韩国传统医学和现代医学是完全分开的，而在中国中西医结合得如此圆满。"

"我愿在第二故乡，用最简单朴素的方式坚守岗位，守护着韩国大长今的初心。"

Name: Wonsook Hong
Chinese name: 洪原淑
Nationality: ROK
Position: South Korean Physician at Shanghai Minhang TCM Hospital, Associate Professor at Shanghai University of Traditional Chinese Medicine, M.D.

Wonsook Hong:
Staying true to her original aspiration as a doctor in her second hometown

The biggest change in the level of healthcare in Shanghai, I think, is the improvement in medical services.

Wearing a doctor's coat, speaking fluent Chinese, checking the patient by looking, listening, questioning and feeling the pulse, and prescribing appropriate medicines according to the diagnosis, Wonsook Hong, a traditional Chinese medicine (TCM) doctor in Shanghai Minhang TCM Hospital, looks ordinary but is special. Hong, from the Republic of Korea, is one of the first foreign practitioners to be certified as a TCM practitioner in China, the first TCM doctor with foreign nationality in Shanghai, the first foreign TCM doctor registered with and employed by a top-level state-owned public hospital in China, and winner of the Shanghai Magnolia Gold Award.

"I have been living in Shanghai for 29 years, longer than my life in the ROK and Shanghai is my second hometown," Hong says emotionally. During these years, Hong has seen the upgrade of the overall quality of the medical care and healthcare service in Shanghai, and has witnessed the rapid development of Shanghai.

Settling down in China for her love of TCM

In 1992, Hong graduated from Dongguk University in the ROK. At that time, her father died of cancer, her elder brother was diagnosed to have lung cancer and her elder sister suffered from systemic lupus erythematosus (SLE), which was incurable with western medicinal treatment. In order to cure the diseases of her family members, Hong gave up an opportunity to teach and came to study TCM in China.

Hong remembers clearly that the campus of Shanghai University of TCM on Lingling Road was rather small and the traffic was not convenient. At that time, there were very few Korean restaurants in Shanghai. When she missed her family and the taste from her hometown, Hong had to meet up with other international students and go there by bus. "It was such a long ride that I could go there only

Wonsook Hong:

Staying true to her original aspiration as a doctor in her second hometown

once a year," Hong recalls. But now, the diversity of food in Shanghai meets the needs of people from all over the world.

Hong says: "Obtaining a diploma did not mean that I was able to practice TCM well. The overall environment for TCM in China is better than that in the ROK. Therefore, I chose to stay in Shanghai so as to continually improve my clinical medical skills." During her study in China, the diseases of her brother and sister were under effective control after the treatment with TCM, which strengthened her determination to stay in China and further her research on TCM after graduation.

Acting as the "bridge" out of deep love

In September 2019, Hong got the Foreign Permanent Resident ID Card that she had been longing for. Hong says that she was as excited as when she received the Magnolia Gold Award.

Hong was visiting her mother in ROK when the COVID-19 pandemic broke out. She was very worried at the news that facial masks were badly needed in China. "Shanghai, my second hometown, was in trouble, I was very worried," says Hong. After a lot of efforts, Hong managed to donate 6,000 surgical masks to Shanghai University of TCM and the affiliated hospital.

During the past 29 years, Hong has worked to bridge TCM and traditional Korean medicine. Last September, Hong delivered a video speech on the 2020 International Academic Forum on Korean Medicine, sponsored by the Korea Institute of Medical Sciences in the ROK, introducing China's and Shanghai's COVID-19 TCM treatment to the ROK and the world.

Admiring TCM for its integration nature

In the 29 years of her life in Shanghai, Hong, as a doctor, personally experienced the rapid development of the healthcare condition in the city. She says: "The biggest change in the level of healthcare in Shanghai, I think, is the improvement in medical services." Twenty years ago, many patients lined up at the gate of the hospital, which surprised her very much, because it had never happened in the ROK hospitals. Twenty years later, however, with the online booking system, the patients don't have to wait in the outpatient hall for such a long time. "This is a sweet improvement," says Hong.

TCM is a precious heritage in Chinese history. The Chinese government holds firmly to the policy of attaching equal importance to TCM and western medicine and has launched major projects on revitalization and development of TCM. The practice of integrating TCM with western medicine gives rise to the admiration in Hong's heart. "The practice not only fills me but also the whole Korean medical community with admiration," Hong says. "In ROK, traditional Korean medicine is completely separated from modern western medicine, whereas in China, TCM and western medicine are integrated in such a fulfilling way."

Hong says: "In my second hometown, I will do my job as a doctor and stick to my original aspiration when I became one."

姓　名：Rajnish Sharma
中文名：沙睿杰
国　籍：印度
职　位：印孚瑟斯有限公司助理副总裁、中国区负责人

沙睿杰：
"智慧城市"上海是热情的

上海已经通过数字化转型，成为一座真正意义上的智慧城市。

"2008年我就到过上海，在这里工作生活了3年。2019年当有机会再一次来上海时，我很高兴，带着妻子和孩子们又一次回到了这里。"印孚瑟斯有限公司全球副总裁、中国区负责人沙睿杰时隔8年再一次踏上上海这片土地时，感受到了一个完全不同以往的上海。"上海通过数字化转型，已经成为一座真正意义上的智慧城市。"

来自中国的邀请

印孚瑟斯和中国的不解之缘，得从2002年时任国务院总理朱镕基访问印度说起。

当年1月，时任国务院总理朱镕基在访问印度期间到访印孚瑟斯班加罗尔园区，并进行现场演讲，2000多名员工到场聆听。朱总理在讲话中提到，中国在硬件方面是第一位的，印度在软件方面是第一位的，如果我们能够共同努力一起合作，就可以在更广泛的领域内成为全球第一。这一席讲话极大触动了印孚瑟斯高层，也为印孚瑟斯走向中国种下了种子。

经过一年准备，2003年印孚瑟斯来到中国，在全国各地开展考察调研。最终，上海凭借其高素质的人才优势、强大的文化包容性，以及规范的市场环境赢得了印孚瑟斯青睐。同年，印孚瑟斯在中国设立了第一家全资子公司。

2008年，沙睿杰受派前往位于上海张江的印孚瑟斯中国办公室，在那里度过了难忘的3年时光。"后来我因为工作原因离开上海，带着对上海的

沙睿杰：

"智慧城市"上海
是热情的

满满回忆和不舍。"

此后多年里，沙睿杰在全球各地工作生活，但上海的美好时光时常会浮现在脑海里。

上海转型智慧城市

"你看，地面上我们这套虚拟 3D 飞机发动机，对应着空中一架真实飞机的发动机，可以随时读取数据，这两台发动机就像一对'孪生兄弟'。"在印孚瑟斯紫竹园区"living lab"实验室里，数字科技领域的最新技术一一展示。

2011 年，印孚瑟斯加快布局中国市场，投资 1.5 亿美元在闵行紫竹园区建设海外最大的软件开发中心。此时的上海正提出"创建面向未来的智慧城市"战略，10 年间先后制定出台《上海市推进智慧城市建设三年行动计划 (2011-2013 年)》《上海市推进智慧城市建设三年行动计划 (2014-2016 年)》《上海市推进智慧城市建设"十三五"规划》等政策文件，将上海智慧城市建设从铺设信息高速公路的 1.0 阶段，升级到应用融合创新的 3.0 阶段。10 年来，上海数字经济活力迸发，新生代互联网经济蓬勃兴起。

10 年间，印孚瑟斯和数字经济同步成长，成为下一代数字服务和咨询领域的全球领导者之一，客户覆盖全球 46 个国家和地区。

"这 10 年，我发现中国正处于一个巨大的数字转型之中，人工智能和互联网技术在线部署，以及从线上到线下的各个领域都在积极快速地发展，无所不在的大数据技术推动了快速增长。"

核心品质不变

两次到访上海，在沙睿杰看来，虽然很多东西都变了，但有一点没有变，那就是上海的核心品质。"它是一座热情的城市，在商业、文化等方面都领先于它的同行者。"沙睿杰说，两段时间的工作生活，让他切身体会到上海政府始终关心着市民，并在提高市民安全感和生活质量方面不懈努力着。

"我和家人在这里生活感觉很自在，我们还有很多来自不同文化背景的朋友，在上海可以共同庆祝不同文化背景下的节日并乐享其中。"

2010 年，沙睿杰在上海体验了世博会，他再次回到中国又遇上了庆祝新中国成立 70 周年，"现在我们全家都在期待 2022 年的北京冬季奥运会了"。

Name: Rajnish Sharma
Chinese Name: 沙睿杰
Nationality: Indian
Position: Head of Infosys China, Associate Vice President of Infosys Limited

Rajnish Sharma:
Shanghai is a welcoming smart city

Shanghai has leapfrogged into being a truly smart and digital city.

"I first came to Shanghai as far back as 2008 and worked here for 3 years. In 2019, when I got another chance to work in Shanghai, I readily accepted it and took my wife and children back here," says Rajnish Sharma, head of Infosys China and associate vice president of Infosys Limited.

When he set his foot on the land of this city again after a lapse of 8 years, he was deeply impressed by how different it was from what it used to be. "Shanghai has leapfrogged into being a truly smart and digital city," he says.

An invitation from China

Infosys' story with China began with the visit of Zhu Rongji, then Premier of the State Council of China, to India in January 2002. During his tour of Infosys Bangalore campus, he addressed a gathering of over 2000 Infoscions, "India is number one in software exports and China is number one in hardware. Together, we'll become the world's number one."

This speech greatly inspired the senior leaders of Infosys and sparked the idea of expanding Infosys' operations to China. After a year of preparation, in 2003, Infosys began to conduct market research across China, and finally, Shanghai stood out as the best choice for Infosys with its large talent pools, inclusive culture, and fair market environment. In the same year, Infosys established a wholly-owned subsidiary in Shanghai, the first one in China.

In 2008, Rajnish Sharma was dispatched to the office of Infosys China located in Zhangjiang, Shanghai, and spent 3 memorable years there. "I later left Shanghai for a new position, full of nostalgic memories of the city," he says.

In the following years, Rajnish Sharma worked across the globe, but memories of the good old days in Shanghai lingered in his mind.

Transformation of Shanghai into a smart city

The latest digital technologies of Infosys China are showcased in its Living

Rajnish Sharma:

Shanghai is a welcoming smart city

Labs in Zizhu Science and Technology Park. "Look, this 3D VR airplane engine is connected to a real one in a flying airplane, and can read data from it at any time. They are like twins," says Rajnish Sharma.

In 2011, Infosys increased its presence in China by investing US$1500 million to build a campus in Zizhu Science and Technology Park in Shanghai, the company's largest software development center outside India.

In the same year, Shanghai initiated the strategy of "building a future-oriented smart city". Over the past 10 years, Shanghai has progressed from Smart City 1.0, featuring the construction of information superhighways, to Smart City 3.0, featuring digital application, integration and innovation, by implementing smart initiatives such as the Three-Year (2011-2013) Action Plan of Shanghai Municipality for Building a Smart City, the Three-Year (2014-2016) Action Plan of Shanghai Municipality for Building a Smart City, and the 13th Five-Year Plan of Shanghai Municipality for Building a Smart City.

The past decade has witnessed a vigorous digital economy and a booming Internet economy in Shanghai, as well as the growth of Infosys into a global leader in next-generation digital services and consulting, with its clients across 46 countries and regions.

Rajnish Sharma says: "In the last decade, China has embarked on a massive digital transformation, and a wide-scale online deployment of artificial intelligence and Internet technologies. Every field is developing very fast both online and offline, a rapid growth driven by ubiquitous data technology."

The unchanged hallmark of Shanghai

Rajnish Sharma finds that many things about the city have changed during his two stints in Shanghai, but one thing stays the same as ever, that is, the essential urban character of Shanghai.

Rajnish Sharma says: "Shanghai remains a very welcoming city. It stands above its peers in culture, commerce and internationalism. Shanghai cares for its citizens and goes above and beyond to ensure the safety of its citizens. That has been the hallmark of Shanghai."

He adds: "My family feels completely at home here. We have many friends from different cultural backgrounds here, and we can have fun celebrating multicultural festivals together in Shanghai."

In 2010, Rajnish Sharma experienced the World Expo in Shanghai, and returned to China at a time that saw the celebration of the 70th anniversary of the People's Republic of China. "Now my family are all looking forward to the Winter Olympics in 2022," he says.

Scan for videos

姓　名：Francois Tardif
中文名：唐德福
国　籍：法国
职　位：佛吉亚中国区总裁

唐德福：
我喜欢用脚步去丈量上海的点滴

不论是个人还是企业都在努力，这对发展非常有利。

虽然来上海的时间不算长，但唐德福的中文进步神速，他说，上海和法国非常像，人们生活精致，都很喜爱美食与时尚。他对这座城市的未来充满了信心，因为这里不仅很有底蕴，更充满了机遇。

对上海的老建筑情有独钟

20世纪90年代，中国经济加速发展，人民生活水平不断提高，汽车也随之"走入"普通百姓家中。唐德福工作的佛吉亚是一家汽车配件公司，随着中国的汽车产业迅猛发展，从1994年开始，唐德福和同事们来中国出差越来越频繁。

2017年，唐德福被派往佛吉亚的中国区总部——上海工作。在上海安家后，唐德福夫妻俩经常四处逛逛，用脚步丈量这座城市。"上海被誉为东方巴黎，在这里有家的感觉，让人舒适和愉快。"

唐德福夫妻俩对上海的老建筑情有独钟，拥有石库门建筑群的新天地是他们常去的地方之一。新老建筑在这里完美融合，修旧如旧的老建筑有了崭新的生命力。从建筑本身到建筑背后的历史，唐德福夫妇都愿意去探究和了解。

为进一步加强红色文物保护，建设守护好中国共产党人的精神家园，以良好面貌迎接中国共产党成立100周年，2020年中共一大会址纪念馆、中共二大会址纪念馆等红色景点闭馆修缮。

唐德福告诉记者，在中共一大会址纪念馆闭馆修缮前，他和太太约朋

唐德福：

我喜欢用脚步去
丈量上海的点滴

友们去过几次。"我们觉得一大会址具有特殊的象征意义，代表着中国发展的一个重要里程碑，非常期待在改造完成之后能再去参观。"

政府懂商业，服务很到位

定居上海前，唐德福并未想到上海的城市活力会是如此旺盛，更没有想到上海的商业氛围如此浓郁。"不论是个人还是企业都在努力，这对发展非常有利。"

唐德福说中国从中央到地方的各级政府对企业发展的支持力度都很大。佛吉亚中国区的总部落户在上海闵行区，企业与区政府交流很多，"上海各级政府对于企业的情况非常了解，包括我们所处的产业竞争格局、发展重点、我们的顾虑和需求，这也使得政府对我们提供的帮助具有针对性。我们非常感激"。

2020年疫情的暴发始料未及。疫情期间一直坚守在中国的唐德福亲眼见证，从中央到地方各级政府采取了一系列行之有效的措施，迅速控制了疫情。随后，各地有序组织复工复产。"我们非常感谢中国各级政府在疫情期间采取的一系列措施，正是因为他们的快速介入和行动，企业的生产才能步入正轨。"

2020年佛吉亚中国区业务有序恢复，取得了良好业绩。唐德福认为，中国的经济始终走在正轨，充满活力，各行各业、各个领域都在快速发展，不断加大投资，促进中国经济进一步的发展。

尤其是汽车产业，发展潜力巨大，唐德福表示，对于佛吉亚这样的企业而言，意味着在中国将会拥有更多的投资机会。

Name: Francois Tardif
Chinese name: 唐德福
Nationality: French
Position: President of Faurecia China

Francois Tardif:
I love to measure every inch of Shanghai with my steps

No matter Individuals or enterprises, they all work hard. This accelerates development.

Tardif has made tremendous progress in his Chinese learning, although he has only been in Shanghai for a short time. He says Shanghai and France share a lot of similarities: people live a sophisticated life; they love food and fashion. He sees this city with full promises, because it is not only rich in cultural heritage, but also harbors great opportunities.

He has a special fondness for the old buildings of Shanghai

The 1990s witnessed rapid economic growth in China and people's living standards were improved steadily, with which automobiles "entered" ordinary residents' life. Faurecia is a company dedicated to the business of automotive spare parts. With the fast development in the automotive industry of China, Tardif and his colleagues have been making increasingly frequent business trips to China since 1994.

In 2017, Tardif was assigned to work in Shanghai, Faurecia headquarters of China. After they settled down in this city, Tardif and his wife roamed around and explored the city with their feet.

He says: "Shanghai is known as the Paris of the East. It feels like home to us, making us happy and comfortable."

Mr. and Mrs. Tardif have their special fondness for the old buildings in Shanghai. Xintiandi, the place with a cluster of Shikumen buildings (the old-fashioned buildings in Shanghai with stone gates), is one of their favorite places to visit. Here, the old and new buildings compromise perfectly. Those old buildings which have been restored to their original looks are now full of vitality. Mr. and Mrs. Tardif are eager to learn about the buildings as well as the history behind them.

In order to strengthen the protection of the red cultural relics, build and

Francois Tardif:

I love to measure every inch of Shanghai with my steps

protect the spiritual home of Chinese Communists, and welcome the 100th anniversary of the founding of the Communist Party of China (CPC), the Memorials of the First National Congress of CPC and the Second National Congress of CPC will be closed for renovation.

Tardif tells us that before the closure of the Memorial of the First National Congress of the Communist Party of China, he and his wife went to visit it several times with their friends.

He says: "We feel that the site has special symbolic significance and represents an important milestone in China's development. We look forward to visiting it once the renovation is complete."

The government understands business and provides good service

Before he settled in Shanghai, Tardif didn't expect Shanghai would be so vibrant. What surprised him more was that the environment for business in Shanghai was so good. "Both individuals and enterprises are working hard, which helps accelerate development," he says.

Tardif says administrations at all levels in China, from the central government to the local divisions, have been very supportive of business development. The headquarters of Faurecia is located in Minhang District, Shanghai. There is a lot of communication between the enterprises and the local administration.

He says: "The administrations at all levels in Shanghai know the enterprises very well, including the competitive environment of the industry, the development priorities, and our concerns and needs, which helps the government's support for us better targeted. We appreciate this very much."

The outbreak of the pandemic in 2020 was unexpected. Tardif, who stayed in China during the pandemic, witnessed that the central government and local administrations took a series of effective measures and managed to bring the epidemic under control within a short time. Subsequently, industrial production all over the country went back on track.

Tardif says: "We are very grateful to the Chinese administrations at all levels for taking those effective measures during the outbreak. It was their quick intervention and reaction that helped our business get back on track."

In 2020, Faurecia's business in China recovered steadily, achieving a satisfying outcome. Tardif believes that China's economy is on the right track and full of vitality. All industries are developing rapidly. Investment is constantly increasing to promote further development of the Chinese economy.

The automotive industry, in particular, has immense growth potential, which means, to Tardif, more investment opportunities in China for companies like Faurecia.

姓　名：Miodrag Colombo
国　籍：意大利
职　位：执行制片人

Mio：
发展电影工业，上海像一辆高速列车

论电影工业，上海要比温哥华和伦敦发展晚。但是上海发展的速度更快，温哥华和伦敦不具备这速度。上海就像一辆高速列车。

上海电影工业发展的亲历者

"虽然上海是超大城市，但给我的印象并不是人声鼎沸、车水马龙。上海十分惬意，是个有底蕴的地方，融汇了中国、欧洲以及亚洲其他国家的文化。"住在武康路附近的 Mio 告诉记者，上海的周末很热闹，但平日里又很静谧，"有时候我会有一种'啊，其实我在中国的上海'这种如梦方醒的惊喜感"。出生在塞尔维亚的 Mio，在意大利长大。因为工作关系，他曾在温哥华、伦敦、米兰、罗马生活。Mio 告诉记者，这些城市的电影业都很蓬勃，但上海在广告业、金融业有更早更成熟的发展。"论电影工业，上海要比温哥华和伦敦发展晚。但是上海发展的速度更快，温哥华和伦敦不具备这速度。上海就像一辆高速列车。"

Mio 与中国的缘分要从 2011 年说起，那时他接到了一个电影项目《雨果》的后期制作任务。第一次到上海，他觉得一切都很新鲜。这也是 Mio 第一次管理一个团队，团队中有 25 个人，一半外籍一半中国籍。电影的后期制作耗时 10 个月，Mio 回忆，团队经历了很多挑战，但最终赢得了奥斯卡最佳视觉特效奖。"上海和北京的团队都参与其中，这也代表了《雨果》的这次奥斯卡奖荣誉也有中国的一份。"

完成工作后，Mio 离开了中国，在加拿大住了一年多。2014 年，角色变成制片人的 Mio 回到中国，并在上海安了家。他坦言，起初并没有在意

Mio：

发展电影工业，上海
像一辆高速列车

中国的变化，但当他开始关心中国的时候，却惊讶地发现，中国正在发生巨变。

"当你有很棒的创意想法的时候，这里的人会给你机会实现。相比之下，其他国家谈事情是很迟缓的。这里对有志向的外国人来说，有着很好的创业环境。"Mio告诉记者，2019年他和上海电影节合作，把外国优秀电影带来中国。

对在中国的未来充满信心

"十三五"以来，电影成为我国文化艺术领域和文化产业的重要亮点，中国已成为全球电影市场的发展主引擎。2016年，全国电影总票房457.12亿元；2017年11月，全国电影总票房首次突破500亿元；2018年12月底，全国电影总票房首次突破600亿元；2019年12月初，全国电影总票房再次突破600亿元。

如今，中国已是全球第二大电影市场。2021年2月份电影票房122.65亿元，创造全球单月单市场票房纪录。身在其中，Mio有着最直观的感受："中国，机会机会机会！"得益于和中国公司的良好合作，Mio有了和西方电影公司高层及业界大咖对话的机会。Mio告诉记者，他现在的工作是帮中国公司从国外买电影，因为有庞大的中国市场做支撑，很多国外企业找到他。

除了感受到中国市场在海外的影响力，疫情期间Mio也感受到了"上海服务"的温度。影视行业受疫情影响比较严重，政府为Mio的公司减免了不少税收。Mio说："这就叫雪中送炭。"Mio透露，希望搭建一个线上电影学院，可以教年轻人学习更好的电影制作技术。

Mio对在中国的未来充满信心。

Name: Miodrag Colombo
Nationality: Italian
Position: Executive Producer

Miodrag Colombo:
With the film industry going strong, Shanghai is driving forward like a high-speed train

In terms of the development of the film industry, Shanghai started later than Vancouver and London, but grew so much faster, like a high-speed train.

A witness of the development of the Shanghai film industry

"Though a megacity, Shanghai is not all hustling and bustling like I imagined it to be. It's actually a very pleasant city inclusive of not only Chinese but also many European and Asian cultures," says Miodrag Colombo, who lives near Wukang Road, adding that weekends in Shanghai are jolly and fun but weekdays are quieter.

Colombo says: "Sometimes I get the feeling like 'Ah, I am actually in Shanghai.' It's like waking up from a sweet dream and still feeling great."

Colombo was born in Serbia and grew up in Italy. He had lived in Vancouver, London, Milan and Rome because of work. Colombo notes that the film industries in all these cities are thriving, but Shanghai has had an earlier and more mature development in advertising and financial industries. "In terms of the development of film industry, Shanghai started later than Vancouver and London, but grew so much faster, like a high-speed train," says Colombo.

Colombo's China story began in 2011 when he received a post-production assignment for the film Hugo. It was the first time Colombo had been to Shanghai and everything was new to him. It was also the first time that Colombo had headed a team. There were 25 people in the team, half of whom are foreigners, and the other half are Chinese. It took Colombo's team 10 months to finish the post-production. Colombo recalls that they had met many challenges but

Miodrag Colombo:

With the film industry going strong, Shanghai is driving forward like a high-speed train

eventually won an Oscar for best visual effects. "Both teams in Shanghai and Beijing were involved in the film, so credit to China too," says Colombo.

Colombo left China after finishing the project and went to live in Canada for more than a year. In 2014, he returned to China as a producer and settled down in Shanghai. At first, he didn't realize the changes that were happening in China, but later when he started paying attention, he was surprised to find that China was undergoing great changes.

Colombo says: "When you have an amazing idea, people here can actually provide you with what it takes to make it happen, which is not the case with other countries where things move much slower. Aspiring foreigners can find a really great entrepreneurial environment here." In 2019 he worked with the Shanghai International Film Festival and brought in some very good foreign films to China.

Full confidence in his future in China

Since the introduction of the 13th Five-Year Plan (2016-2020), the film industry has become an important highlight in China's cultural and arts industry. And China has become the main force driving the development of the global movie market. China's box office reached 45.712 billion yuan (US$7.18 billion) by 2016, over 50 billion yuan by November 2017, 60 billion yuan by the end of December 2018, and 60 billion yuan again by early December 2019.

China is now the second-largest film market in the world. Its box office in February 2021 reached 12.265 billion yuan ($1.93 billion), setting a world record of a single month's sale of movie tickets.

As a participator, Colombo feels the most direct rushes, "China is all about opportunities, opportunities, and opportunities." Thanks to his cooperation with Chinese companies, Colombo has contact with top executives of some western film companies as well as big names in the industry. Colombo says his job now is to help Chinese companies purchase movies from abroad. Supported by China's huge market, Colombo has received many cooperation offers from foreign companies.

In addition to the Chinese market's influence overseas, Colombo also felt the warmth of the "Shanghai service" during the COVID-19 pandemic. The film industry was severely impacted by the pandemic, but the Shanghai government gave Colombo's company a tax break, which, according to Colombo, "is like being given hot charcoals on a snowy night."

Colombo also hopes to build an online film academy that teaches young people filmmaking techniques, and is confident about his future in China.

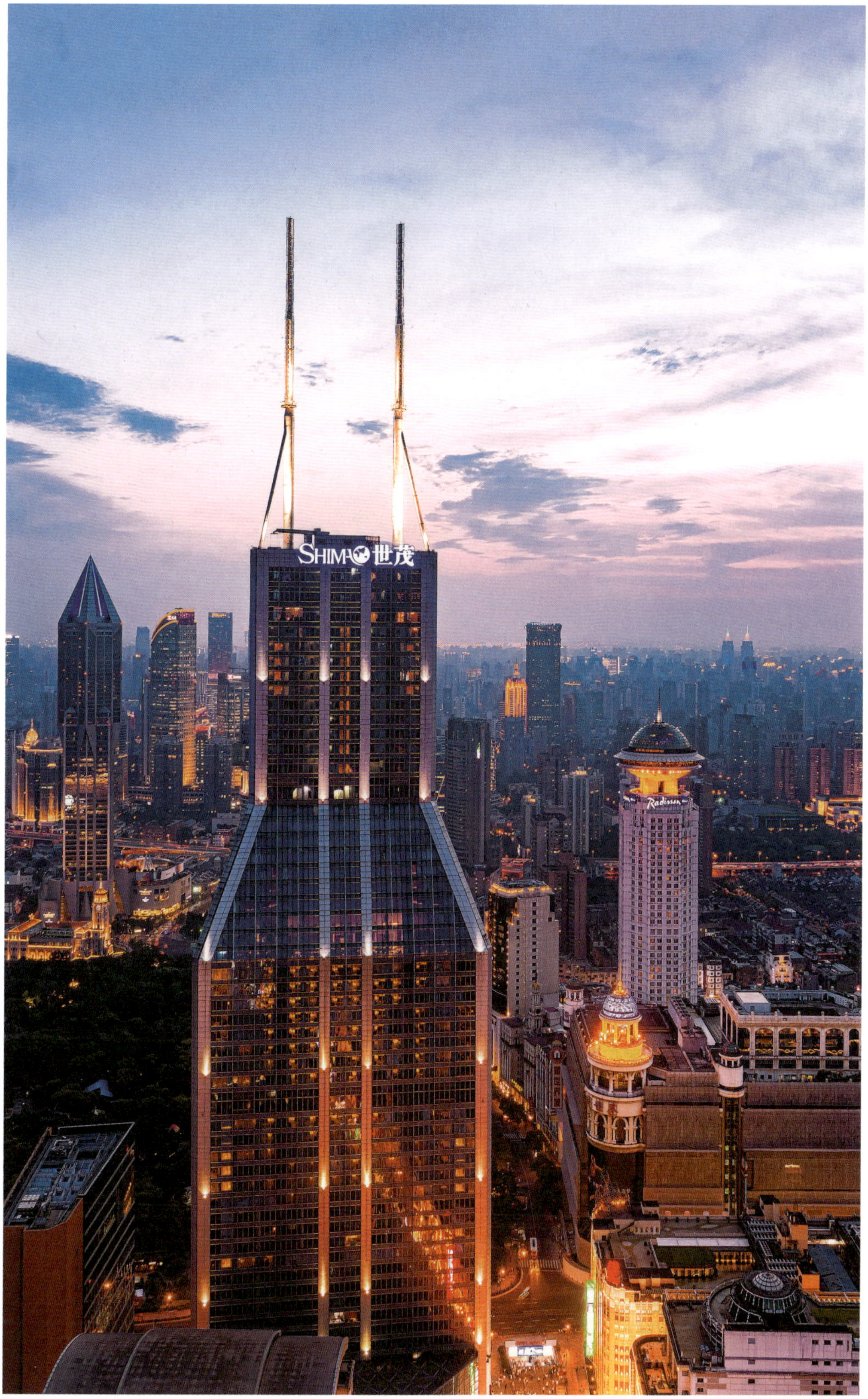
SHIMAO 世茂
Radisson

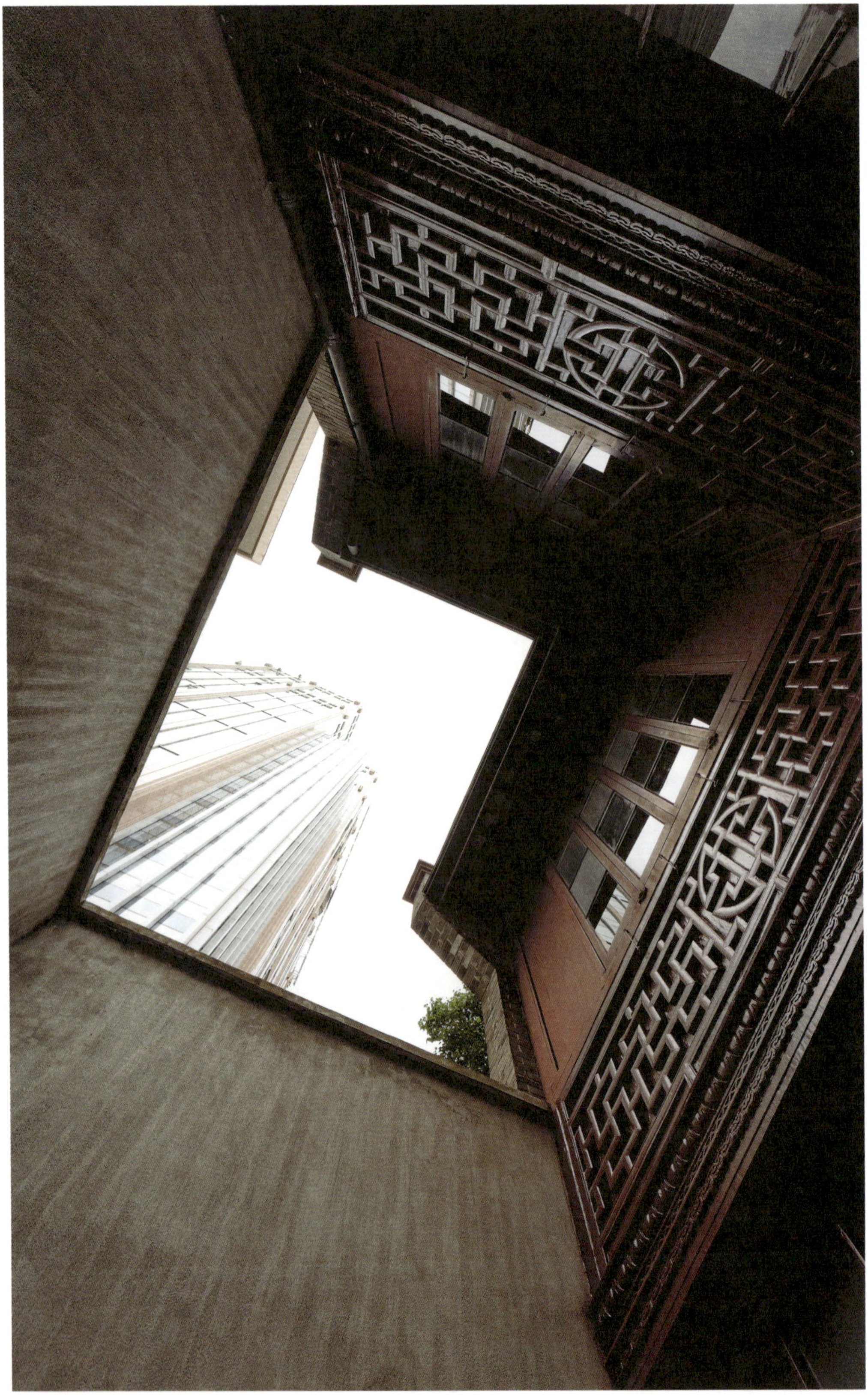

姓　名：Chen-Jiang PHUA
中文名：潘正锵
国　籍：新加坡
职　位：奥特斯（中国）有限公司董事会主席

潘正锵：
上海迸发着热情，一定会继续腾飞！

感谢上海市政府和城市规划师们建设了这样一座美丽的城市。

"我清楚地记得2004年底，总部问我是否有兴趣从香港调到上海接受挑战，我兴奋地同意了。"16年前的那个情形，潘正锵历历在目，他说，事实证明这个决定非常正确。这些年，他不仅见证了自己的进步，也见证了上海的腾飞。

见证上海腾飞

"感谢上海市政府和城市规划师们建设了这样一座美丽的城市。"潘正锵坦言，这16年，上海给他的最大感受就是一直在前进、一直在变化。而这一切都离不开出色的规划。

潘正锵的工作与生活都在闵行，他说自己刚来的时候，闵行不是现在这样，但如今，变化是有目共睹的。"尤其是虹桥枢纽的建设给我留下了深刻印象。15年来，大虹桥发展经历了三个阶段，2006年我刚到上海没多久，虹桥地区刚刚启动建设综合交通枢纽的工程，我眼见着一座现代化商务区因交通而兴。到了2014年，国家会展中心落成。2018年以来，连续三届进博会推动了虹桥商务区成为联动长三角、服务全国、辐射亚太的全球贸易枢纽。"

去年11月，虹桥、莘庄两大城市副中心最新规划设计方案出炉。今年3月，上海加快推进落实《虹桥国际开放枢纽建设总体方案》，绘就了"一核两带"蓝图，以虹桥商务区为核心，南北拓展带将苏浙两省毗邻上海

潘正锵：

上海迸发着热情，
一定会继续腾飞！

的地区连点成线，在打通国内大循环的基础上，一同面向世界，服务于国际国内双循环。春节假期后的第一个工作日，上海市领导又开始实地调研、部署"五个新城"建设。

"和很多国际大都市相比，上海是一座年轻的城市，自由开放、充满活力、激情四射。如果你愿意，每天都可以发掘到不一样的东西。回顾过去十几年，上海取得了很多令人瞩目的成就。直到今天，它依旧在飞速发展中。如今，虹桥国际开放枢纽进入全面实施新阶段，上海'五个新城'建设紧锣密鼓，我相信，在中国共产党的领导下，未来上海一定会继续腾飞！"潘正锵说。

在潘正锵看来，上海的国际化程度首屈一指。他说："来自世界各地不同国籍的人聚居或工作在上海。融合亲和的区域文化、安全便利的人居环境，也是众多跨国企业选择把总部落户上海的原因，我非常荣幸可以参与其中，看到这个不断迸发着热情的城市的成长。"

关爱留守儿童

作为一名企业家，潘正锵也心系社会，主动承担起了企业的社会责任。重庆潼南县，西南部最贫穷的地区之一，距离重庆市区约120公里。从2015年开始，潘正锵和同事们都会定期来到这里的长兴小学看望留守儿童，为他们带去生活和学习用品。

"我们的每一次探访，带给孩子们极大的鼓舞。能带给别人欢乐并改善他们的生活，我觉得非常有意义。"潘正锵感触很深。

习近平总书记在党的十九大报告中提出，坚决打赢脱贫攻坚战，要动员全党全国全社会力量，坚持精准扶贫、精准脱贫，坚持大扶贫格局。

这些年，很多外资企业也都开始深度参与脱贫攻坚战。潘正锵表示他和奥特斯将继续与中国的发展融合，一起前行、进步！

Name: Chen-Jiang PHUA
Chinese name: 潘正锵
Nationality: Singaporean
Position: CEO AT&S Business Unit Mobile Device and Substrates

Chen-Jiang PHUA:
Shanghai oozes warmth; it will continue to thrive

Thank you to the Shanghai Municipal Government and Shanghai's urban planners for making such a beautiful city possible.

"At the end of 2004, when I was in Hong Kong, my company asked me whether I wanted to take up a challenge in Shanghai, and I outright happily accepted the challenge," PHUA says. "I think that is the best decision I ever made in my life."

Over his 16 years in Shanghai, PHUA has seen himself grow and thrive with the city.

Witnessing Shanghai's economic takeoff

PHUA says he is impressed that Shanghai has always been developing and changing over the time he has been here, which wouldn't be possible without excellent city planning.

"Thank you to the Shanghai Municipal Government and Shanghai's urban planners for making such a beautiful city possible," he says.

PHUA works and lives in Minhang District. He says when he first arrived there, Minhang was not what it has become today, and its transformation has been palpable for over a decade and a half.

PHUA says: "The construction of the Hongqiao hub was particularly impressive. The development of the greater Hongqiao area underwent three phases in 15 years. I had just arrived in Shanghai in 2006 when the area's construction of an integrated transportation hub commenced. I witnessed the convenience of transportation giving birth to a modern business district. In 2014, the National Exhibition and Convention Center was completed. Since 2018, three consecutive China International Import Expos fueled the Hongqiao CBD to become an international trading hub that connects the Yangtze River Delta, serves the whole country and bridges up the entire Asia-Pacific region."

Last November, the latest design plan was released for building Hongqiao and Xinzhuang into new centers of the city. In March, the Shanghai Municipal

Chen-Jiang PHUA:

Shanghai oozes warmth; it will continue to thrive

Government accelerated the implementation of an overall plan to develop the Hongqiao International Hub for Opening-up. With its "one core, two belts" layout, the plan will connect the Hongqiao CBD with neighboring areas in Jiangsu and Zhejiang Provinces and will facilitate international trade as part of China's "dual circulation" economic strategy. Immediately after the 2021 Spring Festival holiday ended, Shanghai's authorities unveiled a project to develop five new cities out of five suburban districts in Shanghai.

PHUA says: "Compared with metropolises around the world, Shanghai is a young city that is free, open, energetic and vibrant. If you want, you can discover something different here every day. Over the past decade, Shanghai has made many remarkable achievements. It continues to develop rapidly even today. Now that the establishment of the Hongqiao International Hub for Opening-up and the five new cities is in full swing, I believe Shanghai will continue to thrive under the Communist Party of China's leadership!"

To PHUA, Shanghai's degree of internationalization is impressive. "People of different nationalities from around the world live or work in Shanghai," he says. "The city's inclusive and friendly culture and safe and convenient living environment are both reasons for multinational corporations to establish their headquarters in Shanghai. I feel honored to have been part of it and to experience the growth of this vibrant city."

Caring for "left-behind" children

On top of being a business executive, PHUA cares for his host country and is committed to fulfilling his company's corporate social responsibility. Since 2015, he has regularly traveled to Changxing Elementary School with his colleagues to visit the "left-behind" children there and bring them school and everyday supplies. The school is located in Tongnan County, Chongqing, 120km from downtown Chongqing and one of the poorest areas in southwestern China.

"Every visit of ours motivated the kids massively," he says. "Bringing people happiness and improving their living conditions are things I find meaningful and worthwhile."

President Xi Jinping remarked at the 19th National Congress of the Communist Party of China that winning the battle against poverty requires the mobilization of the energies of the whole Party, the whole country and the whole society, as well as the continued implementation of targeted poverty reduction and alleviation measures drawing on the joint efforts of government, society, and the market.

Many foreign enterprises have joined China's poverty alleviation campaign in recent years. PHUA says his and AT&S's future will be inseparable from China's future and that he and his company will continue to grow and thrive with China.

姓　名：Tarik Temucin
中文名：塔里克·铁穆青
国　籍：土耳其
职　位：上海波特曼丽思卡尔顿酒店总经理

塔里克·铁穆青：
我们用服务传递上海的"温度"

一座酒店的服务"微光"可以照亮城市的美好。

4年前，来自土耳其的塔里克·铁穆青成为上海商城波特曼丽思卡尔顿酒店（以下简称"波特曼丽思卡尔顿"）的"掌门人"。让他倍感自豪的是，作为上海老牌五星级酒店中的佼佼者，波特曼丽思卡尔顿自落成后身披各种荣耀，数不清的国际政要、商界名流来沪都曾下榻此处。近年来，上海国际电影电视节、国际篮联篮球世界杯、中国国际进口博览会等重大盛会接待服务名单中，波特曼丽思卡尔顿也跻身其间，共同参与打响"上海服务"品牌。

展现"上海温度"的窗口

上海是亚洲城市中的一颗璀璨明珠，也是中国最大的经济中心城市，每年有超过1.6亿人次的国内外游客造访上海。中共上海市第十一次代表大会上提出，要用精细化管理打造"有温度的城市"，而酒店服务业正是向海内外游客展现"温度"的窗口之一。

2020年对大多数行业来说，都是"黑天鹅"，酒店服务业更是首当其冲。坐落于静安寺CBD繁华地带的波特曼丽思卡尔顿始终敞开大门，为那些滞留在上海的旅客提供"落脚地"。

疫情还要持续多久？能为这些住客提供什么服务？一系列需要迫切回答的问题摆在了铁穆青面前。

"这是酒店开业22年来从未经历过的。"谈起去年疫情的冲击，铁穆青眉头紧锁，但目光坚定。"那时我们过得非常艰难，属地政府部门在我们

塔里克·铁穆青：
我们用服务传递
上海的"温度"

最困惑的时候，多次走访，并带来了不少有效的防疫建议。"在政府各部门的援助下，酒店防疫物资快速到位，各处防疫关口迅速设立，波特曼丽思卡尔顿由此成为上海应对疫情准备最快最充足的酒店之一。

这一切给了铁穆青极大信心："整个疫情期间，波特曼丽思卡尔顿没有中断运营，始终坚持为全球旅客提供安全优质的服务。"

一座酒店的服务"微光"可以照亮城市的美好。让铁穆青印象深刻的是，疫情期间有两个来自武汉的家庭因为封城回不去，也不敢带孩子们到外面游玩，情绪消沉。波特曼丽思卡尔顿为他们开放了露天屋顶花园，让孩子们能有机会在室外尽情地奔跑；当孩子们回到房间，发现 DVD 已经在播放各种动画片，各种小玩偶、小礼物每天变着花样地出现在他们的房间里……在滞留上海 2 个月后，他们终于回到家乡武汉，第一件事就是给波特曼丽思卡尔顿寄来了一大袋苹果。

"在中国，苹果寓意着平安。"铁穆青动情地说。

卓越城市需要一流酒店

2040 年上海要建成卓越的全球城市，其中，服务功能是上海的核心功能，也是经济中心城市的使命所在。作为上海唯一一家白金五星级酒店，波特曼丽思卡尔顿的服务水准代表着酒店业"上海服务"的标杆。在铁穆青的带领下，波特曼丽思卡尔顿近年参与了多项重大接待任务，提供的高品质服务令人难忘。

如今，铁穆青已经把家搬到了上海。虽然还不会说中文，但他把上海当做了第二家乡。每年中秋，他都会拜访周边养老院，送上月饼和祝福。慈善募捐会上也常能看到他的身影。

去年春节上海气温骤降，铁穆青带着酒店工作人员一起走访附近的居民区、写字楼以及社会机构，为 24 小时坚守岗位的一线工作者送上慰问品。"有位保安接过温热的姜茶时，羞涩地道了一声'谢谢'，脸上洋溢起的笑容，常常让我回味，这就是上海的'温度'。"

Name: Tarik Temucin
Chinese name: 塔里克·铁穆青
Nationality: Turkish
Position: General Manager for Portman Ritz-Carlton, Shanghai

Tarik Temucin:
We give off the "warmth" of Shanghai with our service

The service of a hotel can be "a gleam of light" to shine on the beauty of a city.

Four years ago, Tarik Temucin, who is from Turkey, became the "chief" of the Portman Ritz-Carlton, Shanghai (hereafter referred to as "the Portman Ritz-Carlton"). Temucin takes great pride in the Portman Ritz-Carlton, which, as the leading five-star hotel long established in Shanghai, has received numerous world leaders and renowned businessmen since its opening and has been covered in glory. In recent years, the Portman Ritz-Carlton has provided service for such major events as Shanghai International Film Festival, FIBA Basketball World Cup and China International Import Expo, being one of the brands in the "Shanghai Service" campaign.

A showcase for the "warmth of Shanghai"

As the economic center in China and one of the most prominent metropolises in Asia, Shanghai receives over 1.6 hundred million visits per year from home and abroad. In line with the idea of building the "City of Warmth" with delicate management, which was put forth by the 11th Shanghai Committee of the CPC, hotel service becomes a showcase for the "warmth" to domestic and foreign visitors.

2020 was a "Black Swan" year for most industries, among which hotels were the first to be affected. However, the Portman Ritz-Carlton, situated in the bustling Jing'an Temple CBD, kept its door open and became a temporary "haven" for those held up in Shanghai by the pandemic.

How long would the pandemic last? What service should be provided for those guests? Temucin was faced with questions screaming for an answer.

"We have never met such situations since the hotel opened 22 years ago,"

Tarik Temucin:

We give off the "warmth" of Shanghai with our service

Temucin says, with furrowed brows but a resolute look in his eyes. "We had a very tough time, but the local government paid us many visits when we were most bewildered, giving us a lot of effective advice for COVID-19 prevention." With the assistance of different government departments, anti-pandemic provisions arrived in time and passes were set up quickly. As a result, the Portman Ritz-Carlton became one of the hotels in Shanghai that responded to the pandemic most fully and quickly.

All these gave Temucin a tremendous boost in confidence. "Throughout the pandemic, the Portman Ritz-Carlton strove to keep running and providing fine and safe service for global travelers," he says.

The service of a hotel can be "a gleam of light" to shine on the beauty of a city. Temucin was impressed by two families from Wuhan during the pandemic. They were very dejected because they neither could return to Wuhan due to the lockdown nor dared to take the kids out. The Portman Ritz-Carlton opened the rooftop garden for them so that the kids could run in the open air freely. When the kids came back to the hotel rooms, they would be showered with various surprises like the cartoons playing on DVD, and all kinds of dolls and gifts. When they finally returned to Wuhan two months later, the first thing they did was sending the Portman Ritz-Carlton a sack of apples.

"In China, an apple is the emblem of safety and health," says Temucin, touched.

An excellent city needs first-rate hotels

By 2040 Shanghai is expected to be an "excellent global city" and service will be its core function as well as a mission that an economic center is supposed to fulfil. Being the only *platinum five-star hotel* in Shanghai, the Portman Ritz-Carlton represents exemplary "Shanghai service." Led by Temucin, it has undertaken a number of major reception tasks, impressing people with high standard service.

Temucin has moved his family to Shanghai now. Though still unable to speak Chinese, he regards Shanghai as his second hometown. Every Mid-Autumn Festival he would visit the neighboring nursing homes with good wishes and mooncakes. He also attends fundraisers for charity frequently.

During the Spring Festival last year, Shanghai turned drastically cold. Temucin took his hotel staff to the residential neighborhoods, office buildings and social organizations, sending gifts of appreciation to the front-line workers who remained at their posts around the clock. "A security guard, upon taking the ginger tea, said 'thank you' to me, with a touch of shyness," he says. "The smile on his face often returns to my mind, and that is the 'warmth' of Shanghai."

姓　名：Upadhyaya Nagendra Rijal
中文名：那哲
国　籍：尼泊尔
职　位：WICRESOFT 上海微创软件股份有限公司 WDI 事业部运营总监

那哲：
我们父子两代人见证上海三十年变迁

现在的每一天，这里都是一个崭新的上海，一个机会多多的上海。

"我已经在上海待了 14 年了！"扳起指头一算，来自尼泊尔的那哲恍然发现："我把青春都献给上海啦！"出生于 1983 年的那哲说着一口流利的普通话，和朋友微信聊天用的也都是中文。在上海的 14 年，他早就在这里找到了家的感觉。

两代人结缘上海滩

"我为什么要来上海？我的父亲三十多年前就是上海的留学生呀。"说起结缘上海，那哲打开了记忆盒子。1984 年 4 月，作为中国首批对外开放的 14 个沿海城市之一，上海迎来了大批海外留学生。1988 年，那哲的父亲作为"留华潮"中的一员，来到上海东华大学（时为中国纺织大学）就读。彼时，距离浦东开发开放还有两年时间，横跨上海黄浦江的首座大桥——南浦大桥刚刚开工奠基。但在那哲父亲的眼里，那时的上海已然是座美丽繁华的东方城市，人民善良可亲。

2005 年，那哲来到中国，第一站是南京。在那里他学习了一年中文。2006 年 10 月，他来到上海，入读上海交通大学电子科学与技术专业。"那会儿从南京到上海，我火车坐了足足 5 个小时。现在呢，1 个小时就够了！"

那哲在上海的 14 年，正是上海经济飞速发展的 14 年，摩天大楼拔地而起，快速路网延伸到角角落落，城市发生着日新月异的变化。"我父亲在上海的时候，轨道交通 1 号线才开始建设，我来的时候上海已经有 3 号线了，

那哲：

我们父子两代人见证
上海三十年变迁

看看现在，15 号线也开通了，这才不到 30 年，发展得太快了。"

最近这几年，父亲常常来上海故地重游。每一次到访，他都会感慨上海发展速度之快，面貌之新。30 多年前父亲就读大学时，校门前那条蜿蜒狭窄的延安路，如今已成齐整宽阔的 8 车道，架起的高架路上车辆川流不息，2017 年上海开通的首条城市中运量公交线路畅通无阻，展现在那哲父亲眼前的是一幅城市快速发展的雄壮蓝图。

说起上海的变化，那哲神采飞扬，"我们父子两代人见证了上海这三十多年的飞速发展，时代的脚步在这里留下了深刻印记。现在的每一天，这里都是一个崭新的上海，一个机会多多的上海。"

我的团队是"小联合国"

那哲如今在 WICRESOFT 微创软件担任 WDI 事业部运营总监，为全球企业客户提供技术支持。他的团队有 100 多人，来自 54 个国家，是个标准的"小联合国"。有些人刚从孟加拉国、印度来上海不久，吃不惯这里的饭菜，那哲就会带他们去吃新疆菜，"我们会点大盘鸡，我们爱咖喱"。

"他们来自全球各地，文化和生活习惯都不一样。不过别担心，我会告诉他们，这就是上海，看看我在这里都生活了那么久，过得有多愉快。"

周末时间，那哲喜欢做菜，邀请三五好友一起来家里吃吃饭聊聊天。"我的拿手好菜是番茄炒蛋，还有大盘鸡、回锅肉，朋友看到我炒炸焖煮样样在行，都说我像个上海好男人。"

遇上好天气，那哲还喜欢爬山和骑行。2008 年他买了辆山地自行车，从闵行出发，一口气骑行到金山。"整整 2 个小时，'吸'了一路乡村美景，那感觉太棒了！"

每年，那哲都会回尼泊尔看望父母。"在尼泊尔街头，如果听到周围有人说普通话，一股亲切感会油然而生，因为那声音是来自我遥远的第二故乡。"

Name: Upadhyaya Nagendra Rijal
Chinese name: 那哲
Nationality: Nepalese
Position: Operations Director of Shanghai Wicresoft Co., Ltd. WDI Division

Upadhyaya Nagendra Rijal:

Both my father and I witnessed Shanghai's transformation over the past 30 years

> In Shanghai, every day is a new day full of opportunities.

Rijal counts nearly a decade and a half since he first arrived in Shanghai. Born in 1983, he is now fluent in Mandarin and uses it to message his friends on WeChat. "I've been in Shanghai for 14 years!" he says. "I've spent my entire youth in Shanghai!"

Rijal says he has found a home in Shanghai in the 14 years he has been here.

Two international students in Shanghai, across two generations

Rijal first came to Shanghai in 2006 as an undergraduate student at Shanghai Jiaotong University. He says what brought him here was his family's connection to the city.

He says: "Why did I come to Shanghai? It's because my dad was also an international student in China."

As one of the first 14 Chinese coastal cities that opened up, Shanghai became a popular destination for international students in April 1984. In 1988, Rijal's father graduated from China Textile University, which is now renamed Donghua University. It was two years before the development and opening-up of Shanghai's Pudong; the construction of Nanpu Bridge, the first bridge across the Huangpu River, had just begun. But to Rijal's father, Shanghai back then was already a beautiful and bustling city with friendly people living and working there.

It was in 2005 that Rijal first arrived in China. His first stop was Nanjing, where he studied Mandarin for a year. In October 2006, he came to Shanghai Jiaotong University as an undergraduate majoring in electronic science and

Upadhyaya Nagendra Rijal:

Both my father and I witnessed Shanghai's transformation over the past 30 years

technology.

Rijal says he has witnessed the rapid development of China's transportation network. "Back then, it took me five hours by train to travel from Nanjing to Shanghai," he says. "Now it takes just one hour!"

The 14 years Rijal has been in this city have been the years of its economic boom. Skyscrapers have risen up, highways have reached destinations near and far, and the city has been evolving every day. Rijal says Shanghai today is much different from the Shanghai his father used to know.

He says: "When my father was in Shanghai, the construction of Metro Line 1 had just begun. And when I first came here, there was already a Line 3. Look at what it's like now – Line 15 is already up and running. All this in 30 years – it's incredible."

In recent years, Rijal's father has often traveled back to Shanghai to visit his home away from home. Every time he visits, he talks about how rapidly Shanghai's development has been and how fresh and new it looks. The narrow, meandering Yan'an Road 30 years ago is now an eight-lane boulevard doubled with a busy elevated road.

Rijal says: "Time has brought many changes to Shanghai. My dad and I have been witnesses to the city's rapid development over the past 30 years. In Shanghai, every day is a new day full of opportunities."

Leading a mini "United Nations" at work

Rijal's team provides technical support for corporations across the world, and it consists of over 100 people from 54 countries, diverse enough to be a mini "United Nations." He says some of his colleagues from Bangladesh and India who have just arrived in Shanghai would say they are not used to the food here, and he would then get them to try Xinjiang cuisine. "We would order *dapanji* (or 'big plate chicken') because we love curry," says Rijal.

He says: "They're from all over the world and have different customs and habits. But I would tell them about my life in Shanghai – how long I've been here and how much I've enjoyed it."

Rijal says he likes to have some friends over and cook for them on weekends. "My best dishes are tomato and egg stir-fry, *dapanji* and twice-cooked pork," he says. "My friends call me a good Shanghainese man because of my cooking skills."

When the weather is nice, Rijal likes to go hiking and ride his bike. He bought a mountain bike in 2008 and rode all the way from Minhang District to Jinshan District. "It took me two hours," he says. "I was spellbound by the beauty of the countryside along the way, and it was an amazing experience."

Rijal says he would go to Nepal every year to visit his parents. Even there, he would sometimes find traces of his second home, China. "I feel touched when I hear people speaking Mandarin in the streets of Nepal because it comes from my other, faraway home," he says.

姓　名：Gordon Boo
中文名：巫国端
国　籍：马来西亚
职　位：曜影医疗整脊科主任

巫国端：
时光经年，对上海的爱正浓

上海汇聚了来自世界各地的人，尤其是怀揣梦想的年轻人。

巫国端是曜影医疗的一名脊骨医疗师，2014年他从马来西亚只身来到上海，今年是他在这里行医的第七年。在巫国端看来，是"一带一路"倡议进一步拉近了中马关系，自那之后，中马两国在经济、文化、人才、技术等方面展开了更为密切的交流合作，而他作为一名脊骨医疗师，也成了双边交流中的一部分。

机遇之都

"中国有句俗语叫'七年之痒'，但如果说上海是我的'恋人'的话，那我们正处于'热恋期'！"巫国端这样形容现在的自己与上海之间的关系。

在做脊骨医疗师之前，巫国端是一名羽毛球运动员，4岁开始接触羽毛球的他曾两次获得马来西亚国家青少年锦标赛冠军。"2011年末我受邀前来上海参加红牛杯比赛，这是我和上海的第一次见面。"巫国端回忆自己因羽毛球与上海结缘的往事并谈及自己对这座城市的初印象："舒适宜居、规划良好，那时我就感受到上海的与众不同。"

当时，上海世博会刚刚落幕。在八年的筹备期里，上海市政府将迎世博和改善民生结合起来，城市面貌变化显著。也正是因为对上海有如此好的第一印象，之后，巫国端便欣然接受了公司把他从新加坡外派到上海的安排。

"2013年，中国国家主席习近平提出'一带一路'倡议，马来西亚是最早、

巫国端：

时光经年，对上海
的爱正浓

最积极响应的国家之一，我想我之所以选择踏出家门、远赴上海，冥冥之中或许正是受到了这一倡议的指引，因为当时有太多的马来西亚企业和马来西亚人对中国以及与中国合作充满热情与期待。"

"上海是一个对外国人十分友好的城市。这些年，上海向全球人才发出'英雄帖'并屡推入境新政，给我们外国人士在沪居留创业营造了良好的环境。"巫国端一想到自己能带领团队和技术走出国门，并且能在异国他乡"开花结果"——加入曜影医疗并成立整脊科，他就无比感恩中国以及上海能如此友好地向他"敞开大门"。

"上海汇聚了来自世界各地的人，尤其是怀揣梦想的年轻人，在我的客户里，有很多从外国知名大学毕业的外国留学生来上海发展。交流中，我发现他们都将这座具备国际化视野与水平的大都市当作实现理想的地方。"

治愈系城市

因为职业的关系，巫国端每天都会接触到各行各业生活在上海的人们。有人的地方就有故事，巫国端感叹上海是一座充满温暖的治愈之城。

那是发生在 2018 年的事。"那年夏天，一位刚外派来上海的西班牙人在妻子的陪同下来找我问诊。我隐约发现这位西班牙人的妻子沉默寡言、郁郁寡欢。"巫国端说。时间推进到 2019 年中。"我再次接诊了这位病人，惊喜地发现，他的妻子开朗了很多，有说有笑，完全变了一个人。"好奇心驱使巫国端私下询问了这位丈夫他妻子发生转变的缘由。

"原来他的妻子发现上海的生活并不像之前生活在欧洲那么压抑。她在上海结交了很多朋友，一起相约串门、逛街、品尝美食，她现在也不再需要去看心理医生了。更有意思的是，那年的圣诞当他准备回西班牙探亲过节时，他的妻子还哭着吵着说可不可以不回去！"一个小故事，让巫国端深刻体会到外国朋友对上海由衷的喜爱。

上海的温暖还来自于很多细节，比如上海对疫情的有效防控，巫国端坦言生活在上海感觉很安全。他感慨于上海快速的反应与行动力，"不仅体现了高效的城市管理能力，更体现了这座国际化大都市的责任与担当"。

Name: Gordon Boo
Chinese name: 巫国端
Nationality: Malaysian
Position: Head of the Chiropractic Department, SinoUnited Health

Gordon Boo:
My love for Shanghai grows stronger as time passes

Shanghai brings together people from all over the world, especially young people with dreams.

Gordon Boo, a chiropractor at SinoUnited Health, arrived in Shanghai alone from Malaysia in 2014, and this is his seventh year practicing medicine here. In Gordon Boo's view, it was the Belt and Road Initiative that brought China and Malaysia even closer. Since then, the two countries have carried out deeper and more frequent exchanges and cooperation in areas such as economy, culture, talent, technology. As a chiropractor, he has also become a part of that bilateral ties.

A city full of opportunities

"There is a 'seven-year itch', but if Shanghai is my 'lover', then we are now still passionately in love!" Gordon Boo thus describes the relationship between himself and Shanghai.

Now a chiropractor, Gordon Boo used to be a badminton player who started playing badminton at the age of four and had twice won the Malaysia National Junior Championships. "I was invited to the Red Bull Cup badminton tournament in Shanghai at the end of 2011, which was the first time I saw Shanghai," says Gordon Boo, reminiscing about his association with Shanghai through badminton. He also talks about his first impressions of Shanghai: "The city was so comfortable, livable and well-planned. Even then, I felt Shanghai was different."

At that time, the Shanghai World Expo had just concluded. The Shanghai government had spent the previous eight years putting everything in order, and had combined the preparation with the improvement of people's livelihood. As a result, the city changed remarkably. It was precisely because of such a good first impression that Gordon Boo readily accepted his company's arrangement to transfer him from Singapore to Shanghai.

Gordon Boo says: "In 2013, Chinese President Xi Jinping put forward the Belt and Road Initiative, and Malaysia was one of the first and also the most

Gordon Boo:

My love for Shanghai grows stronger as time passes

responsive countries. I think my own decision to leave my home and come to Shanghai might well have been inspired by this initiative. There were so many Malaysian businesses, so many Malaysian people who were full of enthusiasm and expectations for China, and the cooperation with China. It was contagious. "

Gordon Boo says: "Shanghai is a very expat-friendly city. In recent years, Shanghai has sent out a call for 'heroes' to global talents, and has kept on simplifying its policies on entry, therefore creating a very benign environment for foreigners to stay and start businesses here in Shanghai." When he thought that he actually led his team and technology abroad and "blossoms and bears fruits" in a foreign land, -- joining SinoUnited Health and setting up the Chiropractic Department, he was grateful that China and Shanghai had so kindly "opened their doors" to him.

Gordon Boo says: "Shanghai attracts people from all corners of the world, especially young people with dreams. Among my clients, many have graduated from prestigious universities around the world and have chosen to come to work in Shanghai. During our exchanges, I found that they all regard this great metropolis with international vision as the ideal place to achieve their dreams."

A city that heals

As a chiropractor, every day Gordon Boo comes into contact with people from all walks of life in Shanghai. Where there are people, there are stories. Gordon Boo exclaims that Shanghai is a warm city that heals.

It was in 2018. "In the summer of that year, a Spaniard who had just been sent to Shanghai visited me, accompanied by his wife. I somehow perceived the Spaniard's wife was typically silent and gloomy," says Gordon Boo. Then, fast forward to mid-2019. "I saw the male patient again and was pleasantly surprised to see that his wife brightened up a lot. She was talking, laughing and was a completely different person now." Intrigued, Gordon Boo asked the husband the reason for his wife's good transformation when the two were alone.

Gordon Boo says: "It turned out that his wife found life in Shanghai was not at all depressing as it used to be in Europe. She had made so many friends here. They visited among themselves, went shopping and tasted delicious cuisines together. She no longer needed to see her therapist. What's more, that year when he was about to go back to Spain for the Christmas holidays, his wife was again in tears. This time she asked if she could choose to stay!" Little stories like that let Gordon Boo understand better the sincere love for Shanghai by countless local expats.

The warmth of Shanghai also radiates from many details, such as the effective prevention and control of the COVID-19 pandemic. Gordon Boo says frankly that he feels very safe living here, and he is most impressed by Shanghai's rapid response and actions. "It not only reflects the efficient city-management but also the conscientiousness and responsibility of this great cosmopolitan city."

姓　名：Akiko Tomonari
中文名：友成晓子
国　籍：日本
职　位：百汇医疗消化内科医师

友成晓子：
我在上海，被暖意包围

人与人之间有了更多善意，城市也更显温度。

友成晓子是一名来自日本北海道的医生。2015年,她和丈夫来到上海,开启了一段不同寻常的"异国之旅"。如今6年过去,友成晓子早已习惯了这里的生活,在她眼中,上海是一座充满善意和暖意的城市,是一座她来了便再也不想离开的城市。

浓浓暖意

"人民城市人民建，人民城市为人民。"2019年习近平总书记考察上海时提出在城市建设中一定要贯彻以人民为中心的发展思想。在友成晓子看来，上海的人文关怀、浓浓暖意体现在社会的方方面面、城市的角角落落以及人与人的交往中。

友成晓子和老公育有两个孩子，她说，在上海，只要是身边人看到她带着两个小孩，都会走上前来伸出援手。

"我清楚地记得，有一次我带着孩子去餐厅吃饭，其中一个宝宝在闹情绪，还有一个宝宝把吃的东西弄得一团糟。这时候，坐在我旁边的一位上海阿姨看到我为了照顾小孩而顾不上吃饭，主动提出为我抱小孩，让我吃点东西。"友成晓子说这位上海阿姨的举动让她分外感动。

这不是友成晓子第一次在上海感受温暖。她说，平日里，上海的年轻人会在公共汽车上给她和宝宝让座，在地铁站，还会有人帮她把婴儿车抬上楼梯。

"人与人之间有了更多善意，城市也更显温度。"友成晓子说上海人的

友成晓子：
我在上海，
被暖意包围

热情和善良是她选择在这里生活的主要原因，而她也在日常生活中真切感受到了上海"海纳百川、大气谦和"的城市精神。

深深情谊

"山川异域，风月同天"是友成晓子非常喜欢的诗句，疫情期间，这句饱含情谊的诗句被附在了日本民间向中国寄送的口罩包装箱上。

新冠肺炎疫情暴发期间，身在异国他乡的友成晓子对家乡甚是牵挂，但当看到中国和日本在困境中互帮互助时，她倍感欣慰。

"我在新闻上看到中国女孩在日本街头免费派发口罩，也看到中国向日本捐赠了大量的防疫物资。"友成晓子觉得患难之下的情谊更显深厚。

2015年，习近平在中日友好交流大会上指出，中日友好的根基在民间，中日关系的前途掌握在两国人民手里。中国共产党和中国政府一直支持两国民间交流，鼓励两国各界人士特别是年轻一代踊跃投身中日友好事业。

置身医疗领域，友成晓子切身体会到两国的友好交往日渐频繁和高质量。"近年来，越来越多的中国医学专业学生来到日本学习医疗技术，而中国又有着科技和生产力方面的优势，向日本输出了大批高精尖的医疗设备。"友成晓子认为中日两国是一衣带水，理应互帮互助。

在上海生活越久，与上海接触越多，友成晓子越能体会到"山川异域，风月同天"这八个字的美好与深意。

友成晓子真心希望中日两国友好能世世代代延续下去。

Name: Akiko Tomonari
Chinese name: 友成晓子
Nationality: Japanese
Position: Gastroenterologist, ParkwayHealth

Akiko Tomonari:
In Shanghai, I'm enveloped in warmth

> There's more kindness among people, which highlights the warmth of this city.

Akiko Tomonari is a doctor from Hokkaido, Japan. In 2015, she and her husband came to Shanghai and started an unusual "exotic journey". Now, six years later, she has long got used to living here. In her eyes, Shanghai is a city full of kindness and warmth, and a city that she never wants to leave once she came here.

The enveloping warmth

"A people's city is built by the people and for the people," said General Secretary Xi Jinping on his visit to Shanghai in 2019, stressing that people-centered development must be implemented in the city construction. Tomonari thinks that Shanghai's humanistic care and enveloping warmth are reflected in all aspects of society, in every corner of the city and human interactions.

Tomonari and her husband have two children. She says that in Shanghai, as long as people see her with her two children, they will come forward to lend a helping hand.

She says: "I remember that once I took my children to a restaurant for supper and of them was in a mood and the other made a mess of the food. At that time, a Shanghai woman sitting next to me saw that and offered to hold the children for me so I could eat something." She was particularly moved by the woman's help.

This is not the first time that she has felt warmth in Shanghai. She says that on weekdays, young people in Shanghai would give their seats to her and her babies on the bus, and at the subway station, there would be someone to help her lift the stroller up the stairs.

"There's more kindness among people, which highlights the warmth of this

Akiko Tomonari:

In Shanghai, I'm enveloped in warmth

city," Tomonari says. The enthusiasm and kindness of the Shanghai people are the main reasons why she chose to live here, and she also truly feels the spirit of this generous and inclusive city in her daily life.

A deep friendship

"Though in different national terrains, we nevertheless share the same skies" is a verse that Tomonari likes very much. During the pandemic, this verse about friendship was attached to the boxes of face masks sent to China from Japan.

During the outbreak of the COVID-19 pandemic, Tomonari, who was in a foreign country, was very concerned about her hometown, but she felt gratified when she saw that China and Japan were helping each other in times of trouble.

"I saw on the news that a Chinese girl distributed masks free of charge on the streets of Japan, and I also saw that China donated a lot of pandemic prevention materials to Japan," says Tomonari. She feels that friendship in times of adversity is more profound.

In 2015, General Secretary Xi Jinping pointed out at the Sino-Japan Friendship Exchange Conference that the foundation of Sino-Japanese friendship lies in the people, and the future of Sino-Japanese relations will also lie in the hands of the two peoples. The Communist Party of China and the Chinese government have always supported non-governmental exchanges between the two countries and encouraged people from all walks of life in both countries, especially the younger generations, to actively participate in the cause of Sino-Japanese friendship promotion.

In the medical field, Tomonari experienced the increasingly frequent and high-quality friendly exchanges between the two countries. "In recent years, more and more Chinese medical students have come to Japan to study medical skills, and China has advantages in terms of technology and productivity, and has exported a large number of sophisticated medical equipment to Japan," she says. She believes that China and Japan as neighbors separated only by a strip of water have every reason to help each other.

As Tomonari has more and more contact with this city, she increasingly appreciates the beauty and profound meaning of the verse, "Though in different national terrains, we nevertheless share the same skies". She earnestly hopes the deep friendship between China and Japan can be passed on generation by generation.

姓　　名：Martin Wawra
中文名：华伟廷
国　　籍：德国
职　　位：福伊特驱动技术系统（上海）有限公司交通事业部执行副总裁兼首席行政官

华伟廷：
上海人的思想非常开放

> 如果离开上海三四个月，回来之后就能感受到许多新的变化。

机遇与挑战

"在上海，变化每天都在发生。"在福伊特驱动（中国）总经理华伟廷眼中，上海是一座兼具开放性与包容性的城市，在这里，机遇与挑战并存。他还清楚地记得，1998年自己第一次来到上海，和朋友站在外滩聊天的场景。"当时浦东只有几幢大楼，通往市中心的高架上没有多少车，还能看到许多农舍和菜地，跟现在看到的完全不一样。我和朋友聊起浦东未来的发展，谁也想不到，短短一段时间里，它会发生如此巨大的变化，上海总能给人带来惊喜。"

2011年，华伟廷和妻子选择搬到上海居住。"之前我已经来过中国三四次了，比较了解上海，我们相信在这里会生活得很好。"每周五晚上，华伟廷和家人会选择外出用餐，"在上海有各式各样的餐厅，不仅菜式丰富多样，而且食物烹饪的质量很高。"

华伟廷对中国文化也情有独钟，他家墙上挂的一幅画就是老上海的街景。"我很喜欢那时的上海，路很窄，人们的穿着也很独特，有一种特别的氛围。"

十年一晃而过，华伟廷和家人见证了上海的变化。"如果把上海和一些欧洲城市作比较，我必须承认，上海是一个先进的、发展得很快的城市。如果离开上海三四个月，回来之后就能感受到许多新的变化。"

华伟廷：

上海人的思想
非常开放

开放与包容

上海的开放与包容也给华伟廷留下了深刻的印象，他说："上海人的思想非常开放。我认为这是上海的一个传统，因为上海是一个海港城市。通常来说，住在沿海区域的人们会对外国人和新鲜事物接受度更高。我们公司在上海刚开始发展的时候，已经有很多同事英语说得很好，这里的人受教育程度很高。"

在华伟廷看来，上海还是一座绿色的城市，四季常青的树木和花草、四通八达的城市地铁和公交线路都是这座绿色城市的标志。"上海的人口密度其实很大，可以用做城市规划的空地并不是很多。但是，上海的绿化面积并不小。有时，我走在绿树成阴的马路上，能够感受到上海的生机与活力。在高架上开车时，总能看到许多防止噪声污染的装置。"

日常出行，华伟廷会选择乘坐公共交通。他认为，上海的交通规划做得很好，目前还在不断增加新的地铁线路，进一步提升了公共交通的便利程度。"这样一来，会有越来越多的人选择乘坐公共交通出行，也有利于改善环境污染的问题。生活、工作在这座城市，又便利、又环保。"

Name: Martin Wawra
Chinese name: 华伟廷
Nationality: German
Position: CEO Mobility at Voith Turbo, Managing Director at Voith Turbo China

Martin Wawra:
Shanghai people are open-minded

If you have been out of Shanghai for three or four months, you would find many new changes when you come back.

Opportunities and Challenges

"Changes are happening every day around Shanghai," says Martin Wawra, CEO Mobility at Voith Turbo, Managing Director at Voith Turbo China & CRRC Voith JV's in Beijing and Shanghai. In his eyes, Shanghai is a city that is open and inclusive, where opportunities and challenges coexist. He still vividly remembers the scene when he first came to Shanghai in 1998 and stood chatting with his friend at the Bund. He says: "At that time, there were only a few buildings in Pudong, not many cars on the elevated road to the city center, and many farmhouses and vegetable fields in sight, which was completely different from what we see now. My friend and I talked about the future development of Pudong, and no one could have imagined that it would change so dramatically in such a short time. Shanghai can always bring us surprises."

In 2011, Wawra and his wife chose to move to Shanghai. He says: "I have been here in China three or four times before and I am quite familiar with Shanghai. We believe that we will live a good life here." Every Friday night, Wawra and his family will go out for dinner. "There are various restaurants and dishes are not only varied but also of a high quality," says Wawra.

Wawra also has a special liking for Chinese culture. A picture hanging on the wall of his home is a street view of old Shanghai. He says: "I like Shanghai of that time very much. The roads were very narrow and people were uniquely dressed. There was a special atmosphere."

Ten years passed quickly, and Wawra and his family have witnessed the changes in Shanghai. He says: "If we compare Shanghai with some European cities, I must admit that it is an advanced and fast-growing city. If you have been out of Shanghai for three or four months, you would find many new

Martin Wawra:

Shanghai people are open-minded

changes when you come back."

Open and inclusive

Wawra is also deeply impressed by Shanghai's openness and inclusiveness. He says: "Shanghai people are open-minded. I think this is a tradition of Shanghai as a seaport. Generally speaking, people living in coastal areas will be more receptive to foreigners and new things. When our company started to develop in Shanghai, many colleagues already spoke very good English. People here were highly educated."

In Wawra's view, Shanghai is also a green city, with evergreen trees and flowers all year round, and the city subway network and bus lines extending in all directions are all symbols of this green city. "Shanghai's population density is actually very high, so there are not many open spaces that can be used for urban planning. However, the green area in Shanghai is not small. Sometimes, when I walk down the tree-lined streets, I can feel the vitality and vigor of the city. When driving on the elevated road, shields to prevent noise pollution are also everywhere to be seen."

For daily travel, Wawra will choose public transportation. He believes that Shanghai has done a good job in transportation planning, and new subway lines are constantly being added, further improving the convenience of public transportation. He says: "In this way, more and more people will choose to travel by public transportation, which is also conducive to alleviating environmental pollution. Life and work in this city are becoming convenient and environmentally friendly."

Scan for videos

姓　　名：Nicolas Poirot
中文名：柏昊天
国　　籍：法国
职　　位：液化空气中国总裁兼首席执行官

柏昊天：
明亮的蓝天和优质的空气总是令我神清气爽

过去几年里，上海的变化让我感到惊讶。

20年间频繁造访上海，城市的快速发展让液化空气集团中国区总裁兼首席执行官柏昊天惊叹不已。

令人惊叹的上海速度

柏昊天出生于法国，加入液化空气集团后，曾在多个国家任职，1999年柏昊天第一次来到上海，记忆中那时的上海还只有虹桥机场，浦东陆家嘴建成开放的地标建筑也只有一座东方明珠。但仅仅2年后，当柏昊天二度造访上海时，迎接他的已是一座巨大而崭新的浦东国际机场，当年，APEC在上海召开，金茂大厦拔地而起，延安路高架全线贯通……上海发展之快，变化之大，让柏昊天惊叹于"上海速度"。此后的上海，每年都以不一样的面貌出现在柏昊天视野中：环球金融中心、上海中心……一座座摩天大楼拔地而起，磁悬浮、高架路、地铁线，密织的交通网延伸至角角落落，20年来，城市的天际线在不断伸长，功能布局在持续完善，每次造访都让柏昊天对上海既熟悉又陌生。

2019年，柏昊天上任液化空气集团中国区总裁兼首席执行官，他带上妻子和两个女儿，把家安到了上海。"过去几年里，上海的变化让我感到惊讶。"日新月异的城市风景线中，柏昊天把陆家嘴列为全球NO.1。"我喜欢在不同的时间、不同的季节，从不同的角度看陆家嘴，全球最美的风景就在这里。"

柏昊天：

明亮的蓝天和优质的空气总是令我神清气爽

看看上海的"水晶天"

然而，多年前上海曾雾霾锁城，柏昊天感慨上海政府的治污决心和魄力。2000年，上海启动环保三年行动计划，到2019年时，上海的空气质量指数（AQI）优良天数已达到309天，全年超八成的日子是"水晶天"。"整个2020年，很少有严重污染的天气，明亮的蓝天和优质的空气总是令人神清气爽，而且这已经成为了常态。"柏昊天说，他常拍下一张张蔚蓝天空的照片发给那些曾在上海工作过的外国同事们，让他们看看这里的空气改善了多少，"他们讶异不已，都想亲自回来看看。"

柏昊天任职的液化空气集团，是全球工业与医疗保健领域气体、技术和服务的领导者之一，业务遍及全球78个国家和地区，从20世纪70年代开始向中国提供空分设备，目前在中国设有近100家工厂，遍布40多个城市。

深耕中国多年，法国液空见证了中国高质量发展的奋斗之路。2019年中法经济峰会上，液化空气集团与中国石化就发展氢能签订战略合作协议，致力服务于中国的能源转型和清洁出行。"我们看到在过去几年中，电动汽车在中国的快速发展，我对未来氢动力出行在中国的发展充满信心。"柏昊天说。

改革开放40多年来，中国经济发展成绩卓越。在全球所有主要经济体中，中国的增长率排名领先，并已成为世界第二大经济体。上海是中国设立最多跨国公司总部的城市，2020年尽管受疫情影响，上海仍获得了超过200亿美元的直接外商投资。

"这是对上海营商环境的有力证明。"随着"十四五"规划的展开，柏昊天相信液化空气集团将从中国高质量发展和开放政策中受益，获得更多机会。

Name: Nicolas Poirot
Chinese name: 柏昊天
Nationality: French
Position: President and CEO of Air Liquide China

Nicolas Poirot:
I always feel refreshed by the bright sky and the clean air

"I am amazed by the changes in Shanghai over the past few years."

Having visited Shanghai frequently over the past 20 years, Nicolas Poirot, President and CEO of Air Liquide China, is amazed by the rapid development of the city.

The amazing speed of Shanghai

Born in France, Poirot has worked in several countries since joining Air Liquide. He remembers that when he first came to Shanghai in 1999, there was only Shanghai Hongqiao International Airport and only one landmark building in Lujiazui in Pudong, the Oriental Pearl TV Tower. But just two years later, when he visited Shanghai for the second time, he was greeted by a huge and brand-new Shanghai Pudong International Airport. APEC was held in Shanghai, the Jinmao Tower rose from the ground, and the Yan'an Road Elevated Line was fully opened. He can't help but marvel at the city's rapid development and extensive changes, all made possible with the "Shanghai speed."

Every year since then, Shanghai impresses him with a different vision: skyscrapers like Shanghai World Financial Center and Shanghai Tower keep rising. A dense transportation network consisting of the maglev, elevated roads and subway lines extends to every corner of the city. In the past 20 years, the city's skyline has been stretching out, and its functional layout has been improving. Every time he visits the city, he feels both familiar and strange.

In 2019, as he took up the position of President and CEO of Air Liquide China, Poirot settled down in Shanghai with his wife and two daughters. "I am amazed by the changes in Shanghai over the past few years," he says. Among the ever-changing cityscape, he ranks Lujiazui as the world's No.1. "I like to see

Nicolas Poirot:

I always feel refreshed by the bright sky and the clean air

Lujiazui from different angles at different times of the day and seasons. It is the most beautiful scenery in the world," he says.

Check out the crystal-clear sky in Shanghai

Years ago, however, the city was plagued with smog. Poirot was impressed by the determination and capability of the Shanghai government to tackle air pollution. The year 2000 saw the launching of a Three-Year Environmental Protection Action Plan by the Shanghai Municipal Government. And the year 2019 saw 309 good days according to the air quality index (AQI), with over 80% of the year's days being "crystal clear" in Shanghai.

"Throughout 2020, there were few seriously polluted days, and the bright blue skies and quality air were very refreshing, and this has become the norm," he says. He often takes a picture of the blue sky and sends it to his foreign colleagues who used to work in Shanghai to show them how much the air has improved. "They are amazed and want to come back and see for themselves," says Poirot.

Air Liquide, one of the world leaders in gases, technologies and services for industry and healthcare, with operations in 78 countries, has been supplying air separation units to China since the 1970s and now has nearly 100 plants in more than 40 cities in China.

Deeply involved in China for many years, Air Liquide has witnessed the country's high-quality development. The Sino-French Economic Summit (2019) saw the signing of a strategic cooperation agreement between Air Liquide and Sinopec on the development of hydrogen energy, dedicated to serving China's energy transition and clean mobility. Poirot says: "We have seen the rapid development of electric vehicles in China over the past few years, and I am confident about the future development of hydrogen-powered mobility in China."

Over the past 40 years of reform and opening up, China's economic development has been remarkable. China leads in growth rate among all major economies in the world and has become the world's second-largest economy. Shanghai is the city with the most multinational companies' headquarters in China and received more than $20 billion in direct foreign investment in 2020 despite the impact of the pandemic.

"This is a strong testament to Shanghai's business environment," Poirot says. As the 14th Five-Year Plan unfolds, he believes that Air Liquide will win more opportunities and benefit from China's high-quality development and opening-up.

姓　　名：Takumi Kato
中文名：加藤巧
国　　籍：日本
职　　位：上海江崎格力高食品有限公司总经理

加藤巧：
爱上海从美食开始

中国政府提出节约粮食的倡导，这并不是一句口号，而是真正落在了实处，大家积极响应，行动起来，我觉得非常好。

2017 年，上海江崎格力高食品有限公司总经理加藤巧来到上海。由于从事与食品相关的工作，偏爱食物与料理的他对上海的美食产生兴趣。上海浓郁的艺术氛围、深厚的文化底蕴也深深吸引着他，让他爱上了这座城市。

这里，汇聚美食

来到中国 4 年多，加藤巧已经游历了中国的 50 多个城市。"每到一个地方我都会品尝当地的各种食物和茶饮，我希望通过体验饮食来接触当地的文化。"中国菜肴里，一年四季都有代表性的食材，春季的新鲜蔬菜、夏季的松茸等菌类、秋季的大闸蟹、冬季的火锅，这些美味刺激着加藤巧的味蕾。他说："上海汇集了国内，甚至世界各地的时尚风格与美味佳肴，让我一来就觉得十分亲切。"

在上海的餐厅里，随处可见"杜绝浪费"的标语，这让加藤巧印象深刻。"我认为这是一件非常棒的事情。别人提供给你的食物要全部吃完，如果剩下了，就会对制作这个食物的人产生一种愧疚的心情。所以中国政府提出节约粮食的倡导，这并不是一句口号，而是真正落在了实处，大家积极响应，行动起来，我觉得非常好。"

对于中国消费者来说，"格力高"是一个家喻户晓的食品品牌。1999 年 8 月，格力高在上海成立了上海江崎格力高食品有限公司，正式进军中国市场，多年来为市场贡献了一系列产品，如百奇、百力滋、百醇等。加

加藤巧：

爱上海从美食开始

藤巧经常在上海参加各类活动，将他们的产品带到福利院和学校，请学生们品尝。"我们为中国消费者特地开发过不少产品。"

便利的上海生活

在加藤巧的印象里，上海作为一个古老的港口城市，在这里生活的人们过得非常精致。上海在继承传统的同时也在不断融合新兴事物，吸引着全球各地的人们来到这里，飞速发展的数字化经济、蓬勃发展的文化产业和便利的生活都给他留下了深刻的印象。"来到上海以后，根本无需使用现金，只要轻点手机屏幕即可付款。在家中，足不出户就能收到想吃的食物、想买的物品。外出时，也可以利用手机打车。"加藤巧笑道，上海的城市数字化提升了他的生活品质，出差回日本时反而有些"不习惯"了。"这些是上海，甚至可以说是中国非常先进和优秀的地方。"

在每一次出行中感受人文气息

闲暇时光里，加藤巧喜欢参观上海的博物馆和美术馆。他说："上海的展览非常多。很多展馆都提供了丰富多样的中外展品。每个场馆的地理位置也都很方便，而且入场费非常便宜，甚至免费。"加藤巧最常去的是上海当代艺术博物馆。"这里经常会有当代艺术的展览，会根据季节设置不同的主题。经常会有我喜欢的艺术家的作品展出，当然从不太熟悉的艺术家的作品中我也能得到新的感悟，所以经常过来。"

加藤巧路过中共一大会址时，常常看到络绎不绝的游客，很感兴趣，也想进去参观，但还没有如愿。"我第一次去的时候没有带护照，没能进馆。第二次去带了护照，但那天排队非常长，不知道要等多久于是就放弃了。后来又去过一次，结果不巧碰到了闭馆。几次尝试都没能成功，希望下次能顺利进馆参观。"

喜欢看书的加藤巧也是上海各大书店的常客，他常常被书店极具特色的建筑外观和品位十足的内部装修吸引。"全上海遍布着设计新颖时尚的书店。最近日本的茑屋书店还有全世界的品牌书店也都进驻上海，让我感受到了上海浓厚的人文气息。"

Name: Takumi Kato
Chinese name: 加藤巧
Nationality: Japanese
Position: General Manager of Shanghai Ezaki Glico Foods Co., Ltd.

Takumi Kato:
A Love for Shanghai starts with food

> The Chinese government's advocacy of saving food is not a slogan, but a real implementation. Everyone responds actively and takes action, which I think is very good.

Takumi Kato, the general manager of Shanghai Ezaki Glico Foods Co., Ltd., came to Shanghai in 2017. As he works in a food-related field, his love for food and cooking makes him interested in the cuisine of Shanghai. Shanghai's strong artistic atmosphere and profound cultural background attract him deeply and make him fall in love with this city.

Here: a gourmet heaven

Kato has traveled to more than 50 Chinese cities since coming to China more than four years ago. "Everywhere I go, I taste a variety of local food and tea, from which I hope to get in touch with the local culture," he says. Chinese cuisine has representative ingredients for all seasons of the year. Fresh vegetables in spring, fungi like matsutake in summer, hairy crabs in autumn and hot pot in winter, all these delicacies stimulate Kato's taste buds. He says: "Shanghai brings together the fashionable styles and delicious foods from all over the country and even the world, making me feel at home as soon as I arrived."

Kato is impressed by the "No Waste" slogan, which can be seen everywhere in Shanghai's restaurants. He says: "I think it's great. It is important to eat all the food that someone else offers you, and if there is any leftover, you will feel a sense of guilt towards the person who made that food. So, the Chinese government's advocacy of saving food is not a slogan, but a real implementation. Everyone responds actively and takes action, which I think is very good."

Glico is a widely known food brand for Chinese consumers. It officially entered the Chinese market with the establishment of Shanghai Ezaki Glico Foods Co., Ltd. in August 1999, and has contributed a series of products to the market such as Pocky, Pretz, Pejoy and so on. Kato often attends various activities in

Takumi Kato:

A Love for Shanghai
starts with food

Shanghai, bringing their products to welfare houses and schools and inviting the students to taste them. "We have developed many products especially for Chinese consumers," he says.

Convenient living in Shanghai

In Kato's impression, people lead an exquisite life in Shanghai, an old port city. While inheriting the tradition, Shanghai also integrates newly sprouted things, attracting people from all over the world. He was impressed by the rapid development of the digital economy, the flourishing cultural industries and the convenience of life in Shanghai, which continues to integrate new things while carrying on its traditions and attracts people from all over the world. Kato says with a smile: "I don't need to carry cash at all in Shanghai. Payment can be achieved by tapping the phone screen. You can receive the food and items you want without leaving your home. When you go out, you can use your phone to hail a taxi." The digitization of the city improves his quality of life and when he returns to Japan on a business trip, he feels a little "uncomfortable." "These are the very advanced and excellent aspects in Shanghai, and also in China," says Kato.

Savoring cultural Shanghai on every outing

In his spare time, Kato likes to visit museums and art galleries in Shanghai. He says: "There are many exhibitions in Shanghai and many offering a variety of exhibits from China and abroad. Every venue is conveniently located and the entrance fee is very cheap, even free." He often visits the Power Station of Art. He says: "There are often contemporary art exhibitions here and different themes are given based on different seasons. Works by artists I like are frequently displayed. I can also get new insights from the works of some less familiar ones, so I come here quite often."

Kato often sees an endless stream of tourists when he passes by the Memorial of the First National Congress of the Communist Party of China. He is interested in going in to visit but hasn't fulfilled this wish. He says: "I didn't bring my passport the first time I went there so I was denied entry. I brought my passport the second time, but the line was very long that day. I didn't know how long I had to be waiting, so I gave up. I went there again later, but unfortunately, it was closed on that day. I hope I will be fortunate enough to go inside next time."

Kato likes to read and is also a frequent visitor to major bookstores in Shanghai. He is often attracted by the distinctive architectural appearance and tasteful interior decoration of the bookstores. He says: "Bookstores with novel and fashionable designs can be seen all over Shanghai. Recently, Japanese bookstore, Tsutaya Books, as well as other famous bookstores from all over the world, has entered Shanghai, giving me a sense of the city's flourishing culture."

姓　　名：Claude Maillot
中文名：马优
国　　籍：法国
职　　位：必维船级社集团顾问

马优：
未来航运业的主要舞台将是上海

对我们来说，上海是独一无二的选择。未来航运业的主要舞台将是上海。

"我常说中国人勇于拥抱变革，他们运用技术去实现一次次的飞跃。"2008年，法国人马优来到上海，之后他便喜欢上了这座富有魅力的城市。虽然很多东西发生了变化，然而在他心目中，这又是一座没有陌生感的城市，"你会觉得在上海就像在家一样"。

对于上海这座目标剑指国际航运中心的城市，作为航运业资深人士，马优给出了自己的观察结论："对我们来说，上海是独一无二的选择。未来航运业的主要舞台将是上海。"

对中国文化"爱得深沉"

"我最喜欢的诗人是李白和杜甫。"马优捧着中英对照版《唐诗》如是说道。这位儒雅的绅士可以说对中国文化"爱得深沉"。他的家中，随处可以看到中国文化的印记，玄关处摆放着一个紫砂壶与一把写着"随缘"的折扇；客厅里贴着"福"字与春联；卧室里摆放着朋友赠送的字画；书房的柜子里则有一处专门放置与中国相关的书籍，中国历史、文化、建筑都是他的涉猎范围。空闲时间，他还学起了中文，在田字格练习簿上学写"你好""什么"……

疫情暴发前，马优的家人时常会来上海看望陪伴他。"很遗憾今年他们不能来上海共度春节。"他说，儿子对中国文化也十分感兴趣，常常在上海博物馆一呆就是一整天，女儿则更钟情于中国的山川大河。"我很高兴他们

马优：

未来航运业的主要
舞台将是上海

和我一样喜爱中国。"

"上海充满活力与创新，这里显然是一个世界性的商业中心。同时上海也是开放的、友好的，这给我们的生活带来了很多便利，这里的交通网络四通八达，政府机构也给外国人提供了很多支持与帮助……"马优风趣地说，自己无法用一两个词汇来概括上海，关于这座城市他有太多的故事可以讲述，可能花一整个下午都不够，"真是一个令人印象深刻的城市"。

点赞上海航运业发展

"必维与上海这座城市有着深厚的历史渊源。"19 世纪末，必维船级社就曾在外滩开设代表机构，提供在华服务。随着中国改革开放，贸易得到发展，船只的检验需求也相应增大，在这样的背景下，1993 年必维重返中国。

"如今，一流的航运业企业集聚上海。"马优表示，必维的战略正是不断加强在上海的实力。2013 年，必维船级社在上海建立北亚区总部；2014 年，必维在上海设立第二个研发中心，聘请了具有高精尖技术的中国优秀工程师……这一系列举动体现了上海这座城市对于必维的重要性，也表明了必维对中国市场的重视。

过去一年，新冠肺炎疫情给全球贸易及港口运营带来了严重影响，然而上海港贸易却逆势昂扬，宛如全球贸易寒冬中盛开的"白玉兰"。"十四五"时期，上海将深入建设全球领先的国际航运中心。在马优看来，上海和中国将在塑造未来的航运方面发挥主导作用。"我们认为，未来航运业的主要舞台将是上海。"

当今世界面临着诸多挑战，如全球变暖、气候变化，这也给航运业带来了巨大的挑战。随着中国船舶制造工业的迅速发展，世界船舶制造业的中心正在转向中国。"我们正在积极研究，如何将替代性清洁能源应用于船舶等问题。"这也正契合了上海着力推动国际航运中心绿色发展、智慧发展的方向。

马优补充道："必维将和中国航运业以及上海航运业共同完成。"

Name: Claude Maillot
Chinese name: 马优
Nationality: French
Position: Executive Advisor to the President of Bureau Veritas Marine & Offshore Division

Claude Maillot:
Shanghai will take center stage in the global shipping industry

For us, it's a must to be in Shanghai. Shanghai will take center stage in the global shipping industry.

"I often say that the Chinese people have the courage to embrace change and reformation," Maillot says. "They take one stride after another with technology."

Maillot came to Shanghai in 2008 and soon fell in love with this charming city. Although much has changed since, he says he never feels like a stranger in the city. "You would feel that being in Shanghai is like being at home," he says.

As a veteran in the shipping industry, Maillot says Shanghai has the potential to be an international shipping center. "For us, it's a must to be in Shanghai," he says. "Shanghai will take center stage in the global shipping industry."

Enchanted with Chinese culture

"My favorite poets are Li Bai and Du Fu," Maillot says, holding an English-Chinese edition of *Tang Poetry In Paintings*.

Elements of Chinese culture are everywhere in Maillot's home: a Yixing clay teapot and a hand fan with the word 随缘 (sui yuan), or "let it be," rest at the entryway; the character 福 (fu), or "good fortune," and a pair of Chinese spring couplets hang in the living room; works of Chinese calligraphy and painting from his friends sit in his bedroom; while books about China stand in a dedicated cabinet in his study. Chinese history, culture and architecture all interest him. In his free time, Maillot takes Mandarin lessons and practices writing Chinese characters like 你好 (ni hao), or "hello," and 什么 (shen me), or "what," on his Chinese handwriting practice booklet.

Before the COVID-19 pandemic broke out, Maillot's family often came to Shanghai to keep him company. "It's a pity they couldn't come to Shanghai this year to celebrate the Spring Festival with me," he says.

Maillot's son is also fascinated by Chinese culture, often spending whole

Claude Maillot:

Shanghai will take center stage in the global shipping industry

days in Shanghai Museum. His daughter is drawn to China's magnificent natural beauty. "I'm glad they love China as I do," he says.

Maillot says it's hard to put Shanghai in a word or two. He says he has more than an afternoon's worth of stories to tell about the city.

He says: "Shanghai is filled with a vibrant and innovative spirit. It's obviously a global business center, but it's also open and friendly. This makes our lives really convenient. The transportation network reaches everywhere, and government agencies provide a lot of support for foreigners."

"It's a city that truly leaves a deep impression," he says.

Thumbs-up for the growth of Shanghai's shipping industry

"Bureau Veritas' bond with Shanghai goes way back in history," Maillot says. The company set up a representative office as early as the late 19th century. In 1993, Bureau Veritas returned to China as China's international trade took off with the country's reform and opening-up, boosting demand for ship testing and inspection.

Maillot says Bureau Veritas's strategy is to keep strengthening its presence in Shanghai. In 2013, the company built its North Asia Zone head office here. In 2014, the company set up its second laboratory in Shanghai, hiring Chinese engineers with state-of-the-art expertise. These decisions demonstrated the importance of Shanghai and the Chinese market for the company.

"Top companies in the shipping industry are now gathering in Shanghai," he says.

Last year, the pandemic struck global trade and port operations hard. Nevertheless, trade remained strong in the Port of Shanghai like a white magnolia in a global economic winter. From 2021 to 2025, during China's 14th Five-Year Plan, Shanghai will further its development into a leading global shipping center. Maillot says Shanghai and China will be key players in shaping the future of shipping.

Contemporary challenges like global warming and climate change pose great challenges for global shipping. Shanghai is focusing on promoting green and smart development. As China's shipbuilding industry rapidly develops, it is gradually becoming the center of the global shipbuilding industry.

"We are actively researching the application of alternative clean energy in shipping," Maillot says. "Bureau Veritas will accomplish this transformation with China's and Shanghai's shipbuilding industry."

Scan for videos

姓　名：Jeremy Murray
中文名：杰睿
国　籍：加拿大
职　位：中国科学院分子植物科学卓越创新中心研究组长

杰睿：
上海的科研水平已跻身国际一流

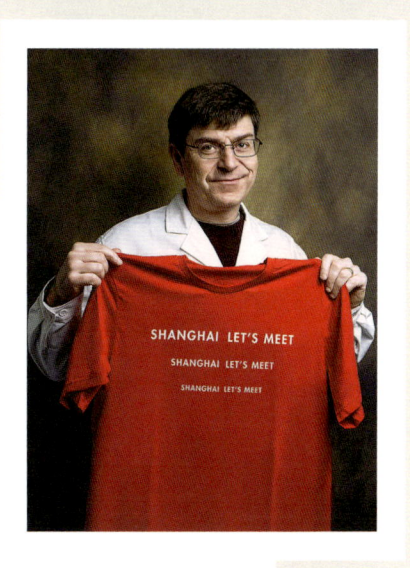

我在很多国家的重点实验室工作过，上海的科研水平和国外一流科研机构不相上下。

在中国科学院分子植物科学卓越创新中心，活跃着一群蓝眼睛高鼻梁的外国人。他们同属于中国科学院－英国约翰·英纳斯中心植物和微生物科学联合研究中心，这座世界植物科学研究的顶尖殿堂。来自加拿大的植物科学家杰睿就是其中之一。2018年来到上海，短短三年时间，他所在的实验室就结出了重量级科研硕果。

"如果这一发现被证实有效，那将为植物研究开辟崭新领域。"个子高大、说话爱笑的杰睿说，得益于上海得天独厚的科创土壤，他的研究在这里取得了突破性进展。"我在很多国家的重点实验室工作过，上海的科研水平和国外一流科研机构不相上下。"

开启上海科研生涯

来上海之前，杰睿就已经"生活在上海"了。杰睿的妻子来自上海，两人在美国相识相恋，日常甜蜜生活里少不了妻子对上海生活点点滴滴的描述。杰睿还有不少杰出科学家朋友，那些年陆续从世界各地奔赴上海开启科研，每次聊天，朋友们都会告诉他不少关于上海的故事。"在我还没有踏足上海前，就已经对这座城市有了相当多的了解。"

10年前，和复旦大学的学术交流让杰睿第一次有机会真正来到上海。"那时候我就发现上海的科学家们非常努力，科研水平、科研环境都蕴藏着无限潜力。"随着2016年国家"十三五"规划纲要提出"科技创新"，上

杰睿：

上海的科研水平
已跻身国际一流

海全力推进建设具有全球影响力的科技创新中心，一大批科学设施启动建设，一大批新型研发机构相继成立。

当年9月，依托于中国科学院分子植物科学卓越创新中心（原中国科学院植物生理生态研究所）创建的中国科学院－英国约翰·英纳斯中心植物和微生物科学联合研究中心上海园区正式揭牌成立，联合中英两国三大研究机构一起，共同应对食品安全和可持续医疗保健面临的全球性挑战，目标直指世界一流科研中心。彼时正在英国约翰·英纳斯中心工作的杰睿，抓住这一良机，将上海视作自己未来科研生涯的重要舞台。经过层层申请严格选拔，最终于2018年成功入驻上海园区。

上海速度不可思议

据上海市科委（市外国专家局）统计，自2016年11月外国人来华工作许可制度在沪试点实施起至2018年底，上海共为外国高端人才办理来华工作许可证超过1.8万份，占外国人来华工作许可总体发证数量的比例超过18%。这一数量在全国稳居第一，并呈明显上升趋势。"在上海做科研与世界其他地方没有差距"，已成为这些顶尖外籍科学家的共同感受。

作为中科院分子植物科学卓越创新中心、植物分子遗传国家重点实验室的研究组负责人，杰睿在这里的研究项目硕果累累，其中一个重要成果就是在植物中发现了参与固氮的蛋白，可以帮助植物吸收更多的氮元素，从而减少氮肥使用。"这一发现将在农业生产和环境保护方面大有作为。"杰睿说。

在上海建设科创中心的热潮下，政府扶持力度不断加大，重点科学项目加快建设，科创中心全球影响力持续增强。"在上海做科研，不用担心经费，只需要考虑有没有好项目。"在杰睿眼中，上海的科研水准已跻身世界顶尖行列，而这距离他第一次来上海才过了短短十年。

"这太不可思议了。"

Name: Jeremy Murray
Chinese name: 杰睿
Nationality: Canadian
Position: Research Group Leader, CAS Center for Excellence in Molecular Plant Sciences

Jeremy Murray:
Shanghai's scientific research is already among the best in the world

I have worked in many key national laboratories and the level of scientific research in Shanghai is on a par with top research institutions in the world.

A group of foreigners with blue eyes and high noses are active in CAS Center for Excellence in Molecular Plant Sciences. They belong to the CAS-JIC Centre of Excellence for Plant and Microbial Science (CEPAMS), the world's top institution for plant science research. One of them is Jeremy Murray, a plant scientist from Canada, who came to Shanghai in 2018, and in just three years, his laboratory has produced significant research results.

"If the discovery has been proved effective, it will blaze a trail for plant research," says Murray. The tall and smiling professor says that his research has achieved a breakthrough thanks to Shanghai's blessed soil for science and innovation. "I have worked in many key national laboratories and the level of scientific research in Shanghai is on a par with top research institutions in the world," he says.

Initiating a research career in Shanghai

Before coming to Shanghai, Murray is already "living in Shanghai". His wife comes from Shanghai, and they met and fell in love in the United States. His wife's description of life in Shanghai filled their sweet life together. He has also made friends with many outstanding scientists, who went to Shanghai from all over the world for scientific research in those years. Whenever he chatted with them, they would tell him many stories about Shanghai. "Before I set foot in Shanghai, I knew quite well about the city," says Murray.

Ten years ago, an academic exchange with Fudan University gave him the first opportunity to come to Shanghai. "At that time, I found out that scientists in Shanghai were working very hard, and that the level of scientific research

Jeremy Murray:

Shanghai's scientific research is already among the best in the world

and the research environment had unlimited potential," says Murray. With the nation's 13th Five-Year Plan in 2016 proposing "scientific and technological innovation", Shanghai has been pushing forward to shape itself into a scientific and technological innovation center with global influence, and the construction of a large number of scientific facilities has started and a large number of new R&D institutions have been established.

In September of that year, the Shanghai Park of the CAS-JIC Centre of Excellence for Plant and Microbial Science (CEPAMS) was established based on the CAS Center for Excellence in Molecular Plant Sciences (formerly Institute of Plant Physiology and Ecology of the Chinese Academy of Sciences). With the three major research institutions in China and Britain in collaboration, it is aimed at addressing the global challenges on food safety and sustainable health care, poised to become a world-class research center. Murray, who was working at the John Innes Center in the UK at that time, seized this opportunity and regarded Shanghai as an important stage for his future scientific research career. After several rounds of strict selection, he was finally admitted to Shanghai Park in 2018.

Shanghai speed is just incredible

According to the statistics of Science and Technology Commission of Shanghai Municipality and Shanghai Administration of Foreign Experts Affairs, from November 2016 when the work permit system for foreigners coming to China was piloted in Shanghai to the end of 2018, the Shanghai authorities handled more than 18,000 work permits for foreign high-end talents, accounting for more than 18% of the total number of work permits issued to all foreigners coming to China. This number ranks first among all cities across the country and shows an obvious upward trend. That "there is no difference between doing scientific research in Shanghai and other parts of the world" has become the shared feeling of these top foreign scientists.

As the head of a research group at the CAS Center of Excellence in Molecular Plant Science and the State Key Laboratory of Plant Molecular Genetics, his fruitful research projects here include the discovery of proteins involved in nitrogen fixation in plants, which can help plants absorb more nitrogen and thus reduce the use of nitrogen fertilizer. "This discovery will make a big difference in agricultural production and environmental protection," he says.

Under the boom of building Shanghai into a science and innovation center, government support has been increasingly boosted, the development of key scientific projects has been accelerated, and the global influence of the science and innovation center continues to grow. Murray says: "When you conduct scientific research in Shanghai, you don't have to worry about funding. You only need to consider whether there are good projects." In his eyes, Shanghai's scientific research level has been among the world's top ranks, and it is only a decade since his first visit to Shanghai.

"This is just incredible." says Murray.

姓　名：Lutz Frankholz
中文名：陆勋海
国　籍：德国
职　位：TÜV 莱茵上海公司执行董事

陆勋海：
上海仿佛机遇之海，触目所及满是生机与希望

> 进博会对于中国和世界而言都意义非凡，这是一个不可或缺的国际盛会。中国用实际行动展示了坚定不移全面扩大开放的决心。

2021 年，是 TÜV 莱茵上海公司执行董事陆勋海来上海的第十年。陆勋海所在的 TÜV 莱茵是一家总部位于德国的检验、检测和认证机构，一直致力于为"中国企业走出去、外国企业走进来"搭建一座双向服务的桥梁。十年来，他不仅见证了自己和公司的成长，也见证了上海这座城市的蜕变。在陆勋海看来，正是开放这张"王牌"让上海成为吸引全球企业目光的热土并推动着上海不断向现代化国际大都市迈进。

政策的力量

检验检测认证服务是国际贸易过程中必不可少的环节。作为国际领先的第三方检验、检测和认证机构，TÜV 莱茵拥有近 150 年的经验，在近 60 个国家和地区建立了 500 多个分支机构。陆勋海于 2012 年来到上海，担任 TÜV 莱茵上海公司执行董事。

在上海的十年里，陆勋海积极响应中国相关政策。"这不仅使公司不断变大变强，还让中外企业的合作发展上了新台阶。"陆勋海感叹。

2013 年，以习近平同志为核心的党中央提出共建"一带一路"倡议，TÜV 莱茵响应国家倡议，成立了专门的工作组，比如在喀麦隆水厂项目上，公司帮助中国机械集团在图纸设计、零部件生产、项目管理、采购、供应

陆勋海：

上海仿佛机遇之海，触目
所及满是生机与希望

商管理、施工、人员培训、标准制定等多维度多领域进行质量把控，使这座非洲最大的水厂成为标杆项目，奠定了中国制造在"一带一路"的声誉。

奇迹在眼前发生。在看到了这些年来"一带一路"倡议给中国及沿线国家带来的积极变化后，陆勋海表示事实已经说明"一带一路"不仅对中国经济发展至关重要，还推动了沿线其他国家的经济发展。

除了"一带一路"，陆勋海还对中国很多具有全局性、前瞻性的政策赞不绝口，"长江三角洲区域一体化发展规划"就在其中。

2019年4月，上海市委市政府召开打响"四大品牌"推进大会，确定了打响"四大品牌"的重要抓手。2019年底发布的《长江三角洲区域一体化发展规划纲要》更明确指出，要"形成有影响力的上海服务、上海制造、上海购物、上海文化'四大品牌'，推动上海品牌和管理模式全面输出，为长三角高质量发展和参与国际竞争提供服务"。

为此，陆勋海积极推动公司作为首批创建单位加入了"上海品牌"国际认证联盟。在助力长三角地区品牌认证的过程中，陆勋海对"长三角区域一体化发展"有了更深刻的感悟："我们一直都在跟着政府的脚步对公司工作进行部署。这些年来，长三角城市之间交往愈发密切，这一部分得益于政府构建了高品质快速轨道交通网，为长三角一带的人员流动、城市生活、沟通交流提供了极大的便利。"

开放的气度

除了享受政策红利，陆勋海还切实感受到开放对于上海成为国际化大都市的重要意义。

2018年11月，TÜV 莱茵以德国总部的身份参加了首届进博会。谈及与会感想，陆勋海表示，上海承办大型展览的能力让人叹为观止，无论是交通布局、展位安排，还是安保设施、人员服务，都是世界顶尖水准。

"进博会对于中国和世界而言都意义非凡，这是一个不可或缺的国际盛会。在进博会上我们近距离接触了全球用户并了解了各自的需求，这不仅有利于把中国产品销往国外，也有助于外国企业更加了解中国市场，这是一种良性的双向互动行为，中国用实际行动展示了坚定不移全面扩大开放的决心。"陆勋海认为。

2020年秋天，当陆勋海再次走进进博会展馆的人海之中时，他说自己仿佛是一条游入机遇之海的鱼，触目所及满是生机与希望。

陆勋海坦言，这种感觉，只在上海体会过。

Name: Lutz Frankholz
Chinese name: 陆勋海
Nationality: German
Position: Managing Director of TÜV Rheinland Shanghai Co., Ltd.

Lutz Frankholz:
Shanghai is a sea of opportunities, brimming with life and hope

The China International Import Expo is an important international event that is of great significance to both China and the world. China has demonstrated its unswerving determination to continue to open up in all respects with concrete actions.

The year 2021 marks the tenth year that Lutz Frankholz, the Managing Director of TÜV Rheinland of Shanghai, has been in Shanghai. TÜV Rheinland, a certificate body with its headquarters in Germany, has been committed to building a two-way service bridge for Chinese companies to go out and foreign companies to come in. Over the decade, Frankholz has not only witnessed the growth of himself and the company but also the great changes of Shanghai.

From Frankholz's perspective, it is the "trump card" of opening-up that transforms Shanghai into a modern metropolis and a hot spot attracting global enterprises.

The Power of Policies

Inspection, testing and certification services are the essential links in international trades. As a leading international third-party certificate body, TÜV Rheinland has nearly 150 years of experience and has established more than 500 branches in nearly 60 countries and regions.

Since his arrival in Shanghai in 2012, Frankholz has been actively responded to China's relevant policies. He exclaims: "This not only makes the company bigger and stronger but also brings the cooperation between Chinese and foreign enterprises up to a new level."

In 2013, Chinese President Xi Jinping proposed the Belt and Road Initiative. In response to the initiative, TÜV Rheinland has set up a special working group. For example, in the Cameroon Water Plant Project, TÜV Rheinland has assisted

Lutz Frankholz:

Shanghai is a sea of opportunities, brimming with life and hope

China Machinery Engineering Corporation in controlling the quality of layout design, components production, project management, procurement, supplier management, construction, personnel training and standard-setting. As a result, this largest water plant in Africa became a benchmark project and established the reputation of Made-in-China among the Belt and Road countries.

Miracles are happening before our eyes

In April 2019, the Shanghai Municipal Committee of the Communist Party of China and Shanghai Municipal People's Government held a conference to advance the building of the city's major four brands. The conference identified an important starting point for building the four brands. The Outline Plan for Integrated Regional Development of the Yangtze River Delta, released at the end of 2019, urged the forming and comprehensive export of the four brands of Shanghai -- services, manufacturing, shopping and culture, setting a management model and providing services for the Yangtze River Delta's high-quality development and participation in international competition.

To this end, Frankholz actively drove the company to join the Shanghai Brand International Certification Alliance as one of the first founding units. He says: "We have been following the footsteps of the government to deploy the company's work. Over the years, cities in the Yangtze River Delta have become increasingly close to each other, thanks in part to the government's construction of a high-quality rail transit network, which has greatly facilitated the personnel flow, urban life and communication in this region."

The spirit of openness

In November 2018, TÜV Rheinland participated in the first China International Import Expo (CIIE) representing the company's German headquarters.

Frankholz says: "The CIIE was an important international event that is of great significance for China and the world. At the CIIE, we came into close contact with global users and learned about their needs, which is not only conducive to selling Chinese products abroad but also helpful for foreign enterprises to have a better understanding of the Chinese market. This is a sound two-way interaction. China has demonstrated its unswerving determination to continue to open up in all respects with concrete actions"

Frankholz says he felt like a fish swimming into a sea of opportunities full of life and hope when he entered the crowded exhibition hall of the CIIE again in the autumn of 2020.

He confesses that he has only experienced this feeling in Shanghai.

姓　名：Krupikova Oksana
中文名：奥克萨娜
国　籍：俄罗斯
职　位：Bodylab 国际舞蹈中心创始人

奥克萨娜：
将祖辈对中国的爱延续到下一代

> 对中国的爱，是我的爷爷分享给我的。从我们小的时候起，他一直和我们说，中国和我们一样，非常努力、非常好、很有发展前景。

生活在有"中国情结"的家族

奥克萨娜是一位非常美丽的俄罗斯女子，她的家族有着浓厚的"中国情结"。爷爷非常喜欢中国的历史，家中因此有很多关于中国的书籍。在奥克萨娜小的时候，爷爷就时常给他们兄妹俩讲中国的故事，在爷爷的讲述中，中俄关系友好，像兄弟一样。耳濡目染之下，奥克萨娜从小就对中国有浓烈的亲近感。"对中国的爱，也是我的爷爷分享给我的。从我们小的时候起，他一直和我们说，中国和我们一样，非常努力、非常好、很有发展前景。"

生性活泼的奥克萨娜热爱运动，小的时候就被父母送到体校学习。通过自己的努力，奥克萨娜成为了一名艺术体操职业运动员，并参加过无数次国际比赛，也去过世界上很多地方。来到中国后，奥克萨娜发现中国和爷爷说的一样好。"中国人都非常善良，对我也非常好。"奥克萨娜回忆道，有趣的是，在中国，每当她向别人介绍自己来自俄罗斯时，大家都会称呼她为"好朋友"。

在上海的创业生活

上海如此吸引她，不仅因为家族的"中国情结"带来的亲近感，还因为这座城市本身的魅力。奥克萨娜觉得上海非常国际化，快速而又充满活

奥克萨娜：

将祖辈对中国的
爱延续到下一代

力的节奏和她的性格完美契合。就这样，奥克萨娜毫不犹豫做出了选择——在上海创业。2016年，她在浦东创办了第一家艺术体操和舞蹈学校，经过5年多的努力，如今已经开设了3家门店。"我们有一家店靠近黄浦江，下班后，我很喜欢去外滩走一走。俄罗斯有一首歌叫《莫斯科郊外的晚上》，外滩和黄浦江的夜晚也一样迷人。"

"共产党员有着诸多优秀品质"

因为爷爷是苏联时代的共产党员，奥克萨娜在中国会比较关注共产党。奥克萨娜知道今年是中国共产党建党一百周年，在她的眼里中国共产党员有着诸多优秀品质。"我们舞蹈中心，有工作人员就是中国共产党员，他们工作特别认真负责，时常工作到深夜。他们对舞蹈中心的事务就像对自己的事业一样热爱，从舞蹈中心创办至今都在这儿工作，非常稳定。"

今年是《中俄睦邻友好合作条约》签署20周年。这将是中俄关系的重要里程碑，更是一个新的起点。如今，奥克萨娜已经在上海安家，儿子7岁，在浦东一家国际学校读书。

奥克萨娜深爱上海，她鼓励儿子从小学好中文，多了解中国文化，承袭来自祖辈的那份"对中国的爱"！

而她，依然会选择在上海继续奋斗，创造出属于她的精彩人生。

Name: Krupikova Oksana
Chinese name：奥克萨娜
Nationality: Russian
Position: Founder of BodyLab Dance Center

Krupikova Oksana:
Carrying my ancestors' love for China to the next generation

The love for China was passed on to me by my grandfather. Ever since we were kids, he has always told us that Chinese people are very hard-working, nice and aspiring, just like us.

Growing up in a family that has "China complex"

Oksana is a very beautiful Russian lady, and her family has a strong "China complex". Her grandfather was very keen on Chinese history, so there were many books about China at her home. When Oksana was a child, her grandfather often told her and her elder brother about Chinese history, and about the friendly and brotherly relations between China and Russia. Under the influence of her grandfather, Oksana grew up with a strong sense of closeness to China.

Oksana says: "The love for China was passed on to me by my grandfather. Ever since we were kids, he has always told us that Chinese people are very diligent, nice and aspiring, just like us."

Start-up in Shanghai

Lively by nature, Oksana loved sports and was sent to a sports school by her parents at a young age. Oksana worked her way up to become a professional artistic gymnast and participated in numerous international competitions, enabling her to travel to many countries. After coming to China, Oksana found that China was as good as what her grandfather told her. "Chinese people were all very kind and treated me very well," Oksana recalls. Interestingly, every time she told people that she came from Russia, they would call her a "good friend."

Shanghai appeals so much to her not only because of her family's "China

Krupikova Oksana:

Carrying my ancestors' love for China to the next generation

complex", but also because of the city's charm. Oksana finds Shanghai very international, with a fast and dynamic pace that fits with her personality perfectly. In 2016, she established her first artistic gymnastics and dance school in Pudong, and after more than five years of hard work, she is now running three schools.

She says: "One of our schools is near the Huangpu River. After work, I'd like to go for a walk along the Bund. There is a Russian song called 'A Night at Moscow Suburb'. Night along the Bund and the Huangpu River is just as charming."

"Members of the Communist Party of China having many excellent qualities"

Because her grandfather was a member of the Communist Party during the Soviet era, Oksana would pay more attention to the Communist Party in China. Oksana knows that this year marks the 100th anniversary of the founding of the Communist Party of China, and she sees many good qualities in the CPC members.

She says: "Some of the staff at our dance center are members of the CPC. They work very hard, sometimes even work late into the night. They take their work in the dance center as their career and are devoted to it, and have been working here since the dance center was founded. They have been settled here."

This year also marks the 20th anniversary of the signing of the China-Russia Treaty of Good-neighborliness and Friendly Cooperation. It will be a milestone and a new starting point for Sino-Russian relations.

Oksana has now settled in Shanghai and her son is seven years old, studying in an international school in Pudong. She loves Shanghai deeply and encourages her son to learn Chinese well, to learn more about Chinese culture and to inherit the "China complex" from her grandparents.

Oksana herself will continue her business endeavor in Shanghai and pursue a colorful life.

Scan for videos

姓　名：Cameron Hume
中文名：何穆凯
国　籍：澳大利亚
职　位：通济隆亚太区执行董事

何穆凯：
很高兴拿到了永居证，长期在中国生活的梦想成真

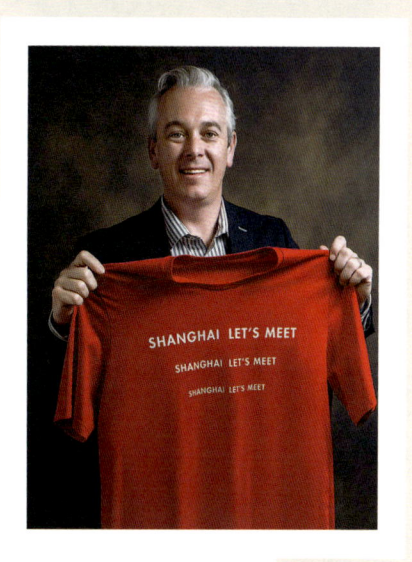

中国共产党出色地完成了让亿万民众摆脱贫困的工作。通过40多年的改革开放，中国已经在很多方面成为世界领先的国家之一。

梦想成现实

在中国生活了20多年的何穆凯前段时间刚拿到中华人民共和国外国人永久居留身份证，这让他长期在中国生活的梦想成为了现实。何穆凯认为，中国共产党出色地完成了让亿万民众摆脱贫困的工作。通过40多年的改革开放，中国已经在很多方面成为世界领先的国家之一。

何穆凯回忆道："小学的时候我的一个朋友碰巧是中国人，我们经常在一起玩。他的妈妈英文不是很好，所以她不得不用中文与我交流。"从那时起，何穆凯开始了解中国，并学习起了中文。

1990年，何穆凯第一次来到中国，那时他便爱上了这个国家。"至今我仍记得那时我回家告诉父母，希望将来有一天可以在中国工作和生活。从此，开始了我和中国的不解之缘。"何穆凯告诉记者，1996年他去了南京学习，拿到奖学金后又去了北京进修经济学。2003年他定居上海。

天时地利人和让他选择上海

据何穆凯介绍，2013年至2014年，通济隆的业务仅服务入境客户，但那时已经看到了中国迅速增长的出境游市场。由于一些旅客无法在国内

何穆凯：

很高兴拿到了永居证，长期在中国生活的梦想成真

兑换到目的地的货币，通济隆开始了和国家外汇管理局、上海外汇管理局的合作。"我们的业务非常依赖跨境旅行的双向流动。中国的出境游市场是世界上最大的旅游市场。越多的国家对中国放松签证限制，对我们的业务就越有利。"何穆凯说。

通济隆作为首批获得国家外汇管理局外币现钞跨境调运及批发业务牌照的三家非银行机构之一，其在中国取得的发展是与中国经济发展、对外开放和改革创新密不可分的。2019年，通济隆正式宣布在上海设立全新的亚太区总部，并以上海为中心辐射香港特别行政区、新加坡、马来西亚、泰国、日本和其他亚太国家及地区的所有业务。

何穆凯用"天时、地利、人和"解释了选择上海的原因。"天时"是指中国正在不断进行的改革开放、"一带一路"倡议的提出以及人民币自由兑换的不断放开；"地利"则因为上海是亚太地区的中心，已建成的基础设施、金融服务，还有机场为进出口货币提供了极大的便利；"人和"有两个层面，一是上海服务型政府的办事效率和良好的营商环境，二是上海的国际化人才资源。

2020年开始，由于新冠肺炎疫情对国际旅行产生了巨大的影响，通济隆外汇兑换业务下降了90%。何穆凯告诉记者，在各级政府和机场的帮助下，通济隆缓解了财务压力。"政府为我们提供了租金减免方案，这也使我们有能力在业务最终复苏前尽可能多地保留工作岗位。"何穆凯认为疫情是一个短期的影响，随着疫苗在国内开始接种，以及最近在亚洲其他地区也开始接种疫苗，国际旅行很快就会开始复苏。

对于中国市场何穆凯充满信心，他称不仅是因为中国本身的市场规模，也在于中国不断地进行改革和提高开放的程度。何穆凯认为，这一切离不开中国共产党的正确决策和领导，也正因为如此，未来中国经济能够继续保持增长势头。

Name: Cameron Hume
Chinese name: 何穆凯
Nationality: Australian
Position: Executive Director (Asia Pacific) at Travelex

Cameron Hume:

I'm very glad to get the Foreign Permanent Resident ID Card and my dream of living in China for a long time has come true

The Communist Party of China has successfully lifted hundreds of millions of people out of poverty. After more than 40 years of reform and opening-up, China has become one of the world's leading countries in many aspects.

A dream coming true

Cameron Hume, who has lived in China for more than 20 years, has just got his Foreign Permanent Resident ID Card of the People's Republic of China recently, which makes his dream of living in China for a long time come true. In Hume's eyes, the Communist Party of China (CPC) has successfully lifted hundreds of millions of people out of poverty. After more than 40 years of reform and opening-up, China has become one of the world's leading countries in many aspects.

"In primary school, one of my friends happened to be Chinese, and we often played together," Hume recalls. "His mother could not speak English, so she had to communicate with me in Chinese." Since then, Hume began to learn about China and study Chinese.

Hume first came to China in 1990, when he fell in love with the country. "I still remember the day when I went back home and told my parents that I hoped to work and live in China one day," Hume says. "From then on, my life has been inextricably bound with China." Hume says that in 1996, he went to Nanjing for school; after receiving a scholarship, he went to Beijing to study economics; in 2003 he settled in Shanghai.

Cameron Hume:

I'm very glad to get the Foreign Permanent Resident ID Card and my dream of living in China for a long time has come true

Shanghai boasting the best timing, location, and people

According to Hume, from 2013 to 2014, the business of Travelex was limited to inbound tourism, but the company had already seen the rapidly growing outbound tourism market in China. Seeing that some tourists could not exchange the currency of the destination country in China, Travelex began to cooperate with the State Administration of Foreign Exchange and Shanghai Administration of Foreign Exchange. "Our business relies heavily on the two-way flow of cross-border tourism," Hume says. "China boasts the largest outbound tourism market in the world, and the larger the number of countries that relax their visa restrictions on China, the better it is for our business."

Travelex is one of the first three non-banking institutions that have obtained the license of the State Administration of Foreign Exchange for cross-border transportation and wholesale of foreign currency notes. Its development in China is closely related to China's economic development, opening up to the outside world, and reform and innovation initiatives. In 2019, Travelex officially established a new Asia Pacific headquarters in Shanghai, with Shanghai as the hub for all its operations in Hong Kong Special Administrative Region, Singapore, Malaysia, Thailand, Japan and other Asia Pacific countries and regions.

Hume explains that he chose Shanghai because the city has the best "timing, location and people." "Timing" refers to the continuous progress of China's reform and opening-up policy, the implementation of the Belt and Road Initiative and the constant liberalization of RMB convertibility. "Location" refers to the fact that Shanghai is the center of the Asia Pacific region, with established infrastructure, financial services, and airports that provide a great convenience for importing and exporting currency. "People" refers to two aspects: first, the service-oriented characteristic of the Shanghai government, manifested in its efficiency in service and the favorable business environment it offers; second, the international talent resources that Shanghai boasts.

Ever since 2020, the foreign exchange business of Travelex has declined by 90% as a result of the huge impact of the COVID-19 pandemic on the international tourism market. Hume says that the governments at all levels and the airports offered timely help for Travelex to relieve its financial burden. "The government has offered us rent reduction and exemption, which helps us to keep as many jobs as possible before the business finally recovers," Hume says. He believes that the impact of the pandemic will be short in term. With the start of vaccination in China and recently in other parts of Asia, international tourism will soon start to recover.

Hume is full of confidence in the Chinese market. According to Hume, it is not only because of the inherent sizable market in China but also because China is forging ahead with the reform policy and keeps opening up to the outside world. Hume believes that all the progress should be contributed to the correct decisions made by the Communist Party of China (CPC) and its wise leadership, and that is why China will be able to sustain its growth momentum in the future.

Scan for videos

姓　名：Philippe Snel
中文名：施菲利
国　籍：比利时
职　位：比利时德沃福律师事务所创始人，上海法国学校董事长

施菲利：
中国在保护知识产权方面取得了巨大进步

当我回顾我在这里的过去十几二十年，我再次感受到这个国家包括这座城市，都经历了令人惊叹的改进。

2001年，比利时人施菲利怀揣着布鲁塞尔律师从业资格证来到了上海。他精通荷兰语、法语和英语，主要工作是协助国外投资者在中国建立和发展业务。20年间，施菲利不仅见证了上海的城市变迁，也亲历了中国的法治化进程。

疫情期间的上海

上海法国学校的董事会主席是施菲利众多头衔中的一个，该校在上海设有杨浦和青浦两个校区。新冠肺炎疫情暴发后，学校从2020年2月至5月都处于关闭的状态，学生也被迫在家上网课。"上海法国学校有大约1600名学生，涉及大约1100个家庭。这里牵涉到了很多人，他们都非常紧张。"施菲利告诉记者，在这样艰难的局面下，沟通变得尤为重要，沟通的对象包括学生家长、老师和多个政府部门。施菲利坦言："不得不提的是，我们与上海的政府部门，尤其是与上海市教育委员会进行了极好的合作。他们总是有问必答，始终保持信息透明化。"

此后，疫情得到控制，为保证学生安全，上海制定了一系列措施和方案，随后，学校重新开放，学生们有序回到课堂。

施菲利：

中国在保护知识
产权方面取得了
巨大进步

这里，有许多机会

17年前，刚来上海的施菲利在水果店认识了一个8岁的小女孩，她经常去店里帮父母的忙，也是家中唯一会说英语的。得益于上海良好的教育，加上她的努力，女孩成功考上了大学并于2021年加入了施菲利所在的律师事务所。施菲利向记者解释道："一个来自农村家庭的女孩儿，即将成为一名律师并开始她自己的职业生涯，这足以说明上海的教育质量。"

疫情也许扰乱了施菲利的"脚步"，却未曾阻碍他带领团队继续发展。虽然因为疫情，很多外国人不能来到上海，但2020年，施菲利所在的律所还是协助客户在闵行的莘庄工业园区完成了一个重大的投资项目。"整个过程中，我们作为客户的代表，成功完成了包括设立合资公司、与园区沟通、合同的协商与订立以及土地的购置等。这些都是在客户不在中国的状态下完成的。"他觉得这一切都证明上海有着大量的机会。

亲历中国的法治化进程

经济的蓬勃发展离不开法律的保驾护航，在中国这样一个超大规模的发展中国家，中国共产党领导的全面依法治国，是中国历史上一次国家治理的深刻变革，也是中华民族走向伟大复兴不可或缺的坚实保障。施菲利对中国的法治化进程深有感触。"我告诉我所有海外的朋友、律师，知识产权在中国已经不是一个问题了。"施菲利认为，随着法律法规的完善和健全，虽然约束更多了，但对于所有人来说也是一种更好的保护。此外，他认为单从知识产权法这个领域讨论，中国已经取得了巨大的进步。

"当我回顾我在这里的过去十几二十年，我再次感受到这个国家，包括这座城市，都经历了令人惊叹的改进。我们继续投入，且继续相信在这个国家，尤其是在这座城市，我们是有未来的。"

Name: Philippe Snel
Chinese Name: 施菲利
Nationality: Belgian
Position: Founder of De Wolf Law Firm in Belgium,
President of Shanghai French School

Philippe Snel:
China has made great progress in IP protection

Looking back on the close to 20 years I've spent here, I feel once again that this country, including this city, has experienced amazing improvements.

In 2001, Philippe Snel, a Belgian and a member of the Brussels Bar, came to Shanghai. He is fluent in Dutch, French and English, and his main job is assisting foreign investors to establish and develop their businesses in China. Over the past two decades, Snel has not only witnessed the changes in Shanghai but also experienced China's transition to the rule of law.

Shanghai during the pandemic

Chairman of the board of Shanghai French School, a school with two campuses in Yangpu and Qingpu Districts, is one of the many titles Snel holds. Due to the COVID-19 pandemic, the school was closed from February to May in 2020, and the students had to do online schooling from home. "Shanghai French School has about 1600 kids and about 1100 families, so it's a lot of people, and they are all very nervous." says Snel.

He also says that in such a difficult situation, it was especially important to communicate with the parents, teachers and related government agencies.

Snel says: "I must say that we've had an excellent collaboration with the Shanghai authorities, particularly with Shanghai Education Commission. They've always given us answers and they've always been, truthfully, they've always been transparent in the information."

Later, when the pandemic was brought under control, Shanghai enacted a series of measures and plans to ensure the safety of students, shortly after which, the school reopened and the students returned to class in an orderly manner.

Philippe Snel:

China has made great progress in IP protection

Here: a land of opportunities

Seventeen years ago, when he first came to Shanghai, Snel met an eight-year-old girl in a fruit shop. She often helped her parents with shop chores there and was the only one in the family that could speak English. Thanks to the good education systems of Shanghai and her own efforts, the girl eventually went on to study in a university, and in 2021 she joined Snel's law firm as a lawyer.

Snel says: "So you see, this girl who came from a family that, honestly, came from the fields, is now a lawyer and can now start her own career. That speaks to the quality of education in Shanghai."

The pandemic might have disturbed Snel's pace, but has never hindered his team from moving forward. Many foreigners were prevented from coming to Shanghai by the pandemic. Nevertheless, in 2020, Snel's law firm helped its clients complete a big investment project in Xinzhuang Industry Park in Minhang District.

He says: "We successfully represented our clients throughout the process of establishing a joint venture, communicating with the industry park, negotiating and concluding contracts, and purchasing land, which was all done when our clients were not in China." He thinks all this shows that Shanghai abounds with opportunities.

Experiencing the rule of law in China

A vigorous economy is inseparable from the protection of the law. For an extraordinarily large developing country like China, a comprehensive rule-of-law regime under the leadership of the Communist Party of China is a profound historical change in national governance, and it is also an indispensable solid guarantee for the great rejuvenation of the nation.

Snel is deeply impressed by how the rule of law has been advanced in China. "I tell all my friends overseas, the lawyers, that intellectual property is no longer a problem in China," says Snel. He believes an improved legal system, though may impose more constraints, will provide better protection for all people. In addition, he points out that in the field of intellectual property protection alone, China has made tremendous progress.

Snel says: "Looking back on the close to 20 years I've spent here, I feel once again that this country, including this city, has experienced amazing improvements. We'll continue to invest here, and we believe that in this country, especially in this city, we have a promising future."

姓　名：Shin Hyungkwan
中文名：辛炯官
国　籍：韩国
职　位：未来益财投资管理（上海）有限公司董事长

辛炯官：
上海是一座很有契约精神的城市

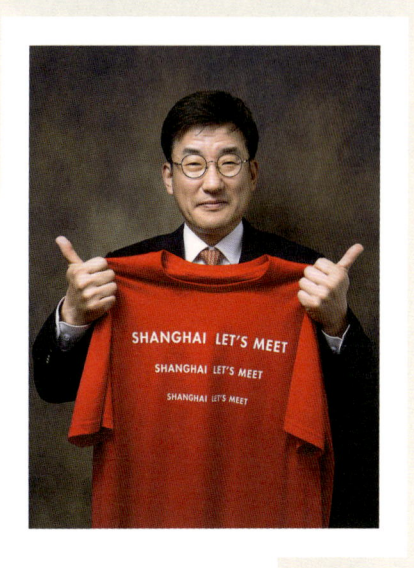

改革开放说起来容易做起来难，但是上海做到了，陆家嘴就是最好的证明。

一晃眼，韩国未来资产集团旗下的未来益财投资管理（上海）有限公司董事长辛炯官已经在上海度过了 13 个春秋。他亲眼见证了上海的变化，也见证了金融行业在浦东陆家嘴的飞速发展。在辛炯官看来，上海是中国改革开放的缩影，是一座有契约精神、充满温度的城市。

上海是中国改革开放的缩影

"浦东开发开放 30 周年是中国改革开放的象征，而未来资产这些年在上海的成长就是浦东开发开放的最好样本。"据辛炯官介绍，早在 2003 年，未来资产就开始了对中国业务的布局。2008 年，未来资产成为第一家取得中国 QFII（合格境外机构投资者）资格和额度的韩国金融公司。2018 年，未来资产集团旗下的未来益财投资管理（上海）有限公司顺利登记为私募证券投资基金管理人，从而成为第一家获准进入中国内地私募基金市场的韩资机构。

值得一提的是，2006 年，刚刚进入中国大陆不久的未来资产，就在高楼林立的陆家嘴片区，斥资 3 亿美元买下了其中的一栋大楼，并以"未来资产"命名。"未来资产集团是世界上唯一一家在上海陆家嘴拥有整楼产权的外资金融机构。当年招商时我们还担心入驻率的问题，但不到一年就基本租满了，可见外资对中国市场的信心和来华投资的热情。"辛炯官说。

在很多外国友人眼里，浦东新区是"中国改革开放的象征"和"上海

辛炯官：

上海是一座很有契约
精神的城市

现代化建设"的缩影。2000年，辛炯官初到上海，那时陆家嘴还没有完全发展起来。2008年，他因工作调动再次来到上海，陆家嘴已经发生了巨大的变化。"改革开放说起来容易做起来难，但是上海做到了。这些年，越来越多的外资企业到上海开公司、开展业务，也有很多朋友向我咨询。我会坚定地告诉他们，浦东陆家嘴是资源与人才的汇集地，是金融投资行业在上海发展的最佳选择。因为，金融产业是人和纸的产业，纸的意思就是合同、契约，是人与人之间连接的工具。上海是一座很有契约精神的城市。"辛炯官说。

上海的优秀，在方方面面

在辛炯官看来，未来资产集团能够在沪顺利发展，与上海的优良营商环境息息相关。"中国投资环境越来越好，政府、中国证监会和基金业协会，上海市金融监督管理局以及陆家嘴全球资管联合会（GAMAL）对于我们私募一级市场、二级市场的布局和未来发展规划都提供了配套和系统性的支持，让我们能够行稳致远。"

在上海生活了13年，辛炯官觉得，这是一座有温度的城市。他喜欢每天骑单车上下班，沿途经过上海的街道，觉得很惬意。

"上海出行很方便，自行车专用车道很多，骑车环保且安全。我每天骑行到码头，然后坐轮渡过黄浦江，和工作人员都很熟悉了。"有一次辛炯官出门忘记戴口罩，被轮渡的工作人员拦下，他去附近的便利店买，发现口罩已经售罄了。十分着急的时候，工作人员专门回到办公室拿了一个新口罩递给他。

"那天虽然天气很冷，但我觉得很温暖。"辛炯官告诉记者。

Name: Shin Hyungkwan
Chinese name: 辛炯官
Nationality: ROK
Position: CEO, Mirae Asset Investment Management (Shanghai) Co., Ltd.

Shin Hyungkwan:
Shanghai embodies the spirit of the contract

It's easier said than done to reform and open up to the outside world, but Shanghai has made it and Lujiazui is the best proof.

Time flies. Thirteen years have passed since Shin Hyuankwan came to Shanghai, working as CEO of Mirae Asset Investment Management (Shanghai) Co., Ltd. affiliated to South Korea's Mirae Asset Group. During his stay, he has witnessed the changes of Shanghai and the rapid development of the financial industry in Lujiazui, Pudong District. He believes that Shanghai is the very epitome of China's reform and opening up, a city beaming with warmth and the spirit of the contract.

Shanghai being the microcosm of China's reform and opening-up

He says: "The 30th anniversary of Pudong's development and opening up showcases China's reform and opening up, while Shanghai Mirae Asset's growth over these years exemplifies Pudong's development and opening up." It was as early as 2003 that Mirae Asset launched its business plan in China. In 2008, Mirae Asset became the first South Korean financial company to obtain China's Qualified Foreign Institutional Investor (QFII) qualification and quota. In 2018, Mirae Asset Investment Management (Shanghai) Co., Ltd. became the first South Korean financial institution to be admitted to China's private equity market, successfully registered as a private equity investment fund manager.

What's worth mentioning is that in 2006, when Mirae Asset newly entered China, it purchased one of the many towering buildings in Lujiazui for $300 million and named it "Mirae Asset".

Shin says: "At that time, Mirae Asset Group was the only foreign financial institution that owned the property right of an entire building in Lujiazui. We were quite worried about its occupancy rate when it was to be leased out, but

Shin Hyungkwan:

Shanghai embodies
the spirit of the contract

only within one year it almost reached its full occupancy, demonstrating foreign investors' interest and confidence in China's market."

In the eyes of many international friends, Pudong New Area is "a symbol of China's reform and opening up" and "the embodiment of Shanghai's modernization drive". When Shin Hyungkwan first came to Shanghai in 2000, Lujiazui was not fully developed, but eight years later when a job transfer brought him back to Shanghai, Lujiazui amazed him with drastic changes.

He says: "It's easier said than done to reform and open up, but Shanghai has made it. In recent years, more and more foreign enterprises have come to Shanghai to set up companies and start businesses, and many friends have come to me for advice. Every time I assure them that Lujiazui, amassing rich resources and talents, is the best choice for financial investment in Shanghai. It's because the financial industry is a trade of people and paper in that paper refers to a contract or an agreement with which people are connected, and Shanghai rightly embodies the spirit of the contract."

A remarkable Shanghai in every way

Shin attributes Mirae Asset Group's successful development in Shanghai to the favorable business environment here.

He says: "Investment environment in China is increasingly optimized. Our steady and long-term development wouldn't be possible without the concerted efforts of the central government, China Securities Regulatory Commission, Asset Management Association of China, Shanghai Municipal Financial Regulatory Bureau and Global Asset Management Association of Lujiazui (GAMAL). They have provided us with consistent and systematic support for the layout and future development of our primary and secondary private equity markets."

Thirteen years' living experience in Shanghai fills Shin with warmth. He cycles to and from work every day, delighted in passing through the city streets.

Shin says: "It's easy to travel in Shanghai. There are many bicycle lanes, so riding a bike is safe and environment-friendly as well. I ride to the dock every day and take a ferry across the Huangpu River. I am well acquainted with the staff there."

Once he forgot to wear a mask which was mandatory in public places for COVID-19 pandemic control, so he was stopped from boarding the ferry. Then he hurried to a store nearby to buy one, only to find none left. One staff member noticed his frustration, returned to her office and got him a new mask.

"It was very cold outside, but I felt warm at heart," Shin says.

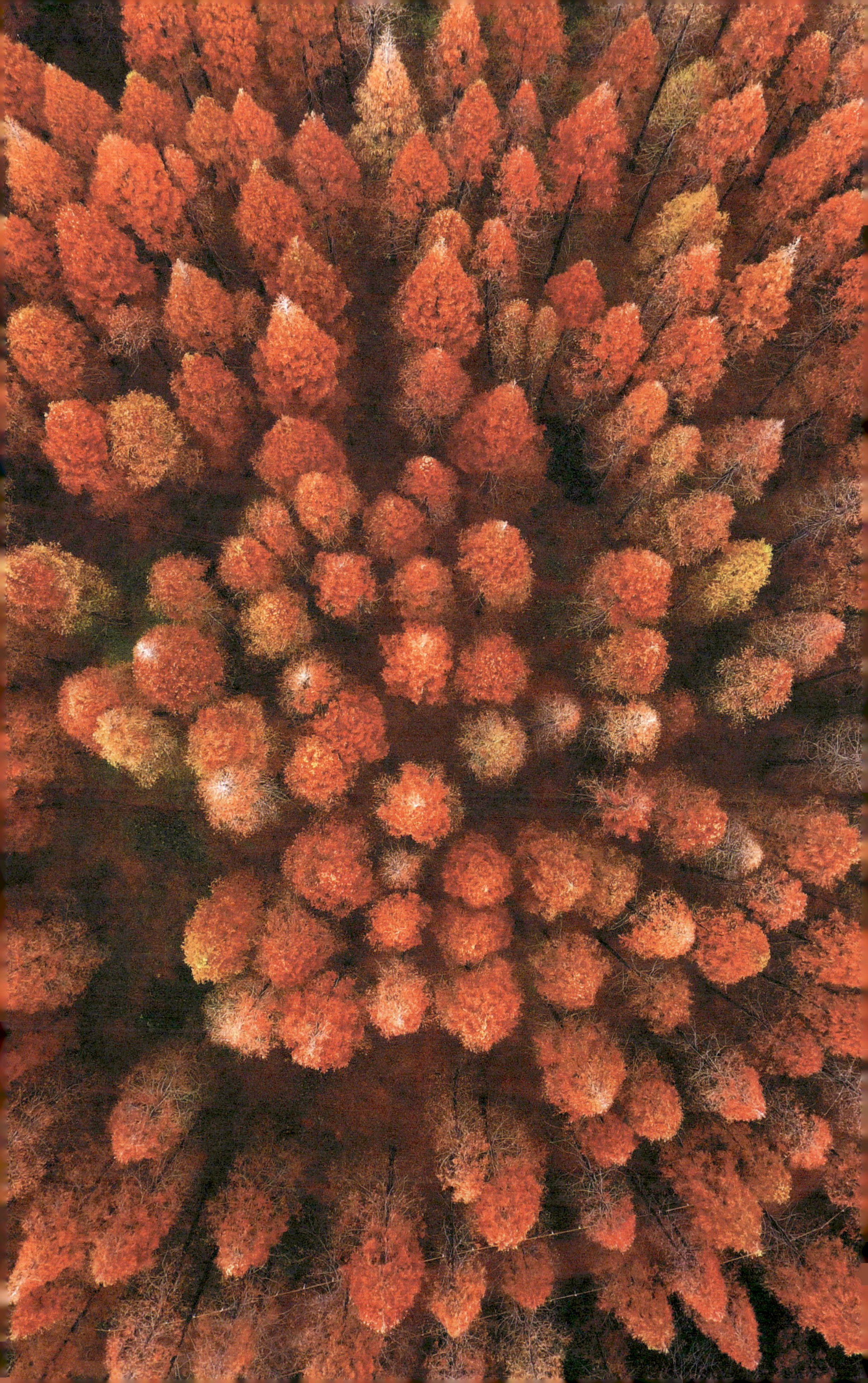

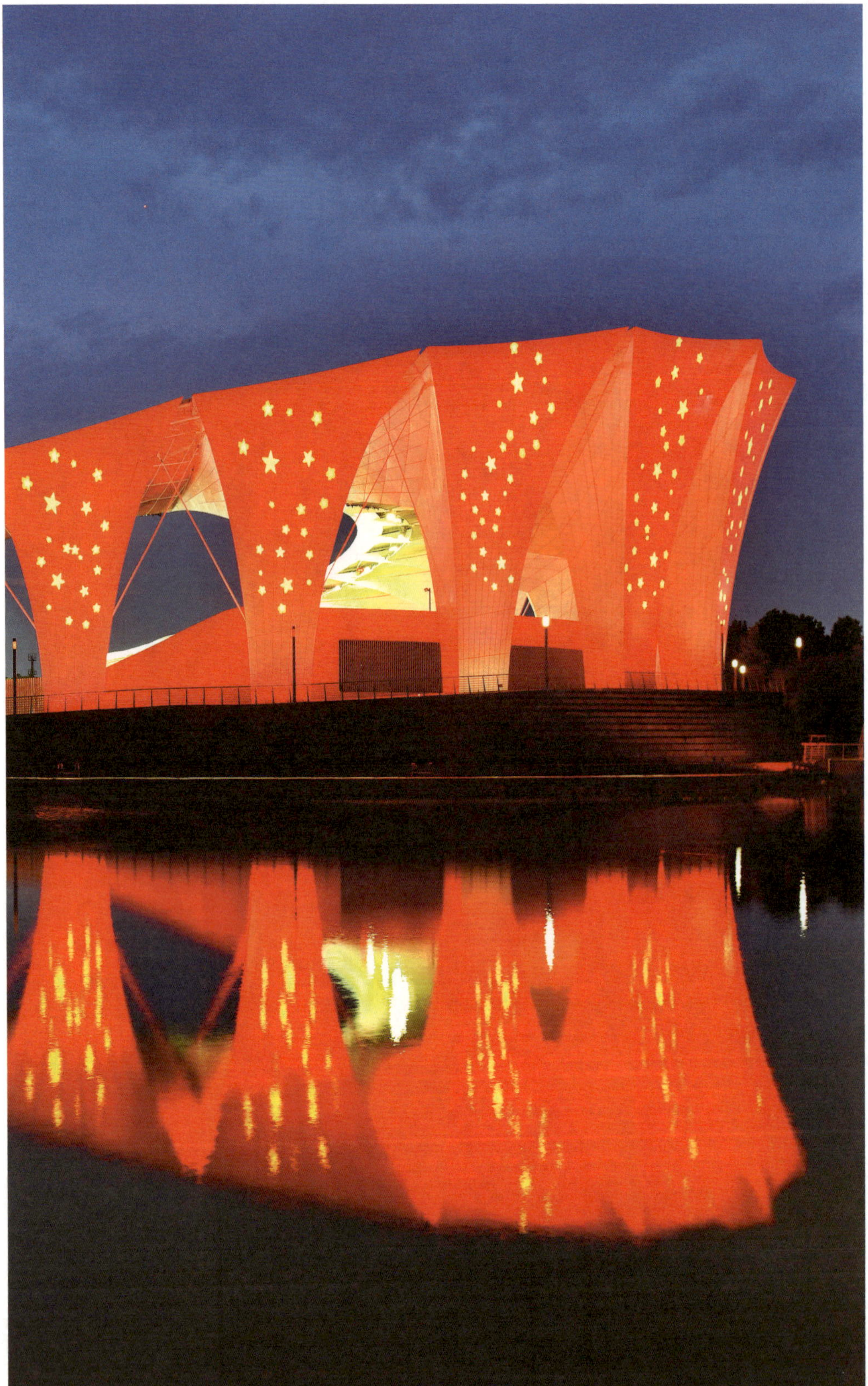

姓　名：DAIMON KAZUTO
中文名：大门和人
国　籍：日本
职　位：威可楷（中国）投资有限公司法人代表兼总经理

大门和人：
我感受到了上海贴心的营商服务

> 在 AI 和高科技的全方位运用方面，中国、上海再一次引领了全球。

虽然常住上海还不到 4 年时间，但大门和人对这里的喜爱溢于言表。思南公馆、新天地留下了他和夫人漫步的身影；夏日里的小龙虾、秋季肥美的大闸蟹都是他的心头好；中国国际进口博览会、G60 科创走廊则给他留下了更为深刻的印象……

大门和人眼中的上海是怎样的？

适宜居住

平日里，大门和人喜欢在上海思南公馆和新天地一带漫步，道路两旁的梧桐和颇具特色的历史建筑，仿佛一位白发老人正娓娓道来他的故事；而浸润在空气中的时尚气息，又为这画面增添了一份特别的意境。

"我最喜欢的要数思南书局。一开始我以为这只是一家开在法式老建筑中的普通书店而已。然而一踏入书局，拾级而上，第一反应便是，我完全小看它了！挑上一本喜欢的书，在咖啡香气的陪伴下，两个小时稍纵即逝。"近年来，包括思南书局在内的一批批新兴实体书店深耕着上海文化沃土，激发全民阅读热情、打响"上海文化"品牌。

除了这座城市的书香气息，大门和人对上海的治安环境同样赞誉有加。2017 年，大门和人的夫人陪同他一起来到上海赴任。他说，上海的治安环境让他可以专注于工作，"有时我工作很晚归家，路上却时不时看到有女性在单独夜跑、锻炼，这一点就足以证明上海治安非常完美。"

大门和人：
我感受到了上海
贴心的营商服务

科技领跑

去年，大门和人收到上海外事办公室邀请参观 G60 科创走廊，感受中国科创的新生机和新力量。"展品使我倍感震惊。"大门和人回忆道，长三角 G60 科创走廊大数据云图令他记忆深刻，城市的各项指标在大屏幕上实时显示，非常先进。

作为全国"一网统管"建设的领跑者，上海一直在积极探索城市数字化转型下的数字治理新理念与新方法，走出了一条中国超大城市管理的新路。大门和人不禁感叹道："在 AI 和高科技的全方位运用方面，中国，上海再一次引领了全球。"

内需主导

诞生于 20 世纪 30 年代的威可楷（YKK）集团，可谓拉链界的鼻祖，这家全球最大的拉链制造公司在 20 世纪末便与上海结下渊源。1992 年，YKK 集团进入上海，然而那时的上海工厂只是做一些代工工作。"随着时代更迭，如今中国的内需潜力不断释放，国内市场持续壮大。我们也从出口导向转变为了内需主导。"大门和人表示，"中国人对穿着要求越来越高，时尚敏感度越来越强，我们也希望在大家对品位的追求方面能够做出更大的贡献。"

2010 年 YKK 在上海临港的新工厂开业，与已有的闵行工厂相结合，上海拥有 YKK 集团最大的产量。"两家工厂在运营中得到了市政府和区政府的大力支持。"大门和人举例道，上海是个对环境要求非常高的城市，在拉链生产环节如何避免环境污染，市、区两级政府在政策与操作层面上给予了 YKK 大量积极指导与帮助，让他感受到了上海"贴心式"营商服务。

"如今，日本与欧美尚未走出疫情阴霾，而中国却以一种惊人的速度恢复到接近正常状态。"谈到对未来中国市场的看法时，大门和人肯定地说道，"我们对中国的市场非常乐观！"

Name: DAIMON KAZUTO
Chinese name: 大门和人
Nationality: Japanese
Position: Corporate Representative & General Manager of YKK (China) Investment Co., Ltd.

DAIMON KAZUTO:
I felt the considerate business-friendly service in Shanghai

In the area of full-scale application of AI and hi-tech, once again China and Shanghai play the leading role in the world.

Although DAIMON KAZUTO has been living in Shanghai for less than four years, he's more than delighted when describing his life here. KAZUTO and his wife love to take a stroll around Sinan Mansions and Xintiandi; the crayfish in summer and hairy crab full of meat and roe in autumn are among his favorite dishes; he is deeply impressed by the China International Import Expo and the G60 Science and Technology Innovation Valley of the Yangtze River Delta…

What does Shanghai look like in KAZUTO's eyes?

Comfortable to Live

When possible, KAZUTO enjoys walking around Shanghai's Sinan Mansions and Xintiandi. The plane trees lined along the streets and the historic buildings with distinctive styles are like senior people in silver hair, full of stories to tell. The fashion ingredients around the corner also add another flavor to the ambiance.

KAZUTO says: "My favorite spot is Sinan Books. In the beginning, I thought it was just an ordinary book store located inside a historic French building. But when I stepped inside and climbed up the stairs, my first response was obviously I underestimated this place. After selecting a pleasant book and immersing myself in coffee aroma, two hours would easily pass before I knew it." In the last few years, a number of new style physical book stores kept propping up in Shanghai, enriching the cultural environment of Shanghai, inspiring more people to read and building a brand of "Shanghai Culture".

Apart from the book reading environment, KAZUTO also highly appraises the public security level in Shanghai. In 2017 he moved to Shanghai together with his wife for a new position. The sound public security helps him be more focused on work.

He says: "Sometimes I go home very late in the night after work, but still I

DAIMON KAZUTO:

I felt the considerate business-friendly service in Shanghai

can see ladies jogging and exercising alone outside. This point alone shows that Shanghai's public security is perfect."

Leading Technology

Last year, KAZUTO was invited by the Foreign Affairs Office of Shanghai Municipal Government to visit the G60 Science and Technology Innovation Valley, as an opportunity to feel the energy and power of China's science innovation. KAZUTO recalls that he was "shocked by the exhibition." He was impressed by the advanced big data cloud map, which could show the real-time major indicators of a city's operation on the big screen.

As a leading city in China's construction of a unified digital governance network, Shanghai has always been exploring new concepts and methods in the digital transformation of the city's governance, which has formed a brand new model for the management of megacity in China. KAZUTO cannot help from saying that "In the area of full-scale application of AI and hi-tech, once again China and Shanghai play the leading role in the world."

Domestic Market Orientation

Established in the 1930s, the YKK Group is one of the earliest companies in the zipper industry. As the world's largest zipper manufacturer, its story with Shanghai dates back to the end of the last century. In 1992, the YKK Group first opened its operation in Shanghai, but the Shanghai factory at that time was only tasked with some assembly processes.

KAZUTO says: "As time changes, now the potential of China's domestic demand is being continuously unleashed. There is fast and strong growth in the domestic market. Our focus has shifted from export-oriented to domestic-market-oriented. Now Chinese people have a higher demand for clothing and also get more sensitive to fashion. We hope to make a bigger contribution in people's pursuit of getting stylish and trendy."

In 2010, YKK's new factory in Shanghai's Lingang Special Area was put into use. Combined with the already existing factory in Minhang, Shanghai boasts the largest manufacturing capacity within the YKK Group. "The two factories get very strong support in the operation from the municipal government and district governments," KAZUTO says. As an example, he says that Shanghai has very high requirements for environmental protection. In order to avoid polluting the environment in the manufacturing of zippers, the municipal government and district governments have given YKK many constructive guidelines and support, both in terms of policy and implementation. In the process, he truly feels the considerate business-friendly service from the government agencies in Shanghai.

"Now when Japan, the EU and the US are still struggling to control the pandemic, China is returning to normal state at an astonishing speed," KAZUTO says. When talking about the future of the Chinese market, he says firmly: "We are very optimistic about the Chinese market!"

Scan for videos

姓　　名：Julie Laulusa
中文名：刘钰涓
国　　籍：法国
职　　位：Mazars 集团董事会成员，Mazars 中审众环执行合伙人

刘钰涓：
我认为上海的成就还仅仅是一个开始

> 上海政府创造了前所未有的历史奇迹，从零打造了一个全球著名的金融中心。

出生在老挝，成长于法国，继而赴美国深造，最终奋斗在上海。这是刘钰涓在"地球村"的简历，亦是她为自己不同人生阶段设定的舞台所在。"在一个人学识精力最为鼎盛的黄金时代，我选择了上海，也是上海选择了我。"

创办上海办公室

走进刘钰涓位于浦东陆家嘴核心地带的办公室，窗外是林立的金融大厦、银行大楼，幕墙反射着耀眼的阳光，远处的上海中心勾勒出一条崭新的城市天际线。谁能想到 30 年前，陆家嘴还只是一片烂泥渡，坊间流传的"宁要浦西一张床，不要浦东一间房"深刻描画着当时浦东的落后面貌。而这一切，从 1990 年初，党中央、国务院做出了开发开放浦东的重大国家战略决策开始改写。"1996 年，我第一次造访浦东。这里到处热火朝天地开工建设，人们朝气蓬勃干劲十足，那一刻我似乎在这里看到了充满无限可能的未来。"

伴随着开发开放的号角，大批外国企业涌入浦东试水。怎么进入中国市场，各类手续怎么办理，认证标准能否对接……外国企业都急切地想要了解浦东，找到答案。作为欧洲第三大会计师事务所——法国 Mazars（玛泽）集团代表，刘钰涓一直以来都希望可以充分利用自己的国际化背景，成为中外合作的桥梁。2001 年，她再次来到浦东，一手创立了 Mazars 上海办公室。

刘钰涓：

我认为上海的成就还
仅仅是一个开始

从"引进来"到"走出去"

在刘钰涓初到上海的十年里，因为对外开放政策的引领，她的工作主要是协助外企落户上海，并且帮助他们在中国扎根和发展。但自从中国成为世界第二大经济体后，越来越多的中国公司开始国际化。最近十年，她的工作重心已变成帮助中国公司走出去。"我们已经在全球50多个国家创建了'中国业务部'，为中国公司到海外发展提供服务。"刘钰涓说，浦东改革开放已经成为中国改革开放的一面旗帜，短短三十年间，浦东就建立了陆家嘴金融贸易区、外高桥保税区、上海自由贸易试验区；引进了3万多家外资企业，其中包括300多家世界五百强；把曾经的农田，华丽转身为GDP总量超1万亿元、摩天大楼林立的世界级经济中心。"在整个过程中，我看到了浦东政府的效率、毅力和决心。"

在刘钰涓眼里，上海的发展速度是国际上任何一个城市都难以企及的。20年来，上海的GDP增长了八倍。作为一个城市，它的GDP已经超越了新加坡、瑞典等发达国家。不管是软实力还是硬实力，都得到了相当大的提升。

刘钰涓还记得2001年她刚来到浦东的时候，陆家嘴只有两座地标性建筑——金茂大厦和东方明珠。20年后，上海已经位列全球第三大金融中心，仅次于纽约和伦敦。"上海政府创造了前所未有的历史奇迹，从零打造了一个全球著名的金融中心。"对上海未来的发展，刘钰涓充满期待："而我认为，上海的成就还仅仅是一个开始。"

Name: Julie Laulusa
Chinese Name: 刘钰涓
Nationality: French
Position: Mazars Group Executive Board Member;
Managing Partner, Mazars Chinese Mainland

Julie Laulusa:
I think the achievement of Shanghai is just a beginning

The Shanghai government has created an unprecedented historical miracle, building a world-famous financial center from scratch.

Laulusa was born in Laos, grew up in France, studied in the U.S. and worked in Shanghai. This is her experience in the global village and also her choice in different stages of life. "At the height of my energy and knowledge, I chose Shanghai and Shanghai chose me as well," she says.

Establishing the Mazars office in Shanghai

Outside Laulusa's office window in Lujiazui, Pudong New Area, Shanghai, the glass walls of towering financial centers and bank buildings shine bright under the sunlight. Shanghai Tower in the distance forms a new city skyline.

Nobody could have imagined that 30 years ago, Lujiazui was just a mud bank. The popular saying "I would rather have a bed in Puxi than a room in Pudong" vividly depicted the backwardness of Pudong at that time. However, things began to change when the Communist Party of China (CPC) Central Committee and the State Council made an important strategic decision on the development and opening up of Pudong in 1990.

Laulusa says: "When I first visited Pudong in 1996, construction work was in full swing everywhere, and people were vigorous and energetic. At that moment, I seemed to see the infinite possibilities of the future."

With the opening up of Pudong, many foreign companies poured into Pudong to test the waters. How to enter the Chinese market? How to handle all sorts of procedures? Whether certification standards can be met? Foreign companies were eager to learn more about Pudong and find the answers to these

Julie Laulusa:

I think the achievement of Shanghai is just a beginning

questions. As one of the delegates of Mazars, the third-largest accounting firm in Europe, Laulusa always hoped to make full use of her international background to bridge the gap between China and the world. In 2001, she came to Pudong again and set up the Mazars office in Shanghai.

From "bringing in" to "going out"

In her first 10 years in Shanghai, thanks to the opening-up policy, Laulusa's main job at that time was to assist foreign companies to settle and grow in China. However, in the recent decade, more and more Chinese companies have started internationalization since China became the second-largest economy in the world. As a result, her focus shifted to helping Chinese companies go global.

"We have established Chinese Service Group in more than 50 countries around the world to provide service for Chinese companies going international," she says. Pudong's development has become a banner of China's reform and opening up. In the past 30 years, Pudong saw the establishment of Lujiazui Finance and Trade Zone, the Waigaoqiao Free Trade Zone and the Shanghai Pilot Free Trade Zone. More than 30,000 enterprises were introduced, including more than 300 out of the Fortune 500 Companies. The former farmland has been turned into a world-class economic center with towering skyscrapers everywhere, generating more than 1 trillion yuan (US$156.8 billion) of GDP. "I saw the Pudong government's efficiency, persistency and resolution during the whole process," Laulusa says.

In Laulusa's eyes, the rapid development of Shanghai is incomparable to any city in the world. In 20 years, Shanghai's GDP has increased eightfold. As a city, it has surpassed some developed countries such as Singapore and Sweden. Shanghai has been greatly enhanced, in both its soft power and hard power.

Laulusa still remembers that when she came to work in Shanghai in 2001, there were only two landmarks in Lujiazui -- Jinmao Tower and the Oriental Pearl TV Tower. Twenty years later, Shanghai has become the third financial center in the world after New York and London. "The Shanghai government has created an unprecedented historical miracle, building a world-famous financial center from scratch," she says. Laulusa is very optimistic about Shanghai's future development. She says: "I think the achievement of Shanghai is just a beginning."

Scan for videos

姓　名：Owen K Messick
中文名：麦欧文
国　籍：美国
职　位：多特瑞中国区总裁

麦欧文：
永久居留身份让我对中国更有归属感

我非常感谢中国政府和上海政府创造的如此好的营商环境，这让我对多特瑞在中国的未来充满信心！

"他们叫我白煮蛋。"多特瑞中国区总裁麦欧文风趣地谈论起自己的外号，他说，因为自己的脑袋像蛋，还因为自己的皮肤是白的，心是"黄"的，有一颗中国心。

麦欧文已经在中国居住了30多年，今年是他在上海生活的第14个年头。"我很爱这座城市，也很爱中国。"麦欧文感慨道，"上海是一个令人着迷的城市，总有全新的东西等待着人们去探索与发现。"

"身份证"让人更有归属感

2019年，麦欧文取得了一张永久居住中国的"身份证"。外国人永久居留身份证、"人才20条"、"人才30条"、人才高峰工程行动方案……近几年，上海推出了一系列政策，加快构建具有全球竞争力的人才制度体系，让越来越多的外籍人才对这座城市青眼有加。

"有了中国身份证后，我在这里生活、工作和旅行变得更加容易了，我不必再续签签证了，这方便了很多。"谈到这张中国"身份证"，麦欧文连连点赞它给自己生活带来的便利。"以前买火车票时，需要在柜台排队购票，而现在网上就可以买票，一刷身份证就可以进站了。"

更为重要的一点是，在麦欧文心里，取得这张"身份证"，让他感到自己被这个国家所接纳，在上海也更有归属感了。

麦欧文和一位中国姑娘恋爱结婚，如今，他们和五个孩子中的两个孩子一起生活在这里。在他心中，上海就如同家一般舒适，"我们都很爱这里。"

麦欧文：

永久居留身份让我
对中国更有归属感

"一个亿"的公益捐赠目标

因为受到了很多帮助，也因为把中国看作是自己的家，麦欧文以及多特瑞也积极回馈着社会。作为全球最大芳香护理和精油企业之一，成立于2014年的多特瑞中国区虽然还很"年轻"，但定下的目标却一点都不小——捐赠一个亿。"这是一个十年的长期目标，累积到现在我们的捐款已经超过了4400万元人民币。"麦欧文表示。

这种"施以援手""助人为乐"的精神无疑是多特瑞的企业文化，与此同时，在麦欧文看来，如今的消费者，尤其是年轻消费者，往往会寻找与他们产生共情的品牌。他们想要找一个可以信赖的公司，一个愿意回馈社会、帮助社会的公司。"上海是中国最发达的城市之一，有着最现代、最前卫的思想，所以我相信我们的顾客一定会支持这样的理念。"

"大功臣"助力提升知名度

作为一家国际企业中国区的掌舵人，麦欧文说自己切实地感受到了中国政府和上海政府营造的良好营商环境以及中国市场的强劲潜能。"政府给了我们相当大的帮助与支持。"麦欧文说，起初自己还有些不习惯，"有趣的是，工作人员会上门来询问我们，并清楚地解释他们可以如何帮助我们，这给多特瑞在上海、在中国开展业务提供了很大信心。"

2021年2月，位于静安区丰盛里的多特瑞生活馆正在如火如荼地建设中。"区政府在公司发展遇到困难之时给了我们很多建议。"

来上海的这14年间，麦欧文见证了高水平营商环境奇迹般的效率。每年，多特瑞会从世界各地进口大量精油。"在过去几年里，海关通关提速约50%。这一点对我们而言非常重要。"2019年的降低增值税"大礼包"也让多特瑞获益匪浅。麦欧文表示，企业在此期间节省了大约8000万元人民币，这有助于公司进行更好的发展与布局。

在麦欧文看来，多特瑞在中国市场逐渐打响名号，背后还有一个"大功臣"——中国国际进口博览会。9㎡、108㎡、150㎡，这是多特瑞在此前三届进博会上分别租用的展台面积。借助进博会这个大舞台带来的关注度和令人欣喜的业绩，多特瑞在上海建立了中国工厂和首个海外实验室。"目前我们已经签约了第四届进博会，并将进一步扩大我们的展区。"

"我非常感谢中国政府创造的如此好的营商环境，这让我对多特瑞在中国的未来充满信心！"

Name: Owen K Messick
Chinese name: 麦欧文
Nationality: American
Position: China President of dōTERRA

Owen K Messick:
Permanent residence status gives me a sense of belonging in China

I'm grateful to China and Shanghai for creating such a friendly business environment. It gives me confidence about the future of dōTERRA in China!

Messick has lived in China for over 30 years and in Shanghai for 14 years. "I love this city," he says. "Shanghai is an enchanting city. There's something brand new for people to explore and discover every day."

A card, an identity, a sense of belonging

In 2019, Messick obtained his China Foreign Permanent Resident ID Card, allowing him to live and work here for as long as he wants.

In recent years, the Shanghai Municipal Government has rolled out the overseas talent permanent residence permit, the "20 articles" and "30 articles" providing favorable policies for overseas talents and a master plan for attracting high-end talents. These incentives accelerated Shanghai's establishment of an internationally competitive talent attraction system as more and more foreign talents now favor living and working in this city.

"With my Chinese identity card, it's much more convenient for me to live, work and travel here," he says. "I don't need to renew my visa anymore, and it's made things much easier."

Messick praises his Chinese "ID card" for making his life more convenient. "I used to have to line up at the counter to buy my train tickets," he says. "Now I can simply purchase my tickets online and swipe my ID card to enter the train station."

More importantly, Messick feels that he is accepted by this country and belongs to Shanghai now that he holds this "ID card".

Messick found his love in China. He and his Chinese wife now live here with two of their five children. He says that Shanghai gives him the comfort of a home, and they all love it here.

Owen K Messick:

Permanent residence status gives me a sense of belonging in China

A goal of ¥100M for charity

Messick and dōTERRA are actively giving back to their Chinese home by donating to charities. dōTERRA is one of the world's largest sellers of aromatherapy products and essential oils. Founded in 2014, dōTERRA China is still young, but it sets an ambitious goal of donating ¥100 million to charities.

"This is a 10-year long-term goal," Messick says. "So far we have donated over ¥44 million."

Charity and care for the community are parts of dōTERRA's corporate culture. Messick says he believes today's consumers, especially young consumers, often look for brands they can bond with. He says they want to look for a trustworthy company, a company willing to give back to the community.

"Shanghai is one of China's most developed cities and is where you find the most modern ideas," Messick says. "I believe our customers support our corporate ideals."

An expo helps raise brand awareness

As the president of an international corporation's China office, Messick says he has experienced the friendly business environment in China and Shanghai and has sensed the strong potential of China's market.

"The government has given us a lot of help and support," Messick says. He says he did not expect the enthusiasm of those who offered help.

"Interestingly, administrative staff would come to our doorstep, ask what we need help with and explain clearly how they can help us," he says. "This boosted dōTERRA's confidence of expanding its business in Shanghai and China."

Messick says the local government was helpful when the company was setting up its store in Jing'an District in February. "The district government gave us a lot of advice when the company was going through a challenging time," he says.

Every year, dōTERRA imports large quantities of essential oil from around the world. In his 14 years in Shanghai, Messick witnessed the miraculous efficiency of a top-notch business environment. "In the past couple of years, our essential oils' customs clearance has been 50% faster," he says. "This is very important for us."

The "gift package" of China's 2019 value-added tax reform also benefited dōTERRA. Messick says the company saved roughly ¥80 million from this reform, boosting its growth in China.

Messick says the company's participation in the Chinese International Import Expo (CIIE) is a major factor in raising its brand recognition in the Chinese market. dōTERRA attended the expo for three consecutive years and expanded its booth from 9m^2 in the first year to 108m^2 and then to 150m^2 last year. The company has now built a Chinese factory and its first overseas lab in Shanghai, in part because of the brand recognition and business deals accomplished through the expo's platform.

"We have now signed up to attend the fourth CIIE and will further increase the size of our booth," Messick says.

"I'm grateful to China and Shanghai for creating such a friendly business environment," he says. "It gives me confidence about the future of dōTERRA in China!"

Scan for videos

姓　名：Jung Hwanuk
中文名：郑桓旭
国　籍：韩国
职　位：原百盛纽可尔瑞特商贸（上海）有限公司总经理

郑桓旭：
我每天的工作就是服务好上海的消费者

徒步在高楼林立的浦东陆家嘴，我为这座新旧交融的城市着迷。

"我来上海已经 11 年了，刚来上海的时候我可还是个年轻小伙呢！"扳起指头一算，来自韩国的郑桓旭恍然发现，出生于 1981 年的自己已步入了中年。作为上海百盛优客城市广场（以下简称"百盛优客"）最年轻的"一把手"，郑桓旭带领商场团队积极响应上海国际消费城市建设，不断创新消费模式，擦亮"上海购物"底色。

我们的"生意经"

任何时候走进长宁百盛优客城市广场，位于东一楼的特卖场里总是人头攒动。特卖品牌每周一换，这些上海本土商场看不懂的"生意经"却是百盛优客的一大特色。

"上海是个非常国际化的城市，消费者很容易接纳新鲜事物，他们不仅追求卓越的商品品质，而且对性价比也有很高的要求。"在商场 6 楼办公室里，郑桓旭用流利的中文侃侃而谈，"我每天的工作就是服务好上海的消费者，给他们提供好的品牌、合适的价格，以及人性化的服务，这也是上海作为国际大都市所需要的。"

百盛优客的前身是老百货天山商厦，进入新世纪后，几十年来沿袭的传统经营模式逐渐跟不上新时代的节奏，虽历经数度转型，效果却均不理想。2015 年，马来西亚百盛商业集团和韩国衣恋集团联手，决定打造百盛优客城市奥特莱斯。常年销售额不到 2 亿元的商场，转型成功后首年业绩就冲破了 7 亿元人民币，在中国商业地产和零售行业引起轰动。

作为全国首家城市奥特莱斯，郑桓旭十分乐于分享百盛优客的成功秘诀。"我们对消费者的喜好非常敏感，不受欢迎的品牌最短一个月就会被调整离开；小餐饮也经常推陈出新，保持品类的丰富性及品牌的新鲜度；每周一换的特卖品牌也能'吸牢'消费者'常回来看看'。"

"上海速度"令人惊叹

在郑桓旭看来，百盛优客的成功，离不开政府细致的"店小二"服务。从项目启动到正式开业运行，政府一次次实地拜访，协调各方力量，让百盛优客创下四个月就开店的"上海纪录"。"我们在韩国有 50 多家商场，最快的一家也用了一年多时间，这样的'上海速度'令人惊叹。"

在读大学时，郑桓旭就认为中国经济持续良好，市场潜力无限。他一边苦练中文，一边了解中国市场。当毕业后进入韩国衣恋集团时，郑桓旭已经对中国市场有了相当多的了解。2009 年公司准备派员来上海拓展市场时，郑桓旭立即抓住了机会。来到上海后，他从最基层的员工做起，靠着对中国市场的理解，不断创新线上线下销售模式，与电商合作频频擦出火花，销售业绩屡攀新高。11 年间不懈奋斗，郑桓旭迎来了人生的高光时刻，成为百盛优客最年轻的总经理。

"我以前只在照片中见过上海，古旧的老城厢面貌让我印象深刻。我的家人当初也非常担心我在上海的生活。但当我用自己的双眼看到历经百年时光的外滩建筑群，徒步在高楼林立的浦东陆家嘴，我为这座新旧交融的城市着迷。"如今，每到节日郑桓旭都会邀请韩国的家人和朋友一起来上海游玩，他们为不断发展壮大的上海赞叹不已，也非常乐于体验上海的城市发展成果，海昌海洋公园、迪士尼乐园都留下了他们的足迹。

在郑桓旭眼中，经营大型商场，消费环境非常重要。"上海的治安环境非常棒，这座城市已成为世界上最安全的城市之一。"郑桓旭说，就百盛优客而言，每年报案失窃率都在逐步递减，"这要感谢派出所及街道所有职能部门，有了他们的付出和支持，我们才能够更专注地做好自己的商场。所以未来在上海这座城市，我们计划再开 4—5 家商场，期待我们的成功吧！"

Name: Jung Hwanuk
Chinese Name: 郑桓旭
Nationality: ROK
Position: Former General Manager of Parkson Newcore Tianshan Square

Jung Hwanuk:
My job every day was to serve well consumers in Shanghai

Walking among the high-rises in Lujiazui, I'm fascinated by the city where the old meets the new.

"I came to Shanghai 11 years ago," Jung Hwanuk said. "When I first came to China for work, I was still quite young." Born in 1981, Hwanuk is from ROK. Once the youngest "chief" of Shanghai Parkson Newcore Tianshan Square (hereinafter referred to as Parkson Newcore), Hwanuk, 40 this year, had led the mall team to respond positively to the construction of Shanghai as an international consumer city, continuously innovating consumption models and helping in branding Shanghai as a shopping destination.

Our way of doing business

The outlet mall on the east ground floor of Parkson Newcore in Changning District, Shanghai, is always packed with people. Different from many local malls, the brands on sale there change every week, which is a unique feature of Parkson Newcore.

"Shanghai is a cosmopolitan city," said Hwanuk. "Consumers here welcome novelties and require high-quality as well as cost-effective goods." In his office on the 6th floor of the mall, Jung Hwanuk spoke eloquently in fluent Chinese: "My job every day is to serve Shanghai consumers well by offering them good brands, the right prices, and customized service that Shanghai needs as a cosmopolitan city."

Parkson Newcore is a mall transformed from the old Tianshan Department Store. After entering the new century, the traditional business model the old store had followed for decades gradually failed to keep up with the rhythm of the new era, and although it had undergone several transformations, the results were not satisfactory. In 2015, Parkson Malaysia and the E·land Group from ROK joined forces to create Parkson Newcore City Outlet. The successful transformation of the mall, which had annual sales of less than RMB 200 million, led to an RMB 700 million performance in its first year, causing a sensation in China's commercial real estate and retail industry.

Jung Hwanuk:

My job every day was to serve well consumers in Shanghai

Having run the first urban outlet store in China, Hwanuk was delighted to share the success recipe of Parkson Newcore: "We are very sensitive to consumer preferences. The unpopular brands are taken off the shelf in as little as a month; small food and beverage outlets are constantly updated to keep the category rich and the brands fresh; the weekly renewal of brands on sale also attracts consumers to come back often."

The incredible "Shanghai speed"

Hwanuk attributed the success of Parkson Newcore to the meticulous service offered by the government who acts as an attentive shop assistant. From the start of the project to its official opening, the relevant officials visited the site time and time again and coordinated all the efforts, allowing Parkson Newcore to set a "Shanghai record" of opening a shop in four months. "We have more than 50 stores in Korea, and the fastest one took more than a year," Hwanuk said. "This 'Shanghai speed' is incredible."

When he was at university, Hwanuk believed that China's economy continued to do well and that the market had unlimited potential. He practised his Chinese and learned about the Chinese market at the same time. By the time he graduated and joined the Korean E·land Group, he already had a good understanding of the Chinese market, and when the company was ready to send staff to Shanghai in 2009 to expand the market, he immediately jumped at the chance. After arriving in Shanghai, he started as a junior staff member, and with his understanding of the Chinese market, he continued to innovate the online and offline sales model, and collaborated with e-commerce companies to achieve new sales results. Eleven years of hard work had seen him reach one of the highpoints of his life, becoming the youngest general manager of Parkson Newcore.

Hwanuk said: "I had only seen Shanghai in photographs before and I was impressed by the vintage look of the original old town of Shanghai. My family was also very worried about my life in Shanghai at first. But when I saw the century-old buildings at the Bund with my own eyes and hiked around the high-rise Lujiazui in Pudong, I was fascinated by this city where the old meets the new." Today, every holiday season Hwanuk would invite his family and friends from ROK to come and visit Shanghai. They marveled at the ever-growing Shanghai and were very happy to experience the fruits of the city's development, such as Haichang Ocean Park and Shanghai Disneyland.

In Hwanuk's eyes, the consumer environment is very important when running a large shopping mall. "The security environment in Shanghai is fantastic and the city has become one of the safest in the world," said Hwanuk, adding that in the case of Parkson Newcore, the rate of reported thefts had been gradually decreasing every year.

Hwanuk said: "Thanks to the local police and all the functional departments in the subdistrict, with their dedication and support, we are able to focus more on doing a good job in our own mall." He added that in the future, they planned to open 4-5 more malls in Shanghai.

姓　名：Werner Gottschalk
中文名：高查克
国　籍：德国
职　位：上海电气电站设备有限公司上海汽轮机厂副总经理

高查克：
我让孩子学习中国文化，这对他的未来会有很大帮助

20年里，我来了上海三次，你问我有什么变化？
Better City，Better Life！

20年间三度造访上海，两度长期定居，年近60岁的德国"技术控"高查克用"Better City，Better Life"描绘着对上海近年来蓬勃发展、日新月异的切身感受。作为上海电气电站设备有限公司上海汽轮机厂副总经理，他见证了中国汽轮机技术在步入新世纪后不断迭代更新、屡攀高峰的令人瞩目的成就，更感慨于上海科创中心建设持续发力，为装备制造业聚人才、引大单，让有着六十多年技术发展史的上海汽轮机厂在新时代奋发有为、活力无限。

三度造访上海

走进上海电气电站设备有限公司上海汽轮机厂，一栋栋雄阔整齐的厂房矗立在主干道两侧。作为中国最早成立的电站汽轮机制造基地，这里曾创造了中国汽轮机制造史上的二十项"第一"，被誉为"中国汽轮机生产的摇篮"。

毕业于德国多特蒙德大学的高查克，1985年进入西门子工作，一干就是30多年。2002年至2012年间曾两度被派往上海工作，随着西门子和上海汽轮机厂的合作不断推进，2014年高查克又一次被派往上海，出任合资公司上海电气电站设备有限公司上海汽轮机厂的副总经理。

高查克的办公室位于厂区行政楼二层，紧邻的一幢白色大楼就是设计

高查克：

我让孩子学习中国文化，这对他的未来会有很大帮助

处所在地。每每蹦出灵感火花，他就会穿楼而过，展开图纸和设计员们来一场思想的碰撞。

"这里的年轻人都非常积极向上，团队合作精神也很棒。"高查克觉得中国的年轻人充满创造力，"他们和欧洲年轻人没什么不一样，都有国际化视野，有开放的思维，但中国的年轻人比欧洲人更有进取心。"

踏准发展良机

高查克到任不久，上海就迎来了科创发展的黄金时代。"这是我们发展的绝好时机，整个大环境都在蓬勃发力。"

上海汽轮机厂有着 60 多年汽轮机设计、制造经验，德国西门子有近百年的研发技术、制造技术和管理经验积累，东西方两位"大佬"的强强联手，让合资公司上海电气电站设备有限公司上海汽轮机厂不断突破瓶颈，屡屡书写行业奇迹，交出了一张金光闪闪的"成绩单"。

为推动双方的合作共赢，高查克多次策划和组织了上海电气与西门子之间多领域、多形式的交流和合作。

为了表彰高查克的突出贡献，2018 年上海市政府向他颁发白玉兰奖，这是上海市政府向国际友人颁发的最高奖项。

找到人生归宿

"20 年里，我来了上海三次，加起来在上海生活的时间超过了 12 年，你问我有什么变化？Better City, Better Life！"一头银发的高查克俏皮地眨眨眼说。

高查克早已把上海视作自己的第二家乡。说起上海的一张张旅游"名片"，高查克如数家珍，他甚至为到访上海的德国朋友们设计好了参观路线。"新天地是个很特别的地方，那里有中共一大会址，我在那里看到了中国执政党为让这个国家变得更美好的不懈奋斗历程，非常值得一游。"

在上海，高查克不仅成就了事业，也收获了爱情，找到了归宿，如今已有一个 10 岁的儿子。高查克对上海的教育水平赞赏有加，他把儿子送进了上海德法学校。"我的孩子在这里学习汉语和中国文化，这对他的未来会有很大的帮助。"

Name: Werner Gottschalk
Chinese name: 高查克
Nationality: German
Position: Vice general manager, Shanghai Electric Power Generation Equipment Co., Ltd. Shanghai Turbine Plant

Werner Gottschalk:
I require that my child learn Chinese culture, because it will help his future development

I have been to Shanghai three times in the past 20 years. Talking about the changes taking place in Shanghai, I think it's "better city and better life."

Visiting Shanghai three times

Werner Gottschalk, a German technician of near 60 years old, would like to use "better city, better life" to describe the development and changes of Shanghai. As the vice general manager of Shanghai Turbine Plant (STP) with Shanghai Electric Power Generation Equipment Co., Ltd., Gottschalk has witnessed the Chinese achievements in constantly upgrading the turbine technology in the new century. He is impressed by how the Shanghai Science and Technology Innovation Center gathers talents and attracts big orders to rejuvenate the 60-year-old STP.

Entering the STP site, you can see a grand array of evenly distributed factory buildings flanking the main road. As the first power station turbine manufacturing base, STP has produced 20 "firsts" in Chinese history of turbine production, and is called "the cradle of turbine production in China".

Gottschalk graduated from Dortmund University in Germany. He began his work at Siemens in 1985, and has been working for more than 30 years. Between 2002 and 2012, Gottschalk was dispatched to work in Shanghai twice. With the deepening of cooperation between Siemens and STP, he was dispatched to Shanghai once more in 2014 and became vice general manager with STP, a joint venture between Shanghai Electric and Siemens.

Gottschalk's office closely adjoined a white building where the design office is located. Whenever he has an inspiration, Gottschalk will go to the white building, unfold the design drawings and brainstorm with the designers in the design office.

Werner Gottschalk:

I require that my child learn Chinese culture, because it will help his future development

"The youth here are all very positive, and have great teamwork spirit," Gottschalk says. In his opinion, Chinese youth are full of creativity. "They are not different from youth in Europe, and both have an international vision and an open mind, but those in China are more motivated than those in Europe," says Gottschalk.

Seizing the opportunity for development

Not long after Gottschalk assumed his position in STP, Shanghai saw a golden period of technology and innovation development. "This is the best opportunity ever for us to develop since the whole market is booming," Gottschalk says.

STP boasts more than 60 years of experience in designing and manufacturing turbine, and Siemens has accumulated nearly a hundred years of experience in research and development, production and management. The partnership enables STP to break through a series of technical bottlenecks, create a succession of miracles and make a list of dazzling achievements. To promote win-win cooperation between the two sides, Gottschalk has planned and organized many exchanges and cooperation between Shanghai Electric and Siemens in various fields and forms.

In 2008, the Shanghai Municipal People's Government gave the White Magnolia Award to Gottschalk to honor his outstanding contribution to Shanghai. This award is the highest honor that Shanghai government gives to foreigners working and living in Shanghai.

Finding his true love in Shanghai

"I have been to Shanghai three times in the past 20 years, and have lived here for 12 years," says silver-haired Gottschalk with playful winks. "Talking about the changes taking place in Shanghai, I think it's 'better city and better life.'"

Gottschalk has already taken Shanghai as his second hometown. He has all the scenic spots in Shanghai at his fingertips. He even designed routes for his German friends who came to Shanghai for a visit. "Xintiandi is a very special place," says Gottschalk. "The Memorial of the First National Congress of the Communist Party of China is there, and I can see China's ruling party's relentless struggle to make this country better, so it's really worth a visit."

In Shanghai, Gottschalk has not only achieved a lot at work, but also found his true love and set up a family. His son is 10 years old this year. He thinks highly of the education in Shanghai, and has sent his son to the Deutsche Schule Shanghai. "My son studies Chinese language and culture here, which will contribute a lot to his future development," says Gottschalk.

Scan for videos

姓　名：Carsten Arntz
中文名：安克诚
国　籍：德国
职　位：上汽大众汽车有限公司财务执行总监

安克诚：
非常幸运，我在上海事业进步，还收获了爱情

> 在来上海前，我生活过的最大城市也才有 2 万人口，而现在我住在一个拥有常住人口 2000 多万的城市，你可以想象，这是一个多么巨大的变化。

47 岁的安克诚在中国居住了 18 年，其中上海就有 11 年。在他的办公桌上，放着一张夫妻二人的婚纱照，已经结婚 15 年，但当他和记者讲起那段爱情故事时，仍然一脸甜蜜，如新婚一般。

与夫人在上海一见钟情

对于从小在小村庄和小城市长大的安克诚来说，上海完全不同，"我很喜欢上海，在来上海前，我生活过的最大城市也才有 2 万人口，而现在我住在一个拥有常住人口 2000 多万的城市，你可以想象，这是一个多么巨大的变化，而遇见我的夫人是我在上海工作生活这么多年的一个重要原因。"

2004 年，他和上海籍的妻子在一个聚会上一见钟情，两年后，他们结婚了。虽然存在一些文化差异，但两人还是很默契、很恩爱。

"我非常幸运在这里得到了事业进步，个人生活也迎来转折。"对他来说，中国文化古老而又新鲜。在周末时，他经常会去青浦白鹤镇陪妻子的家人，享受郊区生活。过年时大家会一起吃年夜饭、看春晚、打麻将，他也越来越享受和中国家人在一起的时光。

安克诚：

非常幸运，我在上海事业进步，还收获了爱情

惊叹上海变化之飞快

安克诚最喜欢的运动是踢足球，他还曾在上海带教过一支韩国球队，"上海很多球场的草坪是真草皮，踢起来感觉很好。"上海的体育设施让安克诚赞不绝口。作为一个外国人，他一直以来都惊叹于上海城市变化的速度。"刚来上海的时候，浦东只有东方明珠和金茂大厦，而今天看浦东，有这么多摩天大楼，这些还是我来上海的头十年建好的。"

最近几年，安克诚住在浦西，他感到最震撼的就是虹桥枢纽，"从整个地区的发展、高速公路和地铁系统的发展来看，上海发生了巨大的变化，这种速度在其他国家是无法想象的。"

长三角一体化进程让安克诚工作的上汽大众获益良多。长三角是中国区域一体化发展起步最早、基础最好、程度最高的地区，除了嘉定安亭总部以外，上汽大众在南京、仪征、宁波等地也都建有生产基地，进一步带动了长三角地区整车和零部件的竞争力。

看好中国汽车市场

安克诚一直关注中国汽车产业的发展。他说，中国不仅是汽车行业的最大市场，以后在技术方面肯定也会领先。中国人对于新技术的接受能力远超其他国家，而且中国政府也非常支持技术创新发展。

他预测，汽车行业的趋势是电动化、数字化，而在中国，V2X 尤其是一个重要的趋势，即自动驾驶中车辆与整个周边环境的交互。中国建设了大量的测试区域，有多样的测试能力，这些是世界上其他地方都不具备的，更为重要的是中国基础设施的建设能力也是独一无二的。

安克诚相信，不少中国自主品牌有竞争力，以后能够走向世界，在国外市场拥有一席之地。

Name: Carsten Arntz
Chinese name: 安克诚
Nationality: German
Position: Finance Executive Director, SAIC Volkswagen

Carsten Arntz:

I am very lucky to have achieved career development and met my love in Shanghai

Before coming to Shanghai, the population of the largest city I had lived in was no more than 20,000, but now I am living in a city with more than 20 million permanent residents, so you can imagine what a dramatic change it is.

Carsten Arntz, 47, has lived in China for 18 years, including 11 years in Shanghai. On his desk, there is a wedding photo of his wife and him, who have been married for 15 years. But when he talks about his love story, Arntz still looks sweet as a newlywed.

Love at first sight with his wife in Shanghai

Growing up in a small village and a small city, Shanghai is completely different for Arntz.

Arntz says: "I really like Shanghai. Before I came to Shanghai, the largest city I had lived in has no more than 20,000 people, but now I am living in a city with more than 20 million permanent residents, so you can imagine what a dramatic change it is to me. Having met my wife is the main reason for me to stay in Shanghai for so many years."

In 2004, Arntz fell in love with his Shanghainese wife at first sight at a party, and two years later, they got married. Despite some cultural differences, the couple is very much in tune and deep in love.

"I am very lucky to have achieved career development here and ushered in a turning point in my personal life," Arntz says. For him, Chinese culture is both old and new. On weekends, he often goes to Baihe Town, Qingpu District

Carsten Arntz:

I am very lucky to have achieved career development and met my love in Shanghai

to spend time with his wife's family and enjoy the suburban life. On Chinese New Year's Eve, everyone in the big family will come together to have a family reunion dinner, watch the CCTV Spring Festival Gala and play mahjong. He is enjoying his time with his big Chinese family more and more.

Marveling at how fast Shanghai has changed

Arntz's favorite sport is playing football, and he has even coached a team from the Republic of Korea in Shanghai. "Many football fields in Shanghai have real turf, and it feels good to play," Arntz says. He thinks highly of the local sports infrastructure. As a foreigner, he always marvels at the speed of change in the city.

He says: "When I first came to Shanghai, there were only the Oriental Pearl Tower and Jinmao Tower in Pudong. But today when I look at Pudong, there are so many skyscrapers, and these were built in my first ten years in Shanghai."

In recent years, Arntz lives in Puxi, and he is most amazed by the Hongqiao Transportation Hub. "Shanghai has undergone tremendous changes in terms of its regional development and the development of expressways and subway systems, with a speed unimaginable in other countries," says Arntz.

The Yangtze River Delta integration process has benefited SAIC Volkswagen, where Arntz works. Among all regional integration initiatives across China, the Yangtze River Delta region boasts the earliest start, best foundation, and highest degree of integration development in China. In addition to the Anting headquarters in Jiading District, Shanghai, SAIC Volkswagen also has production bases in Nanjing, Yizheng and Ningbo, further improving the competitiveness of the vehicles industry in the Yangtze River Delta.

Optimistic about China's auto market

Arntz has always followed China's auto industry closely. He says that China is the largest auto market at present, and will also lead in technology in the future. Chinese people are far more receptive to new technology than those in other countries, and the Chinese government is very supportive of technological innovation.

Arntz predicts that electrification and digitalization are the trends of the auto industry. In China, emphasis will be put on V2X, which features interaction of the vehicles with the entire surrounding environment in automatic driving. China has built many test zones with diverse testing capabilities, which are not available anywhere else in the world. More importantly, China's capacity in building infrastructure is unparalleled.

Arntz believes that many Chinese domestic brands are competitive and will be able to go global and play a role in the overseas markets.

Scan for videos

姓　名：Richard Martin Saul
中文名：肖瑞强
国　籍：澳大利亚
职　位：上海外滩华尔道夫酒店总经理

肖瑞强：
我们家有不少人生重要时刻都是在中国发生

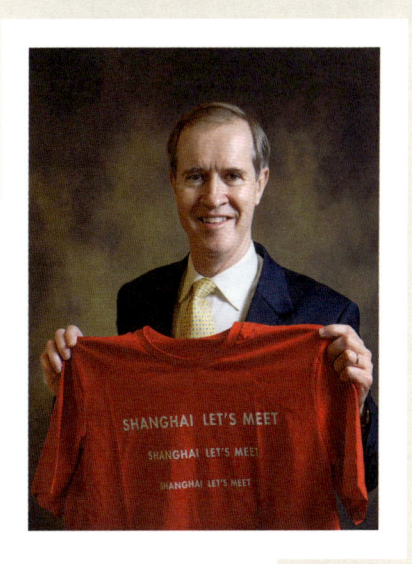

我坚信中国拥有光明的未来，希望我的孩子们从出生到成年都能与中国保持联系。

对眼前这栋历史悠久的建筑，肖瑞强当然知道它的前世今生，曾经是上海总会，后来成为国际海员俱乐部、东风饭店，哪一个身份都载着说不尽的故事，如今，这里又成为外滩华尔道夫酒店，肖瑞强作为酒店的外方总经理，日日漫步于外滩，在这充满故事的地方工作，心生欢喜。

对上海的第一印象

"肖瑞强"，是根据他的英文名音译而来的中文名字。这个来自黄金海岸的澳大利亚人，在中国转眼已待了10多年。对中国这些年的发展变化，他看在眼里，感慨在心。他深深敬佩这个国家一步一个脚印日新月异，城市里笑容随处可见。

"我第一次来中国，就是到的上海，那是2003年1月。我去过世界上很多地方，但我从未见过像上海这样的城市。记得当时我给家里打电话，说上海正在不断蓬勃发展！到处都是起重机，预示着将有巨大的蜕变，当时这座城市正在为举办世博会以及更远的未来进行基础设施建设。"

对上海的第一印象已令肖瑞强难忘，即便之后因为工作原因离开中国，可总也期待能够再回来，回到这座不断创造奇迹的城市。

肖瑞强：

我们家有不少人生重要时刻都是在中国发生

从此，再也不舍离开

2013年，肖瑞强回来了。这次，上海更让他感到惊艳。从此，他就再也舍不得离开了。在上海，肖瑞强一直忙碌在各个著名的酒店管理集团，直到2017年9月，来到外滩华尔道夫酒店。"我每次走出酒店正门，总会驻足停留，看江的这面和对面，看黄浦江上来往的船只。外滩非常有历史感，对岸又是如此繁华。"

肖瑞强想到自己第一次来上海时，从外滩望向对岸的浦东陆家嘴，能看到的最高建筑就是金茂大厦，"那时已是标志性建筑"。

如今，陆家嘴高楼林立，拔地而起的建筑早已赶超了金茂。"那时上海的进口物品不多，不像现在，什么都有，而中国科技的发展让我和我的家乡联络起来非常方便，翻译软件更是帮了我大忙。我现在出门用网约车，平时也会网购，总之，在这里，生活实在是太方便了。"

受新冠肺炎疫情影响，去年至今，占据华尔道夫客流很大份额的外国商务客人骤减，如今来酒店消费的反倒是中国本土客人居多，他除了感叹中国人民在中国共产党领导下拥有的幸福生活，更感谢中国政府出色的疫情防控工作，"中国在抗疫方面做得非常好，我非常欣赏。"

其实，肖瑞强与上海的感情，何止在事业上，他的两个孩子都是在上海出生。2003年3月，他尚在上海扬子江万丽大酒店任总经理时，太太已怀了他们的大儿子约翰，如今，约翰即将在上海完成高中学业，所以，他感慨，"我们一家有不少人生重要时刻都是在中国发生。因此，中国在我们的生活中占有重要地位。"

"我坚信中国拥有光明的未来，希望我的孩子们从出生到成年都能与中国保持联系。"

Name: Richard Martin Saul
Chinese name: 肖瑞强
Nationality: Australian
Position: General Manager of Waldorf Astoria Shanghai on the Bund

Richard Martin Saul:

Many important events of my family took place in China

I firmly believe that China is blessed with a bright future. I hope my children can keep the ties with China from their cradle and well into their adulthood.

Richard Martin Saul surely knows the history of this time-honored building right before his eyes. It used to be Shanghai Club, which later became the International Seamen's Club, and then Dongfeng Hotel. Each of these identities bespeaks endless tales. Today, it has become Waldorf Astoria Shanghai on the Bund. As the foreign General Manager of this joint-venture hotel, Richard saunters along the Bund daily. Working in this place imbued with stories fills his heart with joy.

First impression of Shanghai

"Xiao Ruiqiang" is his Chinese name based on the pronunciation of his English name. As a native from the Gold Coast of Australia, he has been in China for over a decade. The development of China over the years has been witnessed by his eyes, arousing amazement in his heart. He is deeply impressed by the steady and tremendous change of this country, coming across smiling faces everywhere he goes.

Richard says: "My first visit to China is made in Shanghai in January 2003. I have been to many places in the world, but I have never seen such a metropolis as Shanghai. I called my family and exclaimed how vigorously development was carried out nonstop in Shanghai! Crane towers were everywhere, signaling a drastic change in process. Back then this city was undergoing infrastructure construction for the Expo, as well as for the more distant future."

The first impression of Shanghai left an enduring impact on Richard. Therefore, even after job opportunities brought him away from China, he was looking forward to returning to this city that keeps creating miracles.

Richard Martin Saul:

Many important events of my family took place in China

From then on, he could not tear himself away

In 2013 Richard was back. This time, Shanghai enthralled him even more. From then on, he could not tear himself away from this city. In Shanghai, Richard has been busy in various renowned hotel management groups. In September 2017, he came to Waldorf Astoria Shanghai on the Bund.

He says: "Every time I walk out of the front gate of the hotel, I have to stop and catch my breath for a moment, feasting my eyes on both banks of the Huangpu River, and the ships sailing to and fro in the river. Look left up and down the Bund and you see history. Look across the river and you see modernity."

Richard recalls the first time when he was in Shanghai, he stood on the Bund and observed Lujiazui on the opposite side of the Huangpu River. The tallest building he could see was Jinmao Tower, "the landmark at that time."

Nowadays, skyscrapers proliferate in Lujiazui. Newly constructed towering buildings have long since surpassed Jinmao Tower in height.

Richard says: "At that time there were few imported goods in Shanghai. But now we have literally everything. Development in science and technology in China has made it very convenient for me to contact folks in my hometown. The translation software has been a great help indeed. When I go out these days I would book a car online, and I would shop online too. All in all, life here is really convenient."

Ever since last year, there has been a drastic drop in the number of foreign business clients, who used to constitute a lion's share of the customer flow of Waldorf Astoria Shanghai on the Bund. Presently the customers are mainly local clients in China. Richard is impressed by the happy life of Chinese people under the leadership of the Communist Party of China, amazed by the outstanding job done by the Chinese government in pandemic prevention and control. He says, "I think China has done an amazing job in pandemic prevention and control, which I deeply appreciate."

In fact, the bonds between Richard and Shanghai extend beyond his career. Both his children were born in Shanghai. In March 2003 when he was general manager of Renaissance Shanghai Yangtze Hotel, his wife conceived their elder son John. This year John is to complete his high school in Shanghai. Richard says: "Many important events of my family took place in China, so China enjoys an important status in our life."

"I firmly believe that China is blessed with a bright future. I hope my children can keep the ties with China from their cradle and well into their adulthood," says Richard.

Scan for videos

姓　名：Pilar Mejía Buenfil
中文名：逸馨
国　籍：墨西哥
职　位：上海大学上海美术学院在读博士生

逸馨：
上海像支时代万花筒，一眼看尽百年剪影

如今的上海跟老照片上相比完全是另外一个模样。她变化太大了，变得太好了。

从墨西哥到上海

来中国留学前，墨西哥姑娘逸馨一直把上海外滩的图片作为电脑壁纸。"我当时想：以后有机会一定要来这里！"逸馨很早就对中国文化产生了浓厚的兴趣，并自学中文。"自学了三年半后，我就很想来中国留学，刚好申请到了奖学金，得以圆梦。"

五年前，逸馨乘坐航班历经 20 余小时从墨西哥来到上海，开启了留学生活。"从浦东机场到上海大学宝山校区有一定的车程，但上海便捷的交通令我惊叹，我很快就到达了学校。"自此，这位国际留学生便以她独特的视角观察、记录着上海的发展变化。

今年是逸馨从上海大学文学院申请到美术学院读博的第一年。纵观她的求学生涯，从中国历史学，到如今的艺术，跨越了多个学科领域。

作为进博会志愿者的宝贵回忆

2020 年，第三届中国国际进口博览会在国家会展中心（上海）如期举行。逸馨成为一名志愿者，也留下了一段宝贵的回忆。"我朋友告诉我这是一场必须去看看的盛大活动。学校在招志愿者，我便第一时间报名了。在我眼中，

逸馨：

上海像支时代万花筒，
一眼看尽百年剪影

进口博览会是中国向世界展示的窗口。我认为自己的角色就像墨西哥与中国交流的纽带，所以我想体验当一名志愿者，更加深刻地认识中国与墨西哥，以及与其他国家的互通往来。"

进博会是全球首个以进口为主题的国家级展览会。疫情之年，第三届进博会的顺利举办，也向世界传递出特别的信心：面对严峻的全球新冠肺炎疫情，面对罕见大幅下挫的世界经济，中国开放的脚步未曾停下，中国大市场成为全球经济的压舱石。据统计，第三届进博会迎来了更多世界500强及行业龙头企业参展，展览面积也比第二届增加了14%。

逸馨告诉记者，第三届进博会的疫情防控工作做得非常周全，会场内秩序井然，给她留下了深刻的印象。"尽管处于疫情期间，井井有条的管控让我认为这里是最安全的地方。"如今，逸馨已经开始期待今年再次加入第四届进博会的志愿者团队，"希望这场盛会将世界连接得更加紧密"。

通过上海，看见百年

逸馨的博士学术研究方向与她的兴趣十分契合。作为一个热爱中国文化的墨西哥人，她从图像出发，着眼于20世纪上半叶中国和墨西哥的摄影比较，观察两国同一时期的社会、人文差异，并挖掘图片背后的历史故事。"我选择来上海，一方面原因就是我了解到上海的文化资源非常丰富。我是研究摄影历史的，做研究的过程中需要了解相关的史料。我参观了一些上海地区的'红色地标'，也在不同的书籍、档案、文章中认识到中国有很多重要的事情是在上海发生的，比如中共一大。"

通过观看相关影像资料，逸馨惊叹于上海这座城市在一百年间发生的巨大变化，"如今的上海跟老照片上相比完全是另外一个模样。她变化太大了，变得太好了"。

在逸馨心里，上海就像中国近代社会变迁的缩影，像一支时代的万花筒。只需轻轻一瞥，就能看到百年来的缤纷剪影……

Name: Pilar Mejía Buenfil
Chinese name: 逸馨
Nationality: Mexican
Position: Ph.D. candidate of Shanghai Academy of Fine Arts, Shanghai University

Pilar Mejía Buenfil:
Shanghai is a kaleidoscope of the times, a century of silhouettes at a glance

Shanghai today is a completely different place compared to the old photos. She's changed so much, and has become so good.

From Mexico to Shanghai

Before she came to study in China, Pilar Mejía Buenfil, a Mexican girl, used a picture of the Bund in Shanghai as her computer wallpaper. "And I said to myself, someday I will be there, for sure I will be there, I have to be there!" says the young Mexican student. At an early age, Buenfil developed a strong interest in Chinese culture and taught herself the Chinese language. "After studying on my own for three and a half years, I wanted to study in China. I was lucky to get a scholarship and thus realized my dream."

Five years ago, Buenfil took a 20-hour flight from Mexico to Shanghai and started her life studying in China. "It's quite a long distance from Pudong Airport to Shanghai University's Baoshan District campus, but I was amazed by the convenient transportation in Shanghai, and it didn't take me long to get to the campus." Ever since then, this international student has observed and recorded the development and changes of Shanghai from her unique perspective.

This has been the first year since Buenfil successfully applied for a Ph.D. in the Shanghai Academy of Fine Arts as a student originally in the College of Liberal Arts of Shanghai University. Throughout her schooling, she has spanned several subject areas, from Chinese history to the arts.

Working as a CIIE volunteer

In 2020, the third China International Import Expo (CIIE) was held as scheduled in the National Convention and Exhibition Center in Shanghai. Buenfil

Pilar Mejía Buenfil:

Shanghai is a kaleidoscope of the times, a century of silhouettes at a glance

became a volunteer, and also left with a precious memory. "Because I heard from my friend that CIIE is a big event and you have to go and see it, so when the school was recruiting volunteers, I decided to apply. In my eyes, the CIIE is a window for China to show to the world. And I see my role as a link between Mexico and China, so I want to join the volunteers to gain a deeper understanding of China and Mexico, as well as the interconnection between China and other countries."

CIIE is the world's first national-levelled exhibition that features import as the main theme. In the year of pandemic, the successful holding of the third CIIE conveyed special confidence to the whole world: in face of the severe pandemic of COVID-19 and the unheard-of sharp decline of the world economy, China has not stopped her pace of opening up, and the great Chinese market has become the ballast of the global economy. According to statistics, the third CIIE actually ushered in more of the world's top 500 and industry-leading enterprises than ever before. The exhibition area is also increased by 14% than the second CIIE.

Buenfil told reporters that the pandemic prevention and control work of the third CIIE was totally thorough and orderly, which left a deep impression on her. "Even in the middle of this world pandemic, I still think it's the safest place to be here because it's so well managed," says her. Now Buenfil is looking forward to joining the volunteer team of the 4th CIIE again this year. "I hope such a grand event will bring the world even closer."

Seeing a hundred years of history in Shanghai

Buenfil's Ph.D. academic research is a good fit with her interests. As a Mexican who loves Chinese culture, she started from images, focusing on the photographic comparison between China and Mexico in the first half of the 20th century, observing the social and cultural differences between the two countries in the same period, and excavating the historical stories behind those pictures.

Buenfil says: "I chose to come to Shanghai partly because I had learned that Shanghai always has rich cultural resources. I majored in the history of photography, and in the process of doing research, I need to know the relevant historical materials. I have visited some of the 'red landmarks' in the Shanghai area and learned from different books, archives and articles that many important events in China happened in Shanghai, such as the First National Congress of the Communist Party of China."

Through watching the relevant videos, Buenfil was, again and again, amazed at the great changes that have taken place in Shanghai in the past 100 years. "Shanghai today is a completely different place compared to the old photos," she says. "The city has changed so much, and has become so good."

In Buenfil's mind, Shanghai can be seen as a microcosm of China's modern social changes. The city is like a kaleidoscope of times: with just a glance, you can see the colorful silhouettes of the past century.

Scan for videos

姓　名：Alexander Filippov
中文名：萨沙
国　籍：俄罗斯
职　位：上海交响乐团大号首席

萨沙：
我有一个梦想，为中国培养更多的铜管乐人才

上海的艺术氛围愈加浓厚，一直以来，有很多的乐团来到这座爱乐之城。

在上海住了 22 年

1999 年，上海交响乐团到俄罗斯招募乐手，萨沙放弃了俄罗斯交响乐团大号首席的职位，和其他几名俄罗斯乐手一起来到了上海。他也就此成为改革开放后上海交响乐团最早引进的一批外籍乐手之一。萨沙自己肯定也未曾想到，他和家人在上海一住就是 22 年。

萨沙回忆道，刚到上海时，乐队里几乎都是上海本地的乐手，大家都说上海话。萨沙从一开始的茫然，到现在已经能听懂不少上海话，还会说一些。采访中，不善言谈的萨沙会时不时说几句普通话和上海话来调节气氛。

来上海两个多月后，萨沙就把妻子和两个儿子接来，一家人在这座城市开启了全新的生活。他们适应了这里的食物，学上海话，探索这座城市的各个角落。

作为亚洲地区历史最悠久的交响乐团，上海交响乐团前身为 1879 年成立的上海公共乐队，1922 年改称上海工部局乐队，1956 年正式定名为上海交响乐团。2014 年，迁建后的上海交响乐团音乐厅在复兴中路 1380 号正式揭幕。对于现在的演奏厅，萨沙认为地理位置、大小、专业度上都堪称完美。"22 年间，上海发生了很大变化，例如我脚下的这个地方，最初是一个跳水池，然后是网球中心，几年后，变成了我们美丽的音乐厅。"

萨沙：

我有一个梦想，为中国培养更多的铜管乐人才

上海是"爱乐之城"

这些年，上海的艺术氛围愈加浓厚。萨沙在包括上海音乐厅、大剧院在内的诸多地方演出过。"一直以来，有很多的乐团来到上海这座爱乐之城，我遇到很多老同学、老同事。"

萨沙的到来为上海铜管乐的发展起到了不小的作用。除了和乐团其他铜管乐手们一起组建了东方铜管五重奏，萨沙还坚持在上海音乐学院进行大号教学，培养未来的铜管乐手。如今萨沙依旧喜欢骑着自行车在上海音乐学院和上海交响乐团之间穿梭。"我时常想，能不能挖个地道，让我一下就到了，这样就太好了。"萨沙开玩笑道。

在上海的 22 年间，伴随萨沙的除了大号还有乒乓球。"当我还是个孩子的时候，乒乓球在俄罗斯就非常流行。每个学校都在打乒乓球，有些人打得还很不错。我对乒乓球一见钟情。"来到上海后，萨沙经常和同事们去打乒乓球。

回望自己的上海生活，萨沙总感觉到阵阵暖意。22 年来，世界各地的乐手来来往往，换了一茬又一茬，唯独萨沙，至今仍坐在上海交响乐团的大号席上。

他有两个梦想，除了为中国培养更多的铜管乐人才，还希望有机会能带着中国人民的情谊回到家乡莫斯科演出。

Name: Alexander Filippov
Chinese name: 萨沙
Nationality: Russian
Position: Principal Tuba of the Shanghai Symphony Orchestra

Alexander Filippov:

I have a dream of training more brass talents for China

Shanghai has become more artistic, and the big city always attracts many orchestras to come.

Living in Shanghai for 22 years

In 1999, the Shanghai Symphony Orchestra went to Russia to recruit musicians. Filippov abandoned the position of Principal Tuba of the Russian State Symphony Orchestra, and came to Shanghai with several other Russian musicians, becoming one of the earliest foreign musicians introduced by the Shanghai Symphony Orchestra after the reform and opening-up. Even Filippov himself had not expected that he and his family would have lived in Shanghai for 22 years.

Filippov remembers that when they first arrived in Shanghai, almost all the musicians in the orchestra were locals, and everyone spoke Shanghai dialect. He was puzzled at first, but now, he can understand much Shanghainese and even speak some. During the interview, Filippov, not as talkative as others, occasionally speaks some Mandarin and Shanghainese to enliven the atmosphere.

Two months after coming to Shanghai, Filippov took his wife and two sons over and started their new life in this big city. They have adapted to the local food, learnt to speak Shanghainese, and explored all corners of the city.

Founded in 1879, originally known as the Shanghai Public Band, the Shanghai Symphony Orchestra is the oldest in Asia. It was renamed the Shanghai Municipal Council Symphony Orchestra in 1922, and then officially designated as what it is in 1956. The year 2014 saw the unveiling ceremony of the relocated Shanghai Symphony Orchestra Concert Hall at 1380 Middle Fuxing Road. Filippov considers it perfect in geographical location, size and professionalism.

Alexander Filippov:

I have a dream of training more brass talents for China

He says: "In the past 22 years, great changes have taken place in Shanghai. This place, for example, was originally a diving pool, then a tennis court, and a few years later, it became our beautiful concert hall."

Shanghai: a city of love and music

Over the years, Shanghai has become more immersed in art. Filippov has performed at many venues in Shanghai, including Shanghai Grand Theatre and Shanghai Concert Hall.

He says: "(In Shanghai) I met many, many friends of mine, (some of whom) I studied with together, and some I know from the job before. The big city (always attracts) many orchestras to come."

Filippov plays a notable role in the development of Shanghai's brass music. In addition to composing the Eastern Brass Quintet with the other brass players in the orchestra, Filippov also teaches tuba at the Shanghai Conservatory of Music to train future brass players. Now he still enjoys riding his bicycle between the Shanghai Conservatory of Music and the Shanghai Symphony Orchestra. "I often wonder if I can dig a tunnel to get to my destinations quickly, which would be great," he jokes.

During his 22 years in Shanghai, Filippov also has been enjoying playing table tennis besides the tuba.

He says: "When I was a kid, the ping-pong game came to Russia. It's everywhere. Each school, they have their table tennis and some people play not bad. I tried ping pong the first time and liked it very much." After settling down in Shanghai, he often plays it with his colleagues.

Looking back on his Shanghai life, Filippov's heart is always filled with warmth. Over the past 22 years, musicians from all over the world have come and gone like the flow of water, but Filippov still stays here, cleaving to the seat of Principal Tuba of the Shanghai Symphony Orchestra.

Filippov has two dreams now. One is to cultivate more brass talents for China, and the other is to perform in his hometown Moscow, taking along the sincere goodwill of the Chinese people.

Scan for videos

姓　　名：Alex Kopitsas
中文名：孔文卓
国　　籍：希腊
职　　位：强生全球人才招聘负责人

孔文卓：
我喜欢饺子，每周三是我们家的"饺子日"

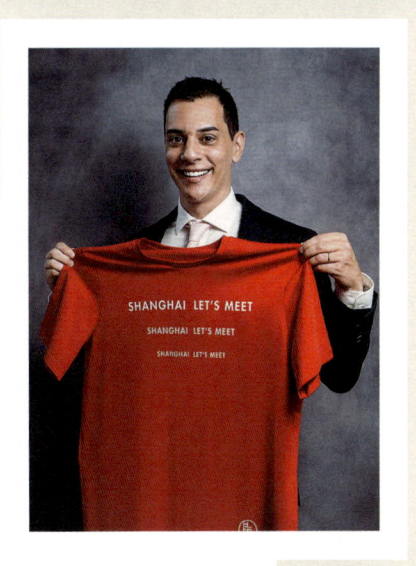

这座城市以多样性与包容性为全世界构建出了一个开放、公平的商业环境。

在过去的 20 年里，强生全球人才招聘负责人孔文卓辗转于世界各个国家工作。他说，自从 2018 年来到上海的那一刻起，就深深地为这座城市的魅力所折服。"上海不仅人文底蕴浓厚，烟火气十足，更是具有全球影响力的科技创新中心、顶尖人才的汇集地。"

这里的年轻人充满朝气

上海是强生中国总部所在地。据孔文卓介绍，2019 年 6 月，强生亚太地区首个创新孵化器 JLABS 在上海开业，目前累计有 50 多家生物科学初创公司入驻。"多年来，我们见证了上海的飞速发展，这座城市以多样性与包容性为全世界构建出了一个开放、公平的商业环境。"孔文卓表示，在过去的一年里，强生在中国的业务实现了大幅增长，正在创造新的就业机会，招聘更多的人才，以更好地服务中国的消费者。

"当我们与新一代的求职者交谈时，我们发现这里的年轻人才充满激情，有抱负和想法。他们经常问'我能从这份工作中学到什么？这家公司如何帮助我成长？'并直言不讳地表达自己的理想，希望在一家与他们有共同目标和价值、能够帮助他们实现职业抱负的公司工作。在强生，我们很重视这些宝贵的品质。我们对年轻人的独特观点持开放态度，为他们提供所有他们需要的平台和资源，将他们的想法付诸实践。"

孔文卓：

我喜欢饺子，每周三是我们家的"饺子日"

据悉，强生在中国拥有超过 11000 名员工，尽管受疫情的影响，这家公司在 2020 年仍新增大约 4400 个工作岗位。"我们相信，随着更多人才加入我们，我们可以共同为改变人类健康的轨迹做出更大的贡献。"

我爱上海

孔文卓认为，上海作为一个国际化大都市，多样性与包容性是它的文化基因。"双语标识在公共场所随处可见，对于外国人来说，即使第一次来上海，在这里转转也不是一件难事。"

2018 年，孔文卓与家人初到上海时，对这座城市的第一印象便是"很绿、很美、很干净"。他惊喜地发现上海有可以随时租用的共享单车，这让热爱骑自行车的他非常兴奋，"我可以用很便宜的价格租到它们，然后在这座城市里自由自在地骑行，十分便捷"。

孔文卓还是一个美食爱好者，有时他漫步在上海的街头，闻到香气四溢，就会想知道："这是什么味道？它叫什么？上海的人们都吃些什么？"孔文卓对饺子情有独钟，每周三的晚上是他们家约定的"饺子日"。

孔文卓有两个儿子，最大的才 10 岁，上海优质的教育资源与环境让孩子们得到快速成长，变得更加成熟与自立。"他们适应了不同的文化和思维模式，结交了许多中国朋友，也更加了解中国的传统文化。"

"我爱上海！"孔文卓的笑容里洋溢着幸福。

Name: Alex Kopitsas
Chinese name: 孔文卓
Nationality: Greek
Position: Head of Global Talent Acquisition & Mobility, Johnson & Johnson

Alex Kopitsas:
I love dumplings. Every Wednesday is "dumpling day" at my home

Shanghai has built an open and fair business environment for the world with its diversity and inclusiveness.

Over the past 20 years, Alex Kopitsas, Head of Global Talent Acquisition & Mobility of Johnson & Johnson, has worked in various countries. He says that since the moment he arrived in Shanghai in 2018, he has been deeply impressed by the city's charm. "Not only does Shanghai boast rich legacies and an incredibly enjoyable life, but it is also a globally influential center of technological innovation and a gathering place for top talent."

Young people here full of energy

Shanghai is home to Johnson & Johnson's China headquarters. According to Alex Kopitsas, in June 2019, JLABS, Johnson & Johnson's first innovation incubator in the Asia Pacific, opened in Shanghai, with a cumulative total of more than 50 bioscience start-ups currently located there. "Over the years, we have witnessed the rapid development of Shanghai, a city that has built an open and fair business environment for the world with its diversity and inclusiveness," says Alex Kopitsas. In the past year, Johnson & Johnson has achieved significant growth in China and is creating new jobs and recruiting more talent to better serve Chinese consumers, according to Alex Kopitsas.

Alex Kopitsas says: "We find that these young talents today are very passionate, purpose-driven, and full of new ideas. As they look for potential employers, they often ask, what can I learn from this job? How can this company help me grow? And they're very vocal about their ambitions and want to work with a company that shares their purpose and value and can help them achieve

Alex Kopitsas:

I love dumplings. Every Wednesday is "dumpling day" at my home

their career inspirations. In Johnson & Johnson, we value such qualities and we're open to the unique perspectives from the young people, giving them all the platforms and resources they need to bring their ideas to life."

Johnson & Johnson reportedly employs more than 11,000 people in China, and despite the impact of the pandemic, this company is adding about 4,400 new jobs in 2020. "We believe that as more talented people join us, together we can make an even greater contribution to changing the trajectory of human health," says Alex Kopitsas.

I love Shanghai

According to Alex Kopitsas, Shanghai is a great cosmopolitan city whose diversity and inclusiveness are in its cultural DNA. "Bilingual signs are everywhere in public places, and it's not difficult for foreigners to get around Shanghai, even if it's their first time," says Alex Kopitsas.

When Alex Kopitsas first arrived in Shanghai with his family in 2018, his first impression of the city was that it was "so green, so beautiful and so clean." He was surprised to find that Shanghai had shared bikes and he could rent a bike at any time, which excited him as he loves cycling. "I can rent them for a very low price and then ride freely around the city, which is very convenient," he says.

Alex Kopitsas is also a food lover and sometimes when he strolls through the streets of Shanghai and smells the aromas, he wonders, "What is this smell? What is it called? What do people in Shanghai eat?" Alex Kopitsas has a passion for dumplings, and every Wednesday evening is "dumpling night" for his family.

Alex Kopitsas has two sons, the oldest being just 10 years old, and the quality educational resources and environment in Shanghai have allowed the children to grow up quickly and become more mature and self-sufficient. "They have adapted to a different culture and mindset, made many Chinese friends, and become more aware of traditional Chinese culture," says Alex Kopitsas.

"I love Shanghai!" says Alex Kopitsas, with a smile of true delight.

Scan for videos

姓　名：Jean-Etienne Gourgues
中文名：高晟天
国　籍：法国
职　位：保乐力加中国董事总经理

高晟天：
喜欢上海，因为这是一座有灵魂的城市

无论白天夜晚，上海都如此令人着迷。

二十年前，高晟天第一次出差到上海，他说，那时的上海就已经是生机勃勃的；二十年后，高晟天来到这座城市工作、定居，他没有想到变化是如此之大，"繁华，摩登，前卫"！

翻天覆地的变化

"我叫高晟天，感谢我的上海朋友给我起了这个好听的名字，但同事们都叫我'天哥'。"2008年到2010年期间，高晟天因为工作原因先后多次来到上海。"那时候正好是上海世博会开幕前夕，我印象深刻的是，几乎每条街道都在施工，整个城市看上去有些'乱'。但很突然，就在世博会开幕前一个月，一切都变得井然有序、生机勃勃，我看到了一座焕然一新的城市，一个全新的上海。"

上海世博会从筹办到举办，历时八年。其间，上海抓住筹办这一重要契机，将迎世博和改善民生结合起来，乘"世"而上，启动了一批惠及民生的市政工程，城市面貌和市民生活发生了显著的变化。

高晟天说自己亲眼见证了这座城市这些年发生的翻天覆地的变化，上海的建设能力让他惊叹。

如灯塔般闪耀的城市

"无论白天夜晚，上海都如此令人着迷。"在高晟天眼中，上海还是一座如灯塔般闪耀的城市。平日里，高晟天有两大爱好。"一是运动，每天早

高晟天：

喜欢上海，因为这是一座有灵魂的城市

上大概 7 点多，我都会在徐汇滨江跑步。"

近几年，经过上海市政府的精心规划和修建，长达 8.4 公里的徐汇滨江成为跑友们心目中的"跑步圣地"，尤其是在春天，跑道两侧的风景美不胜收。

高晟天还喜欢去浦东或佘山骑车。"你知道吗？最有趣的就是去浦东骑车。有时候我会搭乘黄浦江上的渡轮，大概 10 分钟就能从浦西到浦东，1.8 元的票价，真的是物超所值。"

"最近，上海的马路还设置了自行车道，对于酷爱骑自行车的市民来说，这真是太贴心了。"高晟天称赞。

高晟天的第二个爱好是逛美术馆。"龙美术馆和余德耀美术馆都是我的最爱，西岸艺术中心和一些私人画廊也不错。"

夜幕降临的时候，高晟天还会去徐汇区的酒吧坐一坐。"街道两旁，威士忌酒吧、鸡尾酒酒吧遍地开花，人们可以在这里聚会聊天，还可以结交新朋友。"

海纳百川的开放姿态

高晟天认为，开放的姿态是上海这座城市的核心财富之一，这不仅体现在经济上，还体现在人们的日常生活中。

去年，发生在疫情期间的一件事让高晟天印象深刻。"自疫情暴发以来，我们去餐厅或者乘地铁都要出示随申码，作为一个外国人，我目前还不太懂中文，每当我遇到问题，无论是交警还是公交车站、地铁站的工作人员都会热心地帮助我。"

高晟天的公司附近触目可及都是高楼大厦。但与此同时，在这些钢筋水泥丛中，他还总是能看到人们在街心公园里运动、跳舞。

"你可以一边欣赏鸟儿美妙的歌声，一边欣赏这座超级现代化城市的便利。"高晟天坦言，他喜欢上海，因为这是一座有灵魂的城市。

Name: Jean-Etienne Gourgues
Chinese name: 高晟天
Nationality: French
Position: Managing director, Pernod Richard China

Jean-Etienne Gourgues:
I like Shanghai because it is a city with a soul

Day and night, Shanghai is always fascinating.

Twenty years ago, Gourgues came to Shanghai for the first time on business. According to him, Shanghai was already a dynamic city at that time. Twenty years later, Gourgues came to work in the city and settled down. To his surprise, great changes have taken place in Shanghai. "It is prosperous, modern and edgy," he says.

Great changes

Gourgues says: "My Chinese name is Gao Shengtian. Thanks to my Shanghai friends for giving me this nice name, but my colleagues all call me 'Brother Tian'."

From 2008 to 2010, Gourgues had been to Shanghai on business several times. Gourgue says: "At that time, it was just before the opening of the Shanghai World Expo. I could remember very clearly that almost every street was under construction, and the whole city looked a bit chaotic. But all of a sudden, just one month before the opening of the World Expo, everything became orderly and vibrant. I saw a brand-new city, a brand-new Shanghai."

It took eight years to prepare the city for Shanghai World Expo. During this period, the Shanghai municipal government seized the golden opportunity of preparing for the World Expo and took advantage of it to improve people's living conditions. A number of city-planning projects were launched to improve people's livelihood. As a result, remarkable changes have taken place in the city's appearance and people's lives.

Gourgues says that he has witnessed the great changes taking place in Shanghai over the years, and that he was amazed by Shanghai's construction capabilities.

Jean-Etienne Gourgues:

I like Shanghai because it is a city with a soul

A city shining like a lighthouse

"Shanghai is always fascinating, day and night," Gourgues says. In his eyes, Shanghai is a city shining like a lighthouse. On weekdays, Gourgues has two hobbies. "Firstly, I like sports very much," he says. "Every morning at about 7 a.m., I run along the riverside promenade in Xuhui District. "

In recent years, thanks to the careful planning and construction by the Shanghai municipal government, the 8.4-kilometer-long riverside promenade in Xuhui District has become a "running mecca" for runners. The scenery on both sides of the track is very beautiful, especially in spring.

Gourgues also likes to go to Pudong or Sheshan to ride a bicycle. "To me, the most interesting thing is to go to Pudong to ride a bike," Gourgues says. "Sometimes I take the ferry on the Huangpu River, and it takes only about 10 minutes for me to travel from Puxi to Pudong. The ferry ticket is only 1.8 yuan, which is worth the price. "

"Recently, bicycle lanes have been carved out on the streets of Shanghai, which is more than great news to people in Shanghai who love to ride a bike," Gourgues says with appreciation.

Gourgues' second hobby is to visit art museums. "Long Museum and Yuz Museum are my favorites," Gourgues says. "The West Bund Art Center and some private galleries are also very nice."

When night falls, Gourgues will go to the bars in Xuhui District. "There are many whiskey bars and cocktail bars on both sides of the street, where people can party and chat, and make new friends," Gourgues says.

An inclusive and open-minded city

Gourgues believes that an open mind is one of the core assets of Shanghai, which is not only manifest in the economy but also in people's everyday life.

Last year, Gourgues was deeply impressed by people's kindness during the COVID-19 pandemic.

He says: "Ever since the outbreak of the pandemic, we have to show our Shanghai QR Code if we want to go to the restaurant or take the subway. As a foreigner, I don't know much Chinese at that time. Whenever I encountered problems, both the traffic police and the staff at bus and subway stations would be eager to help me."

Gourgues' company is surrounded by tall buildings. But he can always see people exercising and dancing in the street parks in the midst of these steel and concrete.

"You can enjoy the beautiful songs of birds while at the same time enjoy the convenience of this modern city," Gourgues says. He admits that he likes Shanghai because it is a city with a soul.

姓　名：Diego Benedetto
国　籍：意大利
职　位：中国东方航空公司机长

Diego：
身为机长，我期待驾驶中国制造的飞机飞往世界各地

如今我定居中国，不仅是住在这里，更是住在未来里。中国就是未来，一个真正的未来。

中国一直在向前发展

"女士们、先生们，我是来自意大利的 Diego，我是本次航班的机长，祝您旅途愉快……"2018 年，55 岁的 Diego 成功应聘为中国东方航空公司的一名机长，并带着孩子定居中国，开启了他们的"中国生活"。

Diego 告诉记者，从小他就知道中国，但从没想过有朝一日能够来中国工作生活。差不多 40 年前，Diego 因为飞行任务第一次来到中国，那时的中国刚刚改革开放不久。"40 年后，我再次来到中国时，看到这里巨大的发展，这在我的国家是无法想象的。在过去的几十年里，中国一直在向前发展。这真是令人赞叹和敬佩。"

Diego 对虹桥国际机场和浦东国际机场都很熟悉。身为机长，他看机场的视角与乘客不同，每次在上海这两大机场降落时，都能在空中对城市有直观的感受。"在这里工作和飞行是很愉悦和安全的，我非常喜欢这里，很享受。"Diego 毫不掩饰对于上海机场的喜爱。

期待能驾驶中国制造的飞机

2020 年，国产飞机 ARJ21 正式交付，进入我国民航市场。同年 12 月，东航新成立的一二三航空有限公司（简称"一二三航空"）首航，执飞首航

Diego Benedetto：

身为机长，我期待驾驶中国制造的飞机飞往世界各地

航班的国产飞机 ARJ21 从上海飞往北京。

一二三航空计划于 2021 年接收 6 架 ARJ21、2022 年接收 8 架，到 2025 年前，该机型的机队规模将达到 35 架。

同时作为国产大飞机 C919 全球首家启动用户，东航目前已经与中国商飞公司在上海正式签署了 C919 大型客机购机合同，首批引进 5 架，东航也将成为全球首家运营 C919 大型客机的航空公司，在"十四五"开局之年，以"先行者"姿态，在国产大飞机的引进与商业运营上迈出"重要一步"。

在东航工作，能优先接触到中国制造的飞机，这让 Diego 十分激动，他对中国制造的飞机 ARJ21 很好奇，且一直在研究学习中。在 Diego 的眼中，飞机 ARJ21 驾驶舱非常现代化，他期待未来能驾驶中国制造的飞机飞往世界各地。

Diego 坦言，到目前为止，全球飞机制造主要是在欧洲和北美，还有南美一小部分国家。现在中国进入了这个领域，这是非常有趣的。"我很高兴也很惊讶，因为飞机制造是一个非常艰难的领域，很难做得出彩。但是中国做到了。就像造一座水坝，如今中国开始制造飞机，未来'开闸泄洪'，前景势不可挡。"

对于飞行员来说，最重要的使命就是将乘客安全送抵目的地。"女士们、先生们：我们已经抵达上海虹桥国际机场。感谢您搭乘中国东方航空班机。下次旅途再会。"每当广播响起，飞行结束，Diego 总会有一种"使命完成"的强烈感受。

"如今我定居中国，不仅是住在这里，更是住在未来里。中国就是未来，一个真正的未来。"Diego 说。

Name: Diego Benedetto
Nationality: Italian
Position: Captain of China Eastern Airlines

Diego Benedetto:
I'm a pilot who looks forward to flying China-made planes around the world

I'm not just living in China but also the future because China is the real future.

China always moving forward

"Ladies and gentlemen, I am Diego from Italy. I am the captain of this flight. I wish you a pleasant journey…" In 2018, the 55-year-old Italian became a captain of China Eastern Airlines and settled down in China with his children, starting their "life in China."

Diego says that he knew about China since he was little, but never thought he could come to work and live in China one day. He first came here on a flight mission about 40 years ago, shortly after the country's reform and opening up.

He says: "When I came to China again 40 years later, I saw the tremendous development here, which was unimaginable in my country. Over the past few decades, China has been moving forward, which is really amazing and admirable."

Diego is very familiar with both Shanghai Hongqiao International Airport and Shanghai Pudong International Airport. As a captain, he sees the airports from a different perspective than average passengers. Each time he lands at these two major airports in Shanghai, he has a panoramic view of the city from high up in the sky. "It is very pleasant and safe to work and fly here. I really like it here and enjoy every day," says Diego, effusive in his love for Shanghai's airports.

Looking forward to flying China-made aircraft

China's homegrown aircraft ARJ21 officially entered the civil aviation market in 2020. In December, One Two Three Airlines (OTT Airlines), a new subsidiary of

Diego Benedetto:

I'm a pilot who looks forward to flying China-made planes around the world

China Eastern Airlines, debuted its first commercial flight with an ARJ21 jet from Shanghai to Beijing.

OTT Airlines plans to purchase six ARJ21 jets in 2021, eight in 2022, and expects to operate a total of 35 ARJ21 jets by 2025.

Meanwhile, as the first customer of China's homegrown aircraft C919, China Eastern Airlines has signed a purchase deal with its manufacturer Commercial Aircraft Corporation of China. The first five jets will be delivered in the coming years. China Eastern Airlines will also be the first airline in the world to operate a C919. In the first year of the 14th Five-Year Plan, China Eastern Airlines has taken "a major step" as a "pioneer" in the purchase and commercial operation of China-made aircraft.

Working for China Eastern Airlines, Diego is very excited about having access to China-made aircraft. He is interested in the ARJ21 and has been learning about it. In Diego's eyes, the cockpit of ARJ21 is very modern. He looks forward to flying a China-made aircraft around the world sometime in the future.

Diego notes that Europe, North America and a few countries in South America had been the major airplane makers in the global playground until China joined the game, which is fascinating.

He says: "I'm happy about it and amazed too, because airplane manufacturing is a tricky field, one that's extremely hard to prevail at. But China certainly did it, now that it's starting to build airplanes. It's a lot like building a reservoir, at some point in the future, all China will need to do is lift the floodgate, and the water will rush right out, unstoppably."

For a pilot, the most important mission is to deliver passengers safely to their destinations. "Ladies and gentlemen, we have arrived at Shanghai Hongqiao International Airport. Thank you for flying with China Eastern Airlines. See you on your next journey." Every time the radio plays at the end of a flight, Diego always has a strong feeling of "mission accomplished."

"I'm not just living in China but also the future because China is the real future," says Diego.

姓　名：Corentin Delcroix
中文名：戴广坦
国　籍：法国
职　位：厨师

戴广坦：
爱上中餐的法国厨师

> 我的美食生涯最早就是从中国开启的。现在，中国快速发展的新媒体技术又一次成就了我。

帅气阳光、爱笑的戴广坦曾在法国的米其林餐厅工作，现在每天用"二声"普通话在社交平台教人做法餐和融合菜，短短几年就成为拥有百万级粉丝的网红厨师。"我的美食生涯最早就是从中国开启的。现在，中国快速发展的新媒体技术又一次成就了我。"

中国阿姨的美食启蒙

戴广坦出生于法国北部城市里尔。20 岁时，他对遥远的东方产生了浓厚兴趣，只身前往北京学习工商管理。古老的建筑、悠久的历史、完全不同于法国的风景，让戴广坦对中国深深着迷。那会儿，有位中国阿姨教了戴广坦几道家常菜手艺，几乎没下过厨房的戴广坦一下子激发出了对烹饪的热爱，从此一发不可收。炒蛋、豆腐煲、土豆烧刀豆，他的中国同学品尝后都惊讶一个老外能把中餐做得那么地道。

当 4 年后戴广坦回到法国时，他的人生目标已经非常清晰，"我找到了自己热切追求的事业，那就是烹饪"。在里昂顶级厨艺学校博古斯学院学习了两年半后，戴广坦顺利进入法国阿尔萨斯米其林三星餐厅"L'Auberge de L'Ill"。

2010 年上海举办世界博览会期间，法国博古斯学院需要在上海开设分校，有着中国留学背景的戴广坦成为学院主厨的合适人选，也正是这次机会让他重回中国，在上海续写米其林厨师的成功之路，数年间培养出 500

戴广坦：

爱上中餐的
法国厨师

多名和他一样热爱烹饪的中国青年人。

美食博主风生水起

如今，戴广坦在上海已经生活了整整12年，他的身份也从学院主厨变为某儿童食品的创始人、知名餐饮品牌咨询研发与美食博主。三个新身份仍离不了锅碗瓢盆，把他每天的日程挤得满满当当，不过戴广坦乐在其中，美食博主更是做得风生水起。每天，数百万粉丝坐在网络那一端，等着戴广坦一边切配蒸煮，一边用"二声"普通话教他们做出一道道青椒炒肉丝、法式焗蜗牛、苹果卡仕达八宝饭……

"网友们送了我一个名字：'二声教父'。我的普通话发音是有点奇怪，不过做美食博主是真的超级开心。"戴广坦觉得自己能成为"网红"，除了是做菜的一把好手外，中国快速发展的新媒体技术也提供了巨大空间。

这几年里，戴广坦跑了不少地方，世界各地许多城市都留下过他的足迹，不过在他眼里，上海是最舒服最便利的城市之一。"上海这么大的城市，城市规划做得非常好，城市功能布局清晰，去城市任何角落交通都非常便利。"

前不久，戴广坦参加了一场外国人和中共党员的交流活动。和他交流的是一位普通出租车司机。"他告诉我，在世博会和进博会期间，许多党员都去做了志愿者，在推进垃圾分类时，也是党员们站了出来，帮助指导大家。"戴广坦说，这次交流让他有了新的认识。"中共党员不是西方理解的为自己谋福利，在中国，加入共产党意味着要为人民服务。"

Name: Corentin Delcroix
Chinese name: 戴广坦
Nationality: French
Position: Chef

Corentin Delcroix:
French Chef in love with Chinese Cuisine

> My love for cooking started in China, and now the fast-developing new media technology has once again made it possible for me to succeed.

Corentin Delcroix, a handsome and sunny young man from France, had the experience of working for a Michelin-starred restaurant. Nowadays, he is teaching people how to cook French dishes and fusion cuisines on social media, speaking his idiolect Mandarin with a rising tone. In just a few years, Delcroix became a popular chef with millions of followers. "My love for cooking started in China, and now the fast-developing new media technology has once again made it possible for me to succeed," says Delcroix.

Inspiration on cooking from Chinese Ayi

Delcroix was born in Lille, a city in northern France. When he was 20, Delcroix developed a keen interest in China, and left alone for Beijing to study business administration. China's ancient architecture, long history and different landscape from that in France left Delcroix mesmerized. At that time a Chinese Ayi (a middle-aged woman) taught Delcroix a few home-cooked dishes, and Delcroix, who had hardly ever been in a kitchen before, immediately developed a love of cooking that he never recovered from. Scrambled eggs, stewed tofu, sautéed green beans with potatoes…. The food Delcroix cooked made his Chinese classmates very surprised: how could a foreigner cook such authentic Chinese dishes?

Four years later when Delcroix went back to France, he was very clear of the goal of his life. "I've found my career for life-long pursuit, that is, cooking," Delcroix says. After having studied cooking for two and a half years at Institut Paul Bocuse, a top school to learn culinary art in Lille, France, Delcroix successfully landed a job at L'Auberge de L'Ill, a three-star Michelin restaurant in Alsace, France.

Corentin Delcroix:

French Chef in
love with Chinese
Cuisine

In 2010 when Shanghai was holding the World Expo, Institut Paul Bocuse was going to set up an overseas campus in Shanghai. With four years of overseas study experience in China, Delcroix was an ideal candidate for the chef of the institute. This chance brought him back to China to continue his career as a successful Michelin chef. Several years thereafter, he has trained more than 500 Chinese youth who entertain the same enthusiasm for culinary art as him.

Thriving as a food blogger

Up until now, Delcroix has been living in Shanghai for 12 years. He has changed from an institute chef to the founder of a food brand for children, a research and development consultant for famous catering brands and a food blogger. The three new roles are closely related to food, and cram his daily schedule to the brim. Delcroix, however, enjoys himself very much, especially as a food blogger. Every day, millions of fans wait online for Delcroix to show his culinary skills and to teach them in his rising-tone idiolect Mandarin to cook a variety of dishes such as stir-fried shredded pork with green pepper, French baked snails, and apple custard rice.

"My friends on the Internet gave me a nickname, that is, 'rising-tone godfather'," Delcroix says. "My Mandarin pronunciation is a bit odd, but I feel super-happy as a food blogger." Delcroix attributes his success as an "Internet celebrity" not only to his excellent cooking skills, but also to the fast-developing new media technology in China which offers him the opportunity.

In the past few years, Delcroix has traveled to many cities around the world. In his view, however, Shanghai is one of the most pleasant and convenient cities. "Shanghai is very broad in land area, but the city planning is very good in the sense that the layout of urban functions is so clear that it is very convenient to travel to any place in the city," Delcroix says.

Recently, Delcroix has taken part in an event featuring exchanges between foreigners and members of the Communist Party of China (CPC). A taxi driver paired up with him in the activity.

Delcroix says: "He told me that in the 2010 World Expo and the China International Import Expo, many CPC members acted as the volunteers, and in the promotion of the waste sorting in China, it was also the CPC members that offered to help and teach others how to sort the waste."

This event refreshed his knowledge. "CPC members are not people who just solicit benefits for themselves, as what the western countries understood them," Delcroix says. "In China, joining the CPC means to serve the people heart and soul."

Scan for videos

姓　名：Adachi Ken
中文名：安达谦
国　籍：日本
职　位：HIS 国际旅行社中国华东华南大区董事长

安达谦：
希望更多外国朋友来上海，感受中国社会发展的成果

一次长三角之旅，既能看到江南不同地区的文化风俗，又能切身体会中国社会经济快速发展的成果。

HIS 上海总部的办公室位于南京东路繁华街区，窗外上海的地标建筑东方明珠清晰可见。作为日本知名国际旅行社中国华东华南大区的董事长，安达谦多年来深耕上海市场，以外国人独特的视角发掘这座城市无处不在的"宝藏"，用真实、鲜活、动人的方式将这座东方大都市呈现给世界。

上海与初见完全不同

安达谦在日本旅游公司工作了 22 年。2002 年当他第一次到上海出差时，就以旅游人特有的敏锐注视着这座日本的近邻城市。"那时日本人对上海的旅游景点知之甚少，有一种近在咫尺、远在天边的感觉。"回忆起 20 年前的初次造访，安达谦感慨不已，"那会儿上海的地铁还只修到 3 号线，城市里也没有那么多高楼和商场，是一个和现在完全不同的上海。"

此后每隔一年，安达谦就会来上海出差。后来被 HIS 正式派驻上海，出任中国华东地区董事长。"最早我们向日本游客介绍上海时，景点不外乎外滩和豫园。后来每年上海都有新的地标建筑诞生，能逛能吃能玩的地方越来越多，陆家嘴、新天地、田子坊、迪士尼……我们提供给境外游客的旅游路线越做越丰富。"

随着 2006 年"中日旅游交流年"和 2007 年"中日文化体育交流年"的到来，中日间旅游互访达到高峰。仅 2006 年，日本访华人数就达到

安达谦：

希望更多外国朋友来上海，感受中国社会发展的成果

375万人次，占当年中国境外游客总量的22%。

"到今年，我已经在上海待了整整6年。"安达谦动情地说，这6年里他见证着上海翻天覆地的变化，城市天际线不断刷新，服务业水准逐年提高，"不论在景点、商场还是餐厅，人们脸上都洋溢着笑容。"

欢迎更多国际朋友们来到上海

随处可见的手机支付、"隐藏"在街头巷角的中华美食、便捷畅通的交通设施，安达谦希望能让更多的国际朋友们来到上海，"感受一下这里最新的科技发展，以及人们不断变化的生活方式"。

近年长三角一体化持续推进，城际铁路线网密织，高铁班次如公交车一般频繁，国际游客的旅程从上海轻松延伸到周边城市。"长三角一体化发展，对于海外游客来说非常有利。上海、江苏、浙江、安徽，每个地区的景点都独具特色，一次长三角之旅，既能看到江南不同地区的文化风俗，又能切身体会中国社会经济快速发展的成果。"

尽管2020年新冠肺炎疫情对旅游业打击巨大，但在安达谦眼中，中国政府积极防疫抗疫，复工复产快速提振经济，让他对未来仍充满信心。"SARS疫情和东日本大地震这些重创旅游业的事件我都经历过，结束之后都会迎来一个增速明显的市场反弹。眼下旅游业形势虽然还很严峻，但我相信，中国政府、旅行社、酒店、航空业等通力合作，一定会让旅游业尽快恢复活力。"

Name: Adachi Ken
Chinese name: 安达谦
Nationality: Japanese
Position: H.I.S China eastern/southern Area Chairman

Adachi Ken:
I hope more foreign friends come to Shanghai and experience China's social development

A trip to the Yangtze River Delta allows you to see the cultural customs of different regions in Jiangnan and to experience China's rapid socio-economic development.

The office of H.I.S Shanghai headquarters is located in the bustling neighborhood of East Nanjing Road, with the Oriental Pearl TV Tower, the landmark of Shanghai, clearly visible from the window. As the chairman in charge of the east and south China region in a leading Japanese international travel agency, and immersed in the Shanghai market for many years, Adachi Ken has been exploring the city's ubiquitous "treasures" from a foreigner's perspective, and presenting this oriental metropolis to the world in a realistic, vibrant, and appealing way.

Shanghai completely different from the first sight

Adachi Ken has been working in Japanese tourist companies for 22 years. When he first came to Shanghai on business in 2002, he took a keen look at Shanghai, as Japan's neighboring city, with professional sensitivity as a tourism insider.

Looking back at his first visit to Shanghai almost 20 years ago, Adachi Ken recalls, "At that time, Japanese people knew little about Shanghai's tourist attractions, and it's a contradictory feeling of both far and near. At that time, Shanghai's subway was only up to Line 3, and there were not so many tall buildings and shopping malls; it was a completely different city from it is now."

After that, Ken came to Shanghai on business every other year. Finally, he was officially assigned by H.I.S to Shanghai as the chairman of the East China region.

Adachi Ken:

I hope more foreign friends come to Shanghai and experience China's social development

He says: "When we first introduced Shanghai to Japanese tourists, the attractions were no more than the Bund and Yuyuan Garden. Later, every year, new landmarks have mushroomed in Shanghai, and there are more and more places to visit, have meals and play, including Lujiazui, Xintiandi, Tianzifang, Shanghai Disney Resort .... We are offering more and more travel routes to foreign tourists."

With the initiation of the "China-Japan Tourism Exchange Year" in 2006 and the "China-Japan Culture and Sports Exchange Year" in 2007, the mutual visits between China and Japan reached a peak. In 2006 alone, the number of Japanese visitors to China reached 3.75 million, accounting for 22 percent of the total number of tourists from overseas that year.

"By this year, I've been in Shanghai for six consecutive years," says Ken. During these six years, he has witnessed dramatic changes in Shanghai, with the city skyline constantly refreshed and the standards of the service industry raised year by year. He adds, "Whether it's at the tourist attractions, shopping malls or restaurants, people all have smiles on their faces."

Welcoming more international friends to Shanghai

With cell phone payments everywhere, Chinese local delicacies "hidden" in streets and alleys, and convenient transportation facilities, he hopes to bring more international friends to Shanghai to "experience the latest technological developments and the changing lifestyles of the people here."

The Yangtze River Delta Region Integration Initiative has been steadily promoted in recent years. With a dense intercity railway network and high-speed trains as frequent as buses in the streets, it is easy for overseas tourists to extend their journeys from Shanghai to neighboring cities.

He says: "The integrated regional development of the Yangtze River Delta is beneficial to overseas tourists in every aspect. With Shanghai Municipality, Jiangsu Province, Zhejiang Province and Anhui Province each boasting unique tourist attractions, a trip to the Yangtze River Delta will allow you to see the cultural customs of different regions in Jiangnan (referring to regions south of the lower reaches of the Yangtze River), and to experience China's rapid socio-economic development."

Despite the huge blow dealt by the COVID-19 pandemic to the tourism industry in 2020, in Ken's eyes, the effective combat led by the Chinese government against the pandemic and quick boost to the economy by resuming work and production gives him full confidence in the future.

Ken says: "I have experienced the SARS epidemic in 2003 and the 2011 Tohoku earthquake, which hit the tourism industry hard, but later, they both ushered in market rebounds with significant growth rates. The tourism situation is still tough now, but I believe that the full cooperation between the Chinese government, travel agencies, hotels and the airline industry will bring the tourism industry back to vitality as soon as possible."

Scan for videos

姓　名：Divine TUNUNGINI Kiese
中文名：刘迪心
国　籍：刚果（金）
职　位：上海交通大学留学生

刘迪心：
我在上海成了名副其实的"网购达人"

这样的"智慧生活"值得推广到全世界！

"作为一个文化从业者，能近距离了解自己文化之外的其他文化，是件有意思的事儿。"带着这样的想法，来自非洲第二大国刚果金的姑娘刘迪心只身踏上了前往中国上海的求学之路。来到上海后，刘迪心不仅接触到了东方文化，还体验了一把被互联网科技"包围"下的"智慧生活"。

了解全新文化

"我来上海是因为我哥哥就在这边学习，他总是给我发很多照片，向我介绍上海的生活。"刘迪心说，在来上海之前，她对这座城市的所有印象都来自于哥哥的描述。

在家乡学习了六年音乐之后，刘迪心开始为自己的人生做新规划。"那时候，我哥总跟我说上海有很多优秀学府，上海交通大学就是世界上最好的大学之一。"在他的牵引下，刘迪心最终决定前往上海开启全新的人生旅途。

刘迪心是一个敢于挑战、乐于尝试新鲜事物的女孩。原本在高中期间学习生物化学，而后"转行"在刚果首都金沙萨国家艺术学院学习音乐，并获得了学士学位。毕业之后，她又想去接触更多与文化有关的学科。

语言和文化息息相关，语言也是了解一种全新文化的钥匙。2019年，刘迪心远赴上海交通大学学习汉语言专业。"虽然离开自己的舒适区，去往不同的国家，探索未知的世界是一件很酷的事，但来到一个完全陌生的环境，开始总是迷茫的。"刘迪心坦言，无论是语言还是思维方式，她都要从零开始，慢慢适应。

但上海这座城市和上海市民的友好渐渐打消了刘迪心的顾虑和陌生感。"很快，我发现自己身处一个十分温暖的环境，这里的一切让我感到舒适。老师同学非常友善，每当我遇到不懂的问题，他们都会很耐心地解释，直到我弄懂为止。中国人非常乐于助人，如果我迷路了，他们都愿意给我带路。"

刘迪心爱上了中国文化。"中国是一个神秘的国度，不仅有着深厚的历史积淀，还有丰富的文化积累。"

体验"上海生活"

上海吸引刘迪心的地方还有很多。"上海有很多好玩的地方，还汇聚了全球各地的美食，不仅有意大利菜、法国菜，还有日本料理，但我最爱的是意大利菜。"刘迪心觉得除了学习，在上海的生活同样多姿多彩。

让她印象最为深刻的就是中国的互联网"黑科技"给她的生活带来的改变。"在刚果金虽然也可以在网上购物，但我们平时还是要去商店，因为那边网购不是很流行。但在中国，淘宝就能搞定一切。"刘迪心成了名副其实的"网购达人"。

"我不仅可以在淘宝上淘到任何我想买的东西，还能用美团、饿了么点餐，还有许多 App 可以帮助我学中文。"刘迪心说她急着想把中国各种实用方便的 App 介绍给她在刚果金的家人和朋友。

"这样的'智慧生活'值得推广到全世界！"刘迪心兴奋地说。

Name: Divine TUNUNGINI Kiese
Chinese Name: 刘迪心
Nationality: D.R.Congo
Position: International student of Shanghai Jiao Tong University

Divine TUNUNGINI Kiese:
I became a veteran online shopper in Shanghai

Such a smart life is worth worldwide promotion.

"For someone working in the cultural field, it is interesting to look closely into different cultures other than one's own culture." With this thought in mind, Divine TUNUNGINI Kiese, a girl from the Democratic Republic of Congo, the second-largest country in Africa, set off on her own to study in Shanghai, China. After she arrived, Kiese not only came into contact with Eastern culture but also experienced a smart life supported by Internet technology.

Learning about a new culture

Kiese says: "I came to Shanghai because my brother is studying here. Before I came to Shanghai, he sent me some pictures. He talked to me about Shanghai, and how life was like in Shanghai." All she knew about Shanghai came from her brother then.

Having studied music for six years in her hometown, Kiese started making new plans for her life. "At that time, he said that in Shanghai there are so many top universities and Shanghai Jiao Tong University is one of the best universities," Kiese says. Following her brother's lead, she made up her mind to go to Shanghai to start a new chapter in her life.

Kiese is a girl who is willing to embrace challenges and open to new things. She studied biochemistry in high school, and then moved on to study music at the National Academy of Arts in Kinshasa, the capital of the DRC, and obtained a bachelor's degree. After her graduation, she wanted to learn more about culture-related subjects.

Language is closely bound up with culture and is key to learning a new culture. In 2019, she came to learn Chinese at Shanghai Jiao Tong University.

Divine TUNUNGINI Kiese:

I became a veteran online shopper in Shanghai

She says: "Indeed, it is cool to leave your comfort zone to go to different countries and explore the unknown world, but it is always confusing at first when you come to a completely unfamiliar environment." Kiese admits that she had to start from scratch and adapt slowly, both in terms of language and way of thinking.

However, the friendliness of Shanghai and its citizens gradually dispelled Kiese's doubt and sense of strangeness.

She says: "I soon found that I am in a warm environment where I feel at ease with everything. My professors and classmates are very friendly. Every time I am confused about something, they will explain it over and over again until I understand. Chinese people are always ready to help others. If I get lost, they are all willing to show me the way."

Kiese fell in love with Chinese culture. "China is a mysterious country with not only profound historical heritage but also a rich culture," she says.

Experiencing "life in Shanghai"

There are many other things that attract Kiese in Shanghai.

She says: "There are lots of interesting places in Shanghai. You can find Italian cuisine, French dishes and Japanese food, but I like Italian cuisine best." Kiese feels that apart from studying, life in Shanghai is also colorful.

What impresses her most is the changes brought to her life by China's new Internet technology. "In the DRC, although online shopping is also available, we normally go to the stores because online shopping is not that prevalent, but in China, you can buy everything on Taobao," Kiese says. She has become a veteran online shopper now.

"Not only can I buy everything on Taobao, but also I can use Meituan and Eleme to order food. And there're many apps that help me to learn Chinese," Kiese says, adding that she is eager to introduce all kinds of convenient apps to her friends and families back in the DRC.

"Such a smart life is worth worldwide promotion!" Kiese says excitedly.

姓　名：Doruk Keser
中文名：天山
国　籍：土耳其
职　位：土耳其实业银行股份公司上海代表处首席代表

天山：
我是一个中国迷

最近，我去看了莫奈和毕加索的画展，我喜欢这座城市在艺术和文化方面的多样性。

来自土耳其的天山是个名副其实的"中国迷"。谈及中国文化，他如数家珍。在还没来中国之前，天山就已经对这个神秘又古老的国度"魂牵梦萦"。2015年的一天，天山得到了来上海工作的机会，他毫不犹豫地拿着机票，踏上了一段不寻常的"东方之旅"。

文化的魅力

天山对中国的古代艺术有着极大的好奇心。在上海工作之余，最喜欢去的地方就是上海博物馆。"上海博物馆里陈列了许多中国古代的绘画和陶瓷，它们很容易让我想起伊斯坦布尔的托普卡帕皇宫，因为那里收藏了数千件中国陶瓷，尤其是青花瓷。"天山说，"这些中国瓷器不仅是珍宝，更是中土两个文明古国之间长期友好关系的见证。"

天山不仅是古代文化的"忠粉"，也对当代艺术有着浓厚的兴趣。"上海是个非常开放且多元的城市，在这里，我也能欣赏到许多不同的西方艺术。"平日里，天山喜欢去西岸的艺术中心，参观西方艺术家的艺术展，"最近，我去看了莫奈和毕加索的画展，我喜欢这座城市在艺术和文化方面的多样性。"

古代与现代在这里结合，东方与西方亦在这里交汇。天山说，上海完全是他的理想之城。

伟大的政党

天山对中国历史和文化的认知，很大一部分来自书本。"要说中国历史，

天山：

我是一个
中国迷

我其实最喜欢的是中国近代史。"天山知道今年是中国共产党建党一百周年，他说自己通过阅读中国近代史了解到，这是一个多么伟大的政党。

他走到办公室的书架前，拿出一本自己十分珍爱的书籍。"这是1937年的《生活》杂志，里面有美国记者埃德加·斯诺对毛主席的采访。"

"这本杂志上有当时斯诺拍的照片。毛主席和他的同志们在资源如此匮乏的情况下，凭着心中对国家的热爱和忠诚完成了一场重要的革命。"天山感慨，"这种牺牲自我的奉献精神一直深深影响着我。"

今天，在中国共产党的领导下，中国人民经过半个多世纪的艰苦奋斗，国家与个人命运都发生了历史性巨变。

"我认为，'一带一路'是个伟大的倡议。它不仅影响着中国和周边国家，也影响着全球。"天山说。

土耳其地处中东，连接着东西方，连接着欧亚。天山认为，在"一带一路"倡议中，土耳其是中国非常好的合作伙伴。"我认为这不仅是一个双边投资的绝佳机会，也让土耳其与中国文化更加紧密地联系在一起。"

天山相信，中国的明天会更美好。

Name: Doruk Keser
Chinese name: 天山
Nationality: Turkish
Position: Chief Representative of Turkiye Is Bankasi A.S. Shanghai Representative Office

Doruk Keser:
I'm a fan of China

I went to exhibitions of Monet and Picasso recently and I love the diversity of art and culture in this city.

Doruk Keser from Turkey is a veritable fan of China. He talks about Chinese culture with great familiarity. Before coming to China, Doruk Keser had been dreaming of this ancient and unique country for a long time. Once getting the chance to work in China in 2015, Doruk Keser embraced it, took his ticket, and embarked on his unusual "journey to the East" without any hesitation.

The charming culture

Doruk Keser has a keen curiosity for ancient Chinese art, with Shanghai Museum being his favorite place to go in his spare time. The innumerable antique Chinese paintings and porcelain wares there often remind him of Topkapi Palace Museum in Istanbul for its collection of thousands of Chinese ceramics, mostly blue-and-white porcelain, "which are not only fabulous treasures but also a witness to the long-term friendship between the two time-honored civilizations," he says.

Apart from being a dedicated fan of ancient Chinese culture, Doruk Keser also has a strong interest in contemporary art. He says it is the extraordinarily open and diverse cultural atmosphere of the city that makes it possible for him to enjoy art of diversified forms. "West Bund Art Center is another place I'd like to visit," he says. "I went to exhibitions of Monet and Picasso recently and I love the diversity of art and culture in this city."

With the combination of old and new, and the blend of East and West, Shanghai is definitely Doruk Keser's ideal city.

The great Party

Doruk Keser's knowledge of Chinese history and culture is mostly acquired

Doruk Keser:

I'm a fan of China

through reading. When it comes to Chinese history, he says, what he likes best is the modern periods. He knows that 2021 is the 100th anniversary of the founding of the Communist Party of China and that he understands why the Party is so great by reading books on modern Chinese history.

Doruk Keser cherishes a magazine on the bookshelf in his office very much. It is an issue of *Life* in 1937, in which there is a published interview with Chairman Mao by the American journalist Edgar Snow.

"This magazine impressed me with photos taken by Snow. With such a scarcity of resources, Chairman Mao and his comrades went all the way through the important revolution with their deep love for and genuine loyalty to the country," Doruk Keser says, adding he is deeply moved. "Their self-sacrificing dedication has a lasting and intense impact on me."

Today, after more than half a century of arduous struggle, the destiny of the country and people has been historically changed under the leadership of the Communist Party of China.

"The Silk Road, or now the Belt and Road, in my opinion, is a brilliant initiative," Doruk Keser says. "It will affect not only China and the neighboring countries but also globally most of the countries trading with China."

Located in the Middle East, Turkey connects the East and the West, Europe and Asia. Doruk Keser believes that Turkey is surely a very good partner of China in the Belt and Road initiative. "I think this is not only an excellent opportunity for the bilateral investments but also a chance to bring Turkey more closely to Chinese culture," he says.

Doruk Keser sincerely believes that China will have a more promising future.

Scan for videos

姓　名：Jimmer Fredette
中文名：吉默·弗雷戴特
国　籍：美国
职　位：上海久事篮球俱乐部球员

吉默·弗雷戴特：
我憧憬上海体育的未来，希望创造属于自己的奇迹

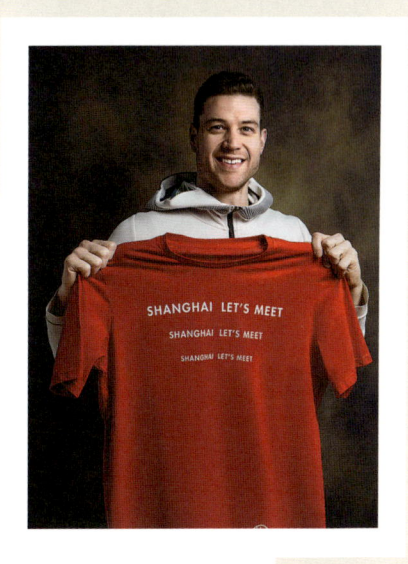

上海将来一定会培养出更多的平民球星，球队也将因此赢下更多比赛。

他生活自律、为人低调谦逊，他用勤奋改变着外援是"打临工"或"淘金者"的形象，他就是CBA现象级的外援吉默·弗雷戴特。"上海将来一定会培养出更多的平民球星，球队也将因此赢下更多比赛，培养出赢球文化。"吉默·弗雷戴特说。

初到上海的"寂寞大神"

1989年，弗雷戴特在纽约州出生。儿时的弗雷戴特未曾想到自己会和大洋彼岸的上海结下不解之缘。2016年，上海男篮宣布与弗雷戴特"牵手"，这也是他首度与CBA接触。就这样，27岁的弗雷戴特第一次来到上海。因为名字发音接近中文的"寂寞"，不少球迷称他为"寂寞大神"。

他是上海男篮阵中乃至全CBA的超级得分手，三分球命中率达40%以上，罚球命中率也始终保持在90%以上，并曾获2016—2017年赛季CBA常规赛外籍球员MVP以及2018—2019年赛季CBA得分王。由于他出色的表现，球迷们还给他打造了专属BGM——"jimmer, jimmer jimmer"。每当赛季结束，球迷们都会对他高喊着"one more year"。

然而因为合同到期，弗雷戴特还是离开了上海。

2019年至2020年间，上海男篮进行了一次"重塑"。2019年，久

事集团完成了对原上海东方篮球俱乐部的股权收购,这标志着上海男篮步入全新的"久事时代"。久事集团的目标是为上海打造一支与城市地位、城市形象相符的球队,助力上海建设全球著名体育城市,打响"上海文化"品牌。

再度回归上海久事男篮

尽管离开了上海,但弗雷戴特一直牵挂着上海男篮,他想回归。就这样双方一拍即合,2020年9月,弗雷戴特宣布回归上海久事男篮。

弗雷戴特告诉记者:"在我离开的这一年,感觉上海改变了很多,城市一直在发展。"他欣喜地发现"家"已经大变样——上海男篮俱乐部新建了专属的训练场,硬件设施大幅提升,而俱乐部位于上海体育馆的主场也正在改造中,设施全面升级后将为球迷带来更好的观赛体验。

对于上海打造全球著名体育城市,弗雷戴特有着自己的理解,他告诉记者,上海无论是篮球还是足球都有过冠军的荣耀。"在姚明时代,上海男篮曾拿过全国冠军,前几年上海的足球俱乐部也夺得了冠军。如果我们也能达到那样的水平,在全国乃至国际,都将拥有一个较高的知名度。"

对于上海男篮、上海体育的未来,弗雷戴特充满了憧憬。他坦言,"最重要的是找到合适的人加入球队,帮助建立成功文化。一旦成功了,其他的东西就会接踵而来。"

弗雷戴特希望能在上海创造属于他的奇迹。

Name: Jimmer Fredette
Chinese name: 吉默·弗雷戴特
Nationality: American
Position: Player of Shanghai Juss Basketball Club

Jimmer Fredette:
I have a yearning for the future of Shanghai sports and hope to work miracles of my own

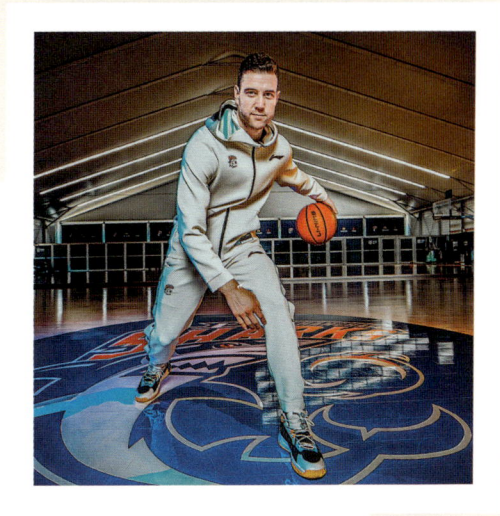

> Shanghai will definitely produce more grassroots basketball stars in the future, and the team will win more games.

He is self-disciplined, keeping a low profile, and he has changed the prejudiced image of foreign players as a "temporary worker" or "gold digger" with his hard work. He is Jimmer Fredette, the phenomenal foreign player in the Chinese Basketball Association (CBA). "Shanghai will definitely produce more grassroots basketball stars in the future, and the team will win more games and develop a 'winning culture,'" Fredette says.

The newly-arrived "King of Loneliness" in Shanghai

Fredette was born in New York State in 1989. As a child, he never expected that fate would someday take him to Shanghai on the other side of the ocean. In 2016, Shanghai Men's Basketball Team announced cooperation with Fredette, which was also his first contact with CBA. In this way, this 27-year-old man came to Shanghai for the first time. Because the pronunciation of his name is close to the Chinese word "loneliness", many fans call him "King of Loneliness".

He is a super scorer in Shanghai Men's Basketball Team and even in the whole CBA, with a 3-point true shooting percentage (TSP) of over 40% and a free throw TSP of over 90%. He has earned his MVP for foreign players in the CBA regular season of 2016-2017 and the scoring champion in the CBA season of 2018-2019. Because of his outstanding performance, the fans also created a

Jimmer Fredette:

I have a yearning for the future of Shanghai sports and hope to work miracles of my own

piece of exclusive background music for him -- *Jimmer, Jimmer, Jimmer*. At the end of a season, the fans will shout "one more year" to him.

However, Fredette left Shanghai as his contract expired.

Between 2019 and 2020, Shanghai Men's Basketball Team has undergone a "reinvention". The year 2019 has seen the acquisition of the former Shanghai Oriental Basketball Club by Juss Group, marking the advent of a "Juss Era" for the Shanghai Men's Basketball Team. The goal of Juss Group is to build a team for Shanghai in line with the city's status and image, to help Shanghai become a globally famous sports city, and to promote the city brand of "Shanghai Culture".

Returning to Juss Men's Basketball Team

Although he left Shanghai, Fredette had been worried about Shanghai Men's Basketball Team and wanted to return. The two sides hit it off at once. In September 2020, Fredette announced his return to Shanghai Juss Men's Basketball Team.

"I feel that, during the year I was away, Shanghai has changed a lot and the city has always been developing," Fredette says. He was delighted to find that his "home" has changed dramatically. Shanghai Men's Basketball Club has built a new exclusive training ground, and its facilities have been greatly improved. The home field of the club located in Shanghai Indoor Stadium is also being renovated, and the comprehensive upgrade of the facilities will bring a better watching experience to fans.

Fredette has his understanding of how Shanghai should strive to become a world-famous sports city. He says: "Shanghai has had the championship in both basketball and soccer. During Yao Ming's time, Shanghai Men's Basketball Team won the national championship, and Shanghai's soccer club also won the championship a few years ago. If we can reach that level, we will have a higher reputation in the country and even in the world."

Fredette has a yearning for the future of Shanghai Men's Basketball and even for Shanghai sports. He says: "The most important thing is to find the right people to join the team and help build a winning culture. Once this is successfully done, other achievements will follow.".

Fredette hopes to create miracles of his own in Shanghai.

姓　名：Betty Barr
中文名：白丽诗
国　籍：英国
职　位：上海外国语大学退休外籍教师

白丽诗：
16 岁那年，我见证了上海解放的历史瞬间

16 岁那年，我见证了上海解放的历史瞬间。

88 岁的白丽诗是一名非常特殊的"上海人"，她这一生都与上海紧密相连。1924 年、1930 年，白丽诗的父母相继从西方来到上海，而后相识相爱。1933 年，白丽诗在上海出生，成为"十里洋场的一名洋人"，她在上海长大而后断断续续在这座城市生活了半个多世纪，遇见了爱情，嫁给了一名上海男人，也见证了上海从沦陷到解放，从苦难到新生，从百废待兴到繁荣昌盛的历程。

在集中营被日军关了 800 多天

在上海市虹口区的家中，白丽诗与丈夫王正文接受了我们的采访。

1941 年 12 月 8 日，白丽诗像往常一样去上学，刚走进校园就听到老师在喊："快回家，战争开始了！"也就是这一天的早晨，日本人占领了上海的公共租界，大街上到处都是日本士兵。

白丽诗的童年就在这样的阴影下度过。1943 年，日军在太平洋战场接连失利，对敌国侨民的政策进一步收紧，把上海的 6000 多名西方人"圈"在多个集中营。白丽诗和家人被带到龙华侨民集中营，她的身份变成了一个编号——22/228。

白丽诗和家人一关就是 800 多天。王正文彼时也在上海，他回忆道，集中营外面的生活更苦，王正文当时在上海住的房屋连窗户都没有，6 平方米的空间挤了 6 个人，夜里甚至有老鼠在舔他的头发。

白丽诗：

16 岁那年，我见证了上海解放的历史瞬间

1944 年 11 月，一批盟军的战机低空飞过集中营，轰炸了附近的龙华机场，白丽诗和家人意识到战争可能快要结束了，1945 年 8 月 15 日，日本宣布无条件投降。白丽诗一家这才走出了集中营，回到了正常的生活状态。

一夜醒来发现解放军在守护学校

随后的三年，白丽诗在上海美国学校继续学业，幸运地见证了上海解放的历史瞬间。"我们意识到中国人民解放军要来了。那一晚我们睡觉时，寂静无声。1949 年 5 月 27 日早上我们从学校窗外看去，一名中国人民解放军站在旗杆下，守护着我们。我们感到很新奇。"

1949 年 7 月 6 日，为庆祝上海解放，上海市近百万军民走上街头举行盛大游行。人们敲锣打鼓，扭着秧歌唱着歌。"我爸爸的学生为了参加游行表演，向我爸爸借了帽子和拐杖，我们一家都去外滩看游行了。"白丽诗回忆。

解放后的上海在人民政府的治理下井然有序，从此开启了新的篇章。1950 年，白丽诗离开中国前往美国。尽管身在海外，白丽诗却一直关注着中国——这个她生于斯长于斯的国度。

改革开放后，白丽诗终于在 1984 年再次回到了上海，从此便扎根于此，一直在上海外国语大学任教，直至退休。

"和平"是他们最大的心愿

对比自己儿时记忆中的上海，白丽诗感叹"变化实在是太大了！"她还记得 80 多年前，她在虹口区的家附近街道上随处可见面黄肌瘦的乞丐，而今天马路上的行人脸上都洋溢着幸福，她记忆中曾经黑臭的苏州河也变成了市民休闲健身的景观带，而这座城市的面貌与综合实力则发生了更为巨大的变化。

岁月荏苒，88 年就这样过去了，如今，白丽诗和丈夫王正文仍旧居住在虹口区，他们每天一起散步、追忆过往，一起继续见证这座城市的成长和巨大的变化。他们祝愿中国迎来更好的发展，祝愿上海拥有更美好的明天。

这对从战争中走来的老人深感和平的珍贵，特意一起弹奏了一曲苏格兰民歌《友谊地久天长》。

Name: Betty Barr
Chinese name: 白丽诗
Nationality: British
Position: Retired foreign expert, Shanghai International Studies University

Betty Barr:
When I was 16 years old, I witnessed the historical moment of Shanghai's liberation

When I was 16 years old, I witnessed the historical moment of the liberation of Shanghai.

Betty Barr, 88, is a very special "Shanghainese". Her entire life has been closely linked to Shanghai. Respectively in 1924 and 1930, Barr's parents came to this city from the Western world, they met and fell in love with each other. In 1933, Barr was born in Shanghai and became "a little foreigner in the Eastern international metropolis". She grew up in this city. Later she has been on and off living here for more than half a century. Here she met and married her love, a local Shanghai man. Also here she witnessed Shanghai's falling and her liberation, her suffering and her rebirth, her journey from healing her scars from the war to the great prosperity of today.

More than 800 days in a concentration camp of the Japanese invaders

Barr and her husband Wang Zhengwen speak to us at their home in Shanghai's Hongkou district.

On December 8, 1941, little Barr went to school as usual. As soon as she entered the campus, she heard her teacher shouting, "Everyone go home! The war has begun!" That morning, the Japanese occupied Shanghai's Public Concession, and in a twinkle of eyes, Japanese soldiers were everywhere in the streets.

Barr's childhood was under such a shadow. In 1943, after the Japanese army suffered successive defeats in the Pacific, its policy towards the expatriates of enemy countries was further tightened. More than 6,000 Westerners in Shanghai were "rounded up" into different concentration camps. Barr and her family were taken to the "Lunghwa Civil Assembly Center" where her name was changed into a mere number -- 22/228.

Barr and her family spent more than 800 days in the camp. Wang Zhengwen, who was also in Shanghai at the time, remembers that life outside the camp was even harder. Wang lived in a windowless room, with six people

Betty Barr:

When I was 16 years old, I witnessed the historical moment of Shanghai's liberation

crammed into a six-square-meter space. Rats sometimes licked his hair at night.

In November 1944, a group of Allied warplanes flew low over across the camp before bombing the nearby Lunghwa Airfield. Barr and her family realized that the war might be coming to an end. On August 15, 1945, Japan announced its unconditional surrender. Only then did the Barrs get out of the concentration camp and returned to their normal life.

Woke up one morning to find the PLA guarding her school

In the following three years, Barr continued her studies at Shanghai American School, where as fate would have it, she witnessed the historical moment of Shanghai's liberation. Barr says: "We realized the People's Liberation Army was coming. When that night came, we didn't hear anything after going to bed. But on the morning of May 27, we looked out of the school window and found a Chinese PLA soldier standing under the flagpole apparently guarding us. We felt it such a novelty."

On July 6, 1949, nearly one million soldiers and civilians took to the streets and held a large victory parade along the Bund. People beat gongs and drums, dancing amid traditional Yangko folk songs to celebrate the liberation and welcome the arrival of the people's army. "My father's hat and stick were borrowed by one of his students to participate in the parade, and our family also went to the Bund to watch the parade," Barr recalls.

After liberation, Shanghai was in good order under the administration of the people's government. The city turned a shining new leaf. In 1950, Barr left China for the United States. Although being abroad, Barr kept her eyes constantly on China, the land where she was born and raised.

After China's Reform and Opening up, in 1984, Barr finally returned to Shanghai, where she stayed and taught at Shanghai International Studies University until her retirement.

"Peace" is their greatest wish

Comparing Shanghai today with the city in her childhood memory, Barr is emotional. "The changes are just too great!" she exclaims. Barr vividly remembers more than 80 years ago in Hongkou district that emaciated and haggard beggars were streaming through her neighborhood streets. Today happiness is written on the face of every pedestrian walking along the new boulevard. The stinky Suzhou Creek in her memory becomes a landscape zone for citizens' leisure fitness.

Eighty-eight years have passed swiftly. Today, Barr and her husband Wang Zhengwen still live in Hongkou District. They take daily strolls together, reminisce about the past, and continue to witness the city's sustainable growth and greater changes together. They wish China an even greater development, and Shanghai an even brighter future.

Having survived a world war, the couple keenly values peace. They played on their piano the Scottish folk song *Auld Lang Syne*.

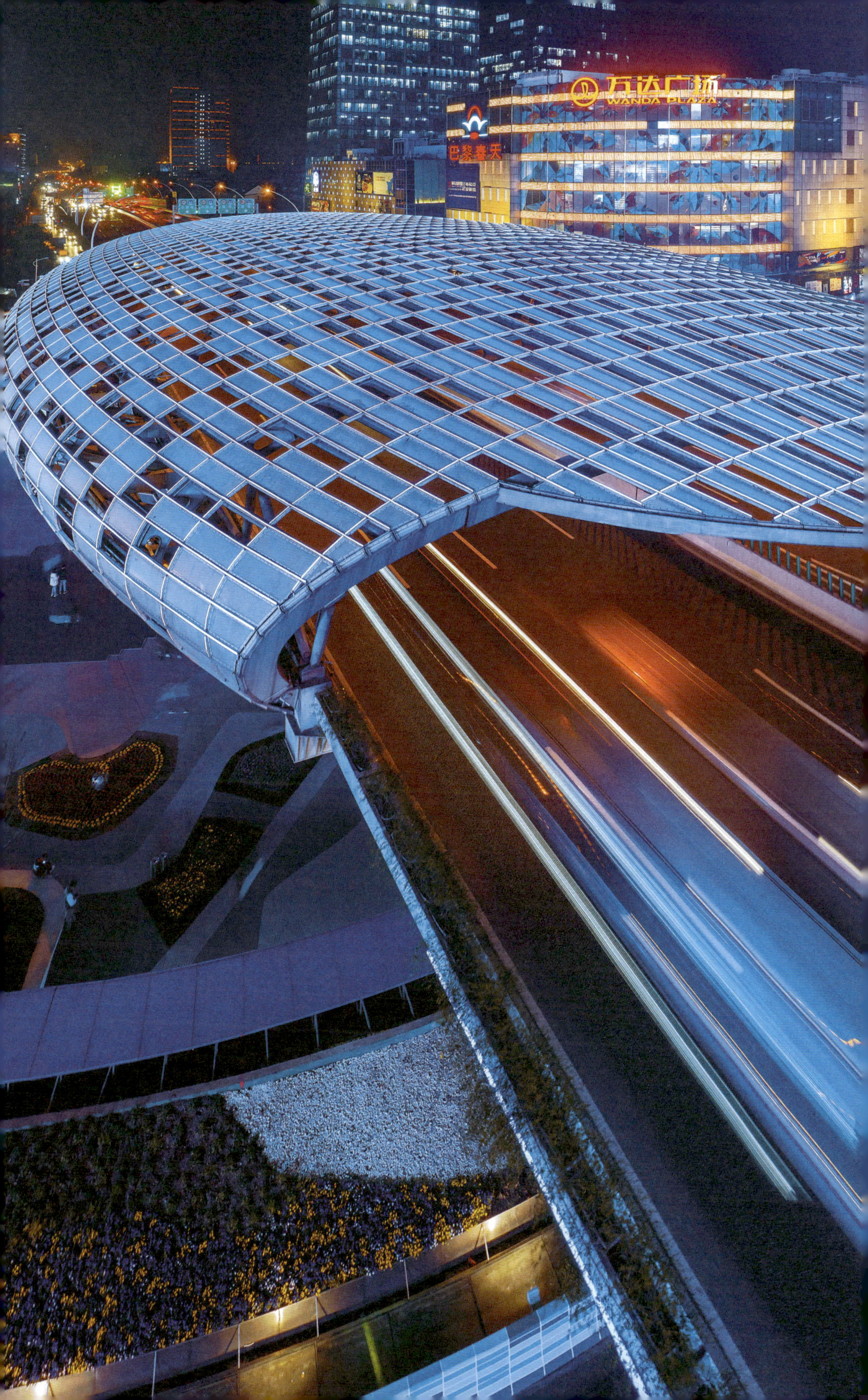

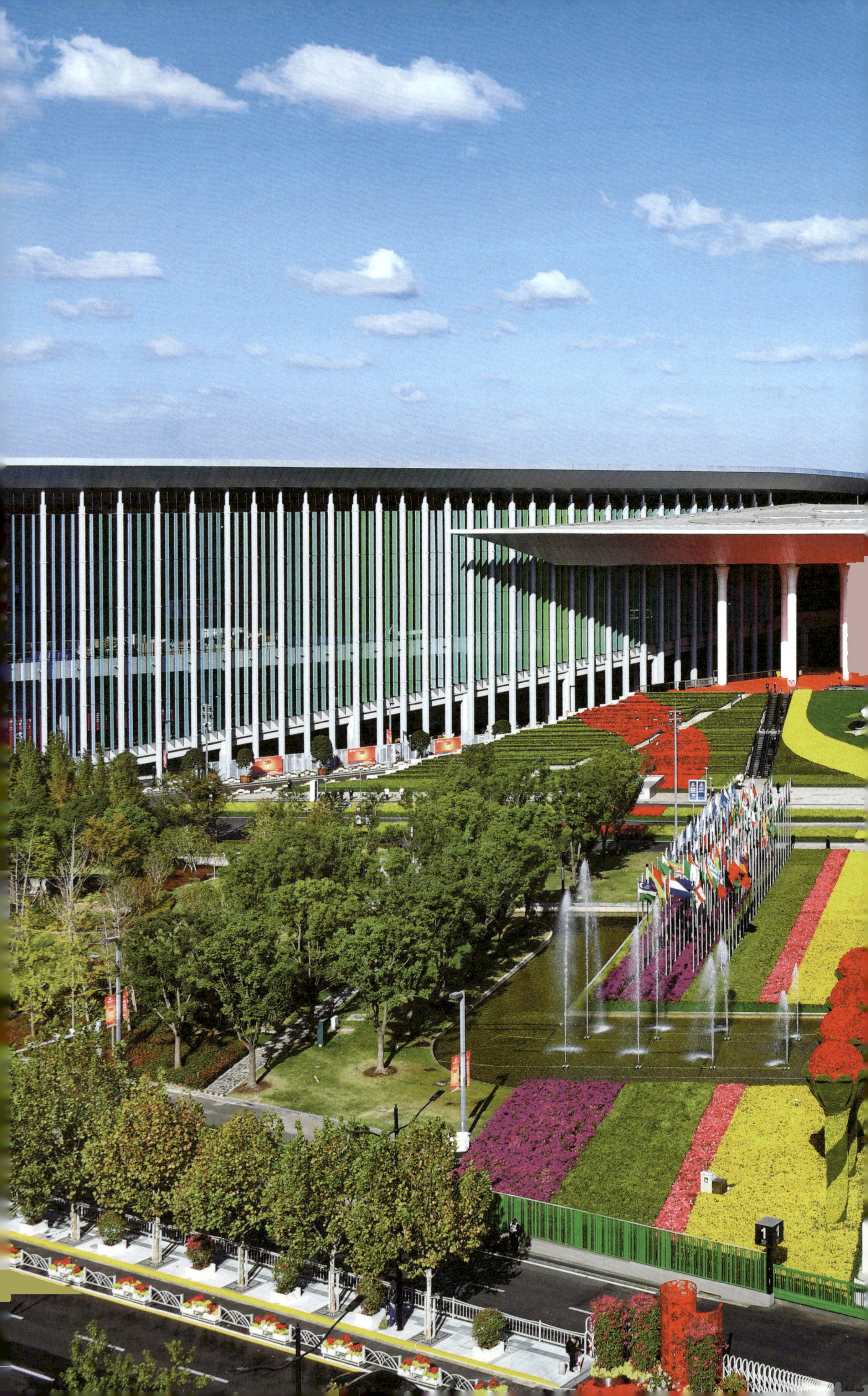

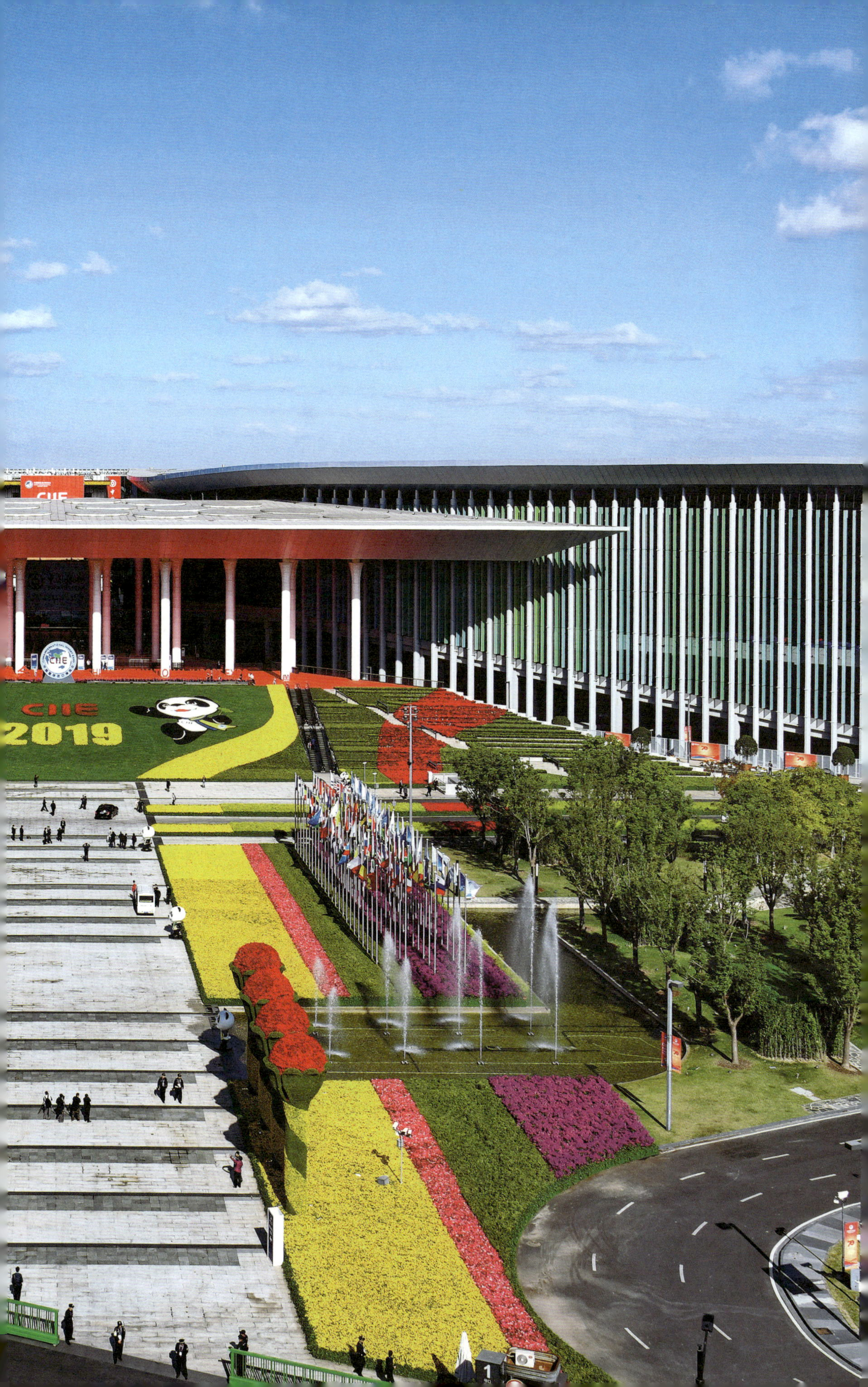
CIIE
2019

1920年毛泽东旧居

姓　　名：Luuk Eliens
中文名：陆可
国　　籍：荷兰
职　　位：XNode 首席商务官

陆可：
我在上海当"梦想推手"

> 我们在好时代里赶上了发展的好时机。中国人民正从这些企业的好项目中受益。

"这里的生活太精彩了，每天都在发生着有意思的事情。"3 年半前，荷兰小伙陆可来到上海开创事业。在这个出生于 1989 年的荷兰小伙眼里，上海是一片充满活力的土地，怀有梦想的人们在这里施展才华。"还有什么事比和一群有想法有创意的人一起工作更吸引人？如果要问我在上海生活的目标，那就是和这些'野心勃勃'的人一起逐梦，一起攀上我们的人生巅峰。"

埋下了闯荡上海的种子

决定来上海，陆可只用了一周时间。

2017 年 4 月，陆可任职的荷兰加速器公司派他来上海开展项目合作。一路从机场到市中心的办公室，城市高楼林立，街道川流不息，都让陆可惊叹不已。"我去过欧洲很多城市，但是在上海，一切都是那么新鲜，一切都在快速运转，我仿佛站到了世界中心。"

在上海的日子里，他的日程表被一个个项目对接会排得满满当当。"看着那些怀揣梦想的人，从会议室里进进出出，为了实现目标而努力'奔跑'，这深深打动了我。"此时的上海正在举办"创业在上海"国际创新创业大赛，近万家企业和团队踊跃报名，火爆程度超过想象。

在那一周里，陆可每天忙忙碌碌，除了办公室和酒店，上海哪里他都没有去成。但正是这段经历在他心里埋下了闯荡上海的种子。

陆可：

我在上海当
"梦想推手"

回到荷兰后，陆可就开始马不停蹄地办理各种离职手续，仅过了两个多月，他就把家搬到了上海。

助推创新者，成就大梦想

来到上海后，陆可担任起 XNode 首席商务官，成为最年轻的"梦想推手"。这是一家面向全球的创新中国引擎平台，通过挖掘好项目、开拓创新渠道，为企业快速发展安上"助推器"，让怀揣"金点子"的创新者们"梦想成真"。

"我们在好时代里赶上了发展的好时机。更重要的是，中国人民正从这些企业的好项目中受益。"与创新者一起改变世界，陆可乐在其中。

英特尔公司有一项 DNA 健康检测系统，通过头发或唾液就能快速筛查早期癌症。"我非常欣赏研发这个项目的工程师，他们雄心勃勃也很努力，让我相信我们可以做得更好。"回忆起和工程师的沟通，陆可说，那是一场激情澎湃的对话。每个人的梦想都是那么清晰，创新思维的碰撞，美好生活的展现，让他当即决定帮助这个项目打开中国市场。

什么才算好项目？陆可的答案是，"能让人们的生活变得更美好"。他在 17 岁时，经常听到荷兰人谈论环境问题，便"脑子一热"创办了一家探查家用电器耗电量的能源企业，人们能通过一套系统查找出家里的"用电大户"，从而减少其使用频率。

"这些能改变人们生活的想法至今看来仍然非常棒，但因为当时我太年轻，没有成熟的商业模式，所以最后都失败了。"陆可笑言，正是一次次"跌倒"，让他意识到，好创意还必须有好推手。

如今，陆可在上海成了一名"梦想推手"，他期待人们在上海这片创业热土上获得成功，成就梦想。

Name: Luuk Eliens
Chinese name: 陆可
Nationality: Dutch
Position: Chief Commercial Officer of XNode

Luuk Eliens:
I am a "dream promoter" in Shanghai

> We have caught up with a good time for development in a good era. Chinese people are benefiting from the good projects of these companies.

"Life here is so brilliant that interesting things happen every day," Luuk Eliens says. Three and a half years ago, the young Dutchman came to Shanghai to start a business. In the eyes of this young man who was born in 1989, Shanghai is a place full of energy and people with dreams come here to showcase their talents. He says: "What could be more attractive than working with a group of people with ideas and creativity? If you ask about my goal of living in Shanghai, my answer will be to chase the dreams with these 'ambitious' people and climb to the top of our lives together."

Preparation for a life of endeavor in Shanghai

It only took Eliens one week to decide on coming to Shanghai.

In April 2017, the Dutch accelerator company where Eliens worked dispatched him to Shanghai to carry out the project cooperation. During the ride from the airport to the office in the city center, Eliens marveled at the city's high-rise buildings and bustling streets. He says: "I've been to many European cities, but in Shanghai, everything is new and running fast. It's like I'm standing in the center of the world."

During his days in Shanghai, his schedule was filled with project matchmaking meetings one after another. He says: "I'm deeply moved by those people with dreams who kept going in and out of the meeting room and tried hard to achieve their goals." At this moment, Shanghai was holding the "Startup in Shanghai" International Innovation and Entrepreneurship Competition with

Luuk Eliens:

I am a "dream promoter" in Shanghai

nearly 10,000 companies and teams enthusiastically signing up. The popularity was beyond imagination.

Eliens was busy every day during that whole week and went nowhere except the office and hotel. But it was this experience that helped prepare for a life of endeavor in Shanghai in his heart.

After returning to the Netherlands, Eliens began various resignation procedures non-stop and moved his family to Shanghai after only two months.

Promoting innovators to fulfill great dreams

After coming to Shanghai, Eliens worked as the Chief Commercial Officer of XNode and became the youngest "dream promoter". This is a Chinese innovative engine platform with a global orientation that provides a "booster" for the rapid development of enterprises by exploring good projects and initiating innovation channels so that the innovators with "golden ideas" can make their dreams come true.

Eliens says: "We have caught up with a good time for development in a good era. What's more, Chinese people are benefiting from the good projects of these companies." He finds happiness in changing the world with innovators.

Intel Corporation has a DNA health testing system that can quickly screen for early-stage cancer through hair or saliva. Eliens says: "I appreciate the engineers who developed this project very much. They are ambitious and hardworking, making me believe that we can do better." Recalling his communication with the engineers, Eliens says that it was a passionate conversation. Everyone's dream was so clear. The collision of innovative thinking and the demonstration of a beautiful life made him immediately decide to promote this project in the Chinese market.

What is a good project? Eliens's answer is "the one that makes peoples' lives better". When he was 17, he often heard Dutch people talking about the environmental problem so he, on the impulse of the moment, established an energy enterprise to detect the power consumption of household appliances. Users can find out the most power-consuming appliances by a system, thus reducing the frequency of use.

"These ideas which can change people's lives still look great today, but they all failed because I was too young at that time and didn't have a mature business model," Eliens says with a smile. It is the repeated "falls" that make him realize that a good idea also takes a good promoter.

Today, Eliens is a "dream promoter" in Shanghai, and he is looking forward to people's success and achieving their dreams in this hotbed of entrepreneurship.

Scan for videos

姓　名：Nishimura Takashi
中文名：西村隆
国　籍：日本
职　位：朝日啤酒（中国）投资有限公司董事总经理

西村隆：
做好中国市场，品质永远是最重要的

上海是我来了就不想离开的城市。

"上海是我来了就不想离开的城市。"站在中信泰富办公室巨大落地窗前，朝日啤酒（中国）投资有限公司董事总经理西村隆俯瞰着脚下川流不息的南京西路繁华街区，内心激荡。自 2009 年来到上海，12 年间见证着这座城市的飞速发展，自己也从一名"中文小白"的 HR，成长为能说一口流利普通话的董事总经理。"奋斗在上海，机遇与挑战并存；生活在上海，便利与高效共享。"西村隆说，自己的未来仍与上海不可分离。

活力上海

2006 年西村隆从东京出差到上海，"没想到上海比东京还要热闹，整个城市充满了朝气。"彼时西村隆眼中的上海正为 2010 年世博会做着准备，城市建设如火如荼，陆家嘴每天都在勾画着新的天际线，老里弄田子坊里开出了一家又一家的创意店铺，游客络绎不绝。

上海的繁华与活力给西村隆留下了深刻印象。当 2009 年朝日啤酒总公司派遣他到上海工作时，一句中文都不会的西村隆欣然接受。为了尽快融入上海，他每天请老师到公司来教授中文，半年下来，他已经能用中文和周围人简单交流了。

克服了语言障碍后，西村隆热情地拥抱起上海的生活，去酒吧、学茶道、练瑜伽；周末徒步在七宝老街、南翔古镇，以各种角度了解上海；到了节假日，搭上高铁就往"一小时同城圈"跑，去苏州逛园子、到杭州游西湖……

西村隆一边尽情体验这里的丰富多彩，一边积极探索上海的消费市场。

西村隆：
做好中国市场，
品质永远是最
重要的

经过一段时间摸索后，他发现上海消费者视野开阔、观念新颖，乐于接受国际化品牌，对产品的要求也非常高。

想要干出一番事业的西村隆坚定了扎根上海的信心。

营商上海

深耕上海市场十几年，西村隆亲历上海营商环境的持续改善。尤其是在去年全球新冠肺炎疫情蔓延背景下，上海市政府先后出台多项惠企政策，不断优化营商环境，打出多套"组合拳"，提振经济复苏的决心和魄力让西村隆印象深刻。在此期间，朝日啤酒响应上海市政府复工复产的号召，推动"夜市经济"发展，在公司附近的安义夜巷也"摆摊"卖起了啤酒。"那时候气温凉凉，完全不是啤酒销售的好季节，但是看到政府那么努力地在恢复经济，我们也都跟着有一股子干劲。"

"上海是我们在中国最重要的市场。"西村隆十分认可上海政府的高效和周到服务，"让外商可以放心地在这里投资"。

眼下，上海正大力推进全方位高水平开放，国内首部地方外商投资条例《上海市外商投资条例》也于去年11月落地实施，进一步实现"对标国际最高标准、最好水平"打造国际一流营商环境的目标。

每年，上海还会举办许多大型展会，企业从中能找到不少发展良机。"不少日本连锁企业负责人和我聊起过投资中国的愿望，我告诉他们，做好中国市场，品质永远是最重要的。"西村隆说。

Name: Nishimura Takashi
Chinese name: 西村隆
Nationality: Japanese
Position: President of Asahi Beer(China) Investment Co., Ltd.

Nishimura Takashi:
Quality is always the most important concern for doing a good job in the Chinese market

Shanghai is a city that I don't want to leave once I come here.

"Shanghai is a city that I don't want to leave once I come here," says Takashi. Standing in front of the huge French window of his CITIC Pacific office, Nishimura Takashi, Managing Director of Asahi Beer (China) Investment Co., Ltd., overlooks the bustling streets of West Nanjing Road at his feet, filled with surging emotion. In the 12 years since he came to Shanghai in 2009, he has witnessed the rapid development of the city and he has grown from an HR who could barely speak Chinese to a fluent Mandarin-speaking managing director. He says: "For people struggling in Shanghai, opportunities and challenges coexist; for those living in Shanghai, convenience and efficiency are both available. And my future is inseparable from Shanghai."

Vitality in Shanghai

In 2006, Takashi went to Shanghai on a business trip from Tokyo. "I didn't expect Shanghai to be livelier than Tokyo, and the whole city is full of dynamism," says Takashi. At that time, Shanghai was preparing for the 2010 World Expo, and the city construction was in full swing. Lujiazui had a new skyline every day, and one creative shop after another was opened in Tianzifang, one of the old neighborhoods of Shanghai, attracting a host of tourists.

The prosperity and vitality of Shanghai left a deep impression on Takashi. When Asahi Beer Corporation sent him to work in Shanghai in 2009, he readily accepted it though he could not speak any Chinese. In order to integrate into the city life here as soon as possible, he hired teachers to come to his company to teach him Chinese every day. Half a year later, he was able to communicate with people around in simple Chinese.

Nishimura Takashi:

Quality is always the most important concern for doing a good job in the Chinese market

After overcoming the language barrier, Takashi enthusiastically embraced life in Shanghai, going to bars, learning the Chinese tea ceremonies and practicing yoga. He would go hiking on Qibao Old Street or in Nanxiang Old Town on weekends to learn about the city from various angles. On holidays, taking advantage of the "one-hour commuting circle" in the Yangtze River Delta, he would take the high-speed train to Suzhou to visit the Chinese gardens, or to Hangzhou to visit West Lake.

Takashi actively explored Shanghai's consumer market while enjoying the rich life here. From his investigation into the local market, he found that Shanghai consumers, with a broad vision and novel concepts, readily accept international brands and have very high requirements for products.

Resolved to do something great here, he has strengthened his confidence in working and living in Shanghai.

Doing business in Shanghai

With intensive business operations in the Shanghai market for more than ten years, Takashi experienced the continuous improvement of Shanghai's business environment. During the COVID-19 pandemic last year, in particular, the Shanghai Municipal Government successively issued a number of policies to benefit enterprises, continuously optimizing the business environment and taking strong measures to boost economic recovery. Takashi was deeply impressed by the government's determination and courage. During this period, Asahi Beer Corporation, in response to the call of the Shanghai Municipal Government to resume work and production and to develop a night-market economy, set up stalls to sell beer in Anyi Night Market near the company. "At that time, the temperature was cool and it was not a good season for beer sales at all, but seeing the government working so hard to restore the economy, we all followed the drive," he says.

"Shanghai is our most important market in China," Takashi says, fully recognizing the efficient and thoughtful service of the Shanghai government. "Foreign investors can then invest here with confidence."

At present, Shanghai is vigorously promoting all-round and high-level opening up, and the first local foreign investment regulation, the Regulations of Shanghai Municipality on Foreign Investment, was implemented in November last year to further achieve the goal of building an international first-class business environment "in line with the highest and best international standards."

Many large-scale exhibitions are held every year in Shanghai, from which enterprises can find many good opportunities for development. "Many heads of Japanese chain companies talked to me about their desire to invest in China. I told them that quality is always the most important concern for doing a good job in the Chinese market," says Takashi.

姓　名：Naomie Fortin
国　籍：加拿大
职　位：卢湾高级中学 BC 课程部负责人

Naomie：
我希望让我的中国学生们更富创造力，更具责任感

我希望给中国的学生们充实"人际沟通""批判型思维""社会责任感"这三大"软实力"。

上海已成为我的家乡

"我在上海生活了 5 年，这里已经成为了我的家乡。回加拿大，对我来说更像是去旅游。"来自加拿大蒙特利尔的 Naomie Fortin 笑声爽朗，充满朝气。作为上海市卢湾高级中学 BC 课程部负责人，她既是上海教育改革的参与者，也从改革创新形成的制度成果中受益匪浅。

在卢高 BC 班，Naomie 能轻松叫出每个学生的名字，课堂讨论或是闲谈时，学生们都爱围绕在这个加拿大大姐姐身边。在执教卢湾高中前，Naomie 就有着丰富的教学经验，她曾在加拿大、韩国教授英文，2012 年来到中国后，又在郑州和常州的国际学校里担任过首席教师。

"2013 年我还在郑州时就来过上海。第一次见到外滩、陆家嘴、新天地，还去了田子坊，这座城市太不一样了。"尽管匆匆造访，但上海给 Naomie 留下了深刻印象。后来到常州任教，她常常趁周末搭上高铁就"飞"来上海。"你知道常州到上海的高铁有多快吗！我太爱上海了。后来我问自己，为什么不留下呢？"从那以后，Naomie 就开始留意上海的教育岗位，2016 年，一个合适的机会让 Naomie 把她的人生舞台正式转到了上海。

Naomie 转战上海，适逢上海大力推进教育综合改革，其中一项重要内容就是实施教育国际化工程。这既是上海建设国际化大都市的必然选择，也是满足上海市民多样化教育需求的重要举措。目前，上海有 20 多所高中

Naomie:
我希望让我的中国学生们更富创造力，更具责任感

开设了国际课程班，为上海市高中阶段学生提供"中外融合"国际课程教育教学服务。足不出沪也能"留学"，对于上海的家长和学生来说已成现实。

Naomie 的教学新尝试

"不同于传统教学模式，卢高 BC 班的课程在形式和内容上有很多创新尝试。"聊起教学话题时，Naomie 严肃而专注。在她的课堂上，会讨论许多有意思的话题，比如"如何进行自我认同""怎样做个好'网民'"等等，这些话题需要学生自己来探索方向，寻找破题路径。

Naomie 还打破了传统年级边界，把高一至高三年级的学生混入一个大班中，3 人一组自由探讨。"这样分组的意义在于能让低年级学生在小组中学习高年级学生相对成熟的思维模式，而高年级学生则会在小组中锻炼领导力。"

相比语数外，她更希望给中国的学生们充实"人际沟通""批判型思维""社会责任感"这三大"软实力"。"这对孩子们的未来至关重要。"Naomie说，卢高 BC 班的教学理念是让学生们变得更独立、更富有创造力，与此同时，让学生们在团队合作中学会为他人着想，承担起对自己、对他人、对社会的责任感。"这一理念将贯穿当下，更为他们将来的学习和职业生涯做好充足准备。"

"上海是个国际大都市，文化多元而互相包容，城市风貌新旧交融，地方特色和世界美食都能轻易找到。"Naomie 和她的外籍同事们在上海生活得很愉快，因为来自靠近北极圈的加拿大蒙特利尔，上海的冬天 Naomie 觉得特别舒服，整年她都乐享户外活动。

"即使冬天，我都能骑自行车上下班，这的确很幸福。"

Name: Naomie Fortin
Nationality: Canadian
Position: Principal of Luwan Senior High School BC Offshore Program

Naomie Fortin:
I hope to make my Chinese students more creative and responsible

I hope to enrich Chinese students with three soft powers: "interpersonal communication", "critical thinking" and "social responsibility."

Shanghai having become my hometown

"I've been living in Shanghai for five years and it has become my hometown. To me, going back to Canada is more like travelling," says Naomie Fortin from Montreal, Canada, laughing heartily. As the principal of the BC Offshore Program of Shanghai Luwan Senior High School, she has not only participated in Shanghai's education reform but also benefited a lot from the institutional outcomes brought by reform and innovation.

In the class of the BC Offshore Program, Fortin can remember everyone's name. Students like to surround this Canadian "big sister" in both in-class discussion or post-class chat. Before teaching at Luwan Senior High School, Fortin has already been experienced in teaching. She has once taught English in Canada and South Korea. After coming to China in 2012, she has worked as the chief teacher in the international schools in Zhengzhou and Changzhou.

Fortin says: "I've traveled to Shanghai in 2013 when I was working in Zhengzhou. That was my first time to see the Bund, Lujiazui, Xintiandi and Tianzifang; the city is so different." Despite a hasty visit, Shanghai impressed Fortin a lot. Later, she went to Changzhou to teach and often took advantage of the weekends to "fly" to Shanghai by taking the high-speed train. She says: "Do you know how fast the train from Changzhou to Shanghai is? I love Shanghai so much that I asked myself: why not stay?" From then on, Fortin began to keep an eye on the education positions in Shanghai and 2016, an appropriate opportunity allowed Fortin to officially move to Shanghai.

Naomie Fortin:

I hope to make my Chinese students more creative and responsible

Fortin's move to Shanghai comes at a time when the city is vigorously promoting comprehensive education reform, one of the key elements of which is the implementation of the Education Internationalization Project. This is a natural choice for Shanghai to become an international metropolis, and an important step in meeting the diverse educational needs of the city's citizens. At present, more than 20 high schools in Shanghai offer international classes, providing "Chinese and foreign" international curriculum education and teaching services for high school students in Shanghai. "Studying abroad" without leaving Shanghai is now a reality for parents and students in Shanghai.

Ms. Fortin's new experiments in teaching

"Different from the traditional teaching model, many innovative attempts have been made in form and content in BC Offshore Program," says Fortin. Fortin is serious and focused when it comes to teaching topics. Many interesting topics are discussed in her class such as "self-identity", "a good netizen" and so on, all of which require the students to explore and learn to solve problems by themselves.

Fortin also breaks the traditional grade boundary by mixing the students from Grade One to Grade Three into a large class and ask them to discuss freely in groups of three. "The point of such grouping is to allow the lower grade students to learn the relatively mature mindset of the higher grade students while the latter can exercise their leadership in groups," says Fortin.

Compared to learning Chinese, Mathematics and Foreign Languages, she hopes the most to enrich Chinese students with three soft powers: "interpersonal communication", "critical thinking" and "social responsibility". "They are crucial to the children's future," Fortin says. The teaching philosophy of the BC Offshore Program is to make the students more independent and creative and at the same time, they can learn to be considerate of others in group cooperation and be responsible for themselves, others and society. "This idea is implemented in their present life and will help them make adequate preparations for their future learning and careers," she says.

Fortin says: "Shanghai is an international metropolis with a diverse and inclusive culture. The city blends the old and the new, and local specialties and world cuisines can be easily found." Fortin and her foreign colleagues live happily in Shanghai. She finds the winter in Shanghai particularly comfortable compared to her hometown, Montreal, Canada, which is close to the Arctic Circle. She can enjoy outdoor activities all year round here.

Fortin says: "Even in winter, I can commute to work by bicycle. This is indeed very pleasant."

姓　名：A.A.M. Muzahid
中文名：安东尼
国　籍：孟加拉国
职　位：上海大学通信与信息工程学院博士研究生

安东尼：
在上海，我感觉自己离梦想更近了

上海是我的第二故乡，我非常喜欢这座城市，我会努力学习，争取留在上海！

在上海，离梦想更近

在孟加拉国的时候，安东尼就对上海这座城市心生向往。2017年，安东尼来到上海求学。他说："在上海，我感觉自己离梦想更近了。"

新中国成立以来，中国的高等教育走过了规模从小到大、实力从弱到强的历程，办学规模、培养质量、服务能力都实现了历史性跃升。尤其是党的十八大以来，我国高等教育与祖国共进、与时代同行，创造了举世瞩目的发展成就。

"你可以在上海的几所一流大学里接受世界一流的教育，与此同时，上海还是一个国际化的大都市，有很多外国人生活在这里，是一个跨文化交流的好地方。"安东尼认为正是因为这些优势，上海才成了他心目中留学的最佳选择地。

"来到上海之后，这里的一切果然没有让我失望。我喜欢上海大学，这里不仅有雄厚的师资力量，还有支持前沿研究的实验室与专项资金。"安东尼坦言："我不仅在这里学习到了前沿科学，还结识了很多上海朋友，他们有着友善温柔、乐于助人、开放包容的优良品质。"学习之余，安东尼很爱社交，他说上海朋友教会了他很多为人处世的道理。

安东尼：

在上海，我感觉自己离梦想更近了

中孟之间的友好情谊令我动容

孟加拉国地处丝绸之路经济带和21世纪海上丝绸之路交汇处，是共建"一带一路"的重要参与者。"自孟加拉国参与共建'一带一路'以来，已经实施了多个项目，每个项目都创造了大量就业岗位，这不仅促进了孟加拉国经济的腾飞，也改善了民生。"安东尼认为："尽管孟加拉国经济的飞速发展有多重原因，但'一带一路'倡议是其中一个重要的原因，这是一项多赢的倡议。"

疫情期间，安东尼多次组织孟加拉国学生为学校捐款捐物，"疫情之下，中孟两国之间的友好情谊让我动容，我觉得自己应该做点什么，为搭起孟加拉国与中国友谊的桥梁添砖加瓦。"

安东尼希望自己能成为一名优秀的院士。"上海是我的第二故乡，我非常喜欢这座城市，我会努力学习，争取留在上海！"

Name: A.A.M. Muzahid
Chinese name: 安东尼
Nationality: Bangladeshi
Position: Ph.D. candidate at School of Communication and Information Engineering, Shanghai University

A.A.M. Muzahid:
In Shanghai, I feel closer to my dream

> Shanghai is my second hometown and I love this city very much. I'll study hard and strive for staying in Shanghai.

Getting closer to his dreams in Shanghai

Muzahid had a longing for Shanghai when in Bangladesh and he came here to pursue his studies in 2017. "In Shanghai, I feel closer to my dream," he says.

Since the founding of the People's Republic of China, higher education has gone through the process from small to large in scale and weak to strong in power. Historical leap has been achieved in terms of school scale, cultivation quality and service capability. Especially since the 18th National Congress of the Communist Party of China, China's higher education has progressed with the motherland and kept pace with time, creating world-renowned development achievements.

Muzahid says: "You can have the world-class education from the top-ranking universities in Shanghai, and at the same time, Shanghai is an international metropolis with a lot of foreigners living here, making it a good place for cross-cultural communication." He believes that it is these advantages that make Shanghai the best choice for studying abroad in his mind.

Muzahid says: "After coming to Shanghai, I found everything here lived up to my expectation. I love Shanghai University not only for its strong faculty, but the labs and special funds to support frontier research as well. I have learned cutting-edge science here and made many local friends who are kind, gentle, obliging, open and tolerant." In his spare time, Muzahid is very sociable and he says that his friends in Shanghai teach him a lot about how to deal with people.

A.A.M. Muzahid:

In Shanghai, I feel closer to my dream

Touched by the friendship between China and Bangladesh

Located at the intersection of the Silk Road Economic Belt and the 21st Century Maritime Silk Road, Bangladesh is an important participant in the joint building of the Belt and Road. Muzahid says: "Since Bangladesh's participation, a range of projects have been implemented and each of them has created a large number of employment positions, which has not only contributed to Bangladesh's economic takeoff but also improved people's well-being. Although there are multiple reasons for Bangladesh's rapid economic development, the Belt and Road Initiative is one of the most important ones. This is a multi-win initiative."

During the pandemic, Muzahid has organized many times the Bangladeshi students to donate funds and items to the school. "I am deeply moved by the friendship between China and Bangladesh during the pandemic, so I think I should do something to contribute more to the friendship between the two countries," says Muzahid.

Muzahid hopes that he can be an excellent academician in the future. He says: "Shanghai is my second hometown and I love this city very much. I'll study hard and strive for staying in Shanghai."

姓　名：Laurent Kneip
中文名：康智文
国　籍：卢森堡
职　位：上海科技大学信息学院研究员、副教授

康智文：
上海蓬勃的科研环境吸引着全球的优秀人才

> 在我去过的城市中，我只推荐上海，我对上海的评价非常高。

"我叫劳伦特·克奈普，我有两个中文名——劳伦特和康智文。"38岁的上海科技大学信息学院研究员、副教授康智文能说一口不错的中文，他在学校创立并领导了移动感知实验室，关注智能移动设备，如自动驾驶汽车。"某种程度上，我们和埃隆·马斯克拥有同样的愿景，即制造一辆不使用激光雷达而只使用摄像头的自动驾驶汽车。"

关注智能驾驶技术

康智文介绍，激光雷达和相机的不同之处在于，激光雷达可以直接感知环境的深度，而相机只能通过投影到平面上来感知环境的外观。他不确定马斯克所说任何押注激光雷达的人将来都注定失败是否正确，但至少从科学和经济的角度来看，依靠相机能实现哪些功能，这仍然是一个非常有趣的话题。

"在移动感知实验室，我们结合了对新型生物视觉传感器、传统几何方法、人工智能和应用驱动的硬件（如环视停车辅助系统）的研究。我们的工作直接促成了一个问题的解决，即自动代客停车。"

经过三年的努力，他的移动感知实验室已经取得了一些突出的成就，例如最近在计算机视觉和模式识别大会（IEEE/CVF）上发表文章，以及

康智文：

上海蓬勃的科研
环境吸引着全球
的优秀人才

在模式识别和机器智能领域的 IEEE 会刊上发表文章。

科研环境有吸引力

康智文在上海已有 4 年多了，他的妻子是中国人，也在上海工作。他认为中国正在迅速发展，对科研人员而言充满机遇。"上海科技大学就是一个很好的例子。这所大学吸引在职业生涯早期的优秀研究人员加入，提供充满了蓬勃生机的科研环境和丰富的资金支持，使我们能实现独立研究。这里也是一个开放的平台，有很多国际交流的机会，非常鼓励多样性，我在这里感到非常开心。"

"上海正投入大量资金进行科研，尽可能给科研人员提供全球最好的基础设施"，康智文分析，从整个国家来说，在月球背面着陆或迅速开发可靠的新冠疫苗等也清楚地证明了中国对科研人员充满机遇。

城市充满新鲜感

康智文在欧洲一个小村庄长大，因而，在他的感知里，中国的城市是庞大而热闹的。初到上海的兴奋劲已经过去，取而代之的是一种亲切感，但这座城市充满活力，日新月异，因而，康智文始终充满新鲜感。

在他看来，上海这座城市很特别，浦西和浦东设法在传统和现代之间取得了良好的平衡。而上海人非常友好，他们知道如何努力工作，同时享受生活；他们也知道如何坚持积极的价值观，同时拥抱有益的新价值观。

"在我去过的城市中，我只推荐上海，我对上海的评价非常高。"

Name: Laurent Kneip
Chinese name: 康智文
Nationality: Luxemburger
Position: Associate Professor of SIST, ShanghaiTech University

Laurent Kneip:
Shanghai's vibrant research environment attracts talents from all over the world

Among the cities I've been to, I only recommend Shanghai, which I think highly of.

"My name is Laurent Kneip and I have two Chinese names—Lao Lunte and Kang Zhiwen," says the 38-year-old associate professor of SIST, ShanghaiTech University, who speaks good Chinese. He founded and led the mobile conception lab which focuses on smart mobile devices such as self-driving cars. "To some degree, we have the same vision as Elon Musk, that is, to make a self-driving car that doesn't use LIDAR but only cameras," says Kneip.

Focusing on intelligent driving technology

Kneip says that the difference between LIDAR and the camera is that LIDAR can directly perceive the depth of the environment while the camera can only perceive the appearance of the environment through the projection on the plane. He is not sure whether Elon Musk's claim that anyone relying on LIDAR is doomed is correct, but at least from a scientific and economic point of view, what functions can be achieved through cameras is still a very interesting topic.

Kneip says: "Researches on new-type biological vision sensor, traditional geometric method, artificial intelligence and application-driven hardware (like the surround-view parking auxiliary system) have been combined in the mobile perception lab. Our work has directly contributed to the solution of the automated valet parking problem."

After three years of hard work, his lab has made some outstanding achievements, such as the articles published on the IEEE/CVF Conference on

Laurent Kneip:

Shanghai's vibrant research environment attracts talents from all over the world

Computer Vision and Pattern Recognition and IEEE Proceedings of Pattern Recognition and Machine Intelligence.

Attractive scientific research environment

Kneip has been in Shanghai for more than four years and his wife, a Chinese woman, also works here. He believes China's rapid development offers plenty of opportunities for researchers. He says: "ShanghaiTech University is a good example. It attracts the participation of excellent academics who are still at the early stage of their careers and provides a vibrant research environment and abundant financial support, enabling us to carry on independent research. It is also an open platform with many international exchange opportunities, which encourages diversity. I feel very happy here."

"Large amounts of money have been invested in scientific research and researchers are provided with the best possible infrastructure in the world in Shanghai," Kneip says, adding that from the perspective of the whole country, the landing on the far side of the moon or the rapid development of reliable COVID-19 vaccines is also clear evidence that to researchers, China is full of opportunities.

A city full of freshness

Kneip grew up in a small village in Europe so he finds cities in China to be large and lively. The initial excitement of his first arrival in Shanghai has passed and is replaced by a sense of intimacy, but the city is vibrant and ever-changing, so it is still new to Kneip every day.

In his view, Shanghai is a special city with Puxi and Pudong striking a nice balance between the traditional and the modern. Being friendly, people in Shanghai know how to work hard and enjoy life at the same time. They also know how to stick to positive values and meanwhile, embrace beneficial new values.

"Among the cities I've been to, I only recommend Shanghai, which I think highly of," Kneip says.

姓　名：Abbigael Clarissa Ford
中文名：小艾
国　籍：英国
职　位：上海康德双语实验学校外籍教师

小艾：
我们培养孩子们的身份认同感，让他们知道要爱护自己的国家

我们希望能培养孩子们的身份认同感，让他们知道自己是中国人，要爱护自己的国家。

她，有着对学生的关爱，对工作的热情，对生活的热爱；她，惊讶于上海鳞次栉比的高楼大厦，漫步在绿树成阴的市民公园，享受着这座城市便捷惬意的生活……她，就是任教于上海康德双语实验学校的外教小艾。

"上海是个不可思议的地方"

两年半前，小艾来到上海。出发前，亲朋好友非常舍不得这个甜美开朗的女孩。"不过后来他们意识到，这或许是一件奇妙的事，因为他们可以来中国看望我了。在我的家乡，人们认为上海是一个很酷、很时髦的地方。"正如小艾想的那样，这些年不少朋友来此探望她后，纷纷表示"上海是个不可思议的地方"。

小艾来自英国中西部的一个小乡村，那里有着大片的田野与草原。"这也是我来到上海后非常兴奋的原因，这里有很多高楼大厦。"她说道。上海便捷的生活和丰富多样的美食令她着迷，并且在这座城市里，可以和来自世界各地的人们打交道，能接触到多元文化，这令她十分激动。

每当小艾想念家乡青草的气息与摇曳的树影，想要短暂逃离都市生活时，她便会去复兴公园漫步。"那里绿草青青，空气清新，是我最喜欢的地

> 小艾：
> 我们培养孩子们的身份认同感，让他们知道要爱护自己的国家

方之一。"小艾如数家珍道，人们可以在公园中心的小咖啡馆里休憩，听爷叔们演奏爵士乐，看阿姨们忘情地舞蹈……所有人都在享受着生活。

谈及为何会选择来上海做老师，小艾说，她在英国时就读于顶尖私立名校英国康德学院——上海康德双语实验学校的姐妹学校。"听到学院要和上海学校合作的消息，我特别高兴，希望可以借此机会来中国教书，于是便递交了申请。"2018年小艾来到上海，加入了上海康德双语实验学校的大家庭，担任英语老师。这就是她和上海、和中国缘分的起点。

中国的学生非常具有上进心

来到中国的时间并不长，但这名英国女孩很快就被源远流长的中国文化所吸引。现在，了解中国、学习汉语，已成为了她的一种爱好。

作为七年级的年级组长，小艾会组织学生开展PSHE，即个人社会健康教育。她希望通过这样一种新式教育，让学生掌握更多学习技能，学会如何更好地与人交流。与此同时，学校不定期开展德育，举办爱国主义歌唱、诗朗诵比赛。"我们希望能培养孩子们的身份认同感，让他们知道自己是中国人，要爱护自己的国家。"

人们常说，教育是最大的民生。2012年，新一届中央政治局常委首次集体亮相，习近平总书记以"十个更好"回应人民关切，"更好的教育"赫然排在首位。在小艾眼中，中国的教育水平位于世界中上行列，并且教育质量正迅速提升，尤其是在上海这样的大都市。

此前，上海的数学教师登上英国课堂，上海的数学教辅书也在英国出版。小艾表示，不同地方的教育进行交流与研讨，或是资源共享与互换，这一点非常重要。

小艾是学生口中的"学霸老师"，严谨却亲切，她的课堂上总是充满欢声笑语。这位英国老师眼中的中国学生又是怎样的呢？

小艾提到了两个关键词："上进"与"尊敬"，"我认为中国学生非常有上进心，并且他们对老师、对整个教育都怀有一颗敬畏之心，这可能是中国学生能在学术上取得成功的原因之一"。

Name: Abbigael Clarissa Ford
Chinese name: 小艾
Nationality: British
Position: Foreign teacher of Shanghai Concord Bilingual School

Abbigael Clarissa Ford:

We hope to foster the children's sense of identity and make them aware that they are Chinese and shall cherish their country

We hope to foster the children's sense of identity and make them fully aware that they are Chinese and shall love their country.

She has a great affection for her students, enthusiasm for work and love for life. She is amazed by the numerous high-rise buildings in Shanghai. She loves strolling in the tree-lined parks and she enjoys the convenience and comfort that the city can offer. She is a young woman named Abbigael Clarissa Ford or Abbi, a foreign teacher of Shanghai Concord Bilingual School.

"Shanghai is an incredible place"

Abbi came to Shanghai two and a half years ago. Before departure, her relatives and friends were very reluctant to see their sweet and cheerful girl leave. "But then they realized that this may be a wonderful thing because they can come to China to visit me. In my hometown, people think Shanghai is a cool and fashionable place," she says. As Abbi had expected, after many of her friends came to visit her over the years, they all said that "Shanghai is an incredible place".

Abbi comes from a small village in the Midwest of Britain, where there are large fields and grasslands. "This is also why I am very excited after coming to Shanghai. There are many high-rise buildings here," she says. She is fascinated by the ease of living in Shanghai and the richness and variety of its cuisine, and is thrilled to be in a city where she can meet people from all over the world and be exposed to diverse cultures.

Whenever Abbi misses the smell of grass and swaying trees in her

Abbigael Clarissa Ford:

We hope to foster the children's sense of identity and make them aware that they are Chinese and shall cherish their country

hometown and wants to escape from urban life for a short time, she will go for a stroll in Fuxing Park. She says: "It is one of my favorite places with green grass and fresh air." She adds that people can relax in the little cafe in the center of the park, listen to Shanghai men play jazz, and watch Shanghai women dance to their hearts' content. Everyone is enjoying life.

Talking about why she chose to be a teacher in Shanghai, Abbi says that she once studied at Concord College, a top private school in the UK and a sister school of Shanghai Concord Bilingual School. "I am very happy to hear that the college is going to cooperate with schools in Shanghai. I hope to take this opportunity to teach in China, so I submitted my application," she says. In 2018, Abbi came to Shanghai and joined the big family of Shanghai Concord Bilingual School as an English teacher. This is the beginning of her relationship with Shanghai and with China, as fate would have it.

Chinese students are highly motivated

She hasn't been in China for long, but this British girl is soon attracted by the profound Chinese culture. Now, understanding China and learning Chinese have become one of her hobbies.

As the leader of Grade 7, Abbi organizes PSHE, that is, Personal, Social, Health, Education, for her students. She hopes that through such a new type of education, students can master more learning skills and learn how to communicate better with others. At the same time, schools carry out moral education from time to time and hold patriotic singing and poetry recitation competitions. "We hope to foster the children's sense of identity and make them aware that they are Chinese and shall cherish their country," she says.

It is often said that education is the greatest livelihood. In 2012, the new Standing Committee of the Political Bureau of the CPC Central Committee made its debut. General Secretary Xi Jinping responded to people's concerns with "ten better" measures, and "better education" came first. In Abbi's eyes, China's education level ranks among the upper middle of the world, and the quality of education is rapidly improving, especially in metropolitan cities like Shanghai.

Previously, Shanghai's math teachers were invited to teach in British classrooms, and Shanghai's math instructional materials were also published in the UK. Abbi says that it is very important for education institutions in different places to communicate and conduct seminars together, or to share and exchange resources.

Rigorous but kind, Abbi is what students call a "Xueba (high-flyer) teacher". Her class is always full of laughter. What, then, are the Chinese students like in the eyes of this British teacher?

Abbi has mentioned two keywords: "motivated" and "respectful". She says: "They take their learning very seriously and they have a great deal of respect for teachers and education as a whole. I think that's related to the academic success of the Chinese students."

姓　名：Michael Kruppe
中文名：迈克尔
国　籍：德国
职　位：上海新国际博览中心有限公司总经理

迈克尔：
我是半个浦东人，用音乐来表达对上海的爱

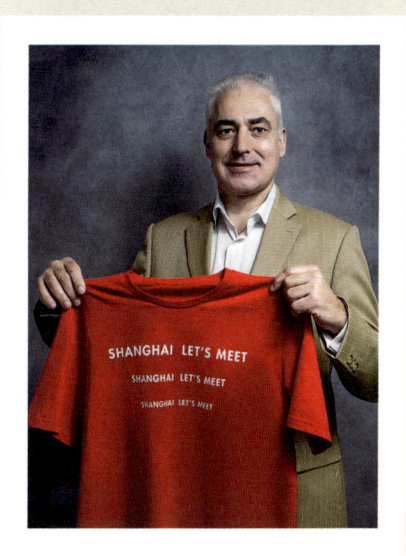

> 在中国，很多人都不止步于已有的成就，而总是会往前看一步，去试想在未来四到五年中会发生些什么。

　　上海新国际博览中心有限公司（以下简称新博）总经理迈克尔在接受采访时，面对镜头侃侃而谈。来到上海 31 年的他，见证了会展行业的发展以及这座城市的巨大变化。如今工作、生活在浦东的他认为自己已经是"半个浦东人"了。

　　这位运营着"全世界最繁忙的会展中心之一"的大忙人，还有着令人意想不到的另一重身份——摇滚乐队 Shanghigh Voltage 的成员。

　　组建乐队，弹着吉他唱着歌，迈克尔用音乐表达着自己对上海的喜爱。

期盼全球早日"面对面"

　　"Face to face,face to face, nothing can replace face to face。"5 年前，迈克尔成立了一支摇滚乐队，名为 Shanghigh Voltage。这首由迈克尔创作的歌曲《Face to face》诞生于新冠肺炎疫情期间。"我创作这首歌曲，是为了激励世界各地的人们不要沮丧。要相信不久的将来，大家都可以像我们在中国这样面对面交流。"

　　谈到为何会起这样一个乐队名，迈克尔解释道："我们想把'上海'融入乐队名中，不过'hai'非'海'，而是'high'（高）。'Voltage'是力量的意思，加起来就是上海和力量。"

　　2020 年，新冠肺炎疫情的影响波及各行各业，而以人员流动、集结、"面

迈克尔：

我是半个浦东人，
用音乐来表达对
上海的爱

对面"为主要特征的会展业首当其冲。迈克尔直呼新博是幸运的，去年新博共举办 83 场展会，接待超 300 万名访客，而且未出现一例新冠确诊病例，成功的背后离不开各方努力。新博制定了严密的安全方案，并购买了如红外测温仪等各类设备，以应对挑战。

"去年疫情的时候，政府给了我们莫大的帮助，包括警方、商务委，还有卫健委、消防等，很多政府部门帮我们一起制定了这份安全计划。"在迈克尔眼中，无论过去还是将来，与政府合作对新博而言都相当重要。

见证浦东腾飞奇迹

在迈克尔眼中，上海就像他的故乡德国汉堡一样，都有港口和一条贯穿城市的河流。"由于港口的缘故，我的故乡在国际贸易方面实力雄厚，上海也是如此。"

1989 年第一次踏足上海，迈克尔便对这座城市"一见钟情"。当时迈克尔住在和平饭店，俯瞰黄浦江对岸，"那时浦东并不发达，我印象里就是一大片空地，再有几个工厂"。

正如迈克尔所说，20 世纪 80 年代的浦东与现在的繁华景象相差甚远。1990 年，一项重大的国家战略——浦东开发开放，把浦东推向了我国改革开放的最前沿。在国家战略的牵引下，这片土地从阡陌农田纵横到摩天高楼林立。东方明珠、上海中心；陆家嘴金融区、上海自贸区……

迈克尔见证了浦东开发的"高度"，体验了浦东开放的"广度"。

亲历会展业快速发展

"在会展业务收益、展会数量指标上，中国已经超越了欧美国家。"迈克尔举例道，正在加速打造世界会展之都的上海，各类专业展览展馆可供展览面积超过 100 万平方米，位列全球主要会展城市第一。

来到中国 30 多年，迈克尔见证了中国市场的韧性发展，在他看来，和欧美不同的是，在中国，很多人都不止步于已有的成就，而总是会往前看一步，去试想在未来四到五年中会发生些什么。

"有了中国人的这种工作精神，以及在开发新产品和服务方面的创意，再加上政府的支持，我很确信更多的国外公司会看到中国市场的增长潜力，来这里投资。"

Name: Michael Kruppe
Chinese name: 迈克尔
Nationality: German
Position: General Manager of Shanghai New International Expo Center

Michael Kruppe:
I am almost a Pudong native now, and I express my love for Shanghai with music

> In China, many people refuse to settle for what they have achieved, but always to look ahead to see what will happen in the next four to five years.

Michael Kruppe, General Manager of Shanghai New International Expo Center (SNIEC), has been in Shanghai for 31 years and witnessed the development of the exhibition industry and the city's great changes. Nowadays, working and living in Pudong, he regards himself as almost a Pudong native.

Everyone can talk to each other "face to face"

"Face to face, face to face, nothing can replace face to face," he sings. Five years ago, the busy German running one of the busiest exhibition centers in the world started a rock band named Shanghigh Voltage. The song "Face to Face" was written by Kruppe during the COVID-19 pandemic. He says: "I wrote this song to inspire people around the world not to be depressed, and to trust that in the near future, everyone can talk to each other face to face, like us here in China."

In 2020, the COVID-19 pandemic affected all sectors. The exhibition industry, featuring people's movements, gathering and "face to face," was hit hard. Kruppe says that SNIEC was fortunate. Last year, SNIEC held 83 exhibitions with over three million visitors, without any confirmed cases of COVID-19, a success inseparable from the efforts of all parties. SNIEC formulated strict safety plans and purchased such equipment as infrared thermometers to meet the challenges.

Kruppe says: "During the pandemic, the government helped greatly. The police departments, Shanghai Municipal Commission of Commerce, Shanghai Municipal Health Commission and the fire departments, all helped us formulate

Michael Kruppe:

I am almost a Pudong native now, and I express my love for Shanghai with music

the safety plans." In Kruppe's eyes, whether in the past or in the future, cooperation with the government is of great importance to SNIEC.

Witnessing Pudong's soaring miracle

In Kruppe's eyes, Shanghai is like his hometown, Hamburg in Germany, both of which have ports and a river running through the city. He says: "Because of the ports, my hometown is strong in international trade, so is Shanghai."

Kruppe fell in love with Shanghai at first sight when he first set foot here in 1989. At that time, he lived in the Peace Hotel, where he could overlook the opposite bank of the Huangpu River. He says: "Pudong was not developed at that time. In my mind, it was a big open space with a few factories."

Just as Kruppe says, Pudong in the 1980s was far from the present prosperity. In 1990, an important national strategy -- the development and opening-up of Pudong pushed this area to the frontier of China's reform and opening-up. Under the leadership of the national strategy, the crisscrossing farmlands has developed into a city full of skyscrapers. The Oriental Pearl TV Tower, Shanghai Tower, the Lujiazui Financial and Trade Zone, the Shanghai Pilot Free Trade Zone… Kruppe has witnessed the "height" of Pudong's development and has experienced the "breadth" of Pudong's opening-up.

In 2014, Kruppe became General Manager of SNIEC. In fact, as an exhibitor, he had been to a food exhibition held in SNIEC 12 years before. SNIEC at that time had only four venues in the first phase with bare surroundings. He says: "I still remember that it was very far away from the so-called 'city center'. Nowadays, it takes only eight minutes by maglev and less than 20 minutes by car from Shanghai Pudong International Airport to SNIEC."

Experiencing the rapid development of the exhibition industry

Kruppe says: "Actually, China has surpassed the European countries and America in terms of exhibition earnings and numbers." He cites Shanghai as an example and says that the city which is accelerating to become the world's exhibition capital has over one million square meters of exhibition space available for various professional exhibition halls, ranking the first among the world's major exhibition cities.

Having been in China for 30 years, Kruppe has witnessed the resilience of the development of the Chinese market. In his view, the Chinese show strong flexibility in offering products, services, and so on. Kruppe says that different from Europeans and Americans, Chinese people refuse to settle for what they have achieved, but always look ahead to see what will happen in the next four to five years.

He says: "With this working spirit of Chinese people, and the creativity in developing new products and services, coupled with government support, I'm sure that more foreign companies will see the growth potential of the Chinese market and invest here."

Scan for videos

姓　名：Alaeddin Ahram
中文名：安明德
国　籍：约旦
职　位：施乐辉大中华区总经理

安明德：
上海人对本地的医疗保健水平感到十分满意与自豪

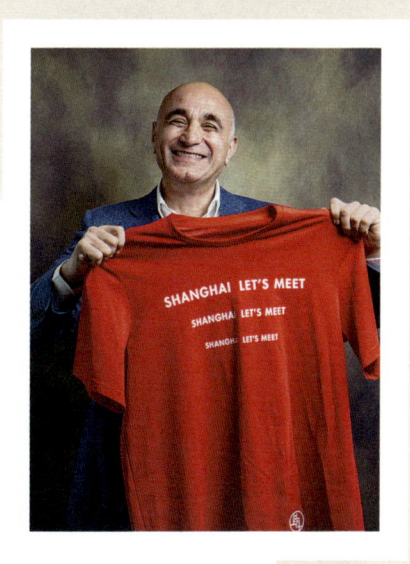

这是一座伟大的城市，这座城市能认可我的贡献以及我们为支持这座城市所做的工作，这种感觉很好，我将永远铭记于心。

施乐辉大中华区总经理 Alaeddin Ahram 有个好听的中文名——安明德，这是 5 年前他刚到上海时，中国同事为他取的。同事告诉他，这名字寓意着友善和睦。"我希望不会辜负这份好意。"这位平易近人的绅士笑着说道。

致力于进口产品"国产化"、响应"中国制造 2025"、积极参与"健康中国 2030"……来中国这些年，安明德带领着这家世界领先的医疗器械公司做了许多尝试。他表示，未来还将继续积极响应中国政府的号召，与这个美好国度共筑"健康梦"。

上海是不二之选

拥有 160 年历史的医疗器械公司施乐辉，是骨科、运动医学与耳鼻喉，以及先进伤口管理领域的全球"领头羊"，运营足迹遍布 110 多个国家和地区。2007 年，施乐辉在苏州建造国内规模最大的高端敷料生产基地；2014 年，在北京建立亚太地区最大的人工关节生产基地；2020 年，在上海设立首家本土化运动医学维修中心……近些年，这家企业的一系列"大动作"，表现出了扎根中国的决心。

为何选择中国、选择上海？"亚洲市场呈上扬态势，我们也意识到中国将引领这一态势。"安明德坦言，中国医药卫生类专业人员需要创新产品

安明德：

上海人对本地的医疗保健水平感到十分满意与自豪

和解决方案来助力他们为患者提供更优质的治疗。"我们希望搭上这艘巨轮并成为其中一员，上海对我们而言正是不二之选。"

来到中国后，安明德相当重视一件事——进口产品"国产化"，即对现有产品进行重新改良和国产化产品设计。

安明德认为，施乐辉对本地化的需求由多种因素驱动：第一，为了积极对接政府颁布的"中国制造2025"政策；第二，针对中国医生和患者的特定需求和要求；第三，基于企业当前在中国的成长。

医疗水平令人满意

"我去过上海许多医院，给我留下了深刻印象。"安明德丝毫不吝啬于对上海医疗水平的夸赞，他表示，这些医院提供的服务和院内的设备让他至今记忆犹新，"他们总是拥有最新、最先进的设备。上海很多医生的技术和经验也是世界级水准"。

曾在美国、欧洲，以及中东和亚洲多个地区生活和工作过的安明德说："与我曾经生活过的许多城市相比，上海的医疗保健水平毫不逊色。上海人应该对本地的医疗系统感到十分满意和自豪。"

人民的健康是立国之基。2016年10月，中共中央、国务院发布《"健康中国2030"规划纲要》，提出了健康中国建设的目标和任务。作为一家医疗器械公司，施乐辉也对此高度关注。

"健康社会必能造就繁荣社会。"安明德表示，"'健康中国2030'是我们希望积极参与并支持的愿景。"

品味城市勃勃生机

安明德时常会站在办公室的落地窗前欣赏这座城市的勃勃生机。办公楼不远处便是静安雕塑公园，暖阳下，公园里成片的郁金香竞相绽放。"无论前往何处，目光所及，绿意盎然。整个城市遍布青葱绿植和娇艳鲜花，如此特别的景致，总是让我发自内心微笑。"安明德欣赏上海的两大优点，其一便是绿化，其二则是上海的文化环境。

他曾参观过不少展览，也去过上海许多博物馆。"上海的文化氛围非常浓厚。"安明德的女儿是一名记者、设计师、艺术家，每次她来上海看望父亲时，安明德总会抽出时间和她一起去逛艺术画廊。

"这是一座伟大的城市，我感到很幸福。"2020年，安明德荣获"白玉兰纪念奖"，他表示："这座城市能认可我的贡献以及我们为支持这座城市所做的工作，这种感觉很好，我将永远铭记于心。"

Name: Alaeddin Ahram
Chinese name: 安明德
Nationality: Jordanian
Position: Managing Director, Greater China
SMITH & NEPHEW

Alaeddin Ahram:
Shanghai people are very satisfied with and proud of the local medical system

This is a great city. I feel gratified that this city can recognize my contribution and our supportive work, and I will always remember that.

Alaeddin Ahram, Managing Director of SMITH & NEPHEW in Greater China, has a nice Chinese name, An Mingde, which was given to him by his Chinese colleagues when he first arrived in Shanghai five years ago. Colleagues told him that the name implies friendliness and harmony. "I hope I will live up to this expectation," the approachable gentleman says with a smile.

Committed to the "localization" of imported products, responding to "Made in China 2025" and actively participating in "Healthy China 2030," Ahram has led the world's leading medical device company to make many attempts in the years since he came to China. He says he will continue to respond to the Chinese government's call to build a "health dream" with this wonderful country.

Shanghai is the only best choice

SMITH & NEPHEW is a 160-year-old "bellwether" medical device company in orthopedics, sports medicine, otolaryngology, and advanced wound management, with operations in more than 110 countries and regions. In 2007, SMITH & NEPHEW built the largest high-end surgical dressings production base in Suzhou. In 2014, the largest artificial joints production base in the Asia-Pacific region was established in Beijing. In 2020, the first localized sports medicine maintenance center was set up in Shanghai. In recent years, a series of "major moves" of this enterprise has shown its determination to settle in China.

Ahram says: "The Asian market is on the rise, and we've realized that China will lead this trend. We want to get on board and be part of this giant ship. Shanghai is the only best choice for us."

Alaeddin Ahram:

Shanghai people are very satisfied with and proud of the local medical system

After coming to China, he attached great importance to one thing — the "localization" of imported products, that is, the improvement of existing products and the localization of product design.

Ahram believes that SMITH & NEPHEW's localization is driven by many factors: the first is to actively meet the "Made in China 2025" policy promulgated by the government; the second is to meet the specific needs and requirements of Chinese doctors and patients; the third is based on the current growth of enterprises in China.

They must be satisfied with Shanghai's medical care

"I have been to many hospitals in Shanghai," says Ahram, adding that the hospitals' services and equipment have impressed him a lot. "They always have the latest and most advanced equipment, and the technology and experience of many doctors in Shanghai are also world-class," says Ahram.

Ahram, who has lived and worked in the United States, Europe, the Middle East and many parts of Asia, says: "Compared with many cities where I have lived, Shanghai's medical care level is not at all inferior. Shanghai people must be very satisfied with and proud of the local medical system."

People's health is the foundation of any country. In October 2016, the Central Committee of the Communist Party of China and the State Council issued the Outline of Healthy China 2030, which put forward the goals and tasks of building a healthy China. As a medical device company, SMITH & NEPHEW also pays close attention to this.

"A healthy society will surely create a prosperous society," Ahram says. "'Healthy China 2030' is a vision we hope to actively participate in and support."

Appreciating the vitality of the city

Not far from Ahram's office building is Jing'an Sculpture Park, where tulips in the park are blooming under the warm sun. "No matter where you go, you can always see greenery. The whole city is covered with lush trees and delicate flowers, and it's such a special sight that it always makes me smile from the bottom of my heart," Ahram says. One of the strengths that he appreciates about Shanghai is its greenery and the other is its cultural environment.

Ahram has visited many exhibitions and museums in Shanghai. "Shanghai has a very strong cultural atmosphere," he says. Ahram's daughter is a journalist, designer and artist. Every time she comes to Shanghai to visit her father, he always takes time to go to art galleries with her.

"This is a great city and I feel very happy," he says. In 2020, Ahram won the Magnolia Silver Award. "I feel so good that this city can recognize my contribution and our work to support it, and I will always remember that," he says.

姓　名：Tolza Simon
中文名：西蒙
国　籍：法国
职　位：上海中医药大学针灸推拿学硕士研究生

西蒙：
把中国作为"研究对象"后，我有了很多发现

这里的人们非常礼貌、友善，在上海生活的每一天，我都充满快乐。

深邃的眼眶、高挺的鼻梁、硬朗的轮廓，西蒙有着一副典型欧洲人的面孔。来自法国的他，能说一口颇为流利的中文，如今是上海中医药大学针灸推拿专业的硕士研究生。上课时，他和中国学生一样，身穿白大褂，对着沙袋练习推拿手法。

作为应届毕业生的他，目前正在准备自己的硕士毕业论文，初定的选题方向是针灸与五音。为何这位法国人会选择来到遥远的中国学习中医？这一切或许要从他幼时看的电影说起……

选择中国作为"研究对象"

"小时候看中国功夫电影，让我喜欢上了汉字。"西蒙解释道，他从小就喜欢画画，年幼的他觉得一个个汉字就像一幅幅画作，还曾误以为中国人是通过画画来沟通的。于是，就读于法国蒙彼利埃大学人类学专业的西蒙，选择了中国作为自己的"研究对象"。

为了更深入地了解这个国家，2003年，西蒙踏上了中国的土地，一边周游中国，一边开展田野调查，北京、上海、新疆等地都留下了他的足迹。

"看到中国电影里人们穿的衣服，觉得设计得特别好看，于是就萌生了来中国看看的念头。"但到了北京后，西蒙发现路上的行人并不像电影里那样穿着唐装马褂，中国和他想象中的并不一样。"只有实地去过，才能了解这个地方，通过电影电视，或许只能获得一个刻板印象。"西蒙笑说，就像大家看电影觉得法国人都很浪漫一样。

西蒙：

把中国作为"研究对象"后，我有了很多发现

2010 年，在新疆研学的西蒙遇到了他的真爱——在喀什旅游的中国妻子，两人结为伴侣后，便到上海定居。

学习针灸，源自好奇

说起学习针灸的缘由，西蒙又提到了"电影"。"在李连杰主演的一部功夫电影里，主角使用银针和敌人交战，这让我很好奇。"西蒙经过一番研究，了解到这部电影融合了武术与中医的元素。"但中医到底是什么？"怀揣着这样的疑问，他选择前往上海中医药大学求学。

西蒙体格健硕，一看就是平日里勤于锻炼的"运动健将"。"我喜欢体操和瑜伽，中医是一种比较自然的治疗方法，能帮助我理解自己的身体，弄清之后也能更好地帮助、治疗其他人。"

除此之外，还有一个理由推动着西蒙学习中医："我的爸爸患有脑瘤，这一疾病引发了他半脸面瘫，我想要为他治疗。"每次回家时，西蒙便会为父亲诊疗一番，"我爸爸的脸已经有了一定的改善，虽然尚未治愈，但越来越好了。"

中医药作为有着数千年历史的文化瑰宝，对中华文明的繁荣发展起到了不可替代的作用。2021 年 5 月 12 日，在河南省南阳市考察的习近平总书记表示，过去，中华民族几千年都是靠中医药治病救人。特别是经过抗击新冠肺炎疫情、非典等重大传染病之后，我们对中医药的作用有了更深的认识。我们要发展中医药，注重用现代科学解读中医药学原理，走中西医结合的道路。

在西蒙眼中，中医、西医各有所长，两套理论体系相辅相成，可以优势互补。

想在法国开针灸工作室

在中国生活了多年的西蒙，对这里很是喜爱。"中国的高铁非常发达，乘坐它可以去到任何地方，又快又方便。"西蒙说，在他的家乡法国，如果想从一个城市去到另一个城市，则需要花费很多时间。

"而且这里的人们也非常礼貌、友善，在上海生活的每一天，我都充满快乐。"即将毕业的西蒙正在思考未来的方向，"因为我妻子是中国人，毕业后我们应该会先留在中国"。

不过，他的心中已经有了一个小目标："我想在法国开一个属于自己的针灸推拿工作室。"

Name: Tolza Simon
Chinese name: 西蒙
Nationality: French
Position: Graduate student of acupuncture-moxibustion and tuina at Shanghai University of Traditional Chinese Medicine

Tolza Simon:
I've made many discoveries since I chose China as my "research subject"

People in Shanghai are very polite and friendly, and I am filled with joy every day I live here.

With deep eyes, a high nose and a well-defined profile, Simon has a typical European face. Although from France, he speaks fluent Chinese and is now a graduate student majoring in acupuncture-moxibustion and tuina (TCM massage) at Shanghai University of Traditional Chinese Medicine. In class, just like his Chinese peers, he wears a white coat while practicing his manipulation on sandbags.

As he is to graduate this year, Simon is currently preparing for his master's thesis, and his topic, for now, is acupuncture and five tones. Then why did this Frenchman choose to come to study TCM in China? Perhaps it all started with the movies he watched as a child.

Choosing China as a "research subject"

"Watching Chinese Kung Fu movies as a child made me fall in love with Chinese characters," Simon says, adding that he grew up drawing, and as a young boy he thought that each Chinese character was like a painting, and had mistakenly thought that the Chinese communicated by drawing. As a result, Simon, who majored in anthropology at Montpellier University in France, chose China as his "research subject."

In order to better understand the country, Simon came to China in 2003 and started traveling around the country while conducting fieldwork, leaving his footprints in Beijing, Shanghai, Xinjiang and other places.

Simon says: "When I saw the clothes people wore in Chinese movies, I found the designs were beautiful, so I came to China to see them with my own eyes." But when Simon arrived in Beijing, he found that the people on the streets were not wearing traditional mandarin coats as in the movies. China was not the same as he had imagined. "The only way to understand a place is to have been there on the ground; through movies and television, you might only get a

Tolza Simon:

I've made many discoveries since I chose China as my "research subject"

stereotype," Simon says.

In 2010, while studying in Xinjiang Uygur Autonomous Region, Simon met his true love, his later Chinese wife, who was visiting Kashgar. After they got married, Simon settled down in Shanghai.

I learned acupuncture out of curiosity

Simon says: "In one martial arts movie, the main character starred by Jet Li uses silver needles to fight against his enemies. This intrigued me." Simon did his own research and learned that the film blended martial arts with TCM. "But what exactly is TCM?" With such questions in his mind, he came to study at Shanghai University of TCM.

Strong and athletic, Simon works out a lot. He says: "I like gymnastics and yoga. And I believe TCM is a more natural way of healing that helps me to understand my body, and I can help and heal others better once I understand it."

Simon says: "My dad has a brain tumor, a condition that triggered half of his face to become paralyzed, and I wanted to treat him." Every time he comes home, Simon treats his father. "My dad's face has improved somewhat, it's not cured yet but it's getting better," says Simon.

As a cultural treasure with a history of thousands of years, TCM has played an irreplaceable role in the prosperity and development of Chinese civilization. During an inspection tour in Nanyang, Henan province, on May 12, 2021, Chinese President Xi Jinping, said that the Chinese nation has relied on TCM to treat diseases and save lives for thousands of years. Having fought against COVID-19, SARS and other major infectious diseases, the Chinese people have a deeper understanding of the role of TCM. Xi highlighted the need to promote TCM development and said efforts should be made to interpret the mechanism of traditional Chinese medicine and pharmacology with modern science and to incorporate both TCM and Western medicine into treatment.

In Simon's eyes, TCM and western medicine each have their own unique strengths. The two theoretical systems dovetail and complement each other.

I want to open an acupuncture studio in France

Simon, who has lived here for years, really loves China. He says: "China's high-speed rail systems are very advanced. You can go anywhere by train fast and convenient."

Simon says: "The people here are very polite and friendly. Every day of my life in Shanghai is filled with joy." Simon, who is about to graduate, is now thinking about his future. "Because my wife is Chinese, we should probably stay in China for a while after my graduation," he says.

However, he already has a goal in mind: "I want to open my own acupuncture and tuina studio in France."

姓　名：Peter Cuthbert
中文名：裴文德
国　籍：美国
职　位：时任上海世博会美国国家馆副馆长

裴文德：
上海实现了 2010 年世博会时的主题——城市，让生活更美好！

上海实现了 2010 年世博会时的主题——城市，让生活更美好！

1992 年，还在美国读大学的 Peter 就开始学习中文，并且产生了一个大胆的想法——去遥远的中国看看。当年，他幸运地拿到了交换生的机会，第一次从美国来到了中国。

在安徽大学，他继续研究中国文化，深入学习中文，因为喜欢书法，中国老师给他取了个有内涵的中文名字"裴文德"。

铁轨上的爱情见证了高铁发展

初来中国，Peter 第一站飞抵上海，然后买了一张火车票从上海火车站出发去安徽合肥。"当时什么也不懂，就买了一张最便宜的火车票，17 元的硬座票，是个慢车，全程需要 9 个半小时。我永远忘记不了当时的情景。"硕士学业完成后，Peter 开始在南京大学 - 约翰斯·霍普金斯大学中美文化研究中心工作，就此留在了中国。

2000 年，已经换工作在美国驻上海总领馆工作的 Peter 认识了现在的太太刘海英，不过，彼时的刘海英在南京，而 peter 却到了上海。

为了见到爱人，Peter 每个周末都要乘火车去南京。"单位的人都知道，周末不要找 Peter，他去南京了。"

裴文德：

上海实现了 2010 年世博会时的主题——城市，让生活更美好！

从绿皮车到快车，再到动车、高铁。Peter 频繁往返于上海和南京之间，也深度体验了中国铁路的变革和技术的巨大进步。

Peter 回忆，2000 年从上海到南京，火车需要约 4 个小时，"那时外国人也比较少，整个南京火车站的乘务员都认识我了。"

2004 年《中长期铁路网规划》发布后，中国开始进入高速铁路的大规模建设时期。2010 年，国产"和谐号"新一代高速动车组，从杭州到上海虹桥试运行途中最高时速达到 416.6 公里，再次刷新运营试验最高速度。

"现在只需要一个小时就能从上海到南京"，因为经常乘坐，Peter 还留意到了高铁沿线城市近年来的发展变化，"九十年代，火车夜里只要开出上海就是黑漆漆一片，现在沿途很亮。"

城市，让生活更美好！

因为中文基础好，加之有领事馆工作的经验，所以 Peter 被聘为 2010 年上海世博会美国国家馆的副馆长，负责接待工作。如今，十年过去了，提及世博会，Peter 还是回味无穷。

2007 年至 2010 年，上海实施了一批以交通基础设施建设为重点的世博配套工程项目，力求打造一个立体化、多元化的综合交通枢纽体系，既方便世博客流的集散，又提升城市综合交通能力。回望上海世博会，Peter 认为当时上海市政府加大对基础设施投入，如虹桥综合交通枢纽公共交通集散中心、轨道交通 7 号线和 9 号线等，不仅服务于世博会，还给现在生活在上海的人带来了便利。

上海世博会是一场让世界惊艳的盛会，结束后，中国馆变身成了一座超大型艺术博物馆——中华艺术宫，"中国馆是独一无二的，无论是建筑外形还是内部的藏品。"Peter 打算找个机会再去参观一趟改造后的中国馆。

"上海实现了 2010 年世博会时的主题——城市，让生活更美好！"Peter 说。

Name: Peter Cuthbert
Chinese name: 裴文德
Nationality: American
Position: Shanghai World Expo United States Pavilion Vice Director

Peter Cuthbert:

Shanghai has translated into reality its Expo vision "Better City, Better Life"

Shanghai has translated into reality its Expo vision "Better City, Better Life".

Cuthbert started learning Mandarin in 1992 when he was a college student in the United States. An idea came to him – seeing what faraway China is like. That year, he got an opportunity to come to China as an exchange student. It was his first visit to China.

Cuthbert continued studying Chinese culture and learning Mandarin at Anhui University. Because of his passion for Chinese calligraphy, his instructor gave him his Chinese name – Pei Wende.

Lovers connected by China's railways

In 1992, Cuthbert flew to his first stop, Shanghai, and bought a train ticket to Hefei, Anhui Province. The long train ride was a memorable experience, he says.

"I didn't know anything about getting around in China, so I bought the cheapest train ticket," he says. "It was a ¥17 (US$2.66) hard seat ticket on a slow train. The trip took nine hours. I can never forget what it was like."

After completing his master's degree, Cuthbert started working at the Johns Hopkins University-Nanjing University Center for Chinese and American Studies and has since stayed in China.

In 2000, Cuthbert first met his wife Liu Haiying. Since she lived in Nanjing while he worked at the U.S. Consulate General in Shanghai, Cuthbert would take a train to Nanjing every weekend to meet his love. "Everyone knew they wouldn't find me in Shanghai over the weekends, because I would be in Nanjing," he says.

Cuthbert says a train ride from Shanghai to Nanjing took four hours in 2000. "There were few foreigners back then,' he says. "All the train attendants at the

Peter Cuthbert:

Shanghai has translated into reality its Expo vision "Better City, Better Life"

Nanjing Railway Station knew who I was."

China entered a period of large-scale construction of high-speed rail after it released the "Mid-term and Long-Term Railway Network Plan" in 2004. In 2010, the "Harmony" CRH-380A, a Chinese-made new-generation high-speed train, reached a maximum speed of 416.6 kph during a test run from Hangzhou to Shanghai, setting a new record of the world's fastest high-speed rail operation speed.

"Now it takes just one hour to get from Shanghai to Nanjing," Cuthbert says.

Chinese railway technology has undergone a massive transformation over the past three decades, from the "green-skinned" slow train to the fast train, and then to the bullet train and now the high-speed train. Cuthbert's rides between Shanghai and Nanjing gave him the chance to experience firsthand such transformation.

From the train carriage windows, Cuthbert also witnessed the development of the cities along the railway lines. "In the 90s, it gets pitch-black at night once the train leaves Shanghai," he says. "Now it's bright along the way."

Better City, Better Life

Cuthbert was hired to work at the USA Pavilion during the 2010 Shanghai World Expo because of his fluency in Mandarin and his experience working at a U.S. consulate. He was in charge of reception as the United States Pavilion Vice Director. A decade has passed, but Cuthbert says he still cherishes his memories at the Expo.

After the Expo, the China Pavilion was transformed into the massive China Art Museum. Cuthbert says he plans to visit the transformed China Pavilion as soon as he can. "The China Pavilion was unique for the building's structure and for its collection," he says.

From 2007 to 2010, in preparation for the Expo, Shanghai implemented a set of development plans with a focus on advancing the city's transportation infrastructure. The purpose was to build a comprehensive three-dimensional transportation system to facilitate visitors' travels to and from the Expo site and to improve the city's transportation capacity.

Looking back at the Shanghai World Expo, Cuthbert says the Shanghai government's investment in infrastructure, such as the construction of the Hongqiao Comprehensive Transportation Hub and Metro Lines 7 and 9, not only served the Expo but also made life more convenient for the city's residents.

"Shanghai has translated into reality its Expo vision 'Better City, Better Life'," he says.

姓　名：Pius S. Hornstein
中文名：贺恩霆
国　籍：瑞士
职　位：赛诺菲大中华区总裁

贺恩霆：
基于一流的营商环境，赛诺菲将中国总部设在上海

上海是中国走向世界的重要门户，是一座经济繁荣、思想开放的城市。正是基于上海一流的营商环境，赛诺菲才将中国总部设在了这里。

1998 年，贺恩霆第一次来到中国，当时是因私旅行；23 年后，当他因工作原因再次来到上海，城市的巨大变化让他惊叹不已。贺恩霆说，上海的许多卓越品质都让他想起了自己的祖国瑞士。

超一流的营商环境

"上海是中国走向世界的重要门户，是一座经济繁荣、思想开放的城市。"贺恩霆说，正是基于上海一流的营商环境，赛诺菲才将中国总部设在了这里。

"前不久，赛诺菲中国研究院在长三角落成，今年 3 月，赛诺菲在上海投资成立了首个智慧健康医疗公司'安睦来'。令人高兴的是，我们还成了首家被上海市政府授予'上海市质量金奖'的跨国药企。可以说，我们公司与上海制造的高品质和创新精神高度一致。"贺恩霆说，赛诺菲在中国的一步步成长，都离不开上海这座城市提供的良好环境和政策支持。

"质量对于医疗和制药企业来说至关重要。"贺恩霆认为，上海注重高质量的环境有利于提高整个行业的质量标准。除此之外，他认为有两项非常关键的政策正在积极推动经济繁荣和医疗健康行业向前发展。

"一个是《'健康中国 2030'规划纲要》的发布，这与我们的追求是高度同步的，而今年的'十四五'规划中也特别强调了如何提高生命质量，

贺恩霆：

基于一流的营商环境，
赛诺菲将中国总部设在
上海

延长总体预期寿命；另一个就是今年公布的《关于全面推进上海城市数字化转型的意见》。"贺恩霆表示，如何通过数字化手段让患者享有更好的医疗服务，也是赛诺菲努力的方向。

强有力的政府支撑

"正因为我们与上海市政府进行了密切的交流与合作，赛诺菲才能够很好地融入本地的医疗和技术生态系统。"贺恩霆对上海市政府在推动医疗领域发展和外资医疗企业本土化发展方面所做出的努力充满感激。

过去一年，还有两件事让贺恩霆深刻感受到政府的责任与担当。"疫情期间，政府通过迅速反应和自律务实的措施很好地进行了疫情防控，这是中国得以在短时间内恢复经济的基础。"贺恩霆感慨，能让每个人、每个企业回到正常的轨道，是一项了不起的成就。

除了疫情防控有力，中国的疫苗研发和接种效率也让贺恩霆赞不绝口。"接种疫苗对我们来说是对抗病毒最好的保护措施，从一开始，我就鼓励公司员工接种。"贺恩霆说，"在上海接种疫苗也十分方便，这也是中国总体疫苗接种率迅速提高的重要原因。"

高品质的都市生活

工作之余，贺恩霆也会走出家门，享受高品质的都市生活。

闲暇时间，贺恩霆喜欢亲近自然。但他无须走得太远，城市中的绿地和公园，就能让他轻松便捷地感受到鸟语花香和自然的气息。"静安公园和复兴公园都是不错的去处，非常适合放松身心。"贺恩霆说。

当他需要一些时间去沉淀或思考时，他就会走进街边静谧的咖啡馆。"上海是全球咖啡馆最多的城市，这里有很多独特又小资的咖啡店，你可以在那里享受休闲时光，也可以静心思考、看书。"贺恩霆很珍惜这样可以独处和"充电"的片刻。

在生活中，贺恩霆还是两个孩子的父亲。他说，他的女儿们和他一样，融入了上海，也深爱着上海。

Name: Pius S. Hornstein
Chinese name: 贺恩霆
Nationality: Swiss
Position: Country Lead, Sanofi Greater China

Pius S. Hornstein:
Sanofi located its China headquarters in Shanghai because of its top-notch business environment

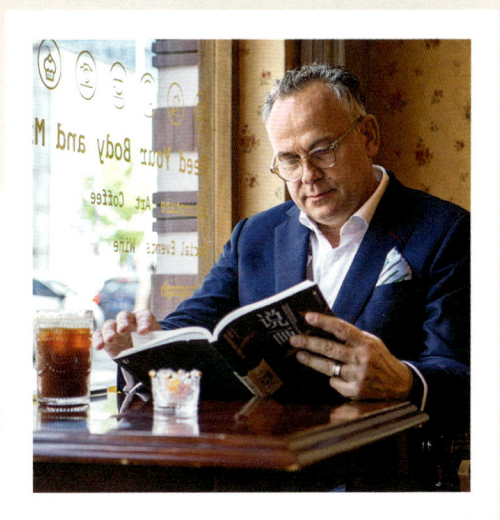

Shanghai is China's key gateway to the world. It is a prosperous and open-minded city. Sanofi locates its China headquarters in Shanghai because of its top-notch business environment.

Hornstein first came to China in 1998 on a private trip. When he returned to Shanghai for work 23 years later, he was amazed by the huge changes in this city. Hornstein says many of Shanghai's outstanding qualities remind him of his home country Switzerland.

A first-class business environment

"Shanghai is China's key gateway to the world. It is a very prosperous and open-minded city," Hornstein says, adding that Sanofi located its China headquarters in Shanghai because of its top-notch business environment.

Hornstein says: "Not long ago, the Sanofi Institute for Biomedical Research was inaugurated in the Yangtze River Delta. In March this year, Sanofi invested in Shanghai to establish the first smart healthcare company 'Amuletcare.' We are very honored that Sanofi also became the first multinational pharmaceutical company to be awarded the 'Shanghai Quality Gold Award' by the Shanghai Municipal People's Government. It can be said that our company is highly aligned with the top quality and innovative spirit of 'Made in Shanghai.'" Sanofi's growth in China has not been possible without the good environment and policy support provided by Shanghai, according to Hornstein.

"Quality is most critical for healthcare and pharmaceutical companies," says Hornstein, who believes that Shanghai's focus on quality is helping to raise standards across the entire industry. Besides, he believes that two key policies

Pius S. Hornstein:

Sanofi located its China headquarters in Shanghai because of its top-notch business environment

are actively driving the economy and the healthcare sector forward.

Hornstein says: "One is the release of the Healthy China 2030 Plan, the goal of which is highly in sync with our own pursuits, while this year's 14th Five-Year Plan also puts special emphasis on improving the quality of life and extending overall life expectancy. The other is the Guideline on Comprehensively Promoting Shanghai's Digital Transformation released this year." Sanofi is also working on ways to give patients better access to healthcare through digital means, according to Hornstein.

Strong government support

Hornstein says: "Because of our close communication and cooperation with the Shanghai government, Sanofi is well integrated into the local healthcare and technology ecosystem." He expresses his gratitude to the Shanghai government for its efforts in promoting the development of the medical sector and localizing foreign medical companies.

In the past year, there were two other events that gave Hornstein a deep sense of the government's responsibility and commitment. He says: "During the pandemic, the government did a good job of preventing and controlling the pandemic through rapid response and pragmatic and disciplined measures, which was the basis for China's ability to recover its economy in a short period of time." He adds that it's a tremendous achievement to get everyone and every business back on track again.

In addition to the effective pandemic prevention and control, China's vaccine development and vaccination efficiency also impressed Hornstein. He says: "Vaccination is the best protection for us against the virus, and I have encouraged our employees to get vaccinated from day one. It's also very easy to get vaccinated in Shanghai, which is an important reason for the rapid increase in overall vaccination rates in China."

High-quality city life

After work, Hornstein often goes out to enjoy the high quality of city life.

During his spare time, Hornstein likes to get close to nature. But he doesn't have to go far. The green oases and parks inside the city allow him to easily smell the roses and listen to the birds. "Jing'an Park and Fuxing Park are both very nice places to go," Hornstein says.

When he needs some quality time to be with himself or to think, he often goes to a quiet cafe down the street. He says: "Shanghai has more coffee shops than any other city in the world now. There are many unique and western-style coffee shops where you can read a book, think or just get relaxed." Hornstein treasures such brief moments when he can be alone and "get back his juice."

Hornstein is now a father of two children, and he says that his daughters embrace and love Shanghai just as he does.

Scan for videos

姓　名：Back István
中文名：贝思文
国　籍：匈牙利
职　位：佰路得信息技术（上海）有限公司 CEO

贝思文：
我是中匈两国友好情谊的见证者，我会在上海停留更久……

中国能控制住疫情，也证明中国人民和中国共产党之间有着非常好的信任和配合。

1918 年，出生于奥匈帝国的邬达克来到上海，在之后的 29 年间，他给这座城市留下了许多建筑，如今，其中一些已成为闻名世界的"上海符号"。2005 年，同样对建筑充满热爱、将邬达克视为偶像的匈牙利人贝思文来到上海，为中欧文化交流贡献着自己的一份力量……

致力于推动中欧文化交流

因为父母都是收藏爱好者，所以贝思文从小就对文化、对博物馆有着浓厚的兴趣。博士毕业后，他来到上海，从此便为推动中欧文化交流而奔忙。

给中国的博物馆、美术馆做数字化展示，提高展览的互动性……贝思文一直致力于文化数字化的创新研发。2014 年，贝思文联合中外行业精英，成功研发了具有完全自主知识产权的专利技术"魔墙"。"魔墙"一经面世，就被广泛推广和运用。

从 2015 年开始，在担任匈牙利国家博物馆驻华代表期间，他为推动匈牙利国家博物馆和上海博物馆以及中国各省级博物馆之间的文化交流而努力着。2017 年，贝思文将《茜茜公主与匈牙利：17—19 世纪的匈牙利贵族生活》大型展览从匈牙利引进到上海博物馆。"没想到，中国观众会对匈牙

贝思文：

我是中匈两国友好情谊的见证者，我会在上海停留更久……

利的文化如此感兴趣。"前来观展的人流量之大让贝思文非常震撼。

由于在文化交流和创新技术上的突出贡献，2020年贝思文获颁"白玉兰纪念奖"。

见证中匈两国友好情谊

常年往返于中匈之间，贝思文也是两国友好情谊的见证者。"中国和匈牙利之间的关系一直非常好。1949年，匈牙利成为第一批和新中国建交的国家之一。"贝思文回忆道。

两国在教育交流方面也展开了很多合作。"位于匈牙利首都布达佩斯的匈中双语学校是中东欧唯一同时使用当地语言和中文教学的全日制公立学校。而复旦大学的首个海外校区也设在了布达佩斯。"贝思文说。

"在中国武汉疫情暴发的时候，匈牙利是最早向中国提供防疫物资的前十个国家之一。此外，匈牙利也是首个批准使用中国新冠疫苗的欧盟国家。我们的总统、总理都先后接种了中国产的新冠疫苗。"

在贝思文看来，突如其来的新冠肺炎疫情更是两国友情的见证。

极具魅力的建筑森林

"更具世界影响力的社会主义国际文化大都市"，这是上海"十四五"规划和二〇三五年远景目标纲要中对上海未来文化建设的定位。

贝思文对上海建筑有着独到的观察，在他看来，老建筑是这座城市的亮丽风景线，更是城市文化"活的记忆"。

"要妥善处理好保护和发展的关系，注重延续城市历史文脉，像对待'老人'一样尊重和善待城市中的老建筑，保留城市历史文化记忆，让人们记得住历史、记得住乡愁。"2019年，在上海考察期间，习近平总书记这样说道。

自从来到上海定居，贝思文在匈牙利的奶奶就开始关注中央电视台的国际频道，开始关注上海。"起初，奶奶并不相信中国发展这么快。"贝思文说，"她在92岁的时候决定来看我，到了上海之后，她被眼前的一切震惊了，她说，如果她再年轻20岁，也想留在上海发展。"

不仅是贝思文的奶奶有这样的感触。上个世纪，邬达克在上海就驻足了近30年。今天，贝思文说，他可能会在这里停留更久……

Name: Back István
Chinese name: 贝思文
Nationality: Hungarian
Position: Back & Rosta (Shanghai) Ltd. CEO

Back István:
I'm a witness to China-Hungary friendship, and I might stay here longer

China's successful control of COVID-19 highlights the trust between Chinese people and the Communist Party of China in their collective efforts to combat the pandemic.

In 1918, Austro-Hungarian László Hudec arrived in Shanghai and, in the following 29 years, designed over 100 buildings in the city, many of which have become Shanghai's world-renowned landmarks.

Viewing Hudec as his idol and following his footsteps, István came to Shanghai in 2005 to contribute his part to China-Europe cultural exchange.

Dedicated to China-Europe cultural exchange

A son of two collectors, István has been deeply interested in culture and museums since childhood. After earning his doctoral degree, he came to Shanghai to contribute his part to China-Europe cultural exchange.

István has been innovating the digitization of culture, such as making digital displays for Chinese museums and galleries to improve the interactivity of exhibitions. In 2014, working with the elites of his industry, István successfully developed the "Magic Wall", patented technology with independent intellectual property rights. The interactive digital wall has been widely promoted and used since its launch.

As a representative of the Hungarian National Museum in China, István has worked to promote cultural exchanges between Hungarian National Museum and Shanghai Museum and other major provincial museums in China since 2015. In 2017, István brought the large-scale exhibition "Princess Sissi and Hungary: Aristocratic Life in 17th–19th Century Hungary" from Hungary to Shanghai Museum.

Back István:

I'm a witness to China-Hungary friendship, and I might stay here longer

He was amazed by the overwhelming popularity of the exhibition in Shanghai.

István was awarded the Magnolia Silver Award in 2020 for his outstanding contributions to cross-cultural exchange and technological innovation.

A witness to China-Hungary friendship

István travels frequently between China and Hungary and is a witness to China-Hungary friendship. "China-Hungary relations have always been good," he says. "Hungary was one of the first countries to establish formal relations with the newly-founded People's Republic of China in 1949."

The two countries have also cooperated extensively in education. "The Hungarian-Chinese Bilingual School in Budapest is the only full-time public school in Central and Eastern Europe that teaches in both Mandarin and the local language," he says. "Fudan University is also building its first overseas campus in Budapest."

István says the friendship between the two countries has been all the more evident during the pandemic.

"When the coronavirus outbreak began in Wuhan, Hungary was one of the first ten countries to provide medical supplies to China," he says. "Hungary was also the European Union's first member to approve China's Sinopharm COVID-19 vaccine. Our president and prime minister were both vaccinated with the Chinese vaccine."

Shanghai – an enchanting forest of buildings old and new

"A socialistic metropolis with global influence" – such is the future role of Shanghai laid out by the city's 14th Five-Year Plan and its long-term vision for 2035.

István says the historical buildings in Shanghai are part of the city's skyline and constitute the city's living memory.

During his visit to Shanghai in 2019, President Xi Jinping spoke of the need to properly balance the relationship between protection and development, and the importance of maintaining a city's historical features. Old architectures in a city, just like elderly people, should be respected and treated well to retain a city's historical and cultural memories so that history and hometown memory can take roots in people's minds, Xi said.

István's grandmother has been watching CCTV International every day for updates about Shanghai since her grandson settled in the city. "At first, my grandma couldn't believe China was developing so fast," he says. "She decided to come and visit me when she was 92 and was shocked by what she saw here. She said if she had been 20 years younger, she would also have wanted to chart her career here."

No less impressed by Shanghai, László Hudec stayed in the city for nearly three decades. Over a century since his idol arrived in the city, István now says he might stay here for even longer.

Scan for videos

姓　名：Anne-Catherine HACHET ep. GUILLOUX
国　籍：法国
职　位：Luneurs 创始人、"网红"冰激凌研发师

Anne-Catherine：
我研发的点心和冰激凌深受上海人喜爱

尽管城市的区域微更新很快，但却保留了原本的历史风貌，这也给居住在这里的人们带去了舒适感。

十几年前，带着 2 个月大的女儿来中国北京时，Anne-Catherine 怎么也不会想到有朝一日可以在中国拥有自己的事业，更不会想到她研发的点心和冰激凌会被中国人喜爱。十几年间，Anne-Catherine 从全职主妇华丽转身为连锁品牌面包店的联合创始人，她希望自己研发的产品能被更多人喜欢，也希望做出更多优质的产品。

对上海毫无陌生感，总联想到家乡

Anne-Catherine 的父亲是一名老师，从小她就跟着父亲去全世界各地游览，母亲是一名家庭主妇，擅长制作美食。在随父亲外出时，母亲会因地制宜地将当地食物与法国料理相结合，做出美味的点心，至今 Anne-Catherine 仍时常回想起那段快乐的时光。也许是受到了母亲的熏陶，Anne-Catherine 自幼对研究美食十分感兴趣。

2012 年，因为丈夫工作调动，Anne-Catherine 又来到了上海，并很快在这里找到了归属感。"上海是一座浪漫的城市，这里的气候和环境都非常舒服。"Anne-Catherine 告诉记者，她对上海毫无陌生感，总联想到家乡。

初到上海时，Anne-Catherine 还是一名家庭主妇，社交圈十分有限，每天除了带孩子就是做饭。随着孩子长大，Anne-Catherine 有了更多自

Anne-Catherine：

我研发的点心和冰激凌
深受上海人喜爱

己的时间，她开始研究各式点心的做法。

点心新鲜出炉后，Anne-Catherine 总会拿去和身边的朋友、邻居们分享。她的好手艺很快就征服了大家的味蕾，在亲友圈里得到了一致认可。一次偶然的机会，她结识了几位法国老乡，就这样，因为一致的理念，几位来自法国的年轻人决定一起创业，Anne-Catherine 负责面包、糕点以及冰激凌的出品和对产品质量的把控。

在餐饮竞争激烈的上海，打造出有自己特色的产品成为 Anne-Catherine 面临的首要难题。不断调试，不断更新实验配方，经过一年多的努力，她研制出的焦糖海盐冰激凌一经推出就得到了大家的喜爱，在上海本地的美食排行榜上长时间蝉联榜首。

上海非常注重历史风貌保护

尽管在餐饮业工作不太会有时间休息，但 Anne-Catherine 只要抽出时间就会带着女儿去公园玩耍。"十三五"期间，上海城市公园从 2015 年的 165 座增加到 2020 年的 406 座，金山廊下等 7 座郊野公园相继建成开放，不仅如此，上海九成的公园延长了开放时间。作为一个外国人，她总能通过新闻获取新公园开放的消息。"只要有新公园或绿地开放，政府都会做大量宣传，让老百姓知道。"对于政府的"广而告之"，Anne-Catherine 表示非常赞赏。

对于这座城市注重历史风貌保护，Anne-Catherine 更是赞不绝口："我发现上海真的很注重修复和保护那些老建筑。"Anne-Catherine 觉得，尽管城市的区域微更新很快，但却保留了原本的历史风貌，这也给居住在这里的人们带去了舒适感。

防控措施成为一道安全屏障

2020 年新冠肺炎疫情的暴发打破了 Anne-Catherine 原有的规律生活，在过去一年多的时间里，她和团队忙着研究如何给客人们提供更安全的服务和食物。作为餐饮从业者，她深知食品安全是底线，必须牢牢守住。

Anne-Catherine 认为中国政府的疫情防控措施十分到位，中国加强了进口食品新冠病毒的检测，从源头上消除不安全的因素，也让食品从业者在使用原材料时更有安全感。政府部门严格的检查机制是守护消费者们的一道屏障。

Anne-Catherine 还在继续学习和研发，她希望能为更多上海乃至中国的消费者提供更加优质安全的美食。

Name: Anne-Catherine HACHET ep. GUILLOUX
Nationality: French
Position: Luneurs Co-founder and Head of Product Innovation

Anne-Catherine HACHET ep. GUILLOUX

My pastries and ice cream are beloved in Shanghai

The city has experienced rapid urban micro-renewal in recent years but has preserved its heritage buildings and old neighborhoods. All these efforts have helped local residents live a more enjoyable life.

When GUILLOUX brought her two-month-old daughter to Beijing over a decade ago, she couldn't have imagined that one day she would build her own business here in China, neither could she have imagined that her pastries and ice creams would be so popular among Chinese customers.

In a decade's time, GUILLOUX changed her life by becoming the co-founder of a bakery chain. She now hopes that more people will love her food and that she can offer better-quality food to her customers.

Shanghai, a déjà vu city

GUILLOUX's father was a teacher who would take his family on trips across the world since she was a child. Her mother was a stay-at-home mom and a good home cook. On these trips abroad, GUILLOUX's mother would make delicious pastries by adding local flavors to her French cooking.

GUILLOUX still has fond memories of those trips today. Somewhat influenced by her mother, she has found a deep interest in cooking and experimenting with food since she was a girl.

In 2012, GUILLOUX moved to Shanghai with her husband and soon felt a sense of belonging. She says she doesn't feel like a stranger in this city because it keeps reminding her of home.

She says: "Shanghai is a romantic city. The climate and the environment

Anne-Catherine Hachet ep. Guilloux:

My pastries and ice cream are beloved in Shanghai

here are very pleasant."

GUILLOUX was a stay-at-home mom when she first arrived in Shanghai. She had a limited social circle and a life revolving around cooking and child-rearing. As her child grew up, GUILLOUX found more time for herself and started learning to make a variety of pastries.

As she honed her skills, GUILLOUX's friends and neighbors soon fell in love with her pastries. It was not long before GUILLOUX ran into several fellow French expats, and the group decided to set up a business together in which she would be responsible for quality control and the development of their bread, pastry and ice cream recipes.

Developing a unique menu in Shanghai's competitive market was the key challenge for GUILLOUX. She put in over a year's worth of effort experimenting with different ingredients and recipes and eventually created her hit caramel sea salt ice cream, which topped Shanghai's food popularity chart for a long time.

Shanghai is serious about preserving its historic buildings

GUILLOUX often takes her daughter to the park when she is free. She says she appreciates that new park openings are always covered in the news and advertised by the local government.

"Whenever there are new parks or public green spaces opening up, the government always lets people know," she says.

As part of Shanghai's 13th Five-Year Plan, the number of public parks in the city increased from 165 in 2015 to 406 in 2020. 90% of the parks extended their opening hours, and seven ecological gardens opened, including the Langxia Ecological Garden in Jinshan District.

GUILLOUX also appreciates the fact that the city takes seriously the protection and preservation of its historic buildings.

She says: "I find that Shanghai focuses a lot on restoring and renovating old buildings. The city has experienced rapid urban micro-renewal in recent years but has preserved its heritage buildings and old neighborhoods. All these efforts have helped local residents live a more enjoyable life."

Sound COVID-19 control safeguards residents' daily life

The COVID-19 outbreak in 2020 disrupted GUILLOUX's daily life. Since the pandemic began, she and her team have ramped up health measures in their cooking and services. Having worked in China's food industry for years, she understands that food safety is a baseline not to be crossed.

GUILLOUX says China's measures to control the pandemic have been sound and effective. China has stepped up SARS-CoV-2 testing on imported food in order to eliminate health concerns at source. The measures also allow workers in the food industry to feel safer when handling ingredients. Strict inspection mechanisms have formed a protective barrier for Chinese consumers.

GUILLOUX is still learning and experimenting with new recipes. She says she hopes to provide higher-quality and safer food for more customers in Shanghai and across China.

姓　名：Thomas Och
中文名：托马斯·奥赫
国　籍：德国
职　位：爱孚迪（上海）制造系统工程有限公司 COO 兼亚洲区域总监

托马斯·奥赫：
上海是一个不夜城，发展得让人难以置信

在上海，能够看到越来越多的充电桩，老百姓的接受程度也很高。无人驾驶可能会是下一个趋势，在上海有很多这类尝试。

50 岁的托马斯·奥赫 3 年前来到上海工作，他所在的爱孚迪（上海）制造系统工程有限公司是为宝马、戴姆勒、大众等国际一线汽车生产商提供整车生产线交钥匙工程、客制化工程设计及各种柔性智能自动化技术支持的战略合作伙伴及核心供应商。订单额从 2016 年的 7.2 亿元增长到了 2020 年的 16.35 亿元。作为 COO 的托马斯·奥赫将此归功于上海蓬勃发展的汽车市场、优秀的企业员工和创新性的技术。

汽车行业发展飞快

托马斯·奥赫认为，中国已然发展成为全球制造技术的引领者之一，实现了从世界工厂到智能制造强国这一角色的转变。而上海因其得天独厚的优势，已成为智能制造或工业 4.0 的标杆，吸引了来自世界各地的有识之士，为智能制造的发展贡献自己的力量。"FFT 致力于将数字化技术运用到自动化生产线中，其中我们数字化双胞胎技术，通过虚拟调试手段对客户的系统进行调试，并对系统的所有元素进行优化，降低风险，提升效率，节约成本。"

对于汽车市场未来的发展趋势，他感到，现在电动汽车会扮演一个越

托马斯·奥赫：

上海是一个不夜城，发展得让人难以置信

来越重要的角色。"特别是在上海，能够看到越来越多的充电桩，老百姓的接受程度也很高。无人驾驶可能会是下一个趋势，在上海有很多这类尝试。上海汽车行业发展飞快，要跟上这样的快节奏，就需要企业始终反应迅速并要将客户需求作为出发点。对于我们FFT而言，现在也是在不断研究新能源电池的相关技术。"

生活惬意品尝美食

托马斯·奥赫眼中的上海，就像一个不夜城，有浓厚的国际氛围、更多的就业机会，人们能够品尝到各地的美食，麻婆豆腐、火锅等重口味的食物是他的最爱。

业余时间他喜欢打高尔夫、骑自行车等。周末会和家人一起去逛各种博物馆。如果有外国朋友来上海的话，他一定会带他们去外滩游览黄浦江，欣赏优美的风景，找个地方喝喝咖啡，非常惬意和享受。如果时间允许，周末他还会跟家人朋友一起去上海周边游玩，之前去过的杭州、苏州、周庄古镇等地都给他留下了美好的印象。

交通便捷办事高效

生活在上海，便捷的交通令托马斯·奥赫印象深刻。首先，对于平时开车的他来说，四通八达的高架让原本可能很远的距离变得很近。其次，地铁、公交等公共交通也很发达，他的太太和孩子平时会乘坐，非常方便。再次，使用打车软件可以很容易就叫到车。"虽然有时候也会堵车，但整体来说还是很好的，上海的交通布局合理，出行非常方便。"

对托马斯·奥赫而言，上海是一个非常有吸引力的国际化大都市，办事高效，充满了活力。上海有很多国际学校，人们不仅可以来上海工作，还可以把家人带来团聚。除了工作以外，上海还有很多展览活动等，人们的业余生活很丰富，可以了解到方方面面的信息。

"上海已成为我的第二故乡"，托马斯·奥赫说。

Name: Thomas Och
Chinese name: 托马斯·奥赫
Nationality: German
Position: COO & Regional Director Asia of FFT Production Systems (Shanghai)

Thomas Och:
Developing amazingly, Shanghai is a city that never sleeps

In Shanghai, more and more charging piles can be seen, and there's a high level of acceptance by the people. Driverless may be the next trend, and there are many such attempts in Shanghai.

Thomas Och, 50, came to work in Shanghai three years ago, and his company, FFT Production Systems (Shanghai), is a strategic partner and core supplier of turnkey projects for complete vehicle production lines, custom engineering design, and technical support for all kinds of flexible intelligent automation for top-tier international car manufacturers such as BMW, Daimler, and Volkswagen. The order volume has grown from 720 million yuan in 2016 to 1.635 billion yuan in 2020. Thomas Och, as COO of the company, attributes this to Shanghai's booming automotive market, excellent corporate staff, and innovative technology.

The automobile industry is developing rapidly

Och believes that China has developed into one of the leaders in global manufacturing technology, achieving the role transformation from a world factory to an intelligent manufacturing force. Due to its unique advantages, Shanghai has become a benchmark for intelligent manufacturing or industry 4.0, attracting talents from all over the world to contribute their own strength to the development of intelligent manufacturing. He says: "FFT is committed to applying digital technology to automated production lines. Among other things, our digital twin technology allows us to commission our customers' systems by means of virtual commissioning and to optimize all elements of the system, reducing risk, increasing efficiency, and saving costs."

Regarding the future development trend of the automobile market, Och

Thomas Och:

Developing amazingly, Shanghai is a city that never sleeps

feels that electric vehicles will be playing an increasingly important role. He says: "Especially in Shanghai, more and more charging piles can be seen, and there's a high level of acceptance by the people. Driverless may be the next trend, and there are many such attempts in Shanghai. The automotive industry in Shanghai is developing rapidly and to keep up with this fast pace requires companies to be responsive and to take customer needs as a starting point. For us at FFT, we are now also constantly researching technologies related to new energy batteries."

Living the good life and tasting the good food

In Och's eyes, Shanghai is a city that never sleeps, with a strong international atmosphere and more employment opportunities. And here, people are able to taste delicious food from all over the world. Mapo Tofu, hot pot, and other heavy foods are his favorites.

In his spare time, he enjoys playing golf and cycling. On weekends, Och goes to various museums with his family. If he has foreign friends coming to Shanghai, he will definitely take them to the Bund to visit the Huangpu River, enjoy the beautiful scenery and then find a place to drink coffee, very relaxing and enjoyable. Time permitting, he will also travel out of Shanghai to neighboring places with his family and friends on weekends. Previously he visited Hangzhou and Suzhou, and such scenic spots as Zhouzhuang Ancient Town, and they have all left a good impression on him.

Easy access to transportation with things done efficiently

Living in Shanghai, Och is impressed by the easy access to transportation. First of all, for him who usually drives, the elevated roads extending in all directions will shorten what might otherwise be a long ride. Secondly, public transportation such as subways and buses are also well developed, which are so convenient that his wife and children usually take them. Thirdly, it is easy to hail a taxi using taxi-hailing APPs. Och says: "Although sometimes there are traffic jams, overall it's still very good. Shanghai's traffic is well laid out and it's very easy to get around."

For Och, Shanghai is a very attractive and cosmopolitan city with high efficiency and a lot of vitality. There are many international schools here and people come to Shanghai not only for work but they are also willing to bring their families here to reunite. After work, if they feel like it, people can attend the many exhibitions and events the city offers, enjoying a rich spare time and getting to learn about all aspects of life.

"Shanghai has become my second hometown," Och says.

姓　名：Ralph Huhndorf
中文名：亨多福
国　籍：德国
职　位：亨多福志愿服务工作室创始人

亨多福：
我是浦东"洋雷锋"，居委会以我的名义成立了志愿者工作室

上海代表了中国的另一面。只要你身在中国，你内心总会有一个声音告诉你，你要去上海。

"在我小的时候，就听过一首由德国著名音乐家创作的关于上海的歌曲。不知为何，从那时起，上海这个地方就一直萦绕在我脑海中，充满了神秘感。"在上海生活、工作了21年的德国人亨多福还记得他对上海这座城市情感的来源，如今他已经完全融入了这座城市，而且还用行动诠释着对这个"家"的理解，成为浦东小有名气的"洋雷锋"。

在上海邂逅了爱情，收获了家庭

2000年，亨多福因为参与一个德国公司的项目，第一次来到上海。他还记得飞机降落在浦东机场时的情景。"那时候，浦东机场只有一个航站楼。飞机落地后，我坐车穿越了大半个浦东，道路很宽敞，沿途也经过一些标志性建筑。"那时的浦东，还没有给亨多福留下车水马龙、高楼林立的印象。而现在，他时常感叹："陆家嘴发生了巨大变化，非常热闹。"

在上海安顿好后，亨多福与朋友们在浦西租了一套公寓。"有时需要出门添置物品，我会先去某一个地方，拿出照片，一些很友好的上海人会帮我看哪里能买到这些东西。"

就这样，亨多福迅速适应了在上海的生活，而且没过多久，就邂逅了

亨多福：

我是浦东"洋雷锋"，居委会以我的名义成立了志愿者工作室

爱情，和一位上海姑娘相识相爱，建立了属于自己的小家庭。

"上海对外界有着很强的吸引力"

21年里，亨多福亲眼见证了上海翻天覆地的变化。在他看来，无论是建筑风貌、人们的生活习惯与生活质量，还是其他方面，上海都在不断进步。"陆家嘴是浦东最先发展起来的地方，但是当时上海的主要城区还是在浦西。说起上海，人们会想起豫园附近的老城厢和历史建筑。现在，我认为陆家嘴成为了上海的名片和对外开放的窗口。即使是在纽约这样的城市，你也找不到类似陆家嘴这样的地方。"

亨多福又谈起了浦西："现在，黄浦江滨江45公里公共空间贯通开放，设置了人行步道，还有很多公园绿地，这是我初次来上海时难以想象的事情。"

"我刚来时，上海人口只有1000万左右，而现在已经超过了2400万，甚至更多。其中有近1000万人并非本地人，但他们都来到了上海，上海对外界有着很强的吸引力。"

"亨多福志愿者工作室"

2014年，亨多福与家人从浦西搬到浦东，居住在中虹佳园。一开始他们还不太适应"这个小区是新小区，我们刚搬来的时候，周围有很多杂物和碎石。我不希望我的孩子每天看到的都是这样的风景"。

为了营造干净舒适的居住环境，亨多福从自家楼道开始整理打扫，楼里楼外、绿地、小区死角……他每天花许多时间来清扫。居民们看到小区焕然一新，也逐渐加入其中。亨多福被称作"洋雷锋"，小区居委会还以他的名义成立了"亨多福志愿者工作室"。

亨多福去过中国的不少城市。"我也去过北京，去过长城和故宫，我认为每个人都应该去那里看一看。"而上海，在他眼里始终有着独特的气质和魅力，"身在中国，你的内心总会有一个声音告诉你，你要去上海。"

Name: Ralph Huhndorf
Chinese name: 亨多福
Nationality: German
Position: The Founder of Huhndorf Volunteer Service Studio

Ralph Huhndorf:

I am "Western Lei Feng" in Pudong and the neighborhood committee has set up the "Huhndorf Volunteers Studio" in my name

Shanghai represents the other side of China. As long as you are in China, there is always a voice in your heart telling you that you should go to Shanghai.

"When I was a child, Shanghai was already coming to my ear in a song written by a famous German musician. I don't know why, from then on, the mysterious Shanghai never got out of my mind," says Huhndorf from Germany. Having lived and worked in Shanghai for 21 years, he still remembers the source of his feeling for Shanghai. Today, being a minor celebrity nicknamed "Western Lei Feng", who is always ready to help others, he has fully integrated into this city and interpreted his understanding of this "home" with his actions.

Meeting love and starting a family in Shanghai

Huhndorf came to Shanghai for the first time in 2000 to participate in a project of a German company. He still remembered the scene when the plane landed at Shanghai Pudong International Airport. He says: "At that time, Pudong Airport had only one terminal. After landing, I passed through most of Pudong by car. Roads were spacious and I passed through some landmark buildings along the way." Pudong at that time didn't impress Huhndorf with heavy traffic and high-rise buildings while nowadays, "Lujiazui has changed dramatically and is very lively," he says with emotion.

Ralph Huhndorf:

I am "Western Lei Feng" in Pudong and the neighborhood committee has set up the "Huhndorf Volunteers Studio" in my name

After settling down in Shanghai, Huhndorf rented an apartment with his friends in Puxi. "Sometimes when I need to buy something, I would go to a certain place firstly, take out some pictures and some friendly Shanghai citizens would help me find where I could buy these things," he says.

In this way, Huhndorf adapted to life in Shanghai soon, and he then met and fell in love with a Shanghai girl, with whom he started a family.

"Shanghai is a strong attraction to the outside world"

In 21 years, Huhndorf has witnessed the earth-shaking changes in Shanghai. In his view, Shanghai has made constant progress in terms of architectural style, people's living habits, quality of life, and many other aspects. He says: "Lujiazui was the first area to develop in Pudong. However, at that time, the main urban area of Shanghai was still in Puxi. When mentioning Shanghai, people would think of the old neighborhoods and historical buildings near Yuyuan Garden. Nowadays, I think Lujiazui has become Shanghai's calling card and the window to the outside world. You can't find a place like Lujiazui even in a city like New York."

"At present, the 45 kilometers of Binjiang public space along Huangpu River has been opened with pedestrian walkways and greeneries, which was unimaginable when I first came to Shanghai," Huhndorf goes on to talk about Puxi.

He says: "When I first arrived, the population of Shanghai was only about 10 million while now, it has exceeded 24 million or even more. Nearly 10 million of them are not residents, but they all came to Shanghai which is a strong attraction to the outside world."

"Huhndorf Volunteers Studio"

In 2014, Huhndorf and his family moved from Puxi to Pudong and lived in Zhonghongjiayuan Estate. At first, they didn't quite fit in. Huhndorf says: "It was a new neighborhood with a lot of debris and rubble around when we first moved here. I didn't want my children to see this view every day."

In order to create a clean and comfortable living environment, Huhndorfs started to clean from his building, inside and outside the building, green areas, and dead-ends in the district… He spent many hours every day cleaning up. The residents saw the new look of the neighborhood and gradually joined in. He is known as the "Western Lei Feng," and the neighborhood committee has set up the "Huhndorf Volunteers Studio" in his name.

Huhndorf has been to many cities in China. He says: "I've also been to Beijing and visited the Great Wall and the Forbidden City. I think everyone should go there and take a look." Shanghai, in his eyes, has its unique temperament and charm. "Being in China, there is always a voice in your heart telling you that you should go to Shanghai," says Huhndorf.

姓　名：Franka Gulin
中文名：古兰兰
国　籍：克罗地亚
职　位：克罗地亚国家旅游局上海代表处主任

古兰兰：
我和"马拉多纳"在上海的快乐时光

这是一个需要你亲身前往，用心感受和发掘，才能正确了解的国家。

说到"马拉多纳"，古兰兰两眼放光，还拿出手机，给记者看她的"马拉多纳"有多好。事实上，这个叫"马拉多纳"的她的至爱，是一只只有几个月大的小狗。偶然间，它从一只浪迹天涯的流浪狗，成了这个克罗地亚姑娘在他乡的"家人"。

为何取名"马拉多纳"？古兰兰说是因为已故球王马拉多纳的母亲就是克罗地亚人。那天看到朋友发来的视频，在上海浦东一个集贸市场的角落有三只流浪小狗，都只有2个多月大。她赶了过去，一开始并没有收养的打算，只是想抱抱，但抱起后便放不下了。最后，她领了其中一只回家。前两周只是想让它活下来，再交给相关的慈善机构，但两周的时间就处出了感情。"我觉得它好棒，这是我到中国9年来第一次养宠物。现在'马拉多纳'已经成为我的家庭成员了。"

中国人的家文化弥足珍贵

事实上，即便没有"马拉多纳"的相伴，古兰兰在上海的生活也不孤单。她在这里认识了很多朋友，每天她都很忙，除了工作，下班后便与朋友聚会。古兰兰两年半前正式从北京来上海。"来上海是因为我得到了克罗地亚国家旅游局的职位，并成为上海代表处的第一任主任，我非常自豪能从事这项工作。实际上，之前我来过上海，第一次来便对她一见钟情。"

古兰兰喜欢这里的老城区，包括弄堂和石库门，她常会去那些地方探

古兰兰：

我和"马拉多纳"
在上海的快乐时光

索，拿着相机，走走拍拍，和居民聊聊天，从中找到家的感觉。"我的家乡和这里的生活非常像，人们喜欢聚在一起，我也喜欢这样的情感交流方式。"这份亲近感，绵延至今，日子越久越浓郁。"在这里，我被当作家人般对待，特别是在疫情期间很难回家乡时。我想说，在上海，有家人真好。"

在中国9年，古兰兰与中国朋友一起度过了很多个春节，大家一起包饺子、吃面条、看春晚，让她很有归属感。"春节时，我会收到红包，也会给别人发红包。我参加过中式婚礼，给过我中国朋友的孩子红包，我让孩子们叫我姐姐而不是叫我阿姨。"她说，"我非常赞同我们大使的观点，那就是中国人的家文化弥足珍贵。"

用心感受与了解中国

古兰兰从小爱读地理和建筑方面的书籍，来中国前，她在一本外国杂志上看到一组上海外滩的照片，"其中一张是没有摩天大楼的老浦东，另一张是与之对比的新浦东。我完全不相信我看到的这两张照片所展示的浦东变化是在15年间发生的。"后来，她真的来到了这片土地。"第一次来上海时，上海中心大厦还在建造，再来，它已建成。那天，我站在（上海中心）门口大概整整半个小时，唯一做的事情就是一直看着它，感觉太棒了。"

如今，她在这座城市住下了，还将继续住下去。"上海有新的产业，带来新的变化。现在，这里到处都有移动支付，这让我不断学习，变得更加聪慧。"

在上海，古兰兰响应这座城市低碳、环保的绿色倡议，还习惯了网购，习惯了垃圾分类。她买了一辆漂亮的自行车，用于日常出行，上下班如此，节假日也会在滨江沿线边骑行边赏景。

她去过两次中共一大会址，了解了中国共产党从成立至今100年的辉煌历程。由此，她更觉得自己应该到中国更多的地方去看看，欣赏中国的各种文化。

"这是一个需要你亲身前往，用心感受和发掘，才能正确了解的国家。"

Name: Franka Gulin
Chinese name: 古兰兰
Nationality: Croatian
Position: Director of Croatian National Tourist Board Shanghai Representative Office

Franka Gulin:
My happy time with "Maradona" in Shanghai

This is a country that you have to visit, feel and discover in person to truly understand.

Speaking of "Maradona", Gulin's eyes lit up. She took out her mobile phone to show the reporter how cute her "Maradona" is. In fact, Maradona, her great favorite, is a puppy only a few months old. By pure accident, he has, from a wandering stray, become this Croatian woman's "family member" in a foreign land.

But why "Maradona"? According to Gulin, it was because the mother of the late football legend Diego Maradona was also Croatian. She recalls seeing a video sent by her friends the other day. There were three abandoned puppies in a market corner in Pudong, Shanghai. All of them were just a little more than 2 months old. She rushed over, initially not intending to adopt, just wanting some hugs, but then couldn't put them down. Finally, she took one of them home. At first, she just meant to keep him alive so he could be handed over to some special charity. But within two weeks a real relationship had developed. Gulin says: "I think he is wonderful. It's the first time I've had a pet since I came to China nine years ago. Now Maradona is my family."

Family is the most precious in Chinese culture

In fact, even without Maradona, Gulin's life in Shanghai cannot be described as lonely. Here she has made a lot of friends who keep her very busy every day. After work, she has parties with her friends. Gulin officially moved to Shanghai from Beijing two and a half years ago. She says: "I came to Shanghai because I was offered a position with the Croatian National Tourist Board and became the first director of its Shanghai office, which made me very proud. But as a matter of fact, I had been to Shanghai before and fell in love with her at the first sight."

Gulin loves the old city center, including its alleys and Shikumen (stone gate) houses. She often goes to explore these places, taking snapshots here and there, and chatting with residents to feel the warmth of home. She says: "In my hometown,

Franka Gulin:

My happy time with "Maradona" in Shanghai

life is quite similar to here. People everywhere like to get together, and I also enjoy this community feeling." Such a feeling of closeness Gulin has been left with from day one has grown stronger with each passing day. She says: "I am treated like a family member here, especially when it is difficult to go home during the pandemic. What I want to express is that it's so great to have a family here in Shanghai."

In her nine years in China, Gulin spent many Spring Festival holidays with her Chinese friends, making dumplings, eating noodles, and watching the CCTV's Spring Festival Gala together, which gave her a strong sense of belonging. Gulin says: "During Spring Festival, I will receive hongbao (red packets containing cash gifts) and, in turn, give hongbao to others. I've been to Chinese weddings. I've given hongbao to my Chinese friends' children too, and I've asked these children to call me sister instead of auntie. I very much agree with our ambassador that family is the most precious in Chinese culture."

To truly feel and understand China

Gulin enjoys reading books on geography and architecture ever since she was a little girl. Before she came to China, she saw a set of photos of the Bund in Shanghai in a foreign magazine. She says: "One of them is the old Pudong without skyscrapers, and the other, in contrast, is the new Pudong. I can't believe that the changes I see in these two photos of Pudong have taken place in 15 years." Later, she did come to this land. Gulin says: "The first time I arrived in Shanghai, Shanghai Tower was still under construction. The next time I was there, it was already completed. That day, I was standing down below for about half an hour and all I could do was to gaze at it. It was mesmerizing."

Now she has settled down in the city and will continue to live here. Gulin says: "Shanghai has new industries, and they bring new changes. Now, mobile payment is everywhere. All these keep me learning and get me smarter."

In Shanghai, Gulin actively responds to the city's green initiative of low carbon and environmental protection. She is used to online shopping and garbage sorting. She bought a cool bike for the commute. Sometimes she would ride along the Huangpu riverside on holidays to enjoy its scenery.

She has twice been to the Memorial of the First National Congress of the Communist Party of China (CPC) and learned about the glorious 100-year history of the CPC from its founding to the present day. As a result, she felt even more compelled to visit more places in China and appreciate its diverse cultures.

Gulin says: "This is a country that you have to visit, feel and discover in person to truly understand."

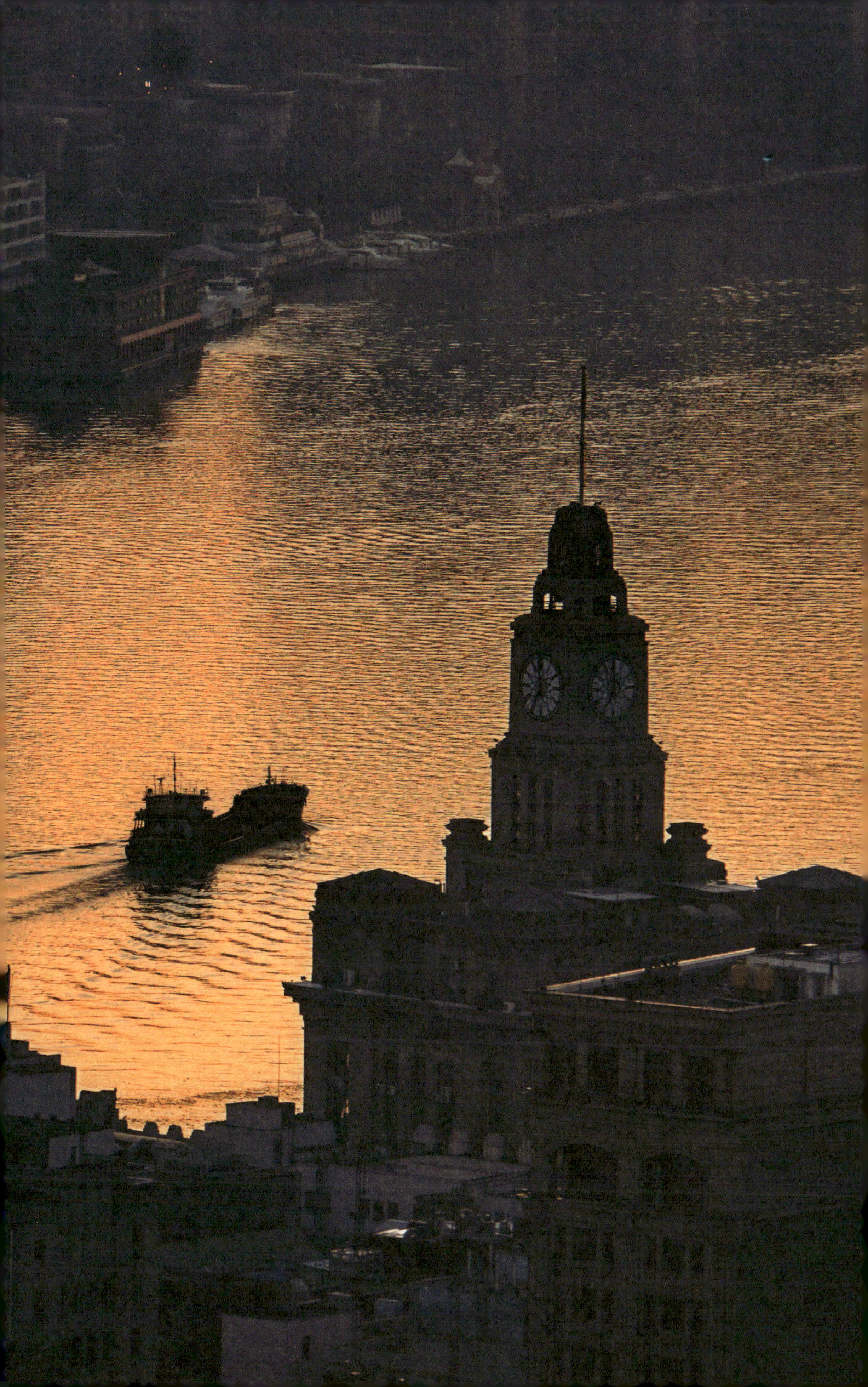

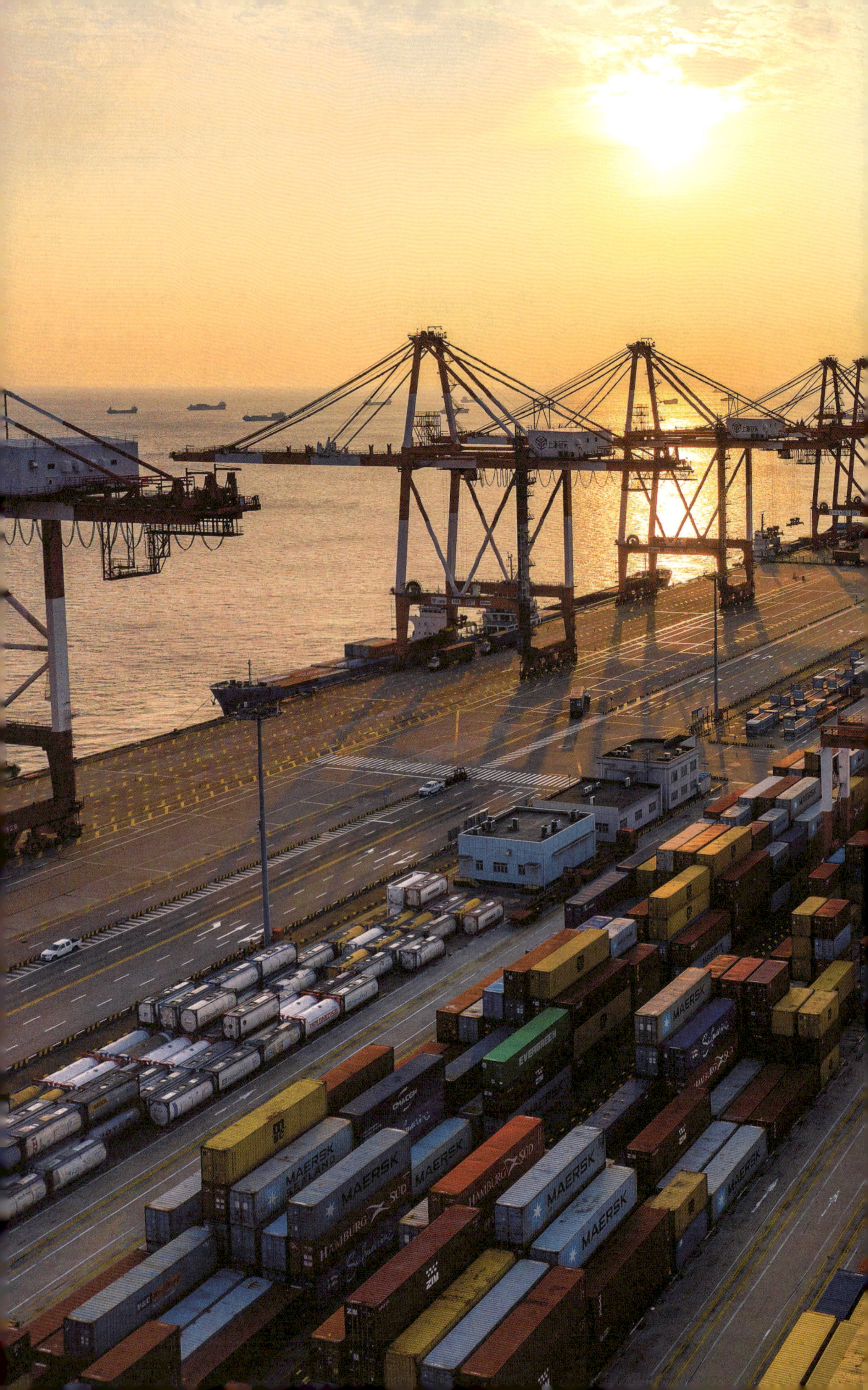
MAERSK
EVERGREEN
HAMBURG SÜD
ZIM

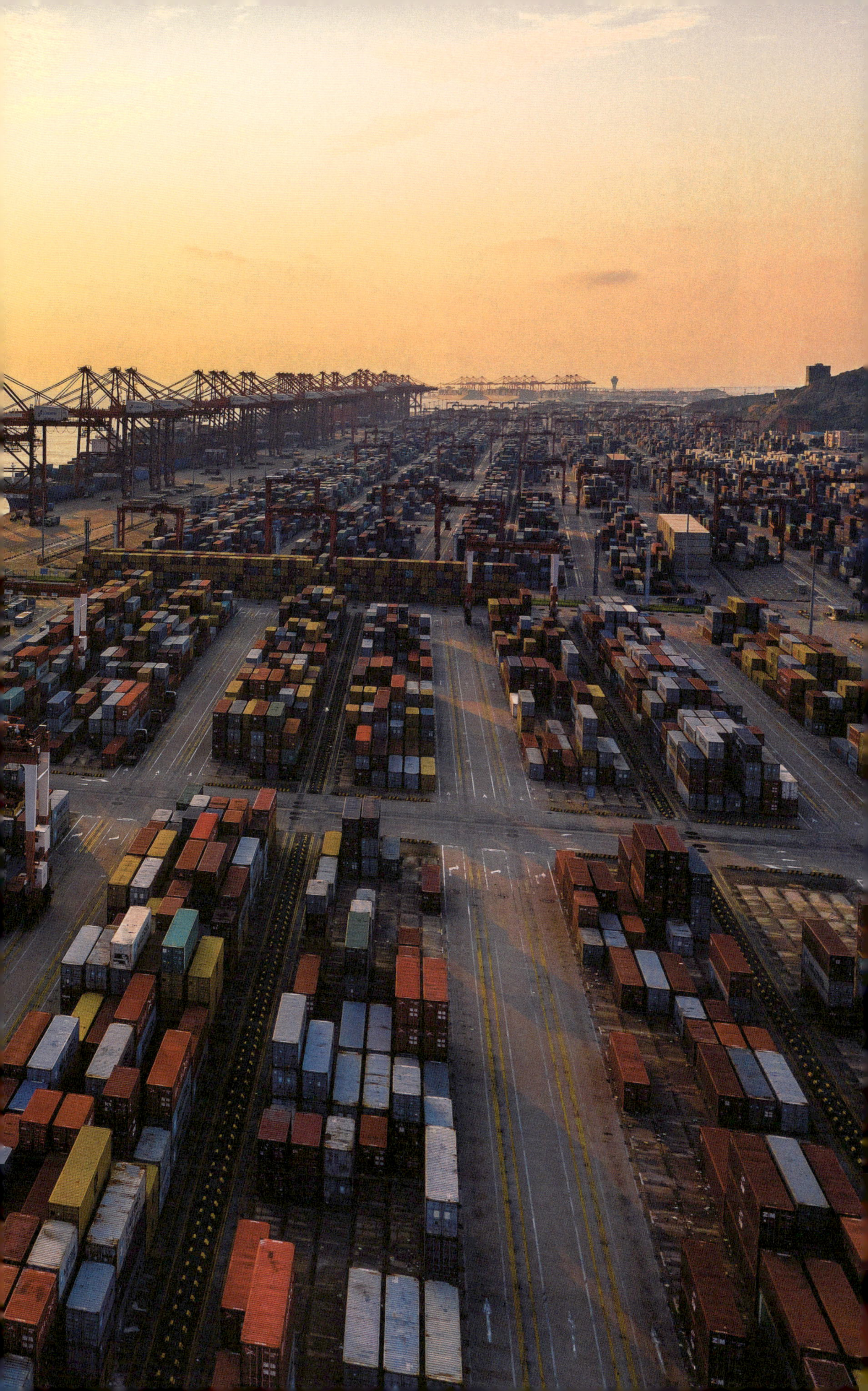

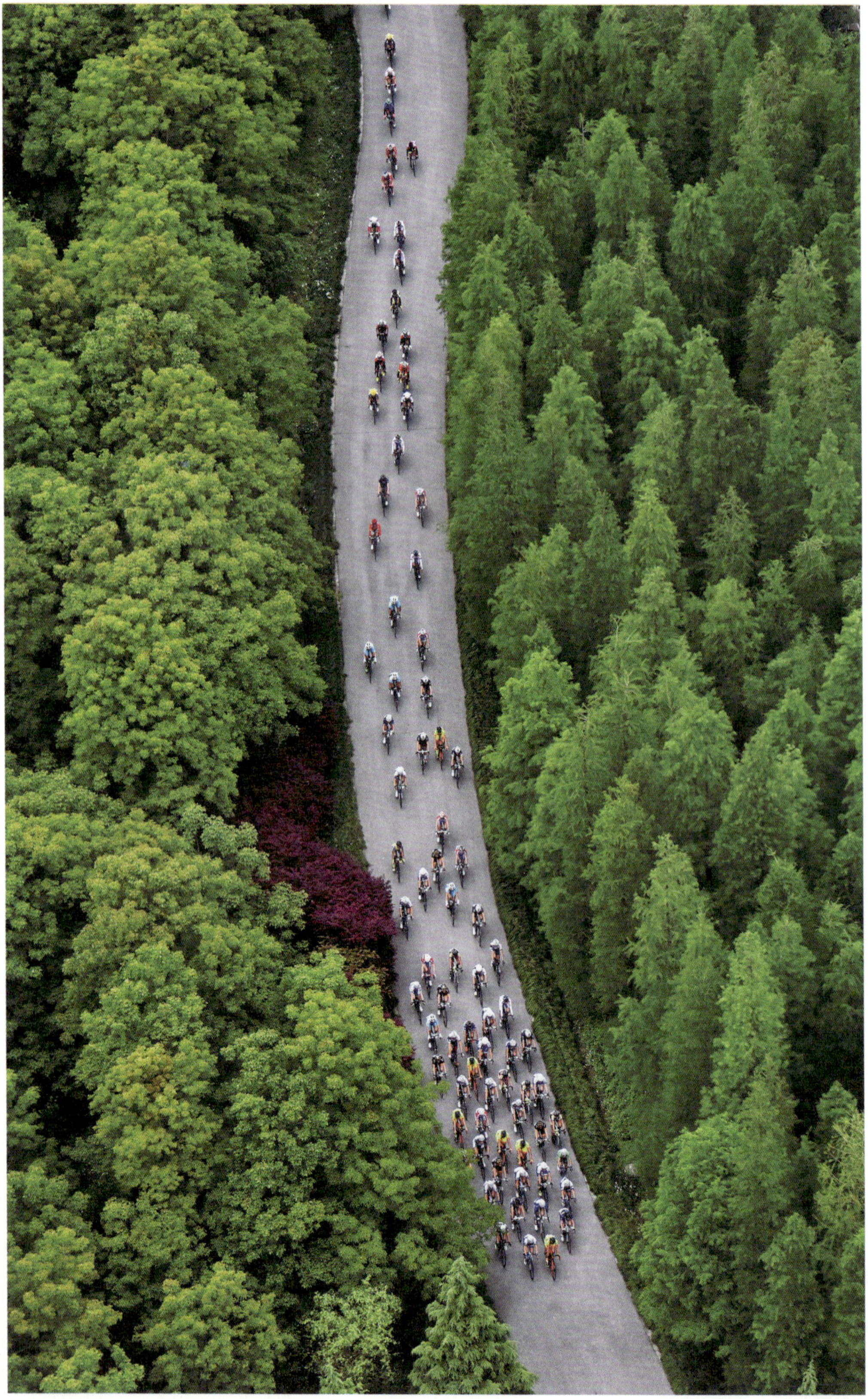

姓　名：Enrico Polato
中文名：里柯
国　籍：意大利
职　位：胶囊上海创始人兼总监

里柯：
中国当代艺术行业的发展非常迅猛

> 我认为中国文化可能会是我了解中国的最好方式。

在上海安福路居民区里，藏着一家名叫"胶囊"的画廊，画廊主人——来自意大利的 Enrico Polato，喜欢别人叫他的中文名字"里柯"。能讲一口流利中文的他，想通过这家小而精致的画廊，给喜爱艺术的人们推荐更多的年轻艺术家以及展现中国当代艺术的魅力。

为了解中国艺术来到上海

里柯从小就对亚洲文化有着浓厚的兴趣。2001 年，他考入威尼斯大学汉学专业。"我认为中国文化可能会是我了解中国的最好方式。"求学期间，他的意大利老师、当代艺术策展人 Monica Dematté，开设了一门介绍中国当代艺术的课程。里柯说，这门课带领他走进了一个关于中国当代艺术的全新世界。

毕业后，里柯获得了意大利政府的奖学金，并前往位于北京的中央美术学院，学习中国当代艺术理论。热爱艺术的里柯，还得到了多个在 798 艺术区工作锻炼的机会。他说："这些是很好的机会，可以让我见到许多艺术家和中国当代艺术的支持者。"

2014 年，在北京居住了 10 年的里柯，决定换个生活环境。在他眼中，当时的上海艺术气息渐浓。"国际画廊、私人博物馆纷纷开始入驻上海，所以我想，到这个城市来生活工作，会是一个不错的选择。"

将画廊开在居民区里

里柯说，自从他 7 年前搬来上海后，这座城市发生了很多变化。"最大

里柯：

中国当代艺术行业
的发展非常迅猛

的变化之一，当数有越来越多的艺术机构落户此地。与此同时，我也见证了其他艺术从业人员逐渐迁移至上海的过程。"他认为其中一个很重要的原因是，上海有着非常国际化的氛围和环境。在这里，有许多机会可以欣赏到来自全球各地的艺术作品，并且接触不同的艺术机构和画廊。

"上海有很多保存完好的历史建筑，我一直很想要一个不同于标准白盒子似的展览空间，一个带有上海地域特色的空间。"不同于许多画廊开设在"高大上"的外滩，或是艺术气息浓厚的西岸艺术区及 M50 创意园，里柯选择将胶囊画廊开在了幽静的安福路上。他介绍，画廊所在地是一幢建于 20 世纪 30 年代的老宅，里面有个很漂亮的花园。

"我一看到就爱上了这个地方，这里让我有一种回到威尼斯的感觉。上海弄堂和邻居们所组成的这种社区感，也和我在家乡生活时的经历非常相似。"里柯颇为感恩地说道，一直以来他都很幸运，因为街坊邻居给了他不少帮助，"住在这里的大多数邻居我都认识，大家一直以来都很支持我们这个小小的文化中心。"

将中国艺术家推广到国际

"目前我的画廊代理了大约 15 位艺术家，他们大部分来自中国。其中几位艺术家参与了 2018 年上海静安国际雕塑展，这对我们来说是一件非常棒的事。"对里柯来说，和当代新兴艺术家打交道的过程也是在创造想法。

在他眼中，胶囊画廊就像一个艺术实验室，可以和艺术家们在不同的项目中一起工作，同时创造一个平台让他们在国内和国际上得到推广。几年前，里柯便已着手在国外推广他代理的中国艺术家。"我们的第一批意大利收藏家，开始对中国艺术家的作品有了更多的了解，这极大地激励着我前行。"

在中国生活的 17 年里，里柯见证了中国当代艺术领域的发展与变化。"当我第一次来到中国的时候，当代艺术还是一个没有太多市场的领域。这些年来，这一领域发生了巨大的改变，很多中国收藏家不仅开始收藏国内艺术家的作品，也开始收藏国外艺术家的作品，并且如今许多年轻的中国艺术家在国内外快速发展起自己的事业。中国当代艺术行业的发展无疑是非常迅猛的。"

Name: Enrico Polato
Chinese name: 里柯
Nationality: Italian
Position: Founder & Director of Capsule Shanghai

Enrico Polato:
Chinese contemporary art industry is developing rapidly

I think Chinese culture may be the best way for me to learn about China.

The gallery named "Capsule" was tucked away in the residential area of Anfu Road in Shanghai and it has an Italian owner -- Enrico Polato, who prefers to be called by his Chinese name "Li Ke." Speaking fluent Chinese, he wants to introduce more young artists to art lovers and showcase the charm of Chinese contemporary art through this small yet exquisite gallery.

Coming to Shanghai to learn about Chinese art

Polato has had a keen interest in Asian culture since he was a child. In 2001, he was admitted to the Sinology major at Ca' Foscari University of Venice. He says: "I think Chinese culture may be the best way for me to learn about China." During his studies, his Italian teacher, the contemporary art curator Monica Dematté, offered a course introducing Chinese contemporary art. Polato says that this course led him into a whole new world.

After graduation, Poalto was awarded a scholarship by the Italian government and went to the Central Academy of Fine Arts in Beijing to study Chinese contemporary art theory. Passionate about art, Polato was also given several opportunities to work and practice in the 798 Art District. "These are great opportunities for me to meet many artists and supporters of Chinese contemporary art," he says.

In 2014, Polato decided to have a change of scene after living in Beijing for 10 years and in his eyes, the artistic atmosphere of Shanghai at that time was growing. "International galleries and private museums were starting to settle in Shanghai so I believed that it would be a good choice to live and work in this city," he says.

Opening a gallery in a residential area

Polato says that since he moved to Shanghai seven years ago, this city has

Enrico Polato:

Chinese contemporary art industry is developing rapidly

changed a lot. He says: "One of the biggest changes is that more and more art institutions have settled here. At the same time, I have also witnessed a gradual migration of other art practitioners to Shanghai." He believes that an important reason is the international atmosphere and environment in Shanghai. Here, people have a lot of chances to appreciate artworks from all over the world and get in touch with different art institutions and galleries.

"There are many well-preserved historical buildings in Shanghai. I always want an exhibition space which is different from the standard white box-like art center, a space with Shanghai's regional features," he says. Unlike many galleries opened at the classy Bund, or the artistic West Bund Art Center and M50 Creative Industry Park, Polato chose to open his Capsule Gallery on the quiet Anfu Road. He introduces that his gallery is located in an old house built in the 1930s with a beautiful garden.

Polato says: "I fell in love with this place at the first sight and it gives me a feeling of being back in Venice. This sense of community composed of Shanghai alley and neighbors is exactly similar to my experience when I lived in my hometown." He says gratefully that he has always been very lucky because his neighbors have helped him a lot. "I know most of the neighbors living here and everyone has always been supportive of my small cultural hub," says Polato.

Introducing Chinese artists to the world

Polato says: "At present, my gallery represents 15 artists and most of them are from China. Several artists participated in the Shanghai Jing'an International Sculpture Project in 2018 and for us, it was wonderful." For him, the process of working with emerging contemporary artists is also about creating ideas.

In his eyes, Capsule Gallery is like an art lab, in which he can work with artists in different projects and create a platform for them to be promoted domestically and internationally. A few years before, Polato had already set about introducing his Chinese artists abroad. He says: "Our first Italian collectors began to learn more about the works of Chinese artists, greatly inspiring me to move forward."

In the 17 years of living in China, Polato has witnessed the development and changes in the Chinese contemporary art field. He says: "When I first came to China, contemporary art was still an underdeveloped field. Over the years, this field has undergone dramatic changes and many Chinese collectors began to collect not only domestic but foreign artists' works as well. Additionally, many young Chinese artists are rapidly developing their careers at home and abroad. The development of the Chinese contemporary art industry is undoubtedly very rapid."

姓　名：Maskay
中文名：阿思势
国　籍：尼泊尔
职　位：上海市血液中心无偿献血志愿者服务总队志愿者

阿思势：
我们在上海组建了一个外籍献血志愿者团队

> 虽然我不是中国人，但我有一颗温暖的"中国心"。

在阿思势的眼中，上海是"Cultural magic"（文化魔都），像沸腾的火锅，让不同文化、不同国籍的人汇聚在一起，形成了一种独特的城市魅力。如今，这位来自尼泊尔的友人已经把上海当做了他的第二故乡，阿思势表示："我爱这座城市，并见证着她的成长。"

2020年，阿思势荣获上海市"白玉兰纪念奖"。获奖后，他不禁感慨："虽然我不是中国人，但我有一颗温暖的'中国心'。"

外籍献血志愿者团队在沪诞生

阿思势的父亲是一名肺科医生，经常免费帮当地的穷人们看病。在父亲潜移默化的影响下，成绩优异的阿思势毅然决然选择学医。2003年，拿到政府奖学金的阿思势第一次来到上海，攻读医学硕士学位，毕业后他进入上海和睦家医院工作。

作为一名外科医生，阿思势深刻地知晓血液在手术中的重要性。他回忆道，一位法国游客在上海旅游时出车祸需要大量输血，她的血型是Rh阴性。这一血型在中国汉族人群中占比很低，仅为3‰；但在外籍人士中占比较高，甚至某些人群可以达到15%~20%。他得知血库储存量不足，立即发了一条朋友圈，令人意想不到的是，很快有80多位好友纷纷表示愿意帮助。

事后，在与其他外籍友人交流时，阿思势发现他们对上海的献血工作不了解，在一次与市血液中心的座谈会上，阿思势突发奇想构思出了外籍献血志愿者团队"Bloodline（血缘）"的架构，希望打造一个向外籍志愿者宣传无偿献血的志愿者团队，发动身边的外籍朋友加入其中。经过

阿思势：

我们在上海组建了一个外籍献血志愿者团队

多方共同努力，上海市血液中心无偿献血志愿者服务总队外籍志愿者队 Bloodline 正式上线。

随着时间的推移，这支献血者的队伍日渐壮大，并将献血理念传播给了其他多个城市的外籍人士。

为上海市民的觉悟点赞

2020 年的开启方式让很多人都始料未及，为了防控疫情，人们减少了不必要的外出活动。春节假期，阿思势在家为 Bloodline 设计宣传资料，制作了防疫的海报和视频。当得知武汉疫情严重后，他还把志同道合的朋友们拉在一起，组建了名为"武汉加油"的微信群，吸引了众多爱心人士。

疫情刚暴发时，由于人们都不敢出门，献血量锐减。"看着很多陌生面孔举起胳膊、卷起衣袖，我激动不已。"阿思势回忆道，政府和社区做了很多工作，上海市血液中心的领导和员工们都出来献血。"武汉加油"微信群里的一些爱心人士也加入了献血的队伍。

对于中国疫情的防控，阿思势认为，以上海为例，政府和人民都做了巨大的贡献。"上海的老百姓非常棒，政府让他们戴口罩，他们就戴口罩；让他们减少外出，街道就变得非常空旷；让他们洗手，大家都认真洗手。"阿思势坦言，这让很多外国人"难以想象"。

办事像网购一样方便

这些年，上海以惊人的速度发展。阿思势回忆道，刚到上海时并不认识中文，即便带着地图出门，也会找不到回家的路。那时很多人也不懂英语，交流起来十分费劲。随着互联网普及，导航、翻译软件、线上支付等人工智能小助手给人们提供了极大的方便。"我再也不用担心找不到回家的路了。"

到政府办事可不可以像网购一样，点按钮下单就能完成？2018 年，上海全力推进"一网通办"的政务服务，让这种想法成为了现实。

一网受理，只跑一次，一次办成，惠及中国老百姓的同时，也让生活在上海的外国人感受到了极大的便利。阿思势说以前办事可能需要跑多个部门，有时还会遇到从第一个窗口问到最后一个窗口的情况。"一网通办"服务实施后，很多需要办理的事情都可以在一个窗口办妥，阿思势赞不绝口。

如今，诞生于上海的 Bloodline 已覆盖到了其他多个城市，成员也不断更换，可能有一天阿思势也会离开上海，但他们曾经在这片土地上献出的热血，永远不会被遗忘。

Name: Maskay
Chinese name: 阿思势
Nationality: Nepalese
Position: Volunteer of Shanghai Blood Donation Volunteer Team Bloodline

Maskay:
We started a blood donation volunteer team of expats in Shanghai

I was not born in China, but I have a Chinese heart.

To Maskay, Shanghai has a certain "cultural magic." People from different cultures and countries are drawn to this magical city and become part of its unique charm. Now, the Nepalese expat has made Shanghai his second home. "I love this city," he says. "And I've been witnessing her growth."

In 2020, Maskay was awarded the Shanghai Magnolia Silver Award. "I was not born in China, but I have a Chinese heart," he said after receiving the award.

A blood donation volunteer team of expats in Shanghai

Maskay's father, a pulmonologist, often treated poor patients in Nepal for free. Influenced by his father, Maskay, who excelled in academics, decided to pursue a medical career.

In 2003, Maskay came to Shanghai for the first time to study in a master's program in general surgery with the help of a government scholarship. After graduating, he started working at Shanghai United Family Hospital.

An orthopedic surgeon, Maskay recalls that once a French tourist in Shanghai was caught in a car accident and needed a massive blood transfusion for her internal bleeding. Her blood type, Rh-negative, was rare among China's Han ethnic majority (3‰) but more common among expats (15%-20%). Learning there wasn't enough supply in the blood bank, Maskay reached out for help on WeChat Moments and, to his delight, received over 80 phone calls that day from people offering to donate blood.

Afterwards, Maskay realized that the expats in Shanghai were not familiar with how blood donation works in Shanghai. In a meeting with Shanghai Blood Center, he proposed to found a blood donation volunteer team made up of expats and name it "Bloodline." After much work, Bloodline was officially registered under the blood center's volunteer service team.

Bloodline has now promoted blood donation among expats in many Chinese

Maskay:

We started a blood donation volunteer team of expats in Shanghai

cities and continues to expand its team.

Thumbs-up for Shanghai residents

After the COVID-19 pandemic broke out at the start of 2020, Maskay created posters and videos for Bloodline, promoting ways for people to avoid infection. He also started a WeChat group named "*Jiayou* Wuhan" (Stay Strong Wuhan), which turned out to attract many caring followers.

At the start of the outbreak, blood donations plummeted because of people's fear of contracting the virus outside their homes. Maskay says during the blood shortage, members of Shanghai Blood Center's staff and leadership team volunteered to donate their blood. Many in the "*Jiayou* Wuhan" WeChat group also joined these blood donation efforts. "I was thrilled to see so many people I had never met lifting their arms and rolling up their sleeves to donate their blood," Maskay says.

Maskay says Shanghai's government and residents, like in many other places in China, all made tremendous contributions to controlling the pandemic. He says these efforts are "unimaginable" to many foreigners. "The Shanghainese are amazing," he says. "They wear masks, avoid travels and wash their hands."

E-government as convenient as e-commerce

Maskay says he couldn't speak or read Mandarin when he first arrived in Shanghai and couldn't find his way home even with the help of a map. With the development of online technologies, software for navigation, translation and online payment has become popular in Shanghai. "I no longer have to worry about getting lost on my way home," Maskay says.

In 2018, Shanghai launched its one-stop online governance platform for government services, Government Online-Offline Shanghai. Citizens could access government services with just a few clicks, much like ordering on e-commerce platforms.

The e-government platform has not only benefited Chinese citizens but also made the lives of expats in Shanghai more convenient. Maskay says he used to have to visit several different government offices to access government services, sometimes being sent from one office to another with no progress. After the launch of Government Online-Offline Shanghai, many government services can be accessed on a single online portal, which Maskay finds deeply impressive.

Maskay's Shanghai-born team Bloodline has now expanded to other cities and has grown its membership. His and his team's passion has left its mark in Shanghai, and their contributions will continue to help make Shanghai a better city.

Scan for videos

姓　名：Mario MORETTI
中文名：马里奥
国　籍：意大利
职　位：意大利船级社亚太区资深总监

马里奥：
上海已经是世界上最大的港口，中国就是我们的未来

上海已经是世界上最大的港口，宁波位列前五，两市仅相隔数百公里，形成了一个巨大的集装箱集群。在城市建设工业园区，对航运中心的发展也有很大的促进作用。

两度定居上海的经历，让意大利船级社亚太区资深总监马里奥坚定地认为"中国就是我们的未来"。今年，因疫情一度滞留新加坡的马里奥，比任何时候都想回到上海。前几天，他终于回到中国，目前正在上海接受隔离观察。

城市天际线变美，老建筑"复活"

2008年，马里奥被集团总部派遣到上海负责新造船项目。工作4年后，马里奥转驻雅加达，离开上海后，马里奥心底始终有一份牵挂，总想回到上海。2018年，升任意大利船级社亚太区资深总监的马里奥如愿以偿，搬回了上海。

两度定居上海，马里奥看到上海城市天际线不断变化和美化，也见证了老建筑的"复活"。马里奥的办公室就在"上生·新所"隔壁的高楼上，对于这里的改造，马里奥看在眼里："上生·新所的改造非常棒。尤其是对我和我的同事来说，有什么比在这个神奇的地方散步，通过享受美食和饮料来舒缓工作压力更好的呢？"

马里奥：

上海已经是世界上
最大的港口，中国
就是我们的未来

"上生·新所"的英文名是 Columbia Circle（哥伦比亚住宅圈），这里曾是在沪侨民的社交休闲场所，由美国建筑师艾略特·哈沙德设计，1924 年建成。中华人民共和国成立后，哥伦比亚住宅圈改名为新华别墅。1951 年，这一带被征用为上海生物制品研究所，那个装饰有马赛克的标志性泳池一度成为上生所职工的内部泳池。

2018 年，更新打造的"上生·新所"重新开放，原有的功能被恢复并拓展，成为民众可漫步进入、开放式的国际文化艺术生活圈。对于城市中老建筑的"复活"，马里奥这样理解："中国有句成语说'鉴往知来'。保存和珍视过去的遗产是我们建立未来的基础。能够将传统建筑与未来项目相结合，是一座城市面向未来、活在当下、汲取历史精华的关键。简而言之，这就是海纳百川，奔涌向前的上海。"

"中国就是我们的未来"

2020 年，上海首次跻身国际航运中心前三强，仅次于新加坡和伦敦。以上海为代表的亚太地区航运中心，保持了良好的上升势头，全球航运资源配置能力加速"东移"。在马里奥看来，"上海已经是世界上最大的港口，宁波位列前五，两市仅相隔数百公里，形成了一个巨大的集装箱集群。此外，在城市建设工业园区，对航运中心的发展也有很大的促进作用"。

马里奥在中国还感受到了"低碳环保"的理念深入人心。各行各业在数字化和脱碳方面投入了大量资金，尤其是在航运方面。马里奥认为，这是任何一个旨在成为全球航运中心的城市都必须掌握的关键之一。

"朝着数字化和脱碳的方向发展，是一个重要而有趣的过程。例如，我们公司目前正与中国船舶工业集团有限公司和招商局国际有限公司合作，开展两个单独的项目，以促进航运业使用无碳燃料。"

"中国就是我们的未来。"马里奥表示，意大利船级社未来将继续在上海和中国投资，增加市场份额。

Name: Mario MORETTI
Chinese name: 马里奥
Nationality: Italian
Position: RINA Italy Classification Society Asia Senior Director

Mario MORETTI:
Shanghai is already the world's biggest port and China is our future

Shanghai is already the world's biggest port and Ningbo is among the top five. Only a couple of hundreds of kilometers separated, the two cities form a huge container cluster. Building industrial parks in the city has also contributed greatly to the development of the shipping center.

Having settled in Shanghai twice, Mario MORETTI, Senior Director of RINA Italy Classification Society Asia, is convinced that "China is our future." This year, MORETTI who was once stranded in Singapore because of the pandemic wanted to return to Shanghai more than ever. Several days ago, he finally returned to China and is under quarantine in Shanghai now.

The urban skyline is more beautiful with the revival of the old buildings

In 2008, MORETTI was dispatched by the group headquarters to Shanghai to take charge of the new shipbuilding project and after working for four years, MORETTI was appointed to Jakarta. Since then, MORETTI has always wanted to return to Shanghai. In 2018, MORETTI finally got the chance to move back to Shanghai as he was promoted to be Senior Director of RINA Italy Classification Society Asia.

Having lived in Shanghai twice, MORETTI has seen the continuous changes of Shanghai's urban skyline and also witnessed the revival of old buildings. MORETTI's office is in the high-rise building next to Columbia Circle and he has witnessed the entire renovation process there. He says: "The renovation of Columbia Circle is great. Especially for me and my colleagues, nothing could be better than taking a walk in this amazing place, relieving the stress of work by

Mario MORETTI:

Shanghai is already the world's biggest port and China is our future

enjoying delicious foods and drinks."

Columbia Circle, whose Chinese name is "Shang Sheng Xin Suo", was once a social and leisure place for the expats in Shanghai. It was designed by the American architect Elliott Hazzard and was completed in 1924. After the founding of the People's Republic of China, Columbia Circle was renamed Xinhua Villa. In 1951, this area was requisitioned as the Shanghai Institute of Biological Products and the iconic swimming pool decorated with mosaic was once used for staff only.

After the renovation, Columbia Circle was reopened in 2018 and the original functions were restored and expanded into an open international cultural and artistic life circle which the public can stroll into. For the revival of the old buildings in the city, MORETTI understands it in this way: "There is a Chinese idiom saying 'consider the past, and you shall know the future.' Preserving and treasuring the heritage of the past is the foundation of our future. Being able to mix heritage buildings with the futuristic project is key to the city's moving towards the future, living in the present and learning from the past. In short, this is the inclusive Shanghai which keeps surging forward."

"China is our future"

In 2020, Shanghai was among the top three international shipping centers for the first time, second only to Singapore and London. The Asian-Pacific shipping center represented by Shanghai has maintained good upward momentum and the global shipping resource allocation capability has accelerated its "shift to the East." MORETTI says: "Shanghai is already the world's biggest port and Ningbo is among the top five. Only a couple of hundreds of kilometers separated, the two cities form a huge container cluster. In addition, building industrial parks in the city has also contributed greatly to the development of the shipping center."

MORETTI also feels that the idea of being "low-carbon and environmentally friendly" has been deeply rooted in the hearts of the people in China. Large amounts of money have been invested in digitalization and decarbonization in all industry sectors, especially in shipping. MORETTI believes that this is one of the keys that any city aiming to be a global shipping center must hold.

MORETTI says: "It is an important and interesting process to develop towards digitalization and decarbonization. For example, our company is currently cooperating with China State Shipbuilding Corporation Limited and China Merchants Holdings (International) Company Limited on two separate projects to promote the use of carbon-free fuels in the shipping industry."

"China is our future," MORETTI says, adding that RINA Italy Classification Society will continue its investment in Shanghai and China in the future to increase its market share.

姓　名：Juergen Beck
中文名：耕贝克
国　籍：德国
职　位：时任勃林格殷格翰中国健康创新事业部负责人

耕贝克：
到上海工作，是令人羡慕的

> 我们把自己在上海的生活情况告诉身在欧洲的三个儿子，孩子们说"到上海工作是令人羡慕的"。

进入著名的上海国际医学中心霁达康复，先进齐全的医疗设备，热情细致的医护人员，干净得会让你主动爱护卫生的氛围，都给人专业而庄重的感觉。有位进入医药和医疗行业近40载的德国人努力在此实现新的梦想——把德国领先的神经康复模式带入中国，帮助卒中患者回归曾经热爱的生活与社会。他就是耕贝克，一个热爱上海并相信能在这里成就事业的"老外"。

我们都要"追求卓越"

耕贝克退休前任职的德国勃林格殷格翰是全球最大的家族制药企业，耕贝克强调，勃林格殷格翰从20世纪30年代起就把医药输出到上海，1995年在上海成立公司，继而在沪建厂，展现了深厚渊源，尤其现在，勃林格殷格翰的创新更与上海这座"海纳百川、追求卓越"的城市息息相关。

从2018年起，耕贝克出任勃林格殷格翰中国健康创新事业部负责人，针对中国老龄化趋势，他率领勃林格殷格翰旗下的霁达康复团队和上海国际医学中心合作，以悠久的德国神经康复理念为背景，基于循证医学经验，将世界公认的一流卒中康复模式带入中国，帮助患者克服功能障碍，重塑日常生活的独立性和适应社会的能力，从而更好回归他们罹患中风前所热爱的生活、工作和社会。

耕贝克认为文化差异不会构成中外人士交往的障碍，反倒会成为他们

耕贝克：

到上海工作，
是令人羡慕的

相互吸引的纽带。得益于浦东新区"只争朝夕"的工作风格，勃林格殷格翰从证照办理到税费缴纳都愈发便捷，他自己所接触的中方办事人员普遍具有精益求精的服务意识。

耕贝克特别强调，在中国的业务不是简单的"Sale to China"（卖产品给中国），而是"Make with China"（携手中国制造），勃林格殷格翰把德国先进方案带进中国，而中国人在数字化方面的领先优势也增进了勃林格殷格翰方案的适应性与推广性。

"举个例子，我们正在推进的 Digital Stroke Rehab（数字化卒中康复）项目，就是一个中国本土创新的杰作，相信将会造福更多的人。"

对历史有一种天然的感情

谈到对上海乃至中国的印象，耕贝克最大的感受是"日新月异"。"我认为两国重要的文化共同点是都喜欢构建自己的生活。"他描述了自己和妻子在上海生活，繁忙的工作之余，他们游览过外滩、中共一大会址、新天地等景点。

他自己还是"骑车控"，有空就骑着自行车走街串巷。"作为国际大都市，上海的魅力在于它不仅有迷人的现代时尚，更有对历史的尊重与保护，这里的人对历史有一种天然的感情，并从中汲取力量，坚定前行。"

耕贝克特别为中国过去一年的抗疫成就点赞，当时他们夫妇俩就在上海，看到那么多中国人坚守岗位，无私奉献，将病毒阴霾逐出生活之外，"我们把在上海的生活情况告诉身在欧洲的三个儿子，尤其当我们说刚去复兴中路听了一场交响乐时，孩子们说'到上海工作，是令人羡慕的'。"

谈到这里，耕贝克不禁笑了。

Name: Juergen Beck
Chinese name: 耕贝克
Nationality: German
Position: Former Head of Healthcare Solutions in Boehringer Ingelheim China

Juergen Beck:
It is enviable to work in Shanghai

> We told our three sons in Europe about our daily life here, and they said: "It is so enviable to work in Shanghai."

When you enter the famous Consanas Rehabilitation in Shanghai International Medical Center, you will at once notice the advanced and complete medical equipment, the enthusiastic and meticulous medical staff, and a level of cleanness that silently keeps you from spoiling it even for a little bit. All these indicate professionalism. A German who has been working in the medicine and medical industry for nearly 40 years is now trying to realize his new dream here, that is, to bring the leading neurological rehabilitation model from Germany to China and to help those stroke patients return to the life and society they once loved. He is Juergen Beck, a "foreigner" who loves Shanghai and believes he can make a great career in this city.

We all need to "seek excellence"

Beck, who works for Germany's Boehringer Ingelheim, the world's largest family-owned pharmaceutical company, emphasizes that Boehringer Ingelheim has been exporting medicine to Shanghai since the 1930s. It established a company first in 1995 in Shanghai and continued to build a factory here. The company not only has a deep root in Shanghai but also with its capability of innovation, is now even more closely linked to Shanghai, an open and inclusive city that always seeks excellence.

Since he started to head Healthcare Solutions in Boehringer Ingelheim China in 2018, in response to China's ageing trend, Beck has been leading Boehringer Ingelheim's Consanas Rehabilitation team in collaboration with Shanghai International Medical Center to bring the world's leading stroke rehabilitation model to China, based on evidence-based medical experience against the backdrop of long-standing German neurological rehabilitation concepts, to help

Juergen Beck:

It is enviable to work in Shanghai

patients overcome their functional impairments and regain their independence in daily life and their ability to adapt to society, so that they can better return to the life, work and society they loved before they suffered a stroke.

Beck believes that cultural differences do not constitute a barrier to interaction between Chinese and foreigners, but rather a bond of mutual attraction. Thanks to Pudong New Area's "just get on with it" style of work, Boehringer Ingelheim has been able to make everything from licensing to tax payments easier, and the Chinese staff he has come into contact with are generally very service-oriented.

In particular, Beck emphasizes that his business in China today is not simply "Sale to China", but "Make with China", with Boehringer Ingelheim bringing advanced German solutions to China, and the Chinese digital leadership enhancing the adaptability and scalability of Boehringer Ingelheim's solutions.

He says: "For example, Digital Stroke Rehab, which we are currently promoting, is a masterpiece of local Chinese innovation that will benefit more and more people."

A natural feeling for history

When it comes to the impression of Shanghai and China, Beck's greatest feeling is "both the city and the country are changing with each passing day." He says: "I think one important cultural common ground is that people of both countries like to build their own unique lives." He describes how he and his wife have lived in Shanghai, and how they have visited local attractions such as the Bund, the Memorial of the First National Congress of the Communist Party of China and Xintiandi, in addition to their busy schedules.

Beck is also a cyclist himself and rides his bike around the streets whenever he can. Beck says: "As a cosmopolitan city, Shanghai's charm lies not only in its glamorous modern fashion but also in its respect and preservation of history, from which people have a natural affinity and draw strength to move forward."

Beck particularly praises China's achievements in the past year's resistance to the raging pandemic. At that time, the couple was right in Shanghai, and they saw many Chinese people holding their positions, selflessly working to fending off COVID-19. He says: "We told our three sons in Europe what our daily life was like in Shanghai, and especially after we let them know that we just returned from a symphony orchestra in Middle Fuxing Road, they all said: 'It is enviable to work in Shanghai.'"

When he mentions this, Beck cannot help chuckling to himself.

姓　名：Shimizu Yasumasa
中文名：清水泰雅
国　籍：日本
职　位：上海清环环保科技有限公司董事长

清水泰雅：
爱上海的理由有很多，这是一座有温度的城市

上海面对问题、解决问题的速度和能力让我惊讶，社区工作人员面对困难时的团结一致、互帮互助让我感动。

娴熟地剥小龙虾、录抖音说"阿拉上海宁"……2021年，是清水泰雅在上海的第16年，他说"自己不仅习惯了这里的生活，也早已爱上了这座充满魅力的城市"。作为日本人，他没有想到这座城市会带给他如此多的惊喜，更没有想到，会与这座城市有如此深刻的连结。

变化中的城市

"时刻处于变化中，是上海最吸引我的地方。"清水泰雅坦言。2005年，清水泰雅来到上海经营一家环保科技公司，此后的16年间，他目睹并亲历着这里日新月异的变化。

说到变化，作为一家环保公司的董事长，清水泰雅的目光首先投向了上海的城市环境。

党的十八大以来，以习近平同志为核心的党中央大力推进生态文明建设，在生态环境保护领域进行了一系列改革创新，生态环境质量得到有效改善。

清水泰雅亲眼见证了上海这些年在环保方面所做出的努力，公司也因此受益。"十几年前我刚到上海，当时偶尔还是能看见有人乱丢垃圾、乱扔烟头，但随着环保教育的普及，如今这些现象有了很大改观。"作为一个细

致的观察者，清水泰雅注意到这些年上海市容市貌和市民素质的改变，他向记者讲述了一件带给他很大触动的身边事——前不久，清水泰雅牵着狗在小区遛弯，一个抽着烟的老人领着孙子走在他前面。没过一会儿，老人将烟蒂丢在了地上，孙子见状立马指出爷爷的不是，并捡起地上的烟蒂，一路拿着最后丢进垃圾桶。

"现在上海小朋友的环保意识太强了！"他感叹道。

暖人心的社区

2020年3月疫情期间，清水泰雅怀着忐忑的心情从日本回到上海长宁区天山华庭小区，成为上海第一批居家隔离的外国居民。如何安全度过隔离期？如何保证这段时间的正常生活？清水泰雅的内心堆积了太多疑虑。

焦虑的并不只有清水泰雅，还有在该小区居住的60户日本居民。社区工作人员迅速采取了行动，在社区微信群里发放注意事项、为隔离者们配送生活用品、体温监测……很快，一切变得安全有序，外国居民悬在半空中的心也跟着落了地。

"上海面对问题、解决问题的速度和能力让我惊讶，社区工作人员面对困难时的团结一致、互帮互助让我感动。"清水泰雅萌生了要在这个非常时期为社区做点什么的念头。

居委会和外籍居民之间的沟通出现了语言障碍，中文水平较高的清水泰雅主动承担起翻译的任务，在社区微信群里对外籍居民的提问进行解答。他还自己动手制作了日语版《天山华庭居家隔离指南》。就这样，清水泰雅从隔离者变成了一位得力的社区志愿者。

"这是一座有温度的城市。"在上海待得越久，和上海走得越近，清水泰雅就越发有这样的感触。

爱上海的理由还有很多。采访结束时，清水泰雅激动地向记者展示了自己去年4月拿到的《外国人永久居留身份证》，在他眼里，这是一种认可与接纳。

16年，清水泰雅将人生中最珍贵的时光留在了上海。他相信这座城市会带给他更多惊喜。

Name: Shimizu Yasumasa
Chinese name: 清水泰雅
Nationality: Japanese
Position: Shanghai Qinghuan Enviro Protech Co., Ltd. CEO

Shimizu Yasumasa:

There are many reasons to love Shanghai, a city filled with warmth

I am surprised at the speed and ability of Shanghai to face and solve the problems, and moved by the solidarity and mutual help of the community workers in the face of difficulties.

Peeling the crayfish skillfully, making short videos on Douyin, and speaking "I am a Shanghainese" in Shanghai dialect... The year 2021 marks Shimizu Yasumasa's 16th year in Shanghai. He says that he has not only got used to living here but also fallen in love with this charming city for a long time. As a Japanese, he didn't expect this city to bring him so many surprises, let alone such a deep connection with it.

A city in change

"What attracts me the most in Shanghai is that the city keeps changing," Yasumasa says. In 2005, he came to Shanghai to run an environmental protection technology company, and in the following 16 years, he has witnessed and experienced the rapid changes here.

Speaking of changes, as the CEO of an environmental protection company, Yasumasa first sets his eyes on Shanghai's urban environment. Since the 18th National Congress of the Communist Party of China (CPC), the Central Committee of the CPC with Xi Jinping as its core has vigorously promoted the construction of ecological civilization and carried out a series of reforms and innovations in the field of ecological environmental protection, which has effectively improved the quality of the ecological environment.

Yasumasa has witnessed all the efforts Shanghai has made on environmental protection over the years and the company has also benefited from it. He says: "When I first arrived in Shanghai more than ten years ago,

Shimizu Yasumasa:

There are many reasons to love Shanghai, a city filled with warmth

sometimes I still could see people throw away rubbish carelessly, like cigarette ends. However, with the popularization of environmental protection education, these phenomena have changed for the better." As a careful observer, Yasumasa notices the changes in Shanghai's city appearance and the improvement of citizen's educational and ethical standards over the years. He tells the reporter about an incident that has touched him deeply. Not long ago, Yasumasa was once walking his dog in his neighborhood, and an old man, smoking, was walking in front of him along with his grandson. After a while, the old man threw the cigarette butt on the ground and his grandson immediately pointed out the mistake, picked up the butt, and took it to the trash can.

"Shanghai children are so environmentally conscious now!" he says.

A heart-warming community

In March 2020 during the COVID-19 pandemic, Yasumasa returned from Japan to Tianshanhuating Estate in Changning District, Shanghai, with great trepidation, becoming one of the first foreign residents to be quarantined at home in Shanghai. How could they safely survive the quarantine period? How to ensure a normal life during this period? Yasumasa had many doubts in his heart.

Yasumasa was not the only one who was worried, but also the 60 Japanese residents who lived in the neighborhood. Community workers took action rapidly by sending precautions in the community WeChat group, delivering daily necessities for the quarantined personnel, and monitoring their body temperature... Soon, everything turned out safe and orderly and these foreign residents finally felt relieved.

He says: "I am surprised at the speed and ability of Shanghai to face and solve the problems and am moved by the solidarity and mutual help of the community workers in the face of difficulties." Yasumasa had an idea that he could do something for the community at this special time.

Whenever language barriers in the communication appear between the neighborhood committee and foreign residents, Yasumasa, with a relatively good command of Chinese, would volunteer to take on the task of translation and answer questions raised by foreign residents in the community WeChat group. He also made a Japanese version of Guideline on Home-quarantine of Tianshanhuating Estate by himself. In this way, Yasumasa became a capable community volunteer while still under quarantine.

He says: "This is a city filled with warmth." The longer he stays in Shanghai and the closer he gets to Shanghai, the more he feels so.

There are more reasons to love Shanghai. Yasumasa received the Foreign Permanent Resident ID Card in April last year. In his eye, it stands for acceptance and recognition.

In these 16 years, Yasumasa has spent the most precious time of his life in Shanghai and he believes that this city will bring him more surprises.

姓　名：Adam Strzep
中文名：亚当斯
国　籍：波兰
职　位：中国科学院上海硅酸盐研究所访问学者

亚当斯：
我期待是中国人再次在月球上留下足迹

我很确定，就在我的有生之年，很有可能是中国人再次在月球上留下足迹，并在月球上建立长期的基地。

喜爱旅游的亚当斯是一个太空迷，他最喜欢的中文书是刘慈欣的《三体》。为了能去中国更多的地方旅行和看更多的中文书籍，亚当斯已经学习起了中文。

"我想阅读更多的中文书籍，以更好地了解中国文化。我名单上的下一本书是《西游记》。"亚当斯告诉记者。

在上海和最优秀的人一起工作

亚当斯毕业于波兰的弗罗茨瓦夫大学，2009年开始学习物理学硕士课程。2014年，亚当斯第一次来到上海，"从那之后我就深深爱上了上海，因为这真的是一个非常棒的城市"。2018年，亚当斯与中国科学院上海硅酸盐研究所的科研团队共同申请了"上海市2018年度'科技创新行动计划''一带一路'国际合作项目"并成功获得资助，成为了中国科学院上海硅酸盐研究所的一名访问学者，也是他们团队中唯一的外国人。

"我在这里遇到的外国人，他们都不想离开，因为在上海的生活很快乐，上海真的有一些特别的东西。"亚当斯坦言，中科院上海硅酸盐研究所是世界闻名的材料科学中心，他想和最优秀的人一起工作。

"来到上海之后，我有幸能够同时从事化学和物理专业的工作。在这里

亚当斯：

我期待是中国人
再次在月球上留
下足迹

我能够重拾幼年时成为化学家的梦想。"亚当斯告诉记者，他其中一项工作就是设计、生成含有不同稀土离子的晶体，并让它们产生不同颜色的荧光。记者在中国科学院上海硅酸盐研究所的实验室内看到，在亚当斯的手中，光线像有了生命一样绽放出五颜六色的光芒。

期待中国航天发展取得更大进步

2021年的全国两会上，载人航天工程、重型火箭研制、火星探测进展等备受瞩目，这一年，中国航天重磅消息频频传出。亚当斯是一个地道的太空迷，对于航天类的新闻总是格外关心，他为中国航天空间技术的飞速发展点赞。

中国航天发展的背后离不开经济的支撑，亚当斯表示很惊讶于中国发展的方式，当审视中国GDP年增长速率并与其他国家相比较时，他确信中国政府做出了更出色的工作。中国政府为工业、贸易和商务的发展创造了一个非常好的环境，这对整个社会都有帮助。谈到这些，亚当斯变得兴奋起来，滔滔不绝地讲述着他的看法："40年前的中国，可能没有人想过太空计划或者去探索火星、月球，更没想过建一个空间站。"亚当斯坚信中国可能将很快完成一个太空空间站的建设。

"我真的很想欣赏人类再次登上月球的一幕。我很确定，就在我的有生之年，很有可能是中国人再次在月球上留下足迹，并在月球上建立长期的基地。我还确定我将成为火星首次载人飞行任务的见证人。"

Name: Adam Strzep
Chinese name: 亚当斯
Nationality: Polish
Position: Visiting Scientist at Shanghai Institute of Ceramics, Chinese Academy of Sciences

Adam Strzep:
I expect that it's the Chinese who will leave a footprint on the Moon again

I'm pretty sure that in my lifetime, it will probably be the Chinese who leave their footprints on the moon again and establish long-term bases there.

Adam Strzep is a space fan who loves to travel, and his favorite Chinese book is Liu Cixin's *The Three-Body Problem*. In order to travel to more places in China and read more Chinese books, he has taken up the learning of the Chinese language.

Strzep says: "I want to read more books in Chinese in order to better understand Chinese culture. The next book on my list is *Journey to the West*."

Working with the best people in Shanghai

Strzep graduated from the University of Wrocław in Poland and entered a master's program in physics in 2009. In 2014, he came to Shanghai for the first time. "I have fallen in love with Shanghai ever since because it is really a great city," he says.

In 2018, Strzep applied for the "Shanghai 2018 'Science and Technology Innovation Action Plan' -- 'The Belt and Road' International Cooperation Project" with the research team from the Shanghai Institute of Ceramics and the Chinese Academy of Sciences (CAS), and successfully received funding to become a visiting scientist at the CAS Shanghai Institute of Ceramics, as the only foreign member on the team.

Strzep says: "The foreigners I've met here don't want to leave because they have got a pretty happy life here in Shanghai, and there's really something

Adam Strzep:

I expect that it's the Chinese who will leave a footprint on the Moon again

special about the city." He says that the CAS Shanghai Institute of Ceramics is a world-renowned center for materials science and he wants to work with the best people.

He says: "After coming to Shanghai, I was fortunate to be able to work in chemistry and physics at the same time. Here I can revive my dream of becoming a chemist when I was young." Strzep says that one of his jobs is to design and generate crystals containing different rare-earth ions and make them produce fluorescence of different colors. In the laboratory of the CAS Shanghai Institute of Ceramics, the light blossoms in Strzep's hands into colorful light as if it has life.

Looking forward to greater progress in China's space development

During the "two sessions" in 2021, China's great achievements on manned spaceflight, heavy rocket development, and Mars exploration progress attracted much attention. This year, big news from China's space industry came up frequently. Strzep is an authentic space fan and always pays special attention to space news. He praises the rapid development of China's space technology.

China's space development cannot be separated from economic support. Strzep expresses amazement at the way China develops. When examining the annual GDP growth rate of China and comparing it with other countries, he is convinced that the Chinese government has done a better job. The Chinese government has created a very good environment for the development of industry, trade, and commerce, which is beneficial to the whole society. When talking about this, Strzep gets excited and rattles off his observation: "Forty years ago, probably no one in China had thought about a space program or exploration of Mars and the Moon, let alone the building of a space station." Strzep firmly believes that China will soon complete the construction of a space station.

Strzep says: "I really want to enjoy the sight of men setting foot on the Moon again. I believe that just in my lifetime, I will see the Chinese leave a footprint on the Moon again and establish long-term bases there. I'm also certain that I will be a witness to the first manned expedition to Mars."

姓　名：Andrea Calducci
中文名：杜安德
国　籍：意大利
职　位：J 酒店上海 101 意大利餐厅厨师长

杜安德：
当我把拍摄的上海的景象发给亲友，他们都震惊到说不出话来

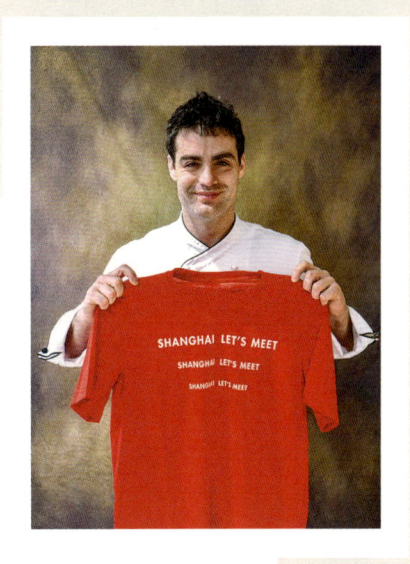

当我来了上海以后，我便立刻爱上了这座城市，无论是这里的环境还是文化。

"在上海工作的感受是独一无二的"

2019 年，研习意大利美食 15 年的杜安德收到了一条来自中国的面试邀请，当时还在筹备中的 J 酒店上海 101 意大利餐厅正在招聘厨师长。怀揣着对"东方神秘古国"的向往，杜安德来到了上海。

杜安德坦言，之前他对中国并不了解，然而，到上海没多久，杜安德就找到了家的感觉，并坚定认为自己的未来就在中国。"当我来了以后，我便立刻爱上了这座城市，无论是这里的环境还是文化，上海的文化和意大利非常相似，尤其是在对美食、家庭及对生活的热爱上。"杜安德解释道，这是一种直觉，很多相似的事物很完美地融合在了一起。

虽然在世界上很多餐厅工作过，但能在世界上最高餐厅之一的 J 酒店上海 101 意大利餐厅工作，杜安德还是表示"很骄傲"。当他第一次来到位于上海中心大厦 101 层的上海 101 意大利餐厅时，也被眼前的美景震撼。杜安德称，这种工作的感受是独一无二的，能体验到诗人杜甫"一览众山小"的感觉。

杜安德的家乡在意大利佛罗伦萨，没有很高的楼。所以每当他在餐厅时，还是会忍不住拿出手机拍摄一些照片发给妈妈和朋友们。"当我拍照片给我

杜安德：

当我把拍摄的上海的景象发给亲友，他们都震惊到说不出话来

的家人朋友时，他们都震惊到说不出话来，尤其是对像我一样来自意大利乡镇的人来说，真的很神奇。当我第一次把在这层楼拍的餐厅景象发给我妈妈时，她回复给我的信息里加了很多表情包，她真的超级开心。"

杜安德告诉记者，妈妈一直在等着国际航线恢复，这样就能来上海了，杜安德的很多朋友也都在"排队"来上海。

"我的未来一定和上海有关"

杜安德有自己的"职业使命"，他想传递更多地道的现代意大利美食来上海。和普通的意大利菜制作不同，101意大利餐厅希望和本地的供应商及农场合作，用就近的食材来烹饪菜品。"我在原本意大利菜的基础上融合中式的食材，制作出更符合中式口味的意大利菜品。"

古丝绸之路从中国的西安出发最后到达了意大利城市罗马，马可·波罗也是第一批到访中国并与中国建立关系的欧洲人。习近平总书记曾说过文明因多样而交流，因交流而互鉴，因互鉴而发展。

定居中国后，杜安德计划去丝绸之路上的城市看看，随着马可·波罗的足迹深入了解中国，他说："丝绸之路无论对于中国还是意大利来说都很重要，马可·波罗来到这里，带回去很多技术，还有信息。"

对于自己的未来，杜安德认为一定和上海有关，他预感未来一定充满激情与挑战。

Name: Andrea Calducci
Chinese name: 杜安德
Nationality: Italian
Position: Head Chef of Centouno at Shanghai Tower J-Hotel

Andrea Calducci:
My family and friends were lost for words when I showed them my photos of Shanghai

Once I arrived in Shanghai, I instantly fell in love with its urban landscape and its culture.

"Working in Shanghai gives me a unique feeling"

In 2019, 15 years of experience in Italian cuisine won Calducci an invitation to a job interview. The position was the head chef of Centouno at Shanghai Tower J-Hotel. Drawn by China's mystical charm, he decided to come to Shanghai.

Although he didn't know much about China, Calducci says he felt at home soon after he arrived in Shanghai.

"Once I arrived in Shanghai, I instantly fell in love with its urban landscape and its culture," he says. "Shanghai's culture is very similar to Italy's, especially in terms of people's love for food, family and life."

Calducci says he went with his intuition and came to Shanghai. He says many similarities between the two cultures worked out well and gave him an enjoyable life here.

Although he has worked in many high-end restaurants around the world, Calducci says he feels "very proud" working at Centouno at Shanghai Tower J-Hotel, one of the highest restaurants in the world. When he first came to the restaurant on the 101st floor of Shanghai Tower, he was amazed by the views. Calducci says working here gives him a unique feeling -- a top-of-the-world feeling famously articulated by the eighth-century Chinese poet Du Fu envisioning himself at the peak of Mount Tai.

Calducci often takes photos of his restaurant for his mother and friends.

Andrea Calducci:

My family and friends were lost for words when I showed them my photos of Shanghai

Florence, his hometown, doesn't have many tall buildings, and the views in his photos often amaze them.

"My family and friends were lost for words when I showed them my photos," he says. "The view is especially magical for me, someone from an Italian town. When I first sent my mother the views from my restaurant, her reply was a flurry of emojis. She was really happy."

Calducci says his mother has been waiting for international flights to resume so that she can come to Shanghai, and many of his friends are also "lining up" to visit Shanghai.

"My future will definitely be tied to Shanghai"

Calducci's ambition is to introduce more authentic modern Italian cuisine to Shanghai. Unlike most restaurants, Centouno hopes to cooperate with local suppliers and farms and use local ingredients in its kitchen. Calducci says the restaurant will incorporate Chinese elements in its Italian dishes.

"I've introduced Chinese ingredients to our Italian dishes so that we can create Italian food that caters to the Chinese palate," he says.

The ancient Silk Road began in Xi'an, China, and ended in Rome, Italy. Italian Marco Polo was one of the first Europeans to visit and explore China and interact with Chinese people. President Xi Jinping remarked in his keynote speech at the Opening Ceremony of the Conference on Dialogue of Asian Civilizations that "diversity spurs interaction among civilizations, which in turn promotes mutual learning and their further development."

Calducci plans to follow Marco Polo's footsteps and explore China along the ancient Silk Road.

"The Silk Road is important for both China and Italy," he says. "After traveling here, Marco Polo brought back many technologies and information."

Calducci says his future will definitely be tied to Shanghai. He foresees a life full of exciting challenges in Shanghai.

姓　　名：Shawn Patrick Tilling
中文名：尚希林
国　　籍：加拿大
职　　位：上海温哥华电影学院 3D 动画与视觉特效系主任

尚希林：
用动画短片讲好上海故事

你知道，住在上海是什么感觉吗？我必须说，这就像身处《银翼杀手》里的电影场景，这里是一座真正的"未来之城"。

2001 年起任教于加拿大温哥华电影学院，2005 年独立创作的短片获得金球奖最佳短片，先后在 DreamWorks、Walt Disney Pictures、MGM 等美国知名影业公司担任 CG 总监，还曾服务于奥林匹克艺术委员会等知名机构……来自加拿大的尚希林职业履历光环闪耀。

2014 年，他心怀助力中国电影发展的梦想来到上海，出任上海温哥华电影学院 3D 动画与视觉特效系主任，在这个遥远的东方大舞台逐梦。"中国已经成为世界上最大的票房市场之一。如果现在还不是最大的票房市场，也会是在不远的将来。"尚希林预判。

从陌生人成为"城市宝藏"挖掘者

尚希林目前正热火朝天地拍摄一部以上海为基底的动画短片，"我让我的小机器人角色们四处游览，只是为了探索上海这个美妙的地方"。这部短片的拍摄灵感来自一个陌生人来到一个美丽的新世界，"探险"路上连连收获惊喜。"这就像在上海，当你转过一个拐角，第一次看到某个新东西时，会感到惊讶，会留下深刻的印象。"

2001 年起，尚希林在加拿大温哥华电影学院任职。7 年前，学校问他是否有兴趣来中国，为中国电影产业大发展设立学习项目时，尚希林欣然应允。"我带着强烈的使命感来到这里。在上海，我们花了很多时间开发 3D 动画与视觉特效这门课程，努力让它成为世界上最好的课程之一，为这个行业培养顶尖人才。"

尚希林：

用动画短片讲好
上海故事

7年间，尚希林在上海不断探索、体验，从一个陌生人成为"城市宝藏"的挖掘者。"这是一座充满活力的城市，激发了我的创作灵感，而且我会一直希望它影响我做的每一件事。"尚希林透露，他还在制作另一部动画短片，故事的女主角克服逆境不断奋斗，最终获得成功。

"这部短片的内容非常人性化。剧本里，我还想要为这个女孩找一个'完美男友'。可是中国版的完美男友是怎样的？我向中国同事求助。他们说，在上海，一个好男友会做饭，会打扫，会拎包，会陪在你身边。你看，我的故事核心和感觉都是非常上海的，我去了解上海的文化，然后把这些写进剧本里。"

"这是一座未来之城"

来上海前，伦敦、巴黎、纽约都曾留下过尚希林的足迹，而现在，他把上海称为自己的家。

"我真的很喜欢这个地方，对我来说最重要的是这里充满着未来主义的感觉，上海绝对是一座属于未来的城市。"说起对上海的体会，尚希林眼中闪耀光芒。"上海有许多经过历史沉淀的老建筑，厚重而古朴；但同时，居民们生活中又使用着各种先进且便捷的应用程序。走在这座城市里，你能看到巨大的屏幕、璀璨的演艺空间，以及众多美妙的小艺术画廊，真是一个非常有趣的城市，比世界上大多数城市都有趣，这让我相信我是居住在未来。"

有了这种强烈的感受，尚希林和世界各地的朋友们聊天时会不时反问："你知道，住在上海是什么感觉吗？我必须说，这就像身处《银翼杀手》里的电影场景，这里是一座真正的'未来之城'。"

用动画讲好上海故事

尚希林连续几年担任中国动漫金龙奖终审评委，这让他有机会看到更多中国以及海外的优秀动画作品。"中国电影业正处于蓬勃发展期，一年比一年好，可以预见的增长也相当可观。对那些优秀的动画作品而言，因为我不是在中国出生和长大的，在文化理解方面会有点脱节，可是当我在这里的时间越久，我就越能理解东方文化的表达方式，对东方文化题材也更加敏感。"

7年的上海生活，让尚希林有了讲"上海故事"的冲动。"我有许多新想法，随着时间的推移，这些想法变得丰富起来。"

尚希林正将这些灵感付诸笔端，不久的未来，上海的身影将出现在更多动画短片中，展现在世界观众面前。

Name: Shawn Patrick Tilling
Chinese Name: 尚希林
Nationality: Canadian
Position: Head of 3D Animation & Visual Effects, Shanghai Vancouver Film School

Shawn Patrick Tilling:
Telling Shanghai stories with animation

Do you know what it feels like living in Shanghai? I must say it's like living in the scenes of the movie Blade Runner. It is really a City of the Future.

Having been teaching at Vancouver Film School in Canada since 2001; winning Golden Globe of independent short film in 2005; serving as CG supervisor for famous clients such as DreamWorks, Walt Disney Pictures, MGM and the International Olymp'Arts Committee… Shawn Patrick Tilling's career is full of these high-profile names and organizations.

In 2014, Tilling came to Shanghai and assumed the position of department head for the 3D Animation and Visual Effect program at Shanghai Vancouver Film School. He aspires to facilitate the development of China's film industry, and he has been pursuing his dream in this far away stage in the East. He predicts: "China has become one of the biggest box office markets. If it is not the biggest one, then it will soon be in the future."

From a stranger to an explorer of "urban treasures"

Now Tilling is fully engaged in producing a short animation film set in Shanghai. He says: "I make my small robot character wandering around, exploring the amazing Shanghai." The inspiration of this short film is the lovely surprises a stranger would run into when he arrives at a beautiful new world. He says: "This is like in Shanghai, when you turn around a corner you would be amazed by something totally new to you and get deeply impressed."

Tilling has been working in Vancouver Film School since 2001. About seven years ago, when China's film industry was about to experience significant growth, the school asked him whether he was interested in China and participating in a study program. He accepted the task with pleasure. He says: "I came here with a strong sense of mission. After arrival in Shanghai, we spent a lot of time developing the program of 3D Animation and Visual Effect. We want to make this

Shawn Patrick Tilling:

Telling Shanghai stories with animation

program into one of the world's best, and produce the top talents for this industry."

Seven years' exploration and immersion have made Tilling no longer a stranger, but a scavager of urban treasures. He says: "This dynamic city is full of inspirations for my creative work, and I hope it'll continue to influence everything I do." He reveals that he is working on another short cartoon film, which is about how a heroine fights against all odds and achieves final success.

He says: "This short film is full of human touch. I also wanted to find a 'perfect boyfriend' for this girl in the script. But what does a perfect boyfriend look like in China? I asked for help from my Chinese colleagues. They told me that in Shanghai, a good boyfriend would cook, do home cleaning, carry his girlfriend's handbag and was always there for her. So apparently my story's core plot and feeling is very close to Shanghai. I tried to understand the Shanghai culture and put these insights into the script."

"This is a city of the future"

Before Shanghai, Tilling left his footprints in London, Paris and New York. And now he takes Shanghai as his home.

With light in his eyes, Tilling talks about his understanding of Shanghai: "I really like this place. The most important reason for me is the futuristic feeling. Shanghai is definitely a city that belongs to the future. Shanghai has many old buildings with many historic stories, marked both by grandeur and simplicity. But at the same time, people here are using all kinds of advanced and convenient apps. Walking inside the city, you can see huge screens, glamorous performance spaces and numerous boutique galleries. It's a very interesting city, more interesting than most of the cities in the world. All these convince me that I'm living in the future."

With this strong feeling, Tilling would usually ask his friends around the world a rhetorical question: "Do you know the feeling of living in Shanghai? I must say it's like living in the scenes of *Blade Runner*. It's really a 'City of the Future.'"

Telling Shanghai Stories with Animation

For several years Tilling has served as a jury member of China's Animation & Comic Competition Golden Dragon Award, which has given him opportunities of seeing many high-quality homemade and international animation films. He says: "China's film industry is in the booming stage and every year sees new progress. The foreseeable future potential is also phenomenal. Because I was not born and raised in China, maybe I can't get immediately the cultural nuances in these good animation films. But the longer I stay here, the more familiar I get with the way of expression in eastern culture, and more sensitive to eastern cultural topics."

After living in Shanghai for seven years, Tilling feels the urge to tell "Shanghai Stories". He says, "I have many new ideas, and as time goes by, these ideas get fleshed out."

Now Tilling is turning these inspirations into scripts and in the near future, Shanghai will make more appearances in animated short films and be seen by more global viewers.

Scan for videos

姓　名：Marie Harder
中文名：玛丽·哈德
国　籍：英国
职　位：复旦大学环境科学与工程系教授

玛丽·哈德：
上海垃圾分类的效果是成功的

两年后的今天，根据测算和研究，上海垃圾分类的效果是成功的。

十年前，一位来自英国的女士带领她的学生们开始在上海的一些小区"捡垃圾"，垃圾分类行为对于当时的小区居民来说还很费劲，这个课题组捡垃圾的行为也不被小区居民理解。然而，最终她给《上海市生活垃圾管理条例》中的一些细则提供了实践与理论支撑。她就是复旦大学环境科学与工程系教授玛丽·哈德。

从不喜欢大城市，到爱上上海

来中国之前，玛丽住在英国，也曾收到过很多学术邀请，但由于"不喜欢大城市"，玛丽都拒绝了。十年前，玛丽收到复旦大学的邀请，这一次玛丽留下了深刻的印象，也改变了对大城市的固有印象，玛丽不仅喜欢上了复旦大学，还爱上了上海。

2011年，玛丽决定和丈夫举家迁往上海。在英国时，玛丽就已经在做商业垃圾分类和居民垃圾分类的研究。据她介绍，垃圾分类在全世界都是很难的。在伦敦城中心，一处只有几十户人家的小区域内，垃圾分类率做到30%已经被认为"非常好"了。而在旧金山城中心，很小的一片住宅内，做到50%的分类率则会感到"十分骄傲"。

到上海后，她发现上海对于垃圾分类有一定认识，但却不如现在那么受到重视。在与朋友、学生们的交流中，玛丽得出一个结论："小区是一个完美的试验场。"由于当时复旦大学在垃圾分类这一议题上，还没有以扎根社区为基础的研究，玛丽和学生们便一起探索新的解决方案。"一开始进入社区搜集数据时，学生们并不想告诉家长自己在社区里做和垃圾相关的工作。"玛丽告诉记者，而对于一个外国人带着中国学生"捡垃圾"，小区居民也觉得很奇怪。

深入社区研究垃圾分类

为了收集到更准确的数据，玛丽带领学生深入社区。作为国内最早关注垃圾分类的高校科研团队之一，复旦大学可持续行为研究课题组进行了10年的跟踪研究，研究城市居民垃圾分类行为如何从建立意愿、开始分类到持续养成习惯。"学生们一开始也不太了解。其实我们在构建一种理论。这些理论需要从小的实验开始，从小区到街道，再扩展到整个上海市。最终，我们提取出上海垃圾分类的几个行为要素。"玛丽解释道。

2019年2月，《上海市生活垃圾管理条例》全文正式公布。条例通过法律的强制性推动垃圾分类，包括固化共识性的管理要求、明确各类责任主体、强制源头减量、落实分类体系的全程监管等。

在上海进入垃圾分类"强制时代"之前，玛丽和她的团队向上海市政府提供了报告，提交了研究中的3个要素，其中包括设施设备的完善和合理、居民对垃圾分类角色的认知、友好的志愿者人际交互值班制度。

玛丽告诉记者，自条例实施以来，成效很快就展现出来了。在两年后的今天，根据测算和研究，目前上海垃圾分类的效果是成功的。

Name: Marie Harder
Chinese name: 玛丽·哈德
Nationality: British
Position: Professor of Department of Environmental Science and Engineering, Fudan University

Marie Harder:
Shanghai's garbage sorting is a success

Now, two years later, according to the calculation and studies, garbage sorting in Shanghai is a success.

Ten years ago, a British professor began to lead her students to pick up garbage in some residential communities in Shanghai. Garbage sorting was a laborious job for the community residents at that time, so the garbage picking of this research group puzzled the residents. However, in the end, she provided practical and theoretical support for some detailed rules in Shanghai's regulation on household waste management. She is Marie Harder, a professor in the Department of Environmental Science and Engineering at Fudan University.

From no liking for big cities to loving Shanghai

Before coming to China, Harder lived in the UK and had received many academic invitations, but she refused them all because she didn't like big cities. Ten years ago, Harder received an invitation from Fudan University, which left her a deep impression and changed her stereotype of big cities. Harder fell in love not only with Fudan University but also with Shanghai.

In 2011, Harder decided to move her family to Shanghai. While in the UK, she was already researching commercial garbage sorting and residential garbage sorting. According to Harder, garbage sorting is a difficult task all over the world. For a small area with only dozens of households in downtown London, a 30% garbage sorting rate can be considered as "very good", while in the city center of San Francisco, residents in a very small area of housing would "be very proud of" themselves if the garbage sorting rate reaches 50%.

After arriving in Shanghai, Harder found that there was some awareness of garbage sorting in Shanghai, but it was not attached so much importance as it

Marie Harder:

Shanghai's garbage sorting is a success

is now. From the communication with friends and students, Harder concluded: "The local neighborhood is a perfect testing ground." Since there was no neighborhood-based research on garbage sorting at Fudan University at that time, Harder decided to explore new solutions with her students.

Harder says: "When they first entered the neighborhood to collect data, the students didn't want to tell their parents that they were doing garbage-related work in a neighborhood." She says that residents there also felt it very strange that a foreigner was leading Chinese students in "picking up garbage".

In-depth residential community research on garbage sorting

In order to collect more accurate data, Harder led her students to go deep into the local residential communities. As one of the earliest university research teams in China focusing on garbage sorting, the sustainable behavior research group in Fudan University conducted a 10-year follow-up study. They studied the process of the urban residents' garbage sorting behavior, from establishing the willingness, starting to sort to developing habits. Harder explains: "The students didn't quite understand it at first. Actually, we were building a theory. These theories needed to start with small experiments, from the residential communities to subdistricts and then to the entire Shanghai. Eventually, we extracted several behavioral essentials of garbage sorting in Shanghai."

In February 2019, the full text of the domestic garbage regulations of Shanghai was officially released. The regulation promotes garbage sorting through mandatory requirements, including consolidating consensus management requirements, clarifying various responsible subjects, enforcing source reduction and implementing the supervision of the sorting system.

Before Shanghai entered the "mandatory era" of waste separation, Harder and her team provided a report to the Shanghai Municipal Government, submitting three elements of the study, including the improvement and rationalization of facilities and equipment, residents' perceptions of their role in waste separation, and a friendly system of interpersonal interaction between volunteers on duty.

Harder says that since the implementation of the regulation, the effects became evident quickly. Now, two years later, according to the calculation and studies, garbage sorting in Shanghai is a success.

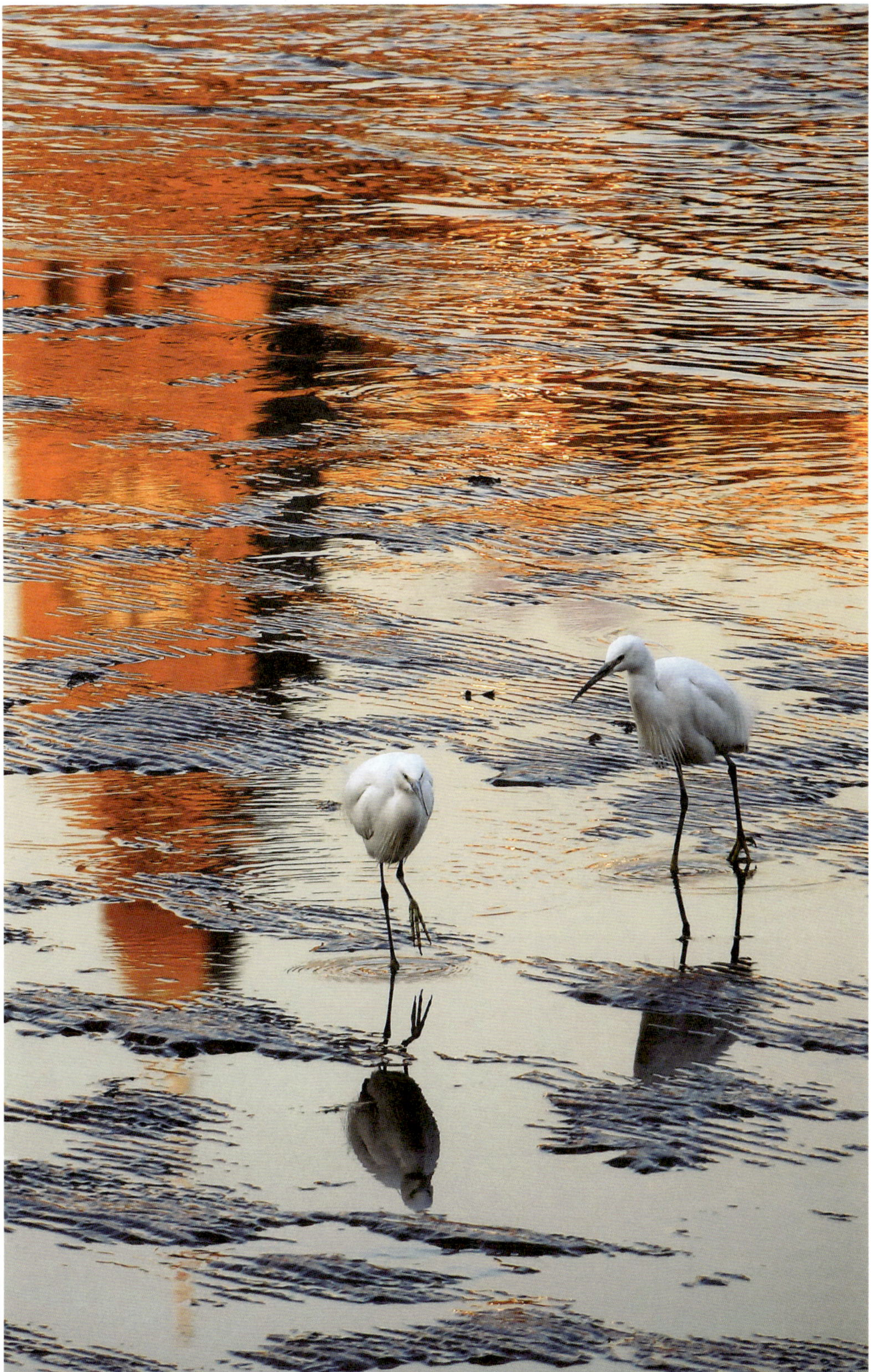

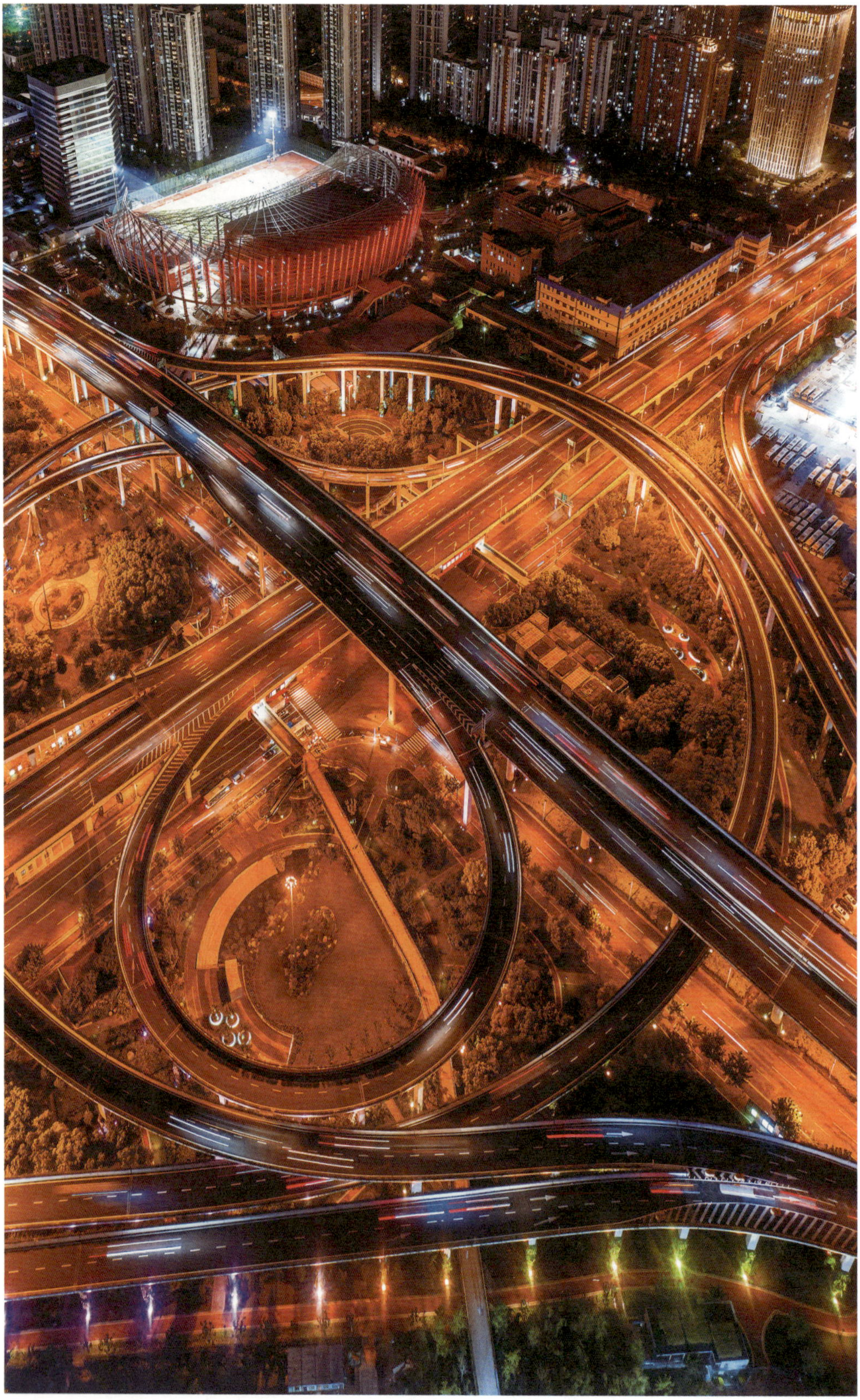

姓　名：Yann Bozec
中文名：杨葆焱
国　籍：法国
职　位：Tapestry 亚太区总裁、Coach 中国区总裁兼首席执行官

杨葆焱：
上海乃至中国正成为世界时尚产业发展的驱动力量

上海乃至中国已经成为全球时尚产业发展的重要驱动力。

"我一直想要探索世界，所以我很幸运能够有机会在莫斯科、东京、巴黎、新加坡等多个城市和国家居住。"2002 年，杨葆焱第一次来到上海，当时便十分感慨上海是一座充满活力、潜力巨大的城市。2006 年，他重新回到了上海，"我惊叹于上海这座城市积极热情的风貌以及高速发展的节奏，希望自己也能成为其中的一分子。"

将"中国时尚"推向国际舞台

杨葆焱尤其喜欢上海的社区氛围，他说："社区就像一个小小的桃源，很亲切。"在杨葆焱看来，是上海多元包容的人文精神和创新进取的氛围，吸引了如此之多才华横溢的人才。

上海已成为当今世界上最重要的时尚和艺术之都之一，作为时尚巨头的"中国当家人"，杨葆焱认为中国消费者已成为全球时尚市场的重要力量，他们的知识与洞察力总是能够为品牌带来许多灵感。

"上海乃至中国正成为世界时尚产业发展的驱动力量。"杨葆焱坦言，他们不仅积极与本土艺术家开展交流，而且致力于将"中国时尚"推向国际舞台，让"中国设计"引领全球风尚，让更多人领略与感受"中国魅力"。

2018 年 12 月，Coach 首次在纽约以外的城市举办时尚大秀，选址

就在上海,展现以"中国设计"为代表的文化自信。

营商环境优化,坚定扎根中国信心

工作之余,杨葆焱喜欢旅行,在游历中国的大好河山的同时,他还关心着中国的传统手工艺。杨葆焱知道中国的每个省市都有着独特的手工艺人,"每次团队向我介绍当地的手工艺术和文化遗产时,我都发自内心地喜爱并感慨中国拥有着如此多元的艺术瑰宝。每个人都有义务并要尽最大的努力来保护这些珍贵技艺。"

对于中国市场,杨葆焱表示,《外商投资法》《优化营商环境条例》等一系列惠企利好政策的实施与推进,都为市场的发展注入了巨大动能,进一步优化了营商环境,也更加坚定了他们扎根中国市场的信心和决心。

2020年5月,在上海市政府与静安区政府的大力协助下,Tapestry集团与中国国际进口博览局签署了全面长期合作备忘录,未来三年(第三届至第五届)将连续参展进博会。

"上海这座城市已经成为我们的家"

尽管受到了新冠肺炎疫情的冲击,中国仍是2020年全球唯一实现正增长的主要经济体。Tapestry也是中国市场利好的获益者。"在过去的2021财年第二季度中,中国市场持续强劲,增长显著,内地市场的营业额同比增长超过30%。"杨葆焱告诉记者。

目前,杨葆焱的大女儿在巴黎生活,但她即将搬来上海,在上海纽约大学继续深造。

杨葆焱说:"上海这座城市已经成为我们的家。"

Name: Yann Bozec
Chinese name: 杨葆焱
Nationality: French
Position: President of Tapestry Asia Pacific & President and CEO of Coach Greater China

Yann Bozec:
Shanghai and China have become the driving force for the development of the world fashion industry

Shanghai and China have become an important driving force for the development of the world fashion industry.

Yann Bozec says: "I have always wanted to explore the world, so I am very lucky to have the opportunity to live in Moscow, Tokyo, Paris, Singapore and other cities and countries." When Yann Bozec first came to Shanghai in 2002, he was very impressed with the city's dynamism and potential, and in 2006, he returned to Shanghai. He says: "I marvel at the city's positive and enthusiastic outlook and its rapid development, and hope I can be part of it."

Pushing "Chinese Fashion" to the international stage

Bozec especially likes the community atmosphere in Shanghai. "The community is filled with a sense of kinship," he says. In his view, it is Shanghai's pluralistic and inclusive humanistic spirit and its innovative and enterprising atmosphere that have attracted so many talented people.

Shanghai has become one of the most important fashion and art capitals in the world today. As the head in China of a fashion giant, Bozec believes that Chinese consumers have become an important force in the global fashion market, and that their knowledge and insight can always bring a lot of inspiration to various brands.

"Shanghai and China are becoming the driving force for the development of the world fashion industry," says Bozec. He admits that they have not only

Yann Bozec:

Shanghai and China have become the driving force for the development of the world fashion industry

an active dialogue with local artists but also a commitment to pushing "Chinese fashion" to the international stage, so that "Chinese design" can lead the global fashion trend and more people can appreciate and feel "Chinese charm."

In December 2018, Coach held its first fashion show in a city other than New York -- Shanghai. The move showcased the cultural confidence represented by "Chinese design".

Business environment optimization and confidence in putting down roots in China

After work, Bozec likes to travel. While admiring the great rivers and mountains of China, he also cares about Chinese traditional handicrafts. He knows that every province and city in China has its own unique craftsmen. He says: "Every time the team introduced me to the local handicraft and cultural heritage, I was struck by how much I loved and how diverse China's artistic treasures are. Everyone has an obligation and must do their best to preserve these precious skills."

For the Chinese market, Bozec says that the implementation and promotion of a series of favorable regulations and policies for enterprises, such as the Foreign Investment Law and the Regulations on Optimizing the Business Environment, have injected great momentum into the development of the market, further optimized the business environment, and strengthened their confidence and determination to put down roots in the Chinese market.

In May 2020, with the great assistance of the Shanghai Municipal Government and Jing'an District Government, Tapestry signed a comprehensive and long-term cooperation memorandum with China International Import Expo Bureau, and will continuously participate in China International Import Expo in the next three years (the third to the fifth).

"Shanghai has become our home"

Despite the impact of the COVID-19 pandemic, China is the only major economy in the world to achieve positive growth in 2020. Tapestry has also benefited from the Chinese market. "In the second quarter of the fiscal year 2021, the Chinese market continued to be strong and grew significantly, with revenue in the mainland market increased by more than 30 percent year-on-year," says Bozec.

At present, Bozec's eldest daughter lives in Paris, but she will soon move to Shanghai to continue her studies at New York University Shanghai.

"Shanghai has become our home," Bozec says.

姓　名：Javier Nieto
中文名：聂威尔
国　籍：西班牙
职　位：西萨化工（上海）有限公司总经理

聂威尔：
中国政治制度巨大的优势是可以做很长远的规划

> 我想了解中国不同的文化。中国这么大的国家，是无法用单一的文化来形容的。

1960 年，聂威尔随家人从西班牙移民到荷兰，定居鹿特丹。2005 年，聂威尔加入了西萨化工集团，担任国际商贸的重要职责，又过了 13 年，聂威尔和家人来到中国，开启了他们的"上海生活"。

用脚步丈量中国

来到中国后，他有了一个响亮的中文名字——聂威尔。尽管来中国的时间不算长，但由于酷爱旅行，只要有空聂威尔就会和家人一起用脚步丈量中国。中国的新冠肺炎疫情率先被控制后，聂威尔继续他的中国深度游。他希望在中国的这段时间，尽可能去更多的地方看看。

在聂威尔接下来的旅游清单上，排在首位的是中国西北地区，他想去走一走古老的丝绸之路，包括西安、张掖、敦煌、吐鲁番、乌鲁木齐、喀什等地。"我想了解中国不同的文化。中国这么大的国家，是无法用单一的文化来形容的。中国有一些地方，也许并不那么为外国人所知，它们和东部沿海地区非常不同。"

除了旅行，聂威尔还是一个美食爱好者，"我基本上尝遍了中国所有的美食，几乎什么都喜欢。在中国，我唯一不喜欢的就是臭豆腐，但是我可以接受鸡脚、肥肠。"

聂威尔：

中国政治制度巨大的优势是可以做很长远的规划

"我认为上海的团队是最好的"

聂威尔能安心游历中国，也得益于他的"上海团队"。"我与世界各地的许多国际团队合作过，我认为上海的团队是最好的。"聂威尔告诉记者，中国的员工总在追求更好的自我，他们有意志和决心，而且适应挑战和变化的速度非常惊人。

除了上海的团队，中国政府的长远规划也让聂威尔觉得很安心。"今年是中国共产党成立 100 周年。我认为目前中国政治制度巨大的优势是可以做很长远的规划。如果你能做长远的规划，你就可以调整并引导你的未来。"聂威尔举例，中国以外的很多国家只能展望 2—4 年，因为 4 年后会进行新的选举。

"从公司的角度来说，中国的发展方式值得信任。我知道我是为了留在中国而来的，我们的公司也是想要长期留下来才来到这里的。如果中国有一个长远的目标，那我也会追逐同样的目标。因为我知道，我将会得到中国共产党和中国政府的支持。"

聂威尔觉得中国的决策非常高效，他举例，面对疫情，中国是第一个采取严格措施的国家，同时还实施了有助于经济继续发展的举措。

"我认为，这只有在中国这样的政治体制下才能做到。我对中国的未来有无穷的信心！"

Name: Javier Nieto
Chinese name: 聂威尔
Nationality: Spanish
Position: General Manager, Cepsa Chemical Shanghai

Javier Nieto:

The huge advantage of the current Chinese political system is that it allows long-term plans

I want to know the various cultures in this country. China is too big to be depicted in one single culture.

In 1960, Javier Nieto emigrated from Spain to the Netherlands with his family and settled in Rotterdam. In 2005, he joined Cepsa Chemical and took up an important position in its international trade. After another 13 years, he and his family came to China and started their life in Shanghai.

Measuring China with his footsteps

After coming to China, Nieto got a cool Chinese name -- Nie Wei'er. He loves traveling so whenever he was free he would travel somewhere in China with his family. After the COVID-19 pandemic was first put under control in China, he continued his in-depth tours in China. He hopes to visit as many places as possible during his stay in China.

Northwest China tops the list of Nieto's next travel. He wants to travel along the ancient Silk Road, including Xi'an, Zhangye, Dunhuang, Turpan, Urumqi and Kashgar. He says: "I want to know the various cultures in this country. China is too big to be depicted in one single culture. There are places in China that may not be so well-known to foreigners, and they are very different from China's eastern seaboard."

In addition to traveling, Nieto is also a food lover. He says: "I've almost tried all the cuisines in China and I like almost everything. The only thing I don't like in

Javier Nieto:

The huge advantage of the current Chinese political system is that it allows long-term plans

China is stinky tofu, but I can accept chicken feet and chitterlings."

"The team in Shanghai is the best"

Nieto can travel around China with no worries thanks to his "Shanghai Team". He says: "I have worked with many international teams around the world, and my Shanghai team is definitely the best." He says that Chinese employees are always pursuing a better self. They have the will and determination, and their speed of adapting themselves to challenges and changes is amazing.

In addition to his team in Shanghai, he also feels reassured by the Chinese government's long-term planning. Nieto says: "This year marks the 100th anniversary of the founding of the Communist Party of China (CPC). I think the huge advantage of the current Chinese political system is that it allows long-term plans. If long-term plans can be made, China will be able to adjust and guide its future." He cites the example that many countries outside of China can only look ahead two to four years because four years later there will be new elections.

Nieto says: "From a company's perspective, China's way of development is trustworthy. So I know that I came to China to stay, and our company is to stay here for a long time. If China has a long-term goal, then I will pursue the same goal, because I know that I will get the support of the CPC and the Chinese government."

Nieto thinks that China's decision-making is very efficient. For example, in the face of the pandemic, China was the first country to take strict measures, and, at the same time, implemented measures to help the economy continue to develop.

He says: "I think this can only be done under a political system like China. I have infinite confidence in China's future!"

姓　名：Lisa Martel De Santis Chisholm
中文名：丽莎·奇泽姆
国　籍：美国
职　位：上海闵行区万科双语学校外方副校长

丽莎·奇泽姆：
上海的教育正变得更加包容

> 当我回美国时，遇到那些对中国有误解的人，我会向他们解释，事实并不是你在美国电视上看到的那样。

"我的名字太长了，所以学校里的人都叫我 Ms.C（C 女士）。"如今任职于上海闵行区万科双语学校的外方副校长丽莎·奇泽姆可以说是经历丰富，她在美国出生、意大利长大，并在欧洲多个国家生活过。

2001 年，来到上海的奇泽姆从幼教做起，她的一句话道出了对这座城市的喜爱之情："我来上海已经有 20 年时间了，并且以后也想一直待在上海。"

为双语教育发展挥洒汗水

"我刚来的时候，浦东还只有东方明珠和金茂大厦。"奇泽姆回忆刚来上海时的情形说，当时她和家人站在外滩看向对面浦东时，不禁发出了"哇哦"的感叹。"中国的建设速度真的很快。在中国，当国家决定要做何事时，立马就能动工、完成。而如果是其他国家，进展速度则会特别慢。"

来上海的第一年，奇泽姆在一所国际学校任教。但在她眼中，这所学校太"不接地气"了。于是，奇泽姆打电话给父母，询问他们的建议。父母告诉她，把姿态放低一点，去本地化一些的学校。"于是我在幼儿园教了 3 年书。"奇泽姆如今任教的上海万科双语学校，前身为创立于 2006 年的复旦万科实验学校"双语 C 班"，而"C 班"正是奇泽姆开启她双语教学生涯的地方。

"这些年间，上海的教育逐渐变得更加包容。"奇泽姆坦言，在十几年前，

丽莎·奇泽姆

上海的教育正变得更加包容

对许多人来说，只有语文、数学和英语等少数科目是重要的，"但现在从这些孩子身上可以看出，上海的教育正努力确保他们的身心健康，我认为这是一件非常好的事情"。

"学党史，初心如磐向未来""'纪念抗美援朝70周年'大型主题班会"……万科双语学校会不定期开展爱国爱党德育活动。奇泽姆说，道德教育课虽然由中国教师来授课，但她同样重视。"这是一个非常严肃的问题，热爱你自己的国家很重要。这15年来，每天早上8时15分国歌响起时，我都会站在孩子们的中间，同样给予国歌尊重。我告诉孩子们，热爱你的国家，尊重你的国家，为你的国家尽最大努力是很重要的。"

与上海在"疫"起

去年新冠肺炎疫情暴发时期，奇泽姆也用自己的行动表达着对这座城市的爱：多次组织社区志愿者宣传防疫安全措施、参与中小学线上双语课程设计工作……

"在新冠肺炎疫情发生后，世界各个国家的处理方法我们都有看到。因为中国政府的正确处理方式，我们现在才能自由地四处走动和生活。"奇泽姆赞叹道。

疫情期间，这位副校长也时刻为复学准备着，2020年2月17日，万科双语学校返沪复工率就已经高达95%。不过奇泽姆也坦言，最初学校采取线上授课时，他们有些措手不及。"孩子们的心理健康是一个大问题。政府给出了很多建议，还给我们分发了口罩。"

奇泽姆说，因为已经在中国住了很久，所以很了解这个国度。"当我回美国时，遇到那些对中国有误解的人，我会向他们解释，事实并不是你在美国电视上看到的那样。"

对于孩子们，她也是这么教导的："如果是一个十五六岁的孩子即将出国，我会让他明白，在外国某处听到的信息并不意味着就是真的，要反复检查、思考。"

Name: Lisa Martel De Santis Chisholm
Chinese name: 丽莎·奇泽姆
Nationality: American
Position: Vice Principal of Western Curriculum, Vanke Bilingual School

Lisa Martel De Santis Chisholm:
Education in Shanghai is getting more inclusive

> When I returned to the United States and met those who have misunderstandings about China, I would explain to them that the facts are not what you saw on American TV.

"Because my name is so long, everybody at school calls me Ms. C," says Lisa Martel De Santis Chisholm, western principal at Vanke Bilingual School Minhang, Shanghai, who has rich life experience. Born in the United States and raised in Italy, she has also lived in several European countries.

Chisholm, who came to Shanghai in 2001 and started as a kindergarten teacher, expresses her love for the city: "I've been here in Shanghai for 20 years, and I would like to stay here forever."

Working hard for the development of bilingual education

"When I first came here, Pudong only had the Oriental Pearl TV Tower and Jinmao Tower," says Chisholm. She recalls when she first came to Shanghai, she stood on the Bund and looked across to Pudong with her family, exclaiming "Wow". She says: "China is developing really fast. When the Chinese government decides to do something, it can be started and finished in a very short time. In other countries, the pace of progress would be particularly slow."

In her first year in Shanghai, Chisholm taught at an international school. But in her eyes, the school was not very "down-to-earth." So she called her parents and asked for their advice. They suggested for her to go local and go to a more localized school. She says: "So I taught in kindergartens for three years." Chisholm now teaches at Shanghai Vanke Bilingual School, formerly known as "Bilingual Class C" at Fudan Vanke Experimental School, which was founded in 2006, and where Chisholm began her bilingual teaching career.

"Over the years, education in Shanghai has become more inclusive,"

Lisa Martel De Santis Chisholm:

Education in Shanghai is getting more inclusive

Chisholm says, adding that a decade or so ago, only a few subjects such as Chinese, Maths and English were attached great importance to. "But now you can see from these children that education institutions in Shanghai are also aimed at ensuring their physical and mental health, which I think is a very good thing," she says.

Vanke Bilingual School will carry out patriotic and Party education activities from time to time, such as "Learning Party History & Staying True to Mission" and "Themed Class Meeting on Commemoration of 70th Anniversary of the War to Resist U.S. Aggression and Aid North Korea." Chisholm says that although moral education is taught by Chinese teachers, she also appreciates it. She says: "This is a very serious matter. It is very important to love your own country. For the past 15 years, when the national anthem sounded at 8:15 every morning, I would stand among the children and pay respect to the national anthem. I told the children that it is very important to love your country, respect your country and do your best for your country."

Together in Shanghai fighting the pandemic

During the outbreak of the COVID-19 pandemic last year, Chisholm also expressed her love for the city with her own actions, like mobilizing community volunteers many times to publicize pandemic prevention measures and participating in online bilingual curriculum design in primary and secondary schools.

Chisholm says: "We have seen the way various countries around the world have handled the COVID-19 pandemic after it happened. We are now able to walk around and live freely because of the right way the Chinese government has handled the situation."

This vice principal was also always ready for the resumption of school during the outbreak. By February 17, 2020, Vanke Bilingual School had reached a work resumption rate of 95%. But Chisholm also admits that they were unprepared at first when the school adopted online teaching. She says: "The children's mental health was a big issue. The government gave a lot of advice and provided us with face masks as well."

Chisholm says that because she has lived in China for a long time, she knows the country very well. She says: "When I returned to the United States and met those who have misunderstandings about China, I would explain to them that the facts are not what you saw on American TV."

Chisholm teaches her students in the same way. She says: "If it was a 15 or 16 years old about to go abroad, I would make sure he understood that just because he heard something somewhere in a foreign country doesn't mean it's true. It would be better to double-check and think over it."

姓　名：Andre Rosendo
国　籍：巴西
职　位：上海科技大学信息学院研究员、助理教授

Andre Rosendo:
放眼全球寻找合适的实验室，我把目光锁定了上海

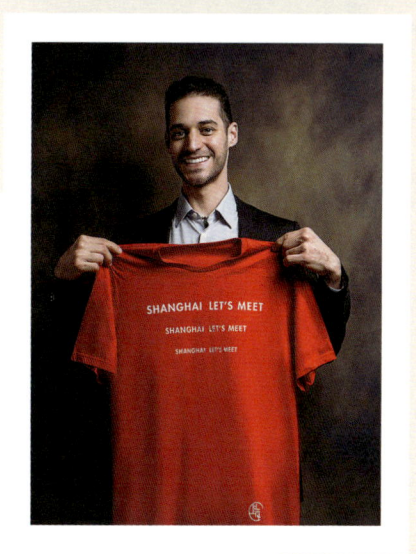

在中国做机器人研发最好的城市，当数上海。

在上海科技大学自动化与机器人中心实验室里，来自巴西的 Andre 手持遥控器向"蹲"在脚边的"小黑"发出一连串指令：快速前进、躲避障碍、原地小跑……一系列动作"小黑"完成得一气呵成。

"小黑"是 Andre 实验室里最新一代机器狗，搜救、测量、物流……未来应用场景广阔。Andre 的工作之一就是让"小黑"变得更聪明，学习在不同场景自主选择行动路径，发生错误也能不依赖人力进行修正。"想象一下未来的机器人，它们能够根据生产线进行自我适应、自我修复，借助人力的地方将会越来越少。"

学霸锁定上海

今年 36 岁的 Andre 是枚妥妥的学霸。在巴西读完机械工程本科后，到日本完成了硕士和博士学业，继而又在英国剑桥大学度过了 3 年博士后研究生涯。2017 年，Andre 想在机器人研究领域有所突破，放眼全球寻找合适的实验室。彼时，上海正加快建设具有全球有影响力的科技创新中心，《2018 上海科技创新中心指数报告》显示，充沛的科研基金、领先的科研机构、高水平的科研基础设施和丰富的科研工作机会等，使上海成为全球科学家最向往工作的中国城市。

在比较了多个城市的重点实验室后，Andre 把目光锁定了上海。"上海和深圳是中国 IT 行业的领头羊。但就研发投入而言，上海的力度是最大的。"

Andre Rosendo:

放眼全球寻找合适的实验室，我把目光锁定了上海

得益于上海人才签证的快速便利，Andre很快办妥了所有手续，成功入驻上海科技大学自动化与机器人中心灵机实验室（Living Machines Lab）。

"你看这个机器人，当我们模拟它的一条腿损坏后，它仍有能力继续走路。"在实验室里Andre大展身手，多个机器人项目上马，智能应用迭代更新。几年间，他带领团队研发了不少能够适应缺陷和故障的机器人：缺损手指的机械臂仍能在生产线上工作，移动测量机器人在缺少一部分腿部支撑后，也能继续执行任务……技术的巨大突破将机器人带入一个新时代。

启蒙小学生编程

来到上海后，Andre曾报名学习中文，但他发现这里不论是学术界大咖，还是求学的莘莘学子，英语水平都可圈可点，交流起来几乎没障碍。"上海有许多国际一流人才，能和他们经常交流让我很开心。"Andre每周都会参加同济大学、上海纽约大学同领域专家的聚会，和这些行业先锋们畅聊机器人发展前景，让他激情澎湃。

工作之余，Andre也闲不住，攀岩、骑行样样拿手。松江区陈春小学买了一批电脑，找不到授课老师，Andre听说后立马自告奋勇要求去当编外老师，巴西人的热情性格在他身上一览无余。"当一个人只有七八岁的时候，很难知道将来会从事什么职业，能够早点让孩子们接触编程，找到兴趣点，这非常有意义。"Andre的课程很受孩子们欢迎，有些小学生在掌握了基础编程后，已经开始向更高难度的编程发起挑战。"当然也有一些学生不喜欢，因为这不是他们将来想要做的事情。不管怎样，我认为这是个很好的方式，我很喜欢它。"

世界大赛展中国实力

去过不少国家，在许多重点实验室里工作过，Andre认为中国机器人水平已经跻身世界一流。"在中国做机器人研发最好的城市，当数上海。"Andre介绍道，2年前他曾带领上科大团队从国内68支队伍中脱颖而出，参加在加拿大举办的世界机甲大师高校人工智能挑战赛，并取得了前八名的好成绩。

Andre摩拳擦掌计划着重出江湖，"我今天已经准备跟团员们开个会，告诉他们去打疫苗，让我们到国际赛事里再展中国实力"。

Name: Andre Rosendo
Nationality: Brazilian
Position: Assistant Professor of SIST, ShanghaiTech University

Andre Rosendo:
Looking for suitable labs in the world, I set my sights on Shanghai

The best city to do robotics R&D in China is Shanghai.

In the lab of ShanghaiTech Automation and Robotics Center, Andre Rosendo from Brazil is holding a remote control and giving a series of instructions to "Xiaohei" who "sits" beside his foot: speed forward, dodge obstacles, trot in place… "Xiaohei" accomplishes all the actions at one go.

"Xiaohei" is the latest generation of robot dogs in Rosendo's lab which can be used in search and rescue, measurement, and logistics, with broad application scenarios in the future. One of Rosendo's jobs is to make "Xiaohei" smarter -- able to learn to choose a path of action independently in different scenarios and correct mistakes without relying on humans. "Imagine the robots of the future. They can adapt and repair themselves based on the production line and there will be less and less human intervention," he says.

The high achiever chose Shanghai

Rosendo, 36, has an exemplary academic record. After receiving a bachelor's degree in mechanical engineering in Brazil, he went to Japan to complete the master's and doctoral programs and then to the University of Cambridge in the UK to carry on three years of post-doctoral research. In 2017, Rosendo wanted to make a breakthrough in the robot research field, so he began to look for a suitable lab around the world. At that time, Shanghai was accelerating its construction of a science and technology innovation center with global influence. Shanghai Science and Technology Innovation Center Index Report 2018 shows that Shanghai has become the most desirable Chinese city to work for scientists worldwide due to its abundant research funds, leading research institutions, high-level research infrastructure, and ample job opportunities.

Rosendo settled in Shanghai after comparing key labs in several cities. "Shanghai and Shenzhen are the bellwethers of China's IT industry while

Andre Rosendo:

Looking for suitable labs in the world, I set my sights on Shanghai

Shanghai has the largest R&D investment," he says. Thanks to the fast and convenient application process for Shanghai talent visa, Rosendo completed all procedures quickly and was successfully admitted to the Living Machines Lab in ShanghaiTech Automation and Robotics Center.

Rosendo says: "Look at this robot. It will keep walking even when we simulate that one of its legs is damaged." In the lab Andre is making his mark, several robotics projects are being launched and smart applications are being updated. Over the years, he has led his team to develop many robots that can adapt to defects and faults: the mechanical arms with missing fingers can still work on the production line; the mobile measuring robot can continue to perform tasks even without part of leg support.

He taught pupils the basics of programming

After coming to Shanghai, Rosendo has signed up to learn Chinese once. However, he found that in Shanghai, whether academic gurus or school students, all can speak praiseworthy English and communicate in English easily. Every week, Rosendo would attend gatherings of experts in the same field from Tongji University and NYU Shanghai. "There are a lot of world-class talents in Shanghai and the frequent exchange with them makes me happy," says Rosendo.

Rosendo is busy even in his spare time. He loves rock climbing and riding. Chenchun Elementary School in Songjiang District purchased a batch of computers but failed to find a teacher. As soon as he heard about it, the warm Brazilian immediately volunteered to teach there.

He says: "When a person is only seven or eight years old, it's hard to know what career he will pursue in the future. It is meaningful to expose children to programming so that they can find their interests at an early age." Rosendo's course is very popular among the children and some pupils have begun to learn more difficult programming after mastering the basics. Rosendo says: "Of course, some students don't like it because it is not what they want to do in the future. Anyhow, I think it is good for them to know something about it, and I like this way."

Showing China's strength in international competitions

Having travelled to many countries and worked in many key labs, Rosendo believes that China's robotics level is already among the world's best. "The best city to do robotics R&D in China is Shanghai," says Rosendo. Two years ago, the ShanghaiTech University team led by him stood out from 68 domestic teams and competed in the RoboMaster University AI Challenge in Canada, achieving a good score in the top eight.

Rosendo is now preparing for a "comeback". He says: "I'll have a meeting today with team members and tell them to have vaccines so that we can show China's strength again in international competitions."

姓　名：Amir Khan
中文名：阿米尔·汗
国　籍：巴基斯坦
职　位：上海市闵行区外籍志愿者

阿米尔·汗：
我不能光索取，也要尽可能为上海做点什么

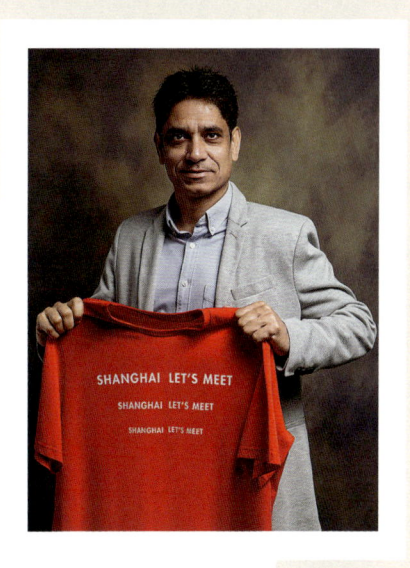

> 中国成功的一大秘诀是有坚强的领导力，而且人民始终是团结而勤奋的。

夹杂着中文和英文的词汇，阿米尔·汗表达着一个外籍人士对上海的印象："她很美，很友善，更关键的是，她充满爱。"这位来自巴基斯坦的职业经理人，已在中国生活了20来年，其中有10余年就在上海，亲眼见证了中国翻天覆地的变化。"中国成功的一大秘诀是有坚强的领导力，而且人民始终是团结而勤奋的。"阿米尔·汗如是说。

从"南亚的上海"来

阿米尔·汗的故乡是巴基斯坦第一大城市卡拉奇，"你们可以看作'南亚的上海'，我们很早就知道中国是巴基斯坦交往的国家里最重要的一个，它是'全天候伙伴'"。几十年来，中巴交往日益深厚，两国间的相互支持、帮助都是慷慨而无私的，更重要的是，这种交往能体现在普通人的生活里。

"我在上海的日子里，很喜欢中国朋友叫我'巴铁'，不光源于巴基斯坦人普遍怀有对中国淳朴的感情，还在于这种友谊植根于两国人民发自内心的'相互尊重'。"阿米尔·汗回忆，中国改革开放以来，经济发展取得长足进步，"但中国人仍然把自己视为发展中国家大家庭的一分子，而不是以'优等生'自居"。阿米尔·汗提到，得益于同中国"一带一路"倡议的对接，巴制造业得到显著发展，"过去我们主要出口棉花、黄麻、矿石等初级产品，但吸纳中国投资，双方企业开展合作后，这些有竞争力的产品得

阿米尔·汗：

我不能光索取，
也要尽可能为
上海做点什么

到深加工，获得更高的附加值，能在国际市场获得更高收益"。

"有'巴铁'这样的称谓，既是荣誉，也是责任。"阿米尔·汗说，去年中国发生新冠肺炎疫情后，正遭受27年来最严重蝗灾的巴基斯坦调集全国公立医院所有库存支援中国，"那个时候，巴国内朋友圈不断转发这样的评论，说得最多的是'我们终于有机会去帮助中国兄弟一把了''我们就该这么做，中国兄弟不会孤军奋战'"。

而当记者向阿米尔·汗展示不久前中国援巴疫苗运抵伊斯兰堡的照片时，他感慨地说："我们的友谊为什么历久弥坚，就是因为我们在各自艰难的时刻都能'有难同当'。"

中国在为未来投资

阿米尔·汗对"巴铁"的理解是"既得到爱，又奉献爱"，把上海乃至中国当作自己挚爱的"第二故乡"。他们家是在2010年搬到上海的。"我和妻子还有两个儿子，在华漕社区住了11年。"阿米尔·汗说，"我不能光索取，也要尽可能为上海做点什么。"

2019年，他得知为帮助越来越多的外籍人士了解本地文化，融入新的生活，华漕金丰国际社区发展促进会（JICDA）发起招募国际志愿者，他率先报名，"我用自己的经历告诉五湖四海的朋友，上海是能实现理想的地方"。特别是在上海的繁荣和美丽之外，更有一份"我为人人，人人为我"的社会氛围。

新冠肺炎疫情期间，阿米尔·汗和许多上海志愿者一道从事社区防疫、物资转运和防疫宣传，"正因为疫情期间一直呆在上海，我得以直观感受到中国在艰难时刻所展现的大国责任与担当。"

阿米尔·汗强调，在上海工作生活都非常方便，营商环境很接地气，"政府提供服务，更多从市场主体出发，实地了解我们需要得到什么支持，我经常被邀请参加他们的重要活动，印象最深刻的是，企业界能发表自己对未来城市基础设施规划的看法，并得到积极回应"。

作为对技术非常敏感的职业经理人，阿米尔·汗非常欣赏中国在5G、数字智慧城市和物联网等"新基建"领域的快速发展，"你们是为未来投资，将获得丰厚回报"。

"我是如此骄傲和幸运，我和家人一起度过了中国发展最快的20年，我相信中国现在和将来都是全球经济的强大支柱。"

Name: Amir Khan
Chinese Name: 阿米尔·汗
Nationality: Pakistani
Position: International Volunteer in Minhang District, Shanghai

Amir Khan:
I can't just take, I have to do as much as I can to give back to Shanghai

> One big secret of China's success is the strong leadership of the country, and the Chinese people have always been united and hardworking.

Speaking with words mixing Chinese and English, Amir Khan describes Shanghai as "beautiful, very friendly and full of love." As a professional manager from Pakistan, Khan has been living in China for over twenty years, including ten in Shanghai and witnessed the tremendous change in China. He says, "One big secret of China's success is the strong leadership of the country, and the Chinese people have always been united and hardworking."

Hometown known as "Shanghai in South Asia"

Amir Khan's hometown is Karachi, the largest city in Pakistan. He says: "You can understand the city's status as Shanghai in South Asia. Since long ago we knew that China was the most important country that Pakistan kept the diplomatic relationship with, known as an 'all-weather friend.'" In the last few decades, China and Pakistan have been deepening the relationship and the mutual support and help have been selfless, and this friendship can be felt in the daily lives of ordinary people.

Khan says: "While living in Shanghai, I like to be called "Batie" (literally "Pakistan iron," a popular term of endearment reserved for Pakistanis, meaning a good friend from Pakistan) by Chinese friends. We get this name because Pakistani people have widespread sincere affection toward China and also because this friendship is based on the heart-felt 'mutual respect' between Chinese and Pakistani people." As Khan remembers, China has made great progress in economic growth since reform and opening-up, "but China still deems itself as a member of the big family of developing countries, instead of complacently labeling itself as 'straight-A student.'" He refers to the Belt and Road initiative as an opportunity to enhance the development of the manufacturing industry in Pakistan. He says: "In the past, we mainly export cotton, jute and

Amir Khan:

I can't just take, I have to do as much as I can to give back to Shanghai

mineral rocks. But with Chinese investment and cooperation between companies from two sides, these competitive products can receive deep processing and achieve higher added value, reaping higher profit from the international market."

Khan says: "The nickname 'Batie' brings both honor and responsibility." Last year when COVID-19 first broke out in China, Pakistan, which is suffering from the worst locust plague in 27 years, mobilized all the public hospitals and sent all the inventory to China. He says: "At that time, some comments were shared a lot in Pakistan's social media, and the most popular ones are 'Finally we have an opportunity to help our Chinese brothers.' and 'We should do this, so the Chinese brothers will not be fighting alone.'"

When the reporter shows the picture of China's vaccines arriving at Islamabad not so long ago, Mr. Khan comments: "The reason why our friendship is so enduring is that whenever there are difficulties on either side, we take on the burden together."

China is investing in the future

Khan moved his whole family to Shanghai in 2010. He says: "Together with my wife and two sons, I have been living in the Huacao community for 11 years. We shouldn't be the people that only take from Shanghai, we should also give back to the city."

In 2019, he learned that in order to help more and more expatriates understand the local culture and integrate into their new lives, the Jinfeng International Community Development Association (JICDA) launched a recruitment drive for international volunteers and he was the first to sign up. He says: "I want to tell friends from around the world my own experience. Shanghai is a place where dreams can become true."

During the fight against COVID-19, together with many Shanghai volunteers, Khan participated in the community quarantine, materials transport and quarantine publicity. He says: "I have been staying in Shanghai throughout the pandemic period, so I could personally witness the courage and sense of responsibility of China as a big country."

Mr. Khan emphasizes that working and living in Shanghai are very convenient, the business environment is very down to earth. He says: "When government agencies provide services, they would try to understand what exactly we need. Frequently I was invited to participate in important activities by government agencies. I'm very impressed that companies can raise their opinions about the city's future infrastructure plans and got timely feedback."

As a professional manager, Khan admires China's fast growth in 5G, smart city and IoT. He says: "You are making an investment into the future and that will generate great returns."

Khan says: "I'm so proud and fortunate that my family and I have spent twenty years in China, which are the fastest-growing period. I firmly believe that China will be an important pillar for the global economy."

Scan for videos

姓　名：Fred Moynan
中文名：莫磊
国　籍：英国
职　位：英雄体育 VSPN 国际战略顾问

莫磊：
上海打造"全球电竞之都"，我想把女友带来中国向她展示这一切

上海政府的大力支持帮助 VSPN 和电竞行业重新振作，也向世界证明上海打造"全球电竞之都"的决心。

从白金汉宫来到黄浦江畔

34 岁的英雄体育 VSPN 国际战略顾问莫磊曾是英国近卫步兵第一团的军官，"当我得知自己将从事电竞行业，我就知道过去的经历都适用于这个全新的领域。我在军队和体育运动中学会的团队精神给到我很多启发"。

作为国际战略顾问，莫磊主要负责 VSPN 的海外推广，踌躇满志的他从白金汉宫来到了黄浦江畔。

在莫磊眼中，电竞是新一代的娱乐方式，也是游戏产业价值链的一环，将来电竞还将被赋予媒介的作用。

"我必须去了解电竞赛事在不同国家的呈现方式和区别。在北美的运营方式可能不适用于中国。"为了学会如何吸引电竞爱好者，莫磊需要观看很多电竞赛事和直播来理解观众的感受以及诉求，以此提供更加丰富的电竞体验。

除了对电竞生态圈的研究，各地政策莫磊也要了然于心。近年来，上海出台关于电竞产业发展的系列措施，2017 年 12 月，上海出台了《关于加快本市文化创意产业创新发展的若干意见》，也就是"文创 50 条"，明确

莫磊：
上海打造"全球电竞之都"，
我想把女友带来中国向她展
示这一切

提出，在动漫游戏产业要聚焦电子竞技这一新兴发展极，做强本土赛事品牌，支持国际顶级赛事落沪，加快全球电竞之都建设。2019年6月，上海市委宣传部、市文化旅游局、市体育局又专门出台了促进电子竞技产业健康发展的20条意见，全方位推进电竞产业发展。

上海是电竞行业发展的乐土

从莫磊这个西方人的角度来看，中外电竞公司最大的区别是中国政府大力支持这个行业。上海出台的这一系列举措向市场发出了信号，优秀电竞人才和企业坚信上海是最为适合发展的地方。

采访中，"政府支持"一词被莫磊频繁提及，受新冠肺炎疫情影响，电竞线下活动一度停摆，重创了海内外的电竞产业。疫情得到控制后，在上海市政府的帮助下，电竞和娱乐回归大众。"VSPN再次能举办大型线下电竞赛事，没有政府的帮助，我们无法做到。去年一整年，海外都无法举办线下赛事，上海政府的大力支持帮助VSPN和电竞行业重新振作，也向世界证明上海打造'全球电竞之都'的决心。"

对电竞产业，社会上存在一些误区，以为电竞选手就是宅在家里打电脑游戏的人。莫磊解释，电竞和传统体育在很多方面有异曲同工之妙。如果想要成为电竞选手，就需要健康饮食、锻炼体魄。"在一个团队中，选手需要有团队精神，就像传统运动一样，无论是足球、橄榄球还是篮球。不管你在任何运动领域，要想成为顶尖选手都是充满挑战性的。"

"之前有人告诉过我一个数据，一些游戏的选手需要在一分钟内点击鼠标300次，这是令人难以置信的。这些选手的反应时间惊人，要想达到这个程度，需要保持训练，保持身心健康。"

上海的"全球电竞之都"建设仍在发力，莫磊的中国电竞梦仍在延续。

莫磊还有一个梦想——把女朋友带到中国，向她展示自己在中国经历的这一切。

Name: Fred Moynan
Chinese name: 莫磊
Nationality: British
Position: VSPN Global Business Strategy

Fred Moynan:

Shanghai is working hard to become "the capital of global eSports," and I want to bring my girlfriend to China to show her all this

The strong support from the Shanghai government helped to revive VSPN and the eSports industry, which proved to the world Shanghai's determination to become "the eSports capital of the world."

From Buckingham Palace to the bank of the Huangpu River

Moynan, 34, VSPN Global Business Strategy Consultant, was once an officer of Grenadier Guards. He says: "When I found out that I was going to be working in the eSports industry, I knew that what I've learned in my previous life was totally applicable to this brand new field. The team spirit I learned in the army and in sports inspired me a lot."

Moynan is primarily responsible for the overseas promotion of VSPN. He moved from Buckingham Palace to the bank of the Huangpu River with an ambitious plan.

In Moynan's eyes, eSports is a new generation of entertainment and part of the value chain of the gaming industry, which will also be given the role of a medium in the future.

He says: "I must learn about the different presentative ways of eSports events in different countries. The operating methods in North America may not be applicable to China." In order to learn how to attract fans, Moynan needs to watch a lot of eSports events and live streaming to acquaint himself with the audience's feelings and demands. This allows him to provide richer eSports experiences.

In recent years, Shanghai has issued a series of measures on the development of the eSports industry. In December 2017, a series of guidelines

Fred Moynan:

Shanghai is working hard to become "the capital of global eSports," and I want to bring my girlfriend to China to show her all this

on accelerating the innovative development of cultural and creative industries in Shanghai were issued, which were also known as 50 articles of cultural and creative industries. It clearly put forward that the animation and gaming industry should focus on eSports as an emerging growth pole, strengthen local eSports brands, support Shanghai in holding international top-level events, accelerate the construction of an eSports capital of the world. In June 2019, the Publicity Department of the CPC Shanghai Committee, Shanghai Municipal Administration of Culture and Tourism, and Shanghai Municipal Administration of Sports jointly issued another 20 guidelines on promoting the healthy development of the eSports industry to push for all-round development.

Shanghai: a paradise for eSports industry

As a Westerner, Moynan believes the biggest difference between Chinese and foreign eSports companies is that the Chinese government supports this industry. The series of measures issued by the Shanghai government signals to the market that Shanghai is the most suitable place for the industry's development.

Affected by the COVID-19 pandemic, the off-line events came to a standstill, which hit hard the eSports industry at home and abroad. After the pandemic was brought under control, eSports and entertainment returned to the public with the help of the Shanghai government.

He says: "VSPN is once again able to hold major off-line eSports events, and we couldn't have done that without the help of the government. Over the last year, it was impossible to hold off-line events overseas. The strong support from the Shanghai government helped to revive VSPN and the eSports industry, which proved to the world Shanghai's determination to become 'the eSports capital of the world.'"

There are some misconceptions in society about the eSports industry that the players are just playing computer games at home. Moynan explains that in many ways eSports is actually quite similar to traditional sports. If you want to be a professional athlete in eSports, you need to eat healthily and you need to stay fit. He says: "In a team, players need to have team spirit, which is similar to traditional sports, whether it's soccer, rugby or basketball. No matter what sport you are in, it is challenging to be a top player."

He says: "Someone told me a statistic before. Some professional eSports players in games have to click a mouse three hundred times in one minute, which is pretty incredible. These players have an amazing reaction time, and to reach that level, they need to keep training and stay mentally and physically fit."

Shanghai is still striving to become "the eSports capital of the world," and Moynan's Chinese eSports dream is continuing.

Moynan also has another dream -- to bring his girlfriend to China, and to show her what he has experienced in China.

Scan for videos

姓　名：Harmen Dubbelaar
中文名：哈曼
国　籍：荷兰
职　位：大仓日航酒店管理公司专务执行董事、中国区总经理

哈曼：
我常常喜欢沿着南昌路一路骑行，了解中国、了解中国共产党

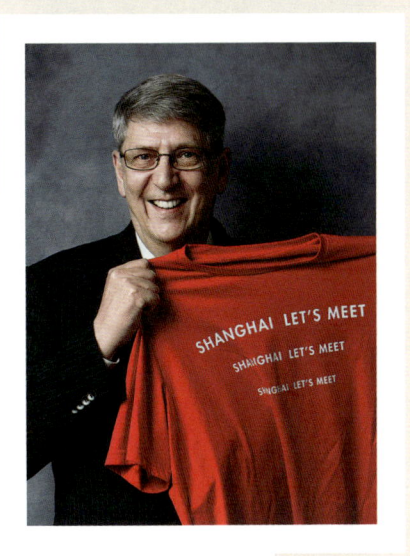

我们正一起招募、组织客人参与红色微旅行，让游客对上海这座梦幻般的城市有更深入的了解。

32 年前，当荷兰人哈曼第一次选择来上海工作时，他的家人、朋友，还有大学同学，都不约而同地问他：为什么不去世界上其他大城市？为什么选择去上海？如今，那些曾经向他发出疑问的人，无不为他当年的选择竖起大拇指。

"这 30 多年的变化，可以称得上是奇迹"

"当时并不是很多人都有兴趣来这里工作，开始新的事业，迈出新的一步。现在人们的想法完全不同了。"哈曼以一个亲历者的身份，把他在中国、在上海的所见所闻和亲身感受告诉远在荷兰的朋友，且不无骄傲地说："我认为上海是我的第二故乡。这不仅仅是一个我工作谋生的城市，也是一个让我感到宾至如归的城市，在这里我可以培养我的兴趣，可以继续在我的工作中取得成功。"

上海于他，是一个真正特别的地方。他的两个女儿都出生在上海，其中一个目前在上海从事设计师的工作，小女儿则在中国香港工作和学习。

其实，32 年前，第一次来到上海，哈曼便爱上了这座城。当时他便感受到这里有一股蓬勃的生机，"城市发展总体规划被完整地一一落实"。他尤其对上海的基础设施建设印象深刻。

哈曼：

我常常喜欢沿着南昌路一路骑行，了解中国、了解中国共产党

如今的上海，已成为一座世界级的大都市。"无论是人们的生活品质，还是年轻人的受教育机会和工作机会，上海这30多年的变化，我认为绝对可以称得上是奇迹。"

喜欢上海，因为上海保留了"旧"

哈曼喜欢骑行，他认为这种方式更贴近这座城市。"上海有美丽的建筑和高楼大厦，有的有几百米高。但实际上，如果放低视线，看看那些街道，就能了解上海人是如何生活的，他们做些什么，他们的幸福指数，他们脸上的笑容，这些都在告诉我们这是一个快乐的城市。"

所以，在哈曼看来，上海是一个很好的居住地，不仅仅对于像他这样的外国人。哈曼喜欢上海，还因为上海保留了"旧"，像公园、庙宇和小巷。"淮海路及其街边小巷，比如南昌路或雁荡路，就拥有非常独特、非常古老的店铺，它们世代相传，我认为把这些老店留在这里很重要。它们是上海的老艺术品，拥有独特的味道。上海不断创新，但上海也尊重这些拥有历史积淀的老产业，新旧结合使上海成为独特的城市。"

让游客对这座城市有更深入的了解

虽然今年6月哈曼离开了他工作5年的花园饭店（上海）总经理岗位，接受总部新的安排，但早在今年年初，他便和他的团队开始讨论花园饭店可以做些什么来庆祝中国共产党成立100周年。"最近，我们开始了红色微旅行的项目。"

哈曼眼中的南昌路，像是建筑史和上海城市发展史中的神秘之地。他喜欢一路沿着南昌路骑行，因为那条街很漂亮。有时，他会沿着南昌路经过大同幼儿园，去新天地附近的中共一大会址。他喜欢这样了解上海的历史，了解中国共产党的历史，深入过后，学着去分享，从而更好地了解和欣赏上海。

如今，这条他了然于心的骑行路线可以与更多人分享，"我们正与锦江饭店和新锦江大酒店一起参与这个城市红色微旅行项目，一起招募、组织客人参与周六下午的红色微旅行，让游客对上海这座梦幻般的城市有更深入的了解"。

哈曼一直庆幸自己身在上海，"我很幸运30多年前便有机会来到这里，我认为上海将继续繁荣。"

Name: Harmen Dubbelaar
Chinese Name: 哈曼
Nationality: Dutch
Position: Senior Managing Executive Officer, General Manager, Okura Nikko Hotel Management Company

Harmen Dubbelaar:
I enjoyed cycling along Nanchang Road to learn more about China and the Communist Party of China

We are working together to recruit and organize guests to participate in the City Walker project to give visitors a deeper understanding of the fantastic city of Shanghai.

When Dutchman Dubbelaar first chose to work in Shanghai 32 years ago, his family, friends and college classmates all asked him the same question: Why not try some other big cities in the world? What made Shanghai so special in his eyes? Today, those who have once doubted him, all give his choice a big thumb up.

"The changes over the past 30 years can be called a miracle"

Dubbelaar says: "At that time, not many people were interested in coming here to work, to start a new career, or just to take a new step. Now people's thinking is different." As an eyewitness, Dubbelaar proudly shared with his friends in the Netherlands what he had seen, heard and felt in China and Shanghai. "I consider Shanghai my second hometown. This is not only a city where I work to earn a living but also a place where I feel at home, where I can cultivate my interests and continue to be successful in my career," he says with pride.

Shanghai is a truly special place for him. His two daughters were both born in Shanghai, one of whom is now a local designer, while the younger one works and studies in the Hong Kong Special Administrative Region, China.

Dubbelaar fell in love with Shanghai 32 years ago when he first came to the city. It was then that he sensed vibrant energy here. "The master plan for urban development was being implemented in its entirety," he says, particularly impressed by Shanghai's achievement in infrastructure development.

Today, Shanghai has become a world-class metropolis. Dubbelaar says:

Harmen Dubbelaar:

I enjoyed cycling along Nanchang Road to learn more about China and the Communist Party of China

"Whether it's the quality of life here, or the educational opportunities and job opportunities for the young people, I think the changes in Shanghai over the past 30 years are miraculous."

I love Shanghai because the city has retained its "historical heritages"

Dubbelaar loves cycling and thinks it's a way to get closer to the city. He says: "Shanghai has beautiful buildings and skyscrapers, some of them hundreds of meters high. But, if you look down and look at the streets, you can see how Shanghai people live, what they do, their happiness, the smiles on their faces, all of which tell us that this is a happy city."

So, in Dubbelaar's opinion, Shanghai is a great place to live, not just for foreigners like him. He loves Shanghai also because the city has retained its "historical heritages" such as its old parks, temples and alleys. He says: "Huaihai Road and its side streets, like Nanchang Road or Yandang Road, have very unique, very old shops that have been passed down from generation to generation, and I think it's important to keep those old shops there. They are old works of art in Shanghai and possess a unique flavor. Shanghai is constantly innovating, but it also respects these old industries with their historical heritage, and the combination of old and new makes Shanghai a unique city."

To give visitors a better understanding of the city

Although Dubbelaar left his five-year post as general manager of Okura Garden Hotel Shanghai in June for a new arrangement assigned by the company headquarters, earlier this year he and his team already began discussing what the hotel could do to celebrate the 100th anniversary of the founding of the Communist Party of China. "Recently, we launched the City Walker project," he says.

In Dubbelaar's eyes, Nanchang Road is a charming place in the history of architecture and Shanghai's urban development. He enjoys riding all the way through Nanchang Road because it is a beautiful street. Sometimes he prefers walking along Nanchang Road, past Datong Kindergarten, on his way to the Memorial of the First National Congress of the Communist Party of China near Xintiandi. He likes this way of learning about the history of Shanghai, the history of the Communist Party of China, and after delving into it, learning to share it so that he can better understand and appreciate Shanghai.

Today, Dubbelaar is more than willing to promote his special and familiar route to more and more people. He says: "We are involving Jin Jiang Hotel and Jin Jiang Tower Hotel to launch this City Walker project together, recruiting, organizing guests to participate in a Saturday afternoon walk to give visitors a deeper understanding of this fantastic city."

"I was lucky to have the opportunity to come here more than 30 years ago, and I think Shanghai will continue to prosper in future," says Dubbelaar, feeling blessed.

Scan for videos

姓　名：Lucie Guyard
国　籍：法国
职　位：插画师

Lucie：
你可以从我那些充满烟火气的画里，感知到中国人当下的幸福生活

如果你看过我书中的漫画或我微信公众号上的漫画，就知道我所要表达的主要是我作为一个法国人在上海的生活。我不需要很宏伟的东西来给我灵感。我可以从非常小的事情中得到灵感。

Lucie 在上海的家位于乌鲁木齐路上一条老式弄堂里。闻着厨房炒菜的油烟味，踩着吱嘎作响的木楼梯上到三楼，就是 Lucie 的家了，这大概就是她要的所谓烟火气吧，内里陈设和上海弄堂人家无异，丝毫看不出房间的主人是一名法国女郎。倒是女主人的画作，成了普通中的不普通。

"这座城市给了我源源不断的创作灵感"

Lucie2010 年来到中国，初到上海，她有些迷茫，语言、文化、周遭的一切如此不同。细想，她是喜欢这种作为一个外地人的感觉的。渐渐地，她不再把自己当外国人或是外地人，而是完完全全融入了这座城市，很自然地，这座城市便给了她源源不断的创作灵感。

"如果你看过我书中的漫画或我微信（公众号）上的漫画，就知道我所要表达的主要是我作为一个法国人在上海的生活。我不需要很宏伟的东西来给我灵感。我可以从非常小的事情中得到灵感。"就像这弄堂里，狭小逼仄的房间，既是她的家，也是她工作的地方。

Lucie：

你可以从我那些充满烟火气的画里，感知到中国人当下的幸福生活

"我在这样的小巷子里工作，常会看邻居窗户外晾晒的衣服，这给了我很大的灵感，这是非常中国化的画面，所有这些，实际上是中国人的日常生活。或者一些小细节，比如一扇门，一个鸟笼，都会给我带来灵感。"

而一些日常小事，也常常会令 Lucie 眼前一亮。有一次，她试着扫码骑共享单车时，一个环卫女工向她走来，提出想来张自拍。"我很高兴，也很吃惊，因为我当时真的不在最佳状态。她自拍了一张照片，我猜她非常高兴能和一个老外自拍，这也让我很开心。她很高兴地说，'非常漂亮。'我说，'好的，谢谢你。'这真的是件很小的事情，但对我来说是件很大的事情。这是你在法国永远不会经历的事情。但只有在中国，你才能体验到这种小事情的大意义。"

"每个人都能从我的画里看到中国元素"

Lucie 说她需要这种很烟火气的生活，所以放弃住那种干净漂亮的公寓，而选择现在的老式弄堂房子。

"上海对我来说，不仅是城市天际线和摩天高楼，还是这个挂着衣服的竹竿。"她的一幅画最近成了网红，画里是上海这座城市的日常。

如今，微信公众号已成为 Lucie 作为一个艺术家展示作品的主要平台，在这个平台上她结识了不少新的朋友。她的微信公众号上关于中国的端午节和中秋节的画也收获不少点赞。"这些节日背后有一些不可思议的故事。我想知道这些故事，并想以一种简单的方式向我的粉丝解释，我的粉丝主要是法国人。为什么在中国会有这些节日，这是几千年前发生的事情，但我们今天仍然在庆祝。"

Lucie 上网做了很多研究，然后画了自己的版本。"通常故事都相当长和复杂，但我把它们画得很简单，让我的粉丝更容易理解这些中国传统文化。"

这就是 Lucie，每个人都能从她的画里，看到一些很中国的元素；从她那些充满烟火气的画里，感知到中国人民当下的幸福生活，很平凡很有滋味。

Name: Lucie Guyard
Nationality: French
Position: Illustrator

Lucie Guyard:

You can feel the happiness of Chinese people in my paintings that are full of scenes of everyday life

> If you look at my comics, either in my book or on my WeChat public account, you will know that I mostly talk about my life here as a French. I don't need big things to be inspired. I can be inspired by very little things.

Lucie Guyard's home in Shanghai is located in an old-fashioned alley on Wulumuqi Road. Smelling the neighbors' cooking and climbing the creaky wooden stairs to the third floor, Guyard has a place that she would like to call home permeated with the smell of everyday life. The furnishings are the same as those in other Shanghainese homes in the alley. There is no sign that the owner of the room is a French woman. It is the paintings of the hostess that have stood out from the ordinary rest.

"The city offers me endless inspirations"

Guyard came to China in 2010. When she first arrived in Shanghai, she was a little confused by the language, the culture, and the fact that everything around her was so different. When she thought about it, she liked the feeling of being a foreigner. Gradually, she stopped thinking of herself as a foreigner or an outsider and became fully integrated into the city, which naturally gave her a constant source of creative inspiration.

Guyard says: "If you look at my comics, either in my book or on my WeChat public account, you will know that I mostly talk about my life here as a French. I don't need big things to be inspired. I can be inspired by very small things." Just

Lucie Guyard:

You can feel the happiness of Chinese people in my paintings that are full of scenes of everyday life

like in this alley, the small, cramped room is both her home and her workplace. "I work in a little lane like this. I often see clothes drying on my neighbor's windows, which gives me a lot of inspiration. It's a very Chinese image, and in fact, it is the daily life of the Chinese. Any small details, like a door or a birdcage, can get me inspired."

Often, some daily things can create refreshing moments for Guyard. Once, when she tried to scan the QR code to ride a shared bike, a sanitation worker came up to her and asked to take a selfie with her. "I was happy and surprised because I was really not at my best on that day. She took the picture and I guessed that she was very happy to take a selfie with a foreigner. This also cheered me up. She said happily that it was very beautiful, and I said 'thank you' to her. This is really a small thing, but it matters to me. This is something you will never experience in France. Only in China can you experience the great significance of such small things."

"Everyone can see the Chinese elements in my paintings"

Guyard says that she wanted to live like a local, so she gave up the shiny apartment and chose the old house on the alley.

"For me, Shanghai is not its city skyline or skyscrapers, but this bamboo pole with clothes hanging on it," says Guyard. One of her paintings has got famous on the Internet recently, showing everyday life in Shanghai.

Now, the WeChat public account has become Guyard's main platform to display her works as an artist, on which she has made many new friends. Her paintings about China's Dragon Boat Festival and Mid-Autumn Festival on the account have received a lot of likes. She says: "There are some incredible stories behind these festivals. I want to know about these stories and, in a simple way, explain to my fans who are mainly French why China has these festivals. These stories all happened thousands of years ago, but we are still celebrating them today."

Guyard has done a lot of research online, and then she has drawn her own version. She says: "Usually the stories are quite long and complicated, but I have made them much simpler, in order to make it easier for my fans to understand the traditional Chinese culture."

This is Guyard. Everyone can see the Chinese elements in her paintings. From the paintings filled with the scenes of everyday life, you can perceive the happy life of the Chinese nowadays, very ordinary but full of taste.

姓　名：Gerd Knaust
中文名：格德·克瑙斯特
国　籍：德国
职　位：静安昆仑大酒店总经理

格德·克瑙斯特：
中国共产党的智慧和决心让人印象深刻

放眼全球，没有哪个政党能够这样持续一百年，坚持初心，始终把广大人民群众的利益放在首位，并且一步步有计划地达成一个个阶段性目标，从而取得前所未有的成就。

"我对中国政府有信心"

格德早在1990年便来到了中国，还娶了一位沈阳姑娘，作为上海静安昆仑大酒店的总经理，格德实实在在感受到酒店业对中国民族品牌的高接受度，让他这个中国女婿也心生自豪。"现在的豪华酒店里有好多是来自我所工作的锦江集团。我们可以清晰地看到民族酒店品牌的崛起之路，越来越多的中国企业有能力打造自己的品牌标准并塑造出能够同时服务好中国以及国际宾客的中国酒店品牌。"

让格德振奋的还有静安昆仑的酒店入住率已全面复苏，无论工作日还是节假日，酒店前台始终有排队等待办入住的客人，大堂咖啡吧，也是一派繁忙景象。他动情地说，这一切都离不开政府的支持。"我们收到来自政府的非常详细的抗疫指南，很好地保护我们的员工和客人。酒店员工还非常幸运地得到政府提供的免费疫苗接种，让我们可以更好地服务客人。"

而疫情期间，政府给予的税收减免政策，对酒店业来说也是雪中送炭。"这让我们即便在疫情形势最严峻的时候，也能维持酒店的正常运作。静安昆仑非常自豪没有因为疫情带来的经营困难而辞退任何员工，也没有员工因为疫情影响到正常收入。"

格德感慨道，他来中国这么多年，对这个国家早已有了深入的感受，

格德·克瑙斯特：

中国共产党的智慧和
决心让人印象深刻

但这一次的新冠肺炎疫情，对他的触动和冲击更大。

"疫情之初，很多老外问我，是留还是回，我毫不犹豫选择留在中国，因为我对中国政府有信心。中国是怎么处理疫情的，其他国家又是怎么对待疫情的，高下立判。"

"要把慈善做强做大"

两年前，格德荣获上海市"白玉兰纪念奖"，还得到了永久居留权。他说自己能获此奖项，得益于静安昆仑一直积极投身各种社区活动和公益慈善项目。"我们酒店有这方面传统，我们有一个叫'昆仑关爱'的组织，专门致力于为各种慈善活动募集善款，同时参与各慈善项目及支持周边社区。"

让格德颇为得意的还有一个已在酒店运作了八九年的慈善项目"制皂希望"。他介绍说，酒店每月约有60—80公斤客人用剩的肥皂，"丢弃会破坏环境，我们就将这些剩余肥皂提供给供应商，让他们聘请残障人士将这些肥皂碾碎再成型，我们支付报酬给残障人士，而成型的肥皂免费送往偏远地区，让那里的人们能有良好的卫生习惯，降低患病概率"。

格德透露，今年静安昆仑还要把慈善做大做强。

"这座城市充满令人赞叹的魅力"

格德很早便知道今年是中国共产党成立100周年的大日子。"我去过新天地附近的中共一大会址，当时排了很长的队。参观时，我非常惊诧。想想一百年前，谁会想到中国共产党能够一步步克服各种艰难险阻，打赢一场场战役，给这个幅员辽阔、人口众多的国家进行彻底全面的改造，进而带领这么多的中国人民走上共同发展、共同富裕的道路？中国共产党的智慧和决心让人印象深刻。放眼全球，没有哪个政党能够这样持续一百年，坚持初心，始终把广大人民群众的利益放在首位，并且一步步有计划地达成一个个阶段性目标，从而取得前所未有的成就。"

对于生活工作的这座城市，格德更是赞不绝口。他年过八旬的父母几年前曾从德国来上海旅游，"他们很喜欢在我们酒店附近散步"。在他看来，酒店所在的静安寺区域正是上海最有魅力的地方之一，"周边梧桐掩映的马路、小咖啡馆、餐厅和精品店都是我喜欢的，我能直观地看到道路的建设、轨道交通和更多的高楼大厦，这一切都是城市发展欣欣向荣的最好证明"。

他赞叹上海的治安非常好，出行完全不需要担心，"我最爱乘坐的71路公交车又快又环保。这座城市充满了令人赞叹的魅力"。

Name: Gerd Knaust
Chinese name: 格德·克瑙斯特
Nationality: German
Position: General Manager of Kunlun Jing An Hotel

Gerd Knaust:
The wisdom and determination of the Communist Party of China are very impressive

No other political party in the world has been able to stay true to its original aspiration for 100 years, always put the interests of the people first, reach one milestone after another in a planned way, and make such unprecedented achievements.

"I have full confidence in the Chinese government"

Knaust came to China as early as 1990 and married a Chinese girl from Shenyang. As general manager of Kunlun Jing An Hotel in Shanghai, he says: "Many of the luxury hotels now come from Jin Jiang Group. We can see the rise of national hotel brands as more and more Chinese companies can develop their own standards and brands, and can serve both Chinese and international guests well."

Knaust is also heartened that his hotel's occupancy rate has fully recovered. Whether on weekdays or holidays, there are always queues of guests waiting to check in at the hotel reception desk, and the lobby coffee bar is also busy. All these, he says emotionally, could not do without the government support. He says: "We have received very detailed guidelines from the government on how to protect our staff and guests from the COVID-19. All hotel staff are lucky to receive free vaccinations provided by the government so that we can better serve our guests."

During the pandemic, the tax relief policy by the government is a great and timely help for the distressful hotel industry. He says: "This allowed us to keep the hotel open even during the worst period of the pandemic. Kunlun Jing An is very proud to say that not a single employee has been laid off because of operational difficulties, and no employee has had any pay cut due to the pandemic."

Knaust says: "At the onset of the pandemic, many expats asked me whether

Gerd Knaust:

The wisdom and determination of the Communist Party of China are very impressive

I would stay or go back. Without hesitation, I chose to stay in China because I have full confidence in the Chinese government. As you can see, there's a stark contrast between how China is handling the pandemic and how other countries are dealing with it."

"We will further step up our charity work"

Two years ago, Knaust was given the city's Magnolia Silver Award and was granted permanent residency in Shanghai. He said he won the honor because Kunlun Jing An has been actively involved in various community activities and charity projects. He says: "We have an organization called Kunlun Care, which is dedicated to raising money for various charity events. We also participate in other charities projects and give support to the surrounding communities."

Nine-year-old Soap Hope Project is one of them. He says: "The hotel collects about 60-80 kilograms of leftover soaps per month. Since discarding them will damage the environment, we provide these remaining soaps to our suppliers, and let them hire some disabled people with salaries paid by us. These disabled people then crush and remold them into new soaps, which are sent to remote areas as gifts, so that people there can also develop good health habits."

Knaust says that this year Kunlun Jing An will further step up its charity work.

"This city is amazingly charming."

Knaust knew early on that this year marks the 100th anniversary of the founding of the Communist Party of China. He says: "I went to the Memorial of the First National Congress of the Communist Party of China near Xintiandi once, and there was already a long queue. During my visit, I was surprised. One hundred years ago, who could have thought that the CPC would be able to overcome all difficulties and obstacles step by step, win battle after battle, thoroughly transform this vast and populous country and lead so many Chinese people onto the road of joint development and common prosperity? The wisdom and determination of the CPC are very impressive. No other political party in the world has been able to stay true to its original aspiration for 100 years, always put the interests of the people first, reach one milestone after another in a planned way, and make such unprecedented achievements."

Knaust thinks the Jing'an Temple area where his hotel is located is one of the most attractive places in Shanghai. He says: "Those streets are lined on both sides with big plane trees and small cafes, restaurants, and boutique shops. I love them all. I can see with my own eyes the construction of roads, subways and more skyscrapers, all of which are a testament to the city's thriving development."

姓　名：Benjamin Travis Wood
中文名：本杰明
国　籍：美国
职　位：伍德佳帕塔设计咨询（上海）有限公司董事长 / 创始人

本杰明：
读懂了中国共产党，我就读懂了今天的中国

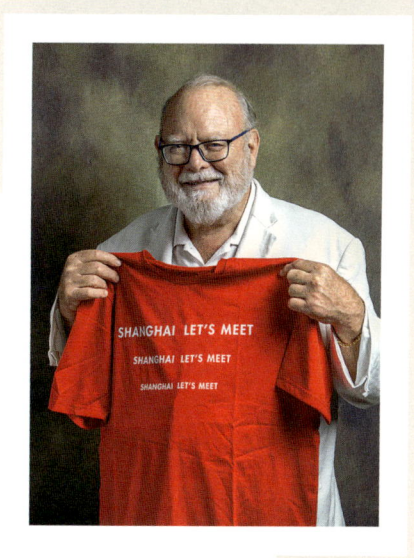

习近平主席曾多次提到"以人民为中心"。有一次我在机场书店看到英文版《习近平谈治国理政》，当场就买下来了。回到家后，我把三卷都读了一遍，这些书帮助我进一步了解了中国。

怀着巨大的责任感参与新天地改造项目

本杰明在上海的家位于新天地一带。站在客厅窗前，便能看到太平湖边被绿树环绕的中共一大纪念馆，这座著名的红色场馆每天游人如织。

这位来自美国的建筑师，职业生涯迄今已有 35 年，其中超过一半时间在中国。本杰明在中国有很多作品，其中最著名的莫过于新天地项目。1998 年，本杰明正是因新天地改造项目而来到上海，他很荣幸自己曾是这个改造项目的主设计师。

中共一大会址就在新天地地域范围内，本杰明回忆道："我有一个在中国长大的同事，他告诉我中国共产党第一次全国代表大会的历史，我于是知道了这是中国历史上的重要里程碑。因此，我满怀敬畏，并确保自己在设计时所做的一切工作都恰如其分。"

新天地如今成了上海驰名中外的地标，而新修建的中共一大纪念馆在党的百年华诞前夕正式对外开放。

本杰明说，虽然自己没有参与中共一大纪念馆的具体设计工作，但作

本杰明：

读懂了中国共产党，我就读懂了今天的中国

为新天地改造项目设计团队中的一员，他也曾向政府建议过如何使一大会址在新天地的两个街区之间变得更美丽。

每每想起这一点，他都感到非常自豪。

"新天地是中国进步的最好证明"

因为职业的缘故，本杰明对建筑充满了天然的兴趣，慢慢地，他在这座城市爱上了漫步。在上海生活越久，本杰明越感受到这是一个很宜居的城市，"公园的数量越来越多，原来的世博园区现在几乎是一个大公园。黄浦江沿岸有许多可以骑自行车的地方。"

"世界各地的人们都希望获得幸福，但不是每个人都能如愿。我知道中国人现在生活得很好，而大部分美国人并不知道这一点。"目睹中国这些年来的变化，本杰明颇有感触，"每天，当我走过新天地，都会看到人们享受着美好的生活。只要来到这里，你就会明白中国在过去的几十年里取得了多大的进步。这是一个持续奋斗的过程，而新天地就是最好的证明。"

本杰明认真研读过《习近平谈治国理政》，"习近平主席曾多次提到'以人民为中心'。有一次我在机场书店看到英文版《习近平谈治国理政》，当场就买下来了。回到家后，我把三卷都读了一遍，这些书帮助我进一步了解了中国。"

翻开第一卷，本杰明就被其中的内容深深吸引住了，"内容是关于习近平主席早期的经历，当时他在一个非常贫穷的省份，我想他了解贫穷意味着什么，就在那时，他决定要帮助尽可能多的人摆脱贫困。这本书让我们真正了解到，为什么习近平主席认为让人们摆脱贫困是如此重要。"

"另外两卷是在他成为中国共产党的领导人之后写的，这两本书同样谈到了人民的重要性。不是关于权力，而是人——如何让人们过上更好的生活。"

这位美国人，就这样用自己的观察读懂了中国共产党，继而读懂了今天的中国。

Name: Benjamin Travis Wood
Chinese name: 本杰明
Nationality: American
Position: Principal/ Founder of Studio Shanghai

Benjamin Travis Wood:

I begin to understand today's China once I have understood the CPC

President Xi Jinping has repeatedly stressed acting on the people-centered philosophy of development. Once I saw the English version of *Xi Jinping: The Governance of China* in an airport bookstore and bought it on the spot. After returning home, I read all three volumes, which helped me further understand China.

Participating in the renovation project of Xintiandi with a sense of responsibility

Benjamin Travis Wood's home in Shanghai is located near Xintiandi. Standing in front of the living room window, he can see the famous Memorial of the First National Congress of the Communist Party of China (CPC) surrounded by trees. The memorial stands by the Taiping Lake and is crowded with visitors every day.

Xintiandi project is Wood's best-known work in China, which brought him to Shanghai in 1998. The American architect with 35 years of experience is proud to have been the lead designer of this renovation project.

The Memorial of the First National Congress of the CPC is within the boundaries of Xintiandi. Wood recalls: "I had a colleague who grew up in China who told me about the history of the First National Congress of the CPC, and I then learned that it was an important milestone in the history of the People's Republic of China. As a result, I was filled with awe and made sure that everything I did in the design was just right."

He says: "I knew the importance of what I was doing, which was to preserve the buildings here. I felt an overwhelming sense of responsibility, and I had to

Benjamin Travis Wood:

I begin to understand today's China once I have understood the CPC

treat the memorial with respect."

Xintiandi is now a famous landmark in Shanghai, and the newly renovated memorial was reopened to the public on the eve of the party's centennial birthday.

Wood says that although he was not involved in the specific design of the memorial, as a member of the design team for the Xintiandi renovation project, he had also advised the government on how to make the memorial more beautiful between the two blocks of Xintiandi.

Every time he thinks of this, he feels very proud of it.

"Xintiandi is the best proof of China's progress"

Because of his profession, Wood has a natural interest in architecture and slowly fell in love with walking in the city. The longer he lives in Shanghai, the more he realizes that Shanghai is a livable city. Wood says: "There are more and more parks, and the former Expo site is now almost one huge park. There are many places for bicycle riding along the Huangpu River."

Wood says: "People all over the world want to be happy, but not everyone gets what they want. I know that Chinese people are now living a good life. However, most Americans don't know that. Every day. when I walk through Xintiandi, I see people enjoying a good life. Just by coming here, you will understand how far China has come in the last few decades. It is a continuous struggle and Xintiandi is the best proof of that."

Wood has carefully studied *Xi Jinping: The Governance of China*. He says: "President Xi Jinping has repeatedly stressed acting on the people-centered philosophy of development. Once I saw the English version of *Xi Jinping: The Governance of China* in an airport bookstore and bought it on the spot. After returning home, I read all three volumes, which helped me further understand China."

Opening the first volume, Wood was fascinated by the content. He says: "It's about President Xi's early political career when he was in a very poor province. I think he understood what it meant to be poor, and it was then that he decided that one day he would help as many people out of poverty as possible. This book gives us a real insight into why President Xi regards it so important to get people out of poverty."

Wood says: "The other two volumes were written after he became the leader of the CPC, and they are about the importance of the people, not the power. They are about how to make a better life for the people."

This American, in this way, used his own observations to read the CPC and then to read today's China.

姓　名：Kris Van Goethem
中文名：柯瑞斯
国　籍：比利时
职　位：Thomas Cook 托迈酷客中国入境业务执行总经理

柯瑞斯：
我的岳父是一名老党员，我和中国共产党之间有一份深厚的感情

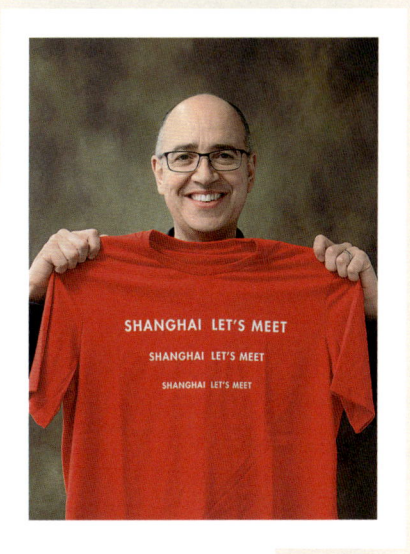

岳父一直说共产党好，没有党就没有他，而我更要说，没有他，也没有今天我的太太，所以，我也要感谢中国共产党。

柯瑞斯站在上海中心大厦 101 层的落地窗前，好似身在云端。脚下是这座城市最核心的风景线，他指着外滩，居然能讲出那每一幢建筑的前世今生，转向浦东，陆家嘴一带的巨变也令他感慨万千。

这个比利时人说着一口流利的汉语，还无比热爱中国文化，这一切都不是无来由的。

因为爱，留在了中国

柯瑞斯从小就喜欢语言，"我中学学的是法语、英语，德语和古希腊语，中学毕业后，打算学一门难度更高的语言，那年我 18 岁，我从俄语、西班牙语和汉语中选择了汉语。因为中国那么大，我想去看看"。

于是，柯瑞斯大学念了汉学，从中了解了中国古今历史。一毕业，便热切地跑来中国旅游。那是 1990 年，他爬上黄山，从那天起，他真正爱上了中国。此后，他走遍中国的山山水水，包括敦煌莫高窟。他得意地说，他看过的中国美景，比他大学的教授还要多。

柯瑞斯深深地爱着中国，最后选择留下。缘分真是奇妙，1995 年，他

柯瑞斯：

我的岳父是一名老党员，
我和中国共产党之间有
一份深厚的感情

带一个英国团来中国旅游，他是领队，在桂林认识了现在的太太，一个做导游的中国姑娘。柯瑞斯那么爱中国，这段感情自然在中国开花结果，成了中国女婿，他更有了留在中国的理由，索性在上海开展起旅游事业，专门接待海外游客，带着老外游中国看中国，将中国文化介绍给更多外国朋友。

2016年，德国多特蒙德球队来上海打比赛。赛事后，柯瑞斯带领上队员游览上海。"他们去豫园、玉佛寺这些中国很传统的地方，也会来上海环球金融中心登高观景，看今天的上海和未来的上海，边看边感叹国外没法和上海比，直呼'中国是未来！'"

即便随便走走，都是件舒服的事

柯瑞斯的家乡安特卫普和上海是姐妹城市，他常和他的外国朋友说，你在上海的日子怎么过，你说了算，这里什么都有。"上海特别适合欧洲人，上海和欧洲的大城市一样，城市中间有水（江河），欧洲人一看就踏实了。"

屈指算来，柯瑞斯在上海已经待了整整5年，之前8年一直在北京。他选择扎根上海，除了这里让他有家乡的亲切感，且非常国际化之外，更在于这里是全中国乃至全亚洲最有发展机会的城市。他有时会略带懊恼地说："我怎么在上海才待了5年呀。"

在柯瑞斯眼里，上海的浦东是看"新"，浦西则新旧兼有，那些老别墅、老洋房，单单看看外观，就已经很值了。即便在上海随便走走，都是件让人舒服的事情。

"我也要感谢中国共产党"

今年是中国共产党成立100周年，柯瑞斯直言应该好好庆祝，因为他和中国共产党之间还有一份深厚的感情在。

原来，柯瑞斯的岳父就是一名老党员。"我岳父1948年入党时只有18岁，如今已是91岁的老人了。每次回我太太老家桂林，岳父都会和我讲以前的故事，讲得很细。比如说土地改革，岳父家分到了一块地，可以在上面种菜，如果没有这块地，他们就没有现在这么好的生活。"

"岳父一直说共产党好，没有党就没有他，而我更要说，没有他，也没有今天我的太太。所以，我也要感谢中国共产党。"

Name: Kris Van Goethem
Chinese name: 柯瑞斯
Nationality: Belgian
Position: Managing Director MICE, LEISURE & SPORT at Thomas Cook China

Kris Van Goethem:
My father-in-law has been a Party member for many years and I have a deep bond with the Communist Party of China

My father-in-law always praises the Communist Party of China (CPC). Without it, there would be no him, then there would be no my wife. So I also need to thank the CPC.

Standing in front of the French windows on the 101st floor of Shanghai Tower, Kris Van Goethem feels like he is in the clouds. Under his feet is the most beautiful landscape of this city. Pointing to the Bund, he is able to tell the past and present of each building. Turning to Pudong, he was also overwhelmed by the dramatic changes in the Lujiazui area.

This Belgian speaks fluent Chinese and loves Chinese culture very much.

Staying in China for love

Goethem has been fond of languages since he was a child. He says: "I learned French, English, German and Classical Greek in middle school and I decided to learn a more difficult language after graduation. I was 18 years old at that time and I chose Chinese instead of Russian or Spanish because China is a big country that I want to visit."

Therefore, Goethem studied Sinology in college and learned about China's ancient and modern history. Then he travelled to China eagerly as soon as he graduated. In 1990, after he climbed Mount Huangshan, he truly fell in love with China. After that, he travelled all over China including Mogao Grottoes in Dunhuang. He says proudly that he has seen more beautiful views of China than his university professors.

Kris Van Goethem:

My father-in-law has been a Party member for many years and I have a deep bond with the Communist Party of China

Goethem was in deep love with China so he decided to stay here. As fate would have it, in 1995, he brought a British group to travel in China, he himself as the group leader, and he met his current wife in Guilin, a Chinese girl who is a tour guide. The relationship has naturally blossomed in China, as he loves China so much. Being a son-in-law, he had more reasons to stay in China and began to launch a tourism business in Shanghai which specializes in receiving overseas tourists, bringing foreigners to travel in China and introducing Chinese culture to more foreign friends.

In 2016, the German Dortmund team came to Shanghai for a match. Goethem then showed the players around Shanghai. He says: "They visited both traditional places such as Yuyuan Garden, the Jade Buddha Temple and modern skyscrapers like Shanghai Tower to see the Shanghai of today and the Shanghai of the future. They exclaimed as they did so that cities abroad can't compare with Shanghai and said, 'China is the future!'"

Even a casual walk is a comfortable thing to do

Goethem's hometown Antwerp and Shanghai are sister cities. He usually tells his foreign friends that you yourself have the final say about how to live your life in Shanghai, as everything is available here. He says: "Shanghai is particularly suitable for Europeans because there is a river running through the city, just the same as the metropolises in Europe. They would feel at ease when they see it."

Goethem has now been in Shanghai for five years after eight years in Beijing. He chose to settle down in Shanghai not only because the city, while being international, makes him feel at home, but also because it is the city with the most development opportunities in China and even in the whole Asia. "How can I only been here for five years," sometimes he complains.

In his eyes, Pudong is the "new" part of Shanghai, while Puxi is a mix of old and new, with old villas and houses that are worth it just to look at. Even a casual walk around Shanghai is a comfortable thing to do.

"I also need to thank the CPC"

This year marks the 100th anniversary of the founding of the Communist Party of China (CPC). Goethem says that he will also give it a good celebration as he has a deep bond with the CPC.

It turns out that Goethem's father-in-law has been a Party member for many years. Goethem says: "When he was admitted to the Party in 1948, my father-in-law was only 18 years old and now he is an old man at the age of 91. Every time I went to my wife's hometown in Guilin, my father-in-law would tell me stories about the past with great details. Taking the Agrarian Reform as an example, my father-in-law's family was allocated a piece of land on which they could grow vegetables. Without the land, they would not have had such a good life as now."

Goethem says: "My father-in-law always praises the CPC. Without it, there would be no him, then there would be no my wife. So I also need to thank the CPC."

姓　　名：Alex Szilasi
中文名：阿莱克斯·西拉西
国　　籍：匈牙利
职　　位：世界著名钢琴家、李斯特音乐节音乐总监

Alex：
中国在抗击疫情方面是正确的榜样

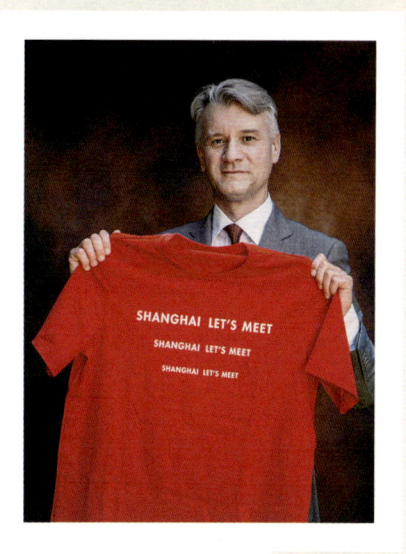

中国在抗击疫情方面是正确的榜样，中国帮助我们走出了困境。我注射了中国疫苗，且我的余生都为此感恩。

来自匈牙利的 Alex 有着诸多身份：他是享誉世界的钢琴家、李斯特第五代嫡系传人、匈牙利音乐博物馆馆长、格德勒皇宫艺术总监……

Alex 对中国有着一份特别深厚的感情，因为中国的历史、文化和艺术深深影响了他的世界观。

从小听"中国故事"长大

1968 年，Alex 出生于意大利帕尔马的一个音乐世家，他的祖父 Imre Csenki 是一位致力于复兴和弘扬匈牙利民族音乐的作曲家、指挥家和音乐教师。

Alex 的家族与中国的缘分可以追溯到 1950 年，他的祖父作为首位访华的中欧音乐家，到访中国时还受到了毛主席的接见。"祖父当时收到的礼品至今仍然伴随着我。他总是告诉我，匈牙利在世界上最亲密的邻居其实是中国，而我也一直确信如此。"

"当我还是个孩子时，中国的历史、文化和艺术就深深地影响和塑造了我的世界观。"Alex 在中华文化和"中国故事"的熏陶中成长，每次来中国，都有回家的感觉。他说："作为匈牙利人，另一个让我非常喜欢上海的原因是匈牙利建筑师拉斯洛·邬达克，他在 20 世纪初居住在上海的时候，为这座城市设计了一百多座建筑。"

Alex：

中国在抗击疫情方面是正确的榜样

艺术家们最著名的聚集点

邬达克、赉安……百年来不少外国设计师在上海留下了他们的作品和故事，这些不同时期、不同风格的建筑，讲述着不同的故事，折射着上海"海纳百川、追求卓越、开明睿智、大气谦和"的城市精神。

Alex说："百年后的今天，上海的音乐厅、博物馆和画廊都汇聚了来自世界各地的艺术家或艺术品。我不得不说，上海是当今艺术家们最著名的聚集点之一。"

2015年，中匈两国签署共建"一带一路"政府间谅解备忘录，这是中国与欧洲国家签署的首份共建"一带一路"政府间合作文件。Alex很高兴看到，文化、教育、商业等方面的交流将两国紧密地联系在一起。

感恩能接种中国疫苗

匈牙利自2020年12月底开始接种新冠疫苗，2021年初，匈牙利总统、总理先后接种了中国疫苗。

Alex也接种了中国的疫苗，"中国在抗击疫情方面是正确的榜样，中国帮助我们走出了困境。我注射了中国疫苗，且我的余生都为此感恩。"

全球疫情得到控制后，Alex想马上回到上海。"我迫不及待地想再次见到我在上海的朋友，欣赏一场音乐会，结束后再次享受世界上最美味的食物，享受和朋友们欢聚在一起的时光。"

Name: Alex Szilasi
Chinese name: 阿莱克斯·西拉西
· Nationality: Hungarian
Position: World-renowned pianist, Music Director of Liszt Festival

Alex Szilasi:
China is the right role model in fighting against the pandemic

China is the right role model in fighting against the pandemic and helps us out of the plight. I've got the Chinese vaccine and I'll be thankful for that for the rest of my life.

Alex Szilasi from Hungary has many identities: a world-renowned pianist, the fifth generation of direct inheritors of Liszt, Curator of Museum of Music History and Artistic Director of Gödöllő Palace…

Szilasi has a particularly profound feeling for China as its history, culture and art have deeply influenced his world-view.

I grew up immersed in "Chinese stories"

Szilasi was born in a musical family in Parma, Italy in 1968. His grandfather, ImreCsenki, was a composer, conductor and music teacher dedicated to the revival and celebration of Hungarian folk music.

The relationship between Szilasi's family and China dated back to 1950, when his grandfather, the first Central European musician to visit China, was received by Chairman Mao in the visit. Szilasi says: "The gift my grandfather received at that time is still with me. He always told me that Hungary's best friend in the world is actually China and I have always been sure of that."

"When I was a child, Chinese history, culture and art deeply influenced and shaped my world view," says Szilasi. Growing up immersed in Chinese culture and "Chinese stories," Szilasi has a feeling of returning home every time he comes to China. He says: "As a Hungarian, the Hungarian architect Laszlo Hudec is another reason why I love Shanghai so much. He designed over 100 buildings for this city when he lived in Shanghai in the early 20th century."

Alex Szilasi:

China is the right role model in fighting against the pandemic

The most famous gathering point for artists

Hudec, Alexandre Leonard… Over the past hundred years, a lot of foreign designers have left their works and stories in Shanghai. These buildings of different periods and styles tell different stories, reflecting the spirit of a generous, enlightened, and inclusive city that always seeks excellence.

Szilasi says: "Today, a hundred years later, Shanghai's concert halls, museums and galleries are filled with artists or artworks from all over the world. I would have to say that Shanghai is one of the most famous gathering points for artists today."

In 2015, China and Hungary signed a memorandum of understanding on jointly building the Belt and Road, the first intergovernmental cooperation document of its kind signed between China and a European country. Szilasi is very happy to see that the exchanges in culture, education and business have closely linked the two countries together.

I am thankful for getting Chinese vaccines

Hungary, since the end of December 2020, has been carrying out vaccination against COVID-19 and at the beginning of 2021, the Hungary President and Prime Minister have received the injection of Chinese vaccines successively.

Szilasi has also received the Chinese vaccine. He says: "China is the right role model in fighting against the pandemic and helps us out of the plight. I've got the Chinese vaccine and I'll be thankful for that for the rest of my life."

Szilasi wants to return to Shanghai immediately after the global pandemic is under control. He says: "I can't wait to see my friends in Shanghai again, enjoy a concert and afterwards have the most delicious food in the world. I am looking forward to the happy reunion with my friends."

姓　名：Astrid Poghosyan
中文名：马星星
国　籍：亚美尼亚
职　位：上海交响乐团团长助理

马星星：
可爱又温暖的上海人，让我找到了家的感觉

这些可爱又温暖的上海人，让我找到了家的感觉，也让我找到了"我的上海"。

"我叫星星，天上的星星！"上海交响乐团团长助理马星星介绍自己时，总是喜欢这样开头。她初来上海时，老师问："你的名字有什么含义吗？"马星星说："我的名字就是'Star'的意思。"于是，"星星"这个中文名字成为了这个自信、开朗的亚美尼亚女孩在上海美好生活的开端。

自 11 年前收到上海音乐学院的录取通知来到上海，从学语言的乌龙糗事，到以成绩优异登上上音留学生手册封面，从获得上海 001 号《留学生在沪工作证》到成为上海交响乐团团长助理……这个 28 岁的亚美尼亚女孩在上海不断完成自己更多的梦想。

300 米的小路见证了她在上海 11 年的故事

2009 年，马星星从遥远的亚美尼亚来到上海，如今，这个酷爱动画片《花木兰》的女孩觉得上海就是她的家，在这里遇到的人和事都让她感到无比温暖。11 年的上海生活在她身上打下了深深的烙印，当她身处其他国家时，每当看到中国的五星红旗，也会由衷地感到激动和骄傲。

"一个地方之所以被称为故乡，就是因为那里有很多的记忆。"马星星告诉记者，从交响乐团走到上海音乐学院的短短 300 米的道路，记录了她与上海 11 年的故事。在那条路上，她总是会遇到很多人，会和保安大叔打招呼，和卖水果的大叔分享故事……这些细节汇聚成的生活碎片，成为她生活、工作在上海的记忆中不可或缺的一部分。"在这 300 米里，我找到

马星星：

可爱又温暖的上海人，让我找到了家的感觉

了我的家，也对这座城市有了依赖感与归属感。"

马星星刚来上海时，人生地不熟，出门需要跟别人比画好久才能问清楚路。张叔叔是她在上海认识的第一位中国邻居。当时，她用在旅行书上唯一学到的一句中文"您好"跟张叔叔打了个招呼。张叔叔回复她："你好！"

这样的对话持续了三个月。马星星的中文日渐进步，她和张叔叔的谈话也从简单的问候扩展到了日常的生活。"张叔叔会给我介绍小区，告诉我最近的菜市场在哪里。我会向他介绍我的国家，向他展示我新学到的中文单词、听到的中文歌。"马星星告诉记者，每次她练完琴回到小区，张叔叔一看到她就会大声地说："星星，回来啦！吃饭了吗？注意不要太累啊！"这些话给了马星星慰藉，让她在陌生的国度也能感受到家的温暖。

"这是一座梦想之城"

说起定居上海的决定，她坦言是因为深刻体会到上海的包容。马星星如今在上海交响乐团从事行政工作。她经常乘坐96路公交车去上班，每次都悄悄许愿，希望能乘上李师傅开的那一辆车。李师傅是96路公交车的司机，和马星星熟识。"李师傅把车停靠在车站以后，如果看到我穿着高跟鞋疯狂赶来，总会开着车门耐心等我，等我上车后还会笑着跟我说'你慢点，慢点！'"

马星星说，自己离开家人，独自生活在上海，有时会感到孤单，也曾遇到过困难，但正因为遇到像张叔叔、李师傅这么好的人，让她感觉一切没有那么难、那么复杂。"这些可爱又温暖的上海人，让我找到了家的感觉，也让我找到了'我的上海'。"马星星说。

在上海待了11年，马星星已经从一个16岁离家求学的小女孩，蜕变成了在异国他乡追寻梦想的大姑娘。工作之余，星星爱去外滩的外白渡桥散散步、看看夜景。"上海每天都有变化，但变化最大的是我本人。我与上海共同成长，这座城市已经成为了我的一部分，我也成为了这座城市的一部分。"

马星星演奏的身影，曾在很多舞台出现。在上音学习期间，她登上过纽约卡耐基音乐厅的舞台，参与过《生活大不同》综艺节目的录制……毕业后就成为了上交团长助理。"助理这个岗位需要有音乐水平，能理解乐团的演奏需求，解决他们的问题，也需要沟通的能力，我的中文还不错，而且我喜欢和人交流。"

"我现在每天的工作都很愉快！"马星星与同事们相处愉悦，对她来说，上海是个"梦想之城"，"只要你真的想要，梦想就会变为现实"。

Name: Astrid Poghosyan
Chinese name: 马星星
Nationality: Armenian
Position: Executive Assistant to the President, Shanghai Symphony Orchestra

Astrid Poghosyan:
The lovely and warm people in Shanghai made me feel at home

The lovely and warm people in Shanghai made me feel at home and discover a Shanghai of my own.

"My name is Xingxing, which means 'stars' in Chinese," says Astrid Poghosyan, executive assistant to the president of the Shanghai Symphony Orchestra. When Poghosyan introduces herself, she always starts with her Chinese name which means the same as her Armenia one.

Since receiving the admission notice from the Shanghai Conservatory of Music 11 years ago, this 28-year-old Armenian young woman has fulfilled one dream after another in Shanghai. When she first arrived, she could barely speak any Chinese. On graduation, she was already featured on the cover of her school's handbook for international students for her excellent grades. She then obtained Shanghai's No.001 "Work Permit for International Students in Shanghai" and became Executive Assistant to the President of Shanghai Symphony Orchestra.

The 300-meter path has witnessed her 11-year story with Shanghai

In 2009, Poghosyan who loves the animated movie *Mulan* came to Shanghai from Armenia and now she feels that Shanghai is her home. The people and things she meets here make her feel warm, and her 11 years in Shanghai have left a deep mark on her. When Poghosyan is in other countries, she feels proud whenever she sees China's national flag.

Poghosyan says: "A place is called a hometown because there are so many memories there." She says that the short 300-meter road from the symphony orchestra to the Shanghai Conservatory of Music has witnessed her 11-year story with Shanghai. On that road, Poghosyan has met a lot of people, greeted the security guard and shared stories with the fruit vendor... These details all make up the tidbits and morsels of her life, a precious piece of her memories of living and working in Shanghai. "Along the 300 meters, I found my home, and also a sense of belonging to the city," she says.

Astrid Poghosyan:

The lovely and warm people in Shanghai made me feel at home

When Poghosyan first came to Shanghai, she was unfamiliar with the city and had to gesture to people for a long time when asking for directions. Uncle Zhang was the first Chinese neighbor she met in Shanghai. At that time, she greeted him with the only Chinese phrase "Ninhao" (meaning "hello") that she had learned in her travel book. Uncle Zhang then replied "Nihao" to her.

Such exchange lasted for three months. Poghosyan's Chinese was improving day by day, and her conversation with Zhang has expanded from simple greetings to chatting a little about daily life. She says: "Uncle Zhang introduced me to the community and told me where the nearest food market was. I introduced my country, and showed him the new Chinese words I learned and the Chinese songs I listened to." She says that every time she returned to the neighborhood after practicing piano, Zhang would speak loudly to her: "Xingxing, you're home now! Have you had your meal? Don't get too tired!" These words comforted her and made her feel the warmth of home in a foreign country.

"This is a city of dreams"

Poghosyan admits that the reason she chose to settle down in Shanghai is the city's inclusiveness. She is now engaged in administrative work in Shanghai Symphony Orchestra. She often goes to work by bus No.96. She makes a wish quietly every time, hoping to get on the bus driven by Li, a driver of the No.96 bus who is familiar with her. She says: "After Li stopped at the bus station, he would always wait for me patiently with the door open if he happened to see me running crazily in high heels. When I got on the bus, he would smile and say to me: 'Slow down, slow down!'"

Poghosyan says that after she left her family and lived alone in Shanghai, she sometimes feels lonely and has encountered difficulties. But because she has met such good people as Uncle Zhang and Li, she feels that everything is not so difficult or complicated. "The lovely and warm people in Shanghai made me feel at home and discover a Shanghai of my own," she says.

After work, she loves to go for a walk on the Garden Bridge and enjoy the night view. She says: "Shanghai changes every day, but the biggest change is in me. I'm growing up with Shanghai, the city has become a part of me, and I have become a part of the city."

During her study at Shanghai Conservatory of Music, Poghosyan performed on the stage of Carnegie Hall in New York and participated in the recording of the variety show "We Are Family." After graduation, she became an executive assistant to the president of the Shanghai Symphony Orchestra. She says: "The position of the executive assistant requires some knowledge of music, an understanding of the needs of orchestra performances, and the ability to solve problems and to communicate with people. My Chinese is not bad, and I like to communicate with people."

Poghosyan says: "I am happy with my work every day now." She gets on great with her colleagues. For her, Shanghai is a "city of dreams." "Your dreams will surely come true if you really want it," she says.

Scan for videos

姓　名：Harald Sturm
中文名：史东
国　籍：德国
职　位：瑞士西卡集团亚太区项目经理

史东：
政府有力支撑了企业发展，我也当起了"河长"参与社会治理

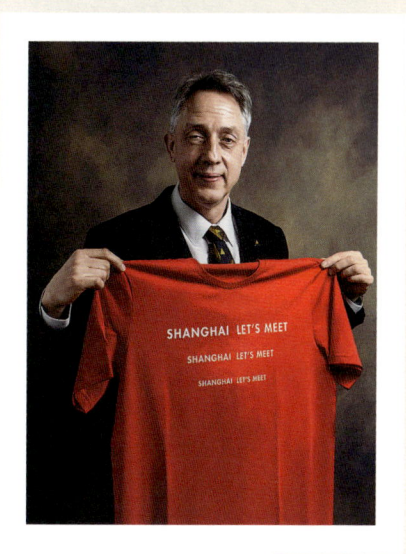

我认为政府部门的领导力将整座城市带入了现代化的世界和数字化的时代，有力地帮助了国家的成长，也为人民带来了财富增长。

"建党百年，是件大事。对于任何组织而言，能够筑基百年都是伟大的。"来自德国的史东感叹道。一个半月前，他到浙江嘉兴，听同事讲述了中国共产党建党百年的故事——中共一大在上海召开，中途转道嘉兴，正是他脚下的这片土地。

更让史东兴奋的是，当他回到上海的办公室，一个25岁的女同事正在申请入党，她向史东描述了中国共产党的崇高与伟大，表达了对成为党员的期盼与向往。"我从她身上看到焕发出来的热情，以及对党的热忱，看到了中国共产党的伟大，也让我感到这个国家未来可期。"史东说。

国家在成长，城市在进步

1998年，史东初次来到上海，在这里度过了十年的时光。2016年，他再度踏足上海，在西卡集团亚太区公司担任项目经理及技术支持。回忆起1998年的上海，他感到恍如隔世。"当时的上海，与现在的上海完全不同。那时，满大街看到的是大众汽车，或是一些日本小轿车。如今，不论是本土的国产品牌还是高端的玛莎拉蒂，在上海的街头都随处可见。这在二十

史东：

政府有力支撑了企业发展，我也当起了"河长"参与社会治理

年前是不可想象的。"

在史东看来，上海这座城市在过去的二十年里迎来了飞速的发展，日新月异的变化让他印象深刻。"我认为政府部门的领导力将整座城市带入了现代化的世界和数字化的时代，有力地帮助了国家的成长，也为人民带来了财富增长。上海人更是拥有勇往直前的拼搏精神，让上海这座城市产生了巨变，我慨叹与佩服！"

政府有力支撑企业发展

西卡上海公司位于莘庄工业区，在政府的支持与关怀下，公司业务不断增长。"去年疫情困难时期，我们被减免三个月的租金。这让公司摆脱了困境。"史东认为，上海将一如既往地快速发展下去，"不得不说，上海，或者说整个中国对于疫情的良好把控使得社会运转恢复良好。正是这样好的态势，让我们公司的业务也得到了意想不到的恢复与增长。去年我们达到了双位数的增长比率，这在全球经济形势不景气的情况下是所有人都难以想象的"。

政府部门还与西卡公司联合组织了各类活动，如绘画、烘焙、心理培训等。史东说："从我的角度而言，这是第一次知道政府与企业的互动可以如此深入而频繁。"

当"河长"参与社会治理

闲暇时光里，史东喜欢烹饪，也酷爱体育运动，比如跑步、骑车、快走等。最近，一个难得的机会让史东投身于莘庄工业区河道管理的工作中。"几个星期前，我和同事路过莘庄工业区的河道时，发现那里布满了垃圾，于是我们劝说钓鱼的人将场地收拾干净再离开，他们毫不犹豫地照做了。"

能够为改善环境尽一份力，这让史东感到欣慰。"政府部门在那里铺设了一条美丽的沿河小道，并种植了绿树与灌木丛加以点缀。现在，我协助照管这块区域，如果发现有任何不妥的地方，我会及时向工业区反映。"

Name: Harald Sturm
Chinese name: 史东
Nationality: German
Position: Project Manager, Asia Pacific at Sika, Switzerland

Harald Sturm:

The government has strongly supported the development of enterprises, and I have also become a "river chief" to participate in social governance

I think the government departments have led the entire city into a modern world and a digital age, which has greatly helped the country develop, and also brought much wealth to the people.

"The 100th anniversary of the founding of the Communist Party of China (CPC) is a great event. For any organization to have maintained a solid presence for as long as one hundred years, it's nothing but greatness," Harald Sturm from Germany says. A month and a half ago, he went to Jiaxing, Zhejiang province, and learned from his colleagues the stories of the CPC in the past 100 years -- the First National Congress of the CPC was held in Shanghai and was then transferred to Jiaxing, which was the very land under his feet.

What made Sturm more excited was that when he returned to his office in Shanghai, a 25-year-old female colleague was applying to join the CPC. She described to Sturm the nobility and greatness of the CPC and expressed her expectations and aspirations for becoming a Party member. "I saw her radiating enthusiasm, her passions for the Party and the greatness of the CPC, which made me feel that a promising future of this country can be expected," Sturm says.

The country is developing and the city is progressing

Sturm first came to Shanghai in 1998 and had stayed for 10 years. In 2016,

Harald Sturm:

The government has strongly supported the development of enterprises, and I have also become a "river chief" to participate in social governance

he set foot in the city once again to work as Project Manager and Technical Support in Sika, Asia-Pacific. Looking back on Shanghai in 1998, he feels like worlds apart now. He says: "Shanghai at that time was a completely different place from what it is now. The roads were filled with Volkswagen or some Japanese cars back then. Today, both domestic brands and high-end Maserati can be seen everywhere on Shanghai's roads, which was unimaginable twenty years ago."

In Sturm's view, Shanghai has undergone rapid development in the past two decades, and he is impressed by the enormous changes. He says: "I think the government departments have led the entire city into a modern world and a digital age, which has greatly helped the country develop, and also brought much wealth to the people. Shanghai people have the fighting spirit of moving forward, contributing to the great changes in this city, which I admire very much!"

Strong government support for the development of enterprises

Located in Xinzhuang Industrial Park, Sika Shanghai has seen continuous growth in business thanks to the support and care of the government. "During the difficult times of the pandemic last year, we were waived three-month rentals which bailed the company out of the plight," says Sturm. He believes that Shanghai will continue to develop rapidly. He says: "I have to say that the good control of the pandemic in Shanghai, even in the whole of China, has allowed the society to recover from the pandemic and function well. It is indeed the favorable condition that helps our business recover and goes beyond our expectations. Last year we reached a double-digit growth rate, which is unimaginable to anyone in the midst of the global economic downturn."

The government departments have also organized various activities with Sika, such as painting, baking and psychological training. "From my perspective, this is the first time I know that the interaction between the government and the enterprises can be so deep and frequent," Sturm says.

Participating in social governance as a "river chief"

In his spare time, Sturm enjoys cooking and exercising such as jogging, cycling and brisk walking. Recently, a rare opportunity came up for him to devote himself to river management in Xinzhuang Industrial Park. Sturm says: "A few weeks ago, when my colleague and I passed by the river in the park, we noticed that it was covered with rubbish, so we persuaded the anglers to clean up the site before leaving. They did so without hesitation."

Sturm is gratified to be able to do his part to improve the environment. Sturm says: "Along the river, the government departments have laid a beautiful path lined with trees and bushes. Now I assist in looking after this area and if I find something improper, I will promptly report to the staff in the industrial park."

姓　名：Geoffrey Alan Rhodes
中文名：陆高安
国　籍：美国
职　位：上海交通大学文创学院教授

陆高安：
上海已成世界级艺术中心，艺术在这里繁荣发展，令人振奋

上海如今已成为世界级的艺术中心，艺术机构和艺术活动都在繁荣发展，令人振奋。

Geoffrey Alan Rhodes 的中文名字是陆高安，因为在他的理解中，他的姓 Rhodes 对应中文的"陆"，而他 2010 年第一次来上海时，居住的地方在高安路。

做新技术的探寻者

陆高安曾在罗彻斯特理工学院的电影和动画学院担任助理教授，并在芝加哥艺术学院担任视觉传达设计系的终身副教授和系主任。2008 到 2010 年间，陆高安出品的几部故事片在美国上映，与此同时，他开始接触新兴的虚拟现实和增强现实等技术，并运用这些新技术进行创作。"我首先和艺术馆、美术馆合作，然后开始与一些机构一起设计项目，在 App 上应用 VR 场景，并向大众普及。"

"与历史博物馆合作的项目才能真正诠释这个想法：让历史照片和影像在我们所处的城市重现，让我们能重见历史。"陆高安告诉记者，1929 年，芝加哥发生了轰动一时的"情人节屠杀"事件。陆高安的团队使用这些照片在芝加哥重建了一个虚拟现实体验的场景，并发布了一个应用程序。这个项目于 2018 年获得美国博物馆联盟"缪斯奖"。在此之后，陆高安主持

陆高安：

上海已成世界级艺术中心，艺术在这里繁荣发展，令人振奋

了一系列项目，持续探索每年最新的技术，把城市故事与技术结合起来。

定居上海开启人生新阶段

2010年，因为妻子的关系，陆高安第一次来到上海。"当时我的妻子在世博会西班牙馆工作。"后来，在定居之前，陆高安又来过上海几次。"我得以回看过去十年间上海艺术界的巨大发展。仅仅从画廊的数量以及新建的博物馆数量来看，都是相当惊人的，而且这种增长势头仍在持续。上海如今已成为世界级的艺术中心，艺术机构和艺术活动都在繁荣发展，令人振奋。"

上海浓郁的艺术气息和上海交大文创学院的邀请等因素促使陆高安一家于2020年开始定居上海。"我的儿子当时刚好一岁半，对他而言，能来到一个没有因为疫情而封闭的城市，和外公外婆在一起，还能正常地去学习，真的很棒。"陆高安表示，特别开心能够在去年夏天来到上海，并以此为契机开启一个新的人生阶段。

完成教学的同时，陆高安也重启了对历史博物馆的探索。他曾参观过中共一大会址，"这里使用了栩栩如生的雕塑来重现中国近现代历史的重要时刻和重大事件。在2021年，人们走进纪念馆后仍然能够感受（一百年前的那段）历史"。

陆高安沉迷于艺术，滔滔不绝地讲述着他的感受。身处上海，他深刻感受到了艺术生产、艺术展览等（艺术活动）在城市中扮演的重要角色，以及艺术活动是如何被用来改变社区的。

"我看到，社区正在发展成不同风格的区域，艺术画廊正在这些区域发挥着作用。"

Name: Geoffrey Alan Rhodes
Chinese name: 陆高安
Nationality: American
Position: Professor of USC-SJTU Institute of Cultural and Creative Industry

Geoffrey Alan Rhodes:

Shanghai has become a world-class art center and it is inspiring to see the arts thriving here

Shanghai is now a world-class art center and it is inspiring to see the prosperity and development of art institutions and art activities.

Being a pioneer of new technologies

Geoffrey Alan Rhodes's Chinese name is Lu Gao'an. In his understanding, his surname Rhodes corresponds to the Chinese word 'Lu', and when he first came to Shanghai in 2010, the place he lived was on Gao'an Road.

Rhodes once worked as an assistant professor in the School of Film & Animation at Rochester Institute of Technology, and the associate professor and department chair of the Department of Visual Communication Design at the School of the Art Institute of Chicago. From 2008 to 2010, several feature films produced by Rhodes were released in the United States and at the same time, he began to learn about emerging technologies such as virtual reality and augmented reality, which he attempted to use for film production. He says: "Firstly I cooperated with some art galleries and art museums. Then I started designing projects with some institutions to apply VR scenes on App and popularize them to the public."

Rhodes says: "The cooperative projects with history museums can truly realize the idea of reproducing the historical pictures and images in our city so that we can visualize the history." Rhodes says that in 1929, the shocking

Geoffrey Alan Rhodes:

Shanghai has become a world-class art center and it is inspiring to see the arts thriving here

"Valentine's Day Massacre" happened in Chicago, and using the pictures of it, Rhodes's team reconstructed a scene for virtual reality experience in Chicago and released an App. This project was conferred MUSE Award by the American Alliance of Museums in 2018. From then on, Rhodes has presided over a series of projects which combined city stories with technology through the continuous exploration of the latest technology each year.

Settling in Shanghai to start a new chapter of life

In 2010, Rhodes came to Shanghai for the first time because of his wife. "At that time, my wife was working in the Spain Pavilion at Shanghai 2010 World Expo," says Rhodes. Later, Rhodes came to Shanghai several times and then he settled down here. He says: "I have the opportunity to get a glimpse of the tremendous development of Shanghai's art scene in the past ten years. The sheer number of galleries and newly-built museums is quite amazing and this growth momentum is continuing. Shanghai is now a world-class art center and it is inspiring to see the prosperity and development of art institutions and art activities."

Shanghai's strong artistic atmosphere and the invitation from USC-SJTU Institute of Cultural and Creative Industry prompted the settling down of the Rhodes family in Shanghai in 2020. Rhodes says: "My son was just 18-month-old at that time, and for him, it was really great to come to a city which is not locked down because of the pandemic, to be with his grandparents and to study normally." Rhodes says that he is very happy to be able to come to Shanghai last summer and, taking this opportunity, to start a new stage of life.

While completing his teaching work, Rhodes also restarted his exploration of history museums. He has visited the Memorial of the First National Congress of the Communist Party of China. He says: "Lifelike sculptures are used here to reproduce the significant moments and important events in Chinese modern and contemporary history. In 2021, people can still experience the history (that happened a hundred years ago) after entering the memorial."

Obsessed with art, Rhodes keeps talking about his feelings. Living in Shanghai, he deeply feels the important role that art production, art exhibitions and other art activities play in cities and how art activities are used to change the community.

"I see that communities are developing into areas with different styles, and art galleries are playing a role in these areas," Rhodes says.

Scan for videos

姓　名：Lena Scheen
中文名：沈雷娜
国　籍：荷兰
职　位：上海纽约大学全球中国学助理教授

沈雷娜：
通过本土作家的小说来感受上海的生活和历史

如果你想了解中国和上海，一定得读本土小说。小说向我们讲述了社会现象和城市文化，也包含了作者自己的故事，这是学术文章无法比拟的。

最爱《长恨歌》与《繁花》

每年到了春光明媚的四月，上海纽约大学全球中国学助理教授沈雷娜都会带领学生们去上海石库门家庭博物馆，接触城市记忆的活标本，感受历史变迁。

来自荷兰的沈雷娜喜欢住石库门房子，是个"上海通"。她说："如果你想了解中国和上海，一定得读本土小说。小说向我们讲述了社会现象和城市文化，也包含了作者自己的故事，这是学术文章无法比拟的。"

王安忆的《长恨歌》和金宇澄的《繁花》是沈雷娜最爱看的，她娓娓诉说着自己的阅读心得："《长恨歌》就像一首永恒的悲伤之歌，上海小姐王琦瑶的故事从20世纪40年代延续到80年代，跟随她的生活，你可以了解上海的历史，包括城市景观。"

另一部小说《繁花》，沈雷娜读完后也直呼"精彩"。通过观察小说中人物的日常生活，沈雷娜更加了解了上海。"《繁花》距离现在更近一些，每个想了解上海的人都应该读一读，小说里还使用了很多上海方言。"

沈雷娜要求学生们每周都要阅读两三位作家的作品，带领学生们一起在文字的世界里追寻上海。

沈雷娜：
通过本土作家的小说来感受上海的生活和历史

带领学生实地感受上海气息

不过，沈雷娜更喜欢实地教学，她会带着学生们走街串巷。在沈雷娜眼中，鲁迅公园是个有烟火气的地方，历经百余年，公园里留下了诸多遗迹，比如鲁迅墓、鲁迅纪念馆等。公园周围还保留了很多漂亮的老房子。"在二十世纪三四十年代的上海，这里曾经生活过很多名人，如今漫步在鲁迅公园内，可以看到人们在练太极、唱歌、跳舞，有时候还能遇到书市。"

同样位于虹口区的上海犹太难民纪念馆也是沈雷娜会带学生去的地方之一。二十世纪三四十年代，纳粹在欧洲疯狂杀害犹太人，上海向犹太人敞开怀抱，先后有数万名犹太人赴上海避难或中转。"现在仍然可以看到他们曾经住过的房子。"

2013年至今，沈雷娜教过来自世界各地的学生，"我的学生都很喜欢走到城市里去实地考察，他们喜欢这些意想不到的发现。这不仅让学生们更好地了解了城市的今天，也让他们获得了与这个城市历史和未来之间的连接。"

沈雷娜写了《上海文学想象——一个转型中的城市》一书，她还做了一个"城市地图"系列，每期请一位上海本地作家写一个关于上海的故事。

8年间，沈雷娜通过文字读懂上海，又留下文字让更多人去读懂上海。她对上海的探究还在继续。

Name: Lena Scheen
Chinese name: 沈雷娜
Nationality: Dutch
Position: Assistant Professor of Global China Studies, NYU Shanghai

Lena Scheen:
I feel Shanghai's life and history through the novels of local writers

If you want to understand China and Shanghai, you must read local novels. The novels, containing the author's own story, tell us about social phenomena and the culture of the city in a way that academic texts cannot match.

The Song of Everlasting Sorrow and Blossoms are her favorites

Every year, in the bright and beautiful April, Lena Scheen, the assistant professor of Global China Studies, NYU Shanghai, would guide her students to Shanghai Shikumen Family Museum to get in touch with living specimens of urban memory and experience the historical changes.

Scheen, though from the Netherlands, knows Shanghai very well, and likes to live in the Shikumen (stone gate) houses. She says: "If you want to understand China and Shanghai, you must read local novels. The novels, containing the author's own story, tell us about social phenomena and the culture of the city in a way that academic texts cannot match."

Wang Anyi's *The Song of Everlasting Sorrow* and Jin Yucheng's *Blossoms* are Scheen's favorites. She says: "*The Song of Everlasting Sorrow* is exactly like its name, filled with eternal grief. The story of the former Miss Shanghai winner, Wang Qiyao, extends from the 1940s to the 1980s. Following her life, readers can learn about Shanghai's history, including the urban landscape."

After reading another novel *Blossoms*, Scheen can't help exclaiming "bravo." In reading about the daily life of the characters in the novel, Scheen has gained a

Lena Scheen:

I feel Shanghai's life and history through the novels of local writers

deeper understanding of Shanghai. She says: "*Blossoms* is closer to the present day. Everyone who wants to learn about Shanghai should read it. The Shanghai dialect is also frequently used in this novel."

Scheen asks her students to read the works of two to three writers every week, and guides them to know more about Shanghai in the world of words.

Taking the students on a field trip to get a taste of Shanghai

Scheen also likes teaching through field trips and she usually shows her students around the streets. In her eyes, Luxun Park, in which a hundred years of history has left its marks, such as Luxun Tomb and Luxun Museum, is nevertheless a lively place. She says: "In the 1930s and the 1940s Shanghai, many celebrities had lived here, and nowadays, strolling in the Luxun Park, you can see people playing Tai Chi, singing or dancing. Sometimes you can even come across a pop-up book market here." Many beautiful old houses around the park are also well preserved.

The Shanghai Jewish Refugees Museum located in Hongkou District is also one of the places that Scheen would take her students for a visit. In the 1930s and the 1940s, the Nazis murdered Jews in Europe and Shanghai opened its arms to the refugees. Tens of thousands of Jews came to Shanghai successively for refuge or transit. "Now, you can still see the houses they used to live in," says Scheen.

Since 2013, Scheen has taught students from all over the world. She says: "My students like to go out into the city for field trips. They like these unexpected discoveries, which offer them not only a better understanding of the city today but also a connection with the history and future of this city."

Scheen wrote a book named *Shanghai Literary Imaginings: A City in Transformation*. She has also started a "City Map" series, where in each issue, a local writer would be invited to write a story about Shanghai.

In the past eight years, Scheen has been reading Shanghai through words, and left her own for more people to read and understand Shanghai.

Her exploration of Shanghai is continuing.

Scan for videos

姓　名：Denis Depoux
中文名：戴璞
国　籍：法国
职　位：罗兰贝格全球管理委员会联席总裁

戴璞：
如果一家公司想要保持全球巨头的地位，就要加入中国市场

> 我仍然记得我在城市规划馆看到的上海未来发展模型，30年后当我看到模型中的一切变成现实之后，我震惊了。

上海对于法国人戴璞而言如同一个魔方，样貌时刻都在改变。虽然在上海已经生活了7年，戴璞却还是时常感觉这座城市是新的。

更全面感受上海，才能更好地为上海服务

戴璞回忆道，1994年，东方明珠、南京西路的波特曼酒店还在建设中，浦东还是一个工业港口。"我仍然记得我在城市规划馆看到的上海未来发展模型，上面显示了城市未来的风景和发展方向，由西到东展示了整座城市。30年后当我看到模型中的一切变成现实之后，我震惊了。现实场景特别像那个模型，我们现在还能在人民广场城市规划馆里看到这个模型。"

更全面感受上海，才能更好地为上海服务。"南京路后街改造项目"是戴璞所在的罗兰贝格公司近年来一个成功的案例。"我们以巴黎、纽约、米兰和东京的中心商业街为对比参照，思考我们如何从中学习，并进行更深入的创新。我们在这里做了非常独特的尝试，在上海静安区的项目获得了巨大成功，现在，你们看到的安义夜巷就是一个很好的例子。"

作为罗兰贝格全球管理委员会联席总裁，戴璞认为未来十年间，

戴璞：

如果一家公司想要保持
全球巨头的地位，就要
加入中国市场

30%—40%的全球GDP增长量将来自中国市场，如果一家公司想要保持全球巨头的地位，就要加入中国市场。

他对中国市场抱有信心，以新冠肺炎疫情期间为例，中国的供应链在疫情期间展现出了非凡的韧劲。虽然在疫情一开始，中国的供应链也经历过短暂的中断，但得益于中国政府果断的措施，迅速从疫情中恢复。

计划搭乘列车再次前往西藏

扎根上海的戴璞对中国非常了解。"长远的规划异常重要。中国共产党具有非常明确的长远规划，无论是对于下一个五十年，还是下一个一百年。他们都能将这些转换为长远的规划，将未来的发展写进一个个五年计划中，并且坚定地落实下去。"

28年前，他第一次来到中国，"当时作为背包客去西藏旅行，坐在大巴上，旅途非常艰辛，路况也很糟糕。不过那时中国已经有了一个计划要在上海和拉萨之间造一条铁路。我当时觉得令人难以置信，是不可能的"。

2006年10月1日，上海开往拉萨的列车首发。戴璞说："这就是一个很好的例子来说明中国共产党可以通过长远的规划来实现目标。"

戴璞敬佩中国在过去三十年间的发展，计划搭乘列车再次前往西藏。

Name: Denis Depoux
Chinese Name: 戴璞
Nationality: French
Position: Global Managing Director of Roland Berger

Denis Depoux:
For any global leading company that wants to keep its position, it must join the Chinese market

I still remember when I first saw the model of Shanghai's future development in the Urban Planning Exhibition Hall. Thirty years later when everything in that model became reality, I was amazed.

Shanghai, in the eyes of Denis Depoux from France, is like a Rubik's cube which is changing every moment. Even though he has been living in Shanghai for seven years, he still feels that the city is new.

Full immersion in Shanghai to better serve the city

As Depoux recalls, in 1994 the Oriental Pearl TV Tower and the Portman Hotel on West Nanjing Road were still under construction, and the river bank on the Pudong side was an industrial harbor. He says: "I still remember when I first saw the model of Shanghai's future development in the Urban Planning Exhibition Hall which showed the future landscape and direction of the city, showing the whole city from west to east. Thirty years later when everything in that model became reality, I was amazed. The real-life scene is very similar to the planning model, which is still on display in the Urban Planning Exhibition Hall in People's Square."

Full immersion in Shanghai is necessary to better serve the city. The Transformation Project of Backstreets along Nanjing Road is a successful case in the last few years by Roland Berger, the company that Depoux works for. He

Denis Depoux:

For any global leading company that wants to keep its position, it must join the Chinese market

says: "We looked into the central commercial streets in Paris, New York, Milan and Tokyo for comparison, thinking about what can be learned and how we can innovate better. We have tried something unique here and the project in Jing'an District proves to be a huge success. Now the Anyi Night Market is a great example of it."

As the global managing partner of Roland Berger, Depoux believes that 30%-40% of the global GDP growth will be contributed by China in the next ten years, and for any global leading company that wants to keep its position, it must join the Chinese market.

He has confidence in the Chinese market. For example, during the outbreak of COVID-19, the supply chain in China showed great resilience. Despite some temporary interruptions at the beginning of the outbreak, the supply chains in China recovered quickly and remain strong thanks to the decisive measures of the Chinese government.

Planning on a second trip by train to the Tibet Autonomous Region

As a resident of Shanghai, Depoux knows China very well. He says: "Long-term planning is of great importance. The Communist Party of China has very clear plans for the next fifty years or the next one hundred years. These long-term goals can be cascaded into interim plans and five-year plans, and implemented with full strength."

His first visit to China was 28 years ago. He says: "I was traveling as a backpacker to Tibet. The trip on the bus was very tough and the roads were pretty bad. But at that time China already had a plan about building a railway between Shanghai and Tibet. I thought the idea was unbelievable and it couldn't be done."

On Oct 1 of 2006, the train from Shanghai to Lhasa was launched. Depoux says: "The railway is a good example to show that the Communist Party of China can achieve goals through long-term planning."

He admires China's development in the last thirty years and plans to make another trip to Tibet by train.

Scan for videos

姓　名：Marc Jaffré
中文名：马锦睿
国　籍：法国
职　位：默克生命科学中国董事总经理、亚太纯水业务副总裁

马锦睿：
身处上海，我总是被浓浓的创新氛围萦绕

在这座城市里，你既可以看到国际化的一面，也能穿行于历史古迹和传统里弄。新与旧，东方和西方，这些元素交织在一起，构成了一幅幅丰富而有趣的城市画卷。

"我的中文名叫马锦睿。龙马精神、马到成功……马在中国传统文化中是勇气、正直、勤奋和力量的象征，而'锦睿'代表着美好、睿智。"2017年，马锦睿带着创造美好未来的希冀来到中国上海，一切，从这个富有寓意的名字开启。

投资经营的理想之地

"多年来，上海不断扩大对外开放，形成了良好的投资环境。"今年，是马锦睿在上海工作的第四年。他说，上海是一个企业投资经营的理想之地。

"在上海的这几年，我欣喜地看到政府在生命科学的人才培养、高科技产业以及学术等多个领域加大资源投入，一个非常活跃的创新生态系统正在这里发展成形。"马锦睿认为，这样的环境无疑是默克这样的生物技术创新企业发展的强劲助力。

"上海市政府也从各个方面推动生物医药领域创新，并将这一计划列为优先选项。"马锦睿说，"举个例子，正是得益于政府的大力支持，默克用于创新生物医药和分析用途的科研材料的进口清关简化了程序和技术档案

马锦睿：

身处上海，我总是
被浓浓的创新氛围
萦绕

需求，海关通关更加便利。这一率先试行的新进口政策的成功标志了一个重要的里程碑，对改善全球科研材料的供应、支持中国生物制药创新、打破科研所用关键材料的进口壁垒，以及确保对挽救生命疗法的关键产品的高效供应，发挥着相当重要的作用。"

2021年1月，上海市"十四五"规划《纲要》出炉。"基本建成令人向往的创新之城、人文之城、生态之城"成为催人奋进的美好愿景。

马锦睿觉得，身处上海，自己总是会被浓浓的创新氛围所萦绕。"人工智能、大数据、区块链、电子商务……上海正在从各个领域推进创新，而移动支付、交通出行、公共服务等方面的创新成果也已渗透到每个人的日常生活中。"

古老与现代交相辉映

"在这座城市里，你既可以看到国际化的一面，也能穿行于历史古迹和传统里弄。新与旧，东方和西方，这些元素交织在一起，构成了一幅幅丰富而有趣的城市画卷。"谈及对上海的印象，"反差"一词闪现在马锦睿的脑海中。

如同了解一个人，在一座城市生活久了，你就能越接近它的内在。马锦睿认为，上海最吸引人的城市品质是"有温度"和"有活力"。

"我住在一个历史与现代交融的社区。在我家附近的街道上，我总能看到一些工匠坐在街边修理皮鞋、皮具，我喜欢看这些老师傅们工作，有时候会主动走上前和他们聊上几句，我还喜欢看一些爷爷奶奶接自己的孙子孙女放学。"马锦睿时常会被这些看似稀松平常却又温暖人心的画面所打动，"在上海总能感觉到和谐、有爱的社会氛围"。

"近几年，上海的城市绿化发生了明显的变化，这其中就包括滨江和苏州河沿岸的改造。"平日里，马锦睿喜欢和妻子在上海沿江、沿河地带骑行。他说，这是他搬来上海后最喜欢、最放松的时刻。

在未来的日子，他想继续探索上海的丰富内涵。

Name: Marc Jaffré
Chinese name: 马锦睿
Nationality: French
Position: Managing Director of Merck Life Science China, Vice President and Head of Lab Water Solutions, APAC

Marc Jaffré:
In Shanghai, I'm always enveloped in a strong atmosphere of innovation

In this city, you can see the cosmopolitan side as well as walk through historical sites and traditional alleys. Old and new, East and West, these elements intertwined to form a rich and interesting urban landscape.

Marc Jaffré: "My Chinese name is Ma Jinrui. 'Ma,' or 'horse' in Chinese, is found in many Chinese idioms with positive meanings. The horse is a symbol of courage, integrity, diligence and strength in Chinese traditional culture, while 'Jinrui' represents beauty and wisdom." In 2017, Jaffré came to Shanghai with the hope of creating a better future for himself. All started from this meaningful name.

An ideal place for investment and business

"Over the years, Shanghai has continuously expanded its opening-up to the outside world and formed a favorable investment environment," says Jaffré. This year is his fourth year in Shanghai. He says that Shanghai is an ideal place for enterprises to invest and do business in.

Jaffré says: "I am pleased to see that in the past few years, the Shanghai government has increased investment in resources in many fields such as personnel training in life sciences, high-tech industries and academia. A very active innovation ecosystem is developing and taking shape here." In his view, such an environment is undoubtedly a strong boost to the development of biotech innovation companies like Merck.

Jaffré says: "The Shanghai government is also promoting innovation in the biomedical field from all aspects and has made this program a priority. As an example, it is thanks to strong government support that the import clearance of Merck's scientific research materials for innovative biomedical and analytical

Marc Jaffré:

In Shanghai, I'm always enveloped in a strong atmosphere of innovation

uses has been streamlined and the need for technical files has been made easier for customs clearance. The success of this pioneering and pilot new import policy marks an important milestone and plays a considerable role in improving the global supply of research materials, supporting biopharmaceutical innovation in China, breaking down import barriers for key materials used in research, and ensuring an efficient supply of critical products for life-saving therapies."

In January 2021, the Outline of Shanghai's 14th Five-Year Plan was released. "Basically completing the building of a desirable city of innovation, humanity and ecology" has become a beautiful vision that inspires people to forge ahead.

Jaffré feels that in Shanghai, he is always enveloped in a strong atmosphere of innovation. He says: "Artificial intelligence, big data, blockchain, e-commerce... Shanghai is promoting innovation in various fields, and innovations in mobile payment, transportation and public services have become part of everyone's daily life."

"The old and the modern intertwined"

Jaffré says: "In this city, you can see the cosmopolitan side as well as walk through historical sites and traditional alleys. Old and new, East and West, these elements intertwined to form a rich and interesting urban landscape." The word "contrast" flashes to Jaffré's mind when talking about his impressions of Shanghai.

Just like getting to know a person, the longer you live in a city, the closer you get to its inner self. According to Jaffré, the most attractive qualities of Shanghai are its warmth and vitality.

Jaffré says: "I live in a community where history and modernity meet. On the streets near my home, I can always see some craftsmen sitting on the sidewalk repairing shoes and leather goods. I like to watch these old masters working, and sometimes I will strike up a conversation. I also like to see some grandparents picking up their grandchildren from school." He is often touched by these seemingly ordinary but heart-warming scenes. "I can always feel the harmonious and loving social atmosphere in Shanghai," says Jaffré.

"In recent years, Shanghai's urban greening has undergone significant changes, including the renovation of the Huangpu Riverfront and the banks along the Suzhou Creek," says Jaffré. He usually likes to ride bicycles with his wife along the rivers in Shanghai. He says this has been his favorite and most relaxing moment since he moved to Shanghai.

Jaffré admits that in the days to come, he wants to continue to explore the unknown richness of Shanghai.

姓　名：Lila
中文名：星悦
国　籍：美国
职　位：歪果仁研究协会副会长、up主

星悦：
我在互联网上通过视频让大家更了解中国

这座城市的活力也激发着年轻人的动力。活力是有感染力的，我的活力在这里被点燃，然后又点燃了其他朋友的活力，我觉得这种感觉很好。

"中国其他地方的人来到上海，世界各地的人也来到上海，上海就像是一份色拉，内容丰富。"星悦形容自己眼中的上海，用了一个非常特别的方式，而随着了解的进一步深入，这位哔哩哔哩up主也对上海心生向往。

能写汉字"太酷了"

星悦与她的团队目前正在从中国的美食、科技以及各种职业的体验等角度出发，制作视频产品向世界介绍中国。在这些节目中，金发碧眼的星悦说着一口流利而地道的普通话，她的叙述逻辑清晰，主持风格颇具特色，给观众们留下了深刻的印象。

但是在生活中，星悦是个腼腆的女生。星悦来自美国加州，她告诉记者，自己高中时就开始学习中文了。"美国的高中要学外语，可以在法语、西班牙语或者另外一种语言中选择。"星悦一开始选了法语，有一天，她和同学补写作业，偶然间瞄到同学在写中文作业。"可以写汉字，这也太酷了吧！我就找中文老师商量，想换到中文班。"就这样，星悦开启了她的中文学习。

高中即将毕业，选择大学时，星悦忽然萌生了一个念头"如果我去中国呢"。从小星悦就是个思维"天马行空"的孩子，加之美国的孩子很少在高中毕业时就去其他国家读书，所以一开始父母都以为她在开玩笑。

星悦开始准备资料，试图向父母证明自己并非一时冲动。发现女儿是

星悦：

我在互联网上通过视频让大家更了解中国

认真的后，父亲非常支持："你真的要去中国？这也太棒了，我觉得很酷，我支持你。"

父亲陪同星悦一起来到中国，进入北京大学校园那一刻，星悦更加认定自己的选择是正确的，"后来我就越来越开心"。

通过视频让大家了解中国

星悦学习的是影视编导专业，她认识了来自以色列的高佑思。几个年轻人产生了一个想法——以在中国生活的外国人为切入点，拍摄一系列视频。"在中国的外国人越来越多，但大家并不知道我们在中国做了些什么。我们不仅想让国外的人看看我们的生活，也想让他们看看中国年轻人的生活。"

他们的视频产品越发在互联网上受到欢迎，起初星悦并不出镜，但一次偶然的机会，她出现在画面中，然后就发现社交账号粉丝数涨了好几万，自己的声音能被更多人听到也是一件很美好的事，就这样星悦从幕后走到了台前。

星悦和伙伴们从中国的美食、科技以及各种职业的体验等角度出发，向世界介绍中国。前段时间，她跟随上海市公安局长宁分局虹桥路派出所民警深入一线，观察并记录民警一天的工作。"很少有这样的机会能和警察长时间接触，深入了解他们的生活。我觉得非常酷。"

星悦觉得中国的警察更亲切，甚至可以像朋友一样。"警察遇到的事，大事小事都有，我很喜欢一名警察告诉我的一句话——执勤的时候既要有制度，也要有温度。"

上海的活力很有感染力

最近，星悦的好多个朋友都搬来了上海，原因不尽相同。由于参加节目《脱口秀大会》的海选，星悦来上海也越来越频繁。她在上海的山羊goat小剧场练习脱口秀，用年轻人喜欢的幽默的方式来讲述中美两国在文化上的差异。

上海的艺术氛围给星悦留下了深刻的印象，这座城市的活力也深深感染了她。星悦说："这座城市的活力也激发着年轻人的动力。活力是有感染力的，我的活力在这里被点燃，然后又点燃了其他朋友的活力，我觉得这种感觉很好。"

星悦期待自己也能在上海留下一段美好的故事。

Name: Lila
Chinese name: 星悦
Nationality: American
Position: Vice President of YChina, Content Creator

Lila:

I make online videos so that everybody will know more about China

The energy of this city also inspires young people. The energy is contagious. My energy is ignited here, which then ignites the energy of my other friends, and I think that's a great feeling.

"People from other parts of China come to Shanghai, and people from all over the world also come here. Shanghai is like a salad, rich in content," Lila describes Shanghai in her eyes in a very special way. As she learns more about the city, this vlogger on Bilibili, one of the largest video websites in China, has also yearned for Shanghai.

It's so cool if I can write Chinese characters

Lila and her team are currently making video products to introduce China to the world from the perspectives of Chinese cuisine, technology and experiences in various occupations. In these programs, this blond girl speaks fluent and authentic Mandarin. Her clear narrative logic and distinctive hosting style leave a deep impression on the audience.

However, Lila is a bit shy in daily life. She comes from California, USA, and began to learn Mandarin Chinese in high school. "High school students in the United States usually learn a foreign language from choices among French, Spanish or other languages," says Lila. She chose French at first. One day when she and her classmates were making up their homework, she happened to notice that her classmates were doing Chinese homework. "It's so cool if I can write Chinese characters! I talked with my Chinese language teacher and said that I wanted to be switched to the Chinese class," she says. Then she started learning Mandarin Chinese.

When she was about to graduate from high school and to choose a university, Lila suddenly had an idea: "What if I go to China?" She has always been a person with a "wild" mind, even in childhood. In addition, American

Lila:

I make online videos so that everybody will know more about China

children seldom go to other countries to study when they graduate from high school, so her parents thought she was joking at first.

Lila began to prepare materials, trying to prove to her parents that her decision was not made on impulse. When discovering that she was serious, her father was very supportive, saying: "Do you really want to go to China? This is great. I think it's cool. I'm on your side."

The moment her father accompanied her to China and entered the campus of Peking University, she became even more determined that she had made the right choice, "and then I just became happier and happier," says Lila.

Making videos so that everybody will know about China

Lila studied film and television directing and later met Raz Galor from Israel. These young people came up with an idea — to shoot a series of videos about foreign citizens living in China. Lila says: "There are more and more foreign people in China, but little is known of our life in China. We want people in other countries to know about not only our lives here but also those of the Chinese young people here."

Their videos became more and more popular on the Internet. At first, Lila did not appear on camera, but for once, when she did appear by chance, she found that the number of her social account followers increased by tens of thousands. It was a wonderful thing that her voice could be heard by more people, so she came to the front stage from behind the scenes.

Lila and her partners introduced China to the world from the perspectives of Chinese cuisine, technology, and experiences in various occupations. She once followed the police officers of Hongqiao Road Police Station of Shanghai Public Security Bureau at Changning District to the front line, observing and recording their work for a day. She says: "It's not often that you get such an opportunity to spend long hours with police officers and get an insight into their lives, which I think is very cool."

Lila felt that these Chinese police officers are more approachable and friendly. "The police encounter all kinds of things, big and small, and I like what a police officer once told me — the police should display both law and leniency when on duty," she says.

Shanghai's energy is very contagious

Recently, many of Lila's friends have moved to Shanghai for various reasons. Thanks to her participation in the audition for the program "Rock & Roast", she has come to Shanghai more frequently. She practiced talk shows at Goat Theater in Shanghai, recounting the cultural differences between China and the United States in a humorous way that young people are fond of.

Lila was deeply impressed by the artistic atmosphere of Shanghai, and the energy of the city also deeply infected her. She says: "The energy of this city also inspires young people. The energy is contagious. My energy is ignited here, which then ignites the energy of my other friends, and I think that's a great feeling."

Lila herself is looking forward to leaving a great story in Shanghai for herself too.

Scan for videos

姓　名：Noyan Rona
中文名：诺扬
国　籍：土耳其
职　位：土耳其担保银行上海代表处首席代表

诺扬：
中国发展到现在这个水平是一个奇迹，但中国人把这个奇迹做出来了

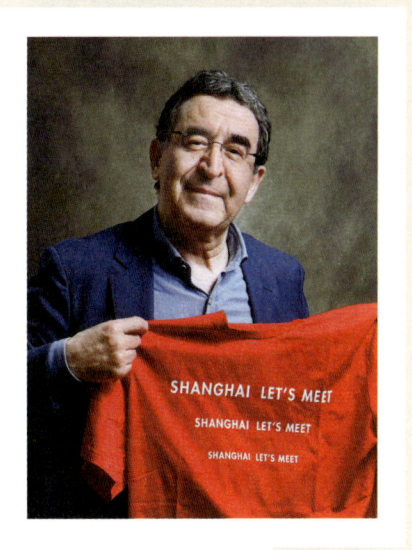

外国人想象不到中国会发展到现在这个水平，这是一个奇迹，但是中国人把这个奇迹做出来了。

诺扬说着一口流利的汉语，在他位于土耳其担保银行上海代表处的办公室里摆满了各种奖状。重要的是，这些荣誉大都来自中国政府的颁授，意义非同一般，诺扬对此非常看重，这是对他在中国这么多年工作的一种肯定。

在中国生活了 38 年

算上今年，诺扬在中国已经生活整整 38 年了，比他在自己的祖国土耳其待的时间还久。从土耳其安卡拉大学汉学系毕业后，1983 年，诺扬作为土耳其第一批公派留学生来到中国，先是在北京语言学院（今北京语言大学）进修汉语，之后在武汉大学攻读历史学硕士学位。硕士毕业后，诺扬先后任职于土耳其外交部、土耳其驻华大使馆、土耳其驻上海总领事馆，1999 年加入土耳其担保银行，成为该行上海代表处首席代表。

土耳其担保银行是改革开放后第一家在中国设立代表处的土耳其银行，看中的正是中国未来的发展潜力，事实证明，他们并未看错。

从武汉到北京，再到上海，三地中，诺扬在上海待的时间最久，迄今已经 25 年，他笑说中国最新一次人口普查结果出炉，他比很多新上海人来上海的日子还要长得多，连儿子都是在 5 岁那年就来了中国，在中国成长，

诺扬：

中国发展到现在这个水平是一个奇迹，但中国人把这个奇迹做出来了

到如今已大学毕业。

"我是上海的一分子"

诺扬感觉这25年来上海的变化是日新月异的，25年来，他尤其关心上海的精神文明建设，并积极参与各项工作，在路口、社区、养老院等地方常常能见到这位土耳其老外的身影。"市民在环境保护、社会秩序、文明礼让等方面都有了长足进步，政府为此做了很多宣传，也收到了成效。"

2005年，诺扬获得了"白玉兰荣誉奖"，7年后，他又被授予"上海市荣誉市民"称号。诺扬还获得了很多荣誉，比如，"上海市社会主义精神文明十佳好人好事""上海市优秀志愿者""全国最美家庭"……

诺扬的办公室里，还有一样宝贝，那就是处于显眼位置的一幅书法，上写"精神文明洋雷锋"。他说这是一个素不相识的中国老人写了赠予他的。"老人看了人民日报对我的报道，知道我是一个热心人，便送我这个称号。"

诺扬说："我是上海的一分子。"把自己看成上海市民，诺扬当然想让城市更美好。

"中国共产党非常有活力"

今年是中国共产党成立100周年。"中国共产党有活力，有自我改革、自我发展的愿望和意志。她所作出的决定非常符合中国国情，对中国百姓非常有利，也因此为百姓所拥护。"

诺扬拿仍在全球肆虐的新冠肺炎疫情来举例，"从中国处理疫情的情况来看，很有中国共产党的特色，其优越性和独特性都得以显示，种种抗疫措施都获百姓支持。从另一个角度解读，因为相信党，百姓才配合。"说这些时，诺扬眼里满是敬佩。

"中国共产党的组织能力很强，影响力和魄力是其他政党不能比的。很多外国人好奇，这么大一个国家，可以发展得这么好，如果不住在中国，不身处这个环境，是很难理解的。"诺扬感慨道，"外国人想象不到中国会发展到现在这个水平，这是一个奇迹，但是中国人把这个奇迹做出来了。"

说到上海的几处红色场馆，诺扬都去过。在他看来，外国人前去参观的目的往往有偏差。"老外是看建筑，是以看名胜古迹的心态去参观，其他的不怎么关心。而我觉得中国共产党的发展历程中有不少事件都是值得我们去了解和学习的。"

Name: Noyan Rona
Chinese name: 诺扬
Nationality: Turkish
Position: Chief Representative of Garanti Bank Shanghai Rep. Office

Noyan Rona:

It is a miracle that China has developed to the level it has, but the Chinese have made it happen

Foreigners can't imagine that China has developed to this level. It's a miracle, but the Chinese have made it happen.

Noyan Rona speaks fluent Chinese, and his office at Turkish Garanti Bank in Shanghai is filled with various awards. What is important is that most of these honors are awarded by the Chinese government, which is of extraordinary significance. He appreciates them very much, as an affirmation of his work in China for so many years.

He has lived in China for 38 years

Rona has lived in China for 38 years, longer than the time he has spent in his home country Turkey. After graduating from the Sinology Department of Ankara University in Turkey, Rona came to China in 1983 as the first batch of government-sponsored international students, first studying Chinese in Beijing Language and Culture College (now Beijing Language and Culture University), and then studying for a master's degree in history at Wuhan University. After graduating with a master's degree, Rona successively worked in the Turkish Ministry of Foreign Affairs, the Turkish Embassy in China, and the Turkish Consulate General in Shanghai. In 1999, he joined the Turkish Garanti Bank and became the chief representative of its Shanghai Representative Office.

Turkish Garanti Bank is the first Turkish bank to establish a representative office in China after the reform and opening-up. They were interested in China's future development potential, and it turned out that they were right.

Rona has been in Shanghai for 25 years now. He laughs and says that he came to Shanghai much earlier than many new Shanghainese. His son also

Noyan Rona:

It is a miracle that China has developed to the level it has, but the Chinese have made it happen

came to China at the age of 5, grew up in China, and now has graduated from university.

"I'm part of Shanghai"

Rona feels that in the past 25 years, Shanghai has been changing with each passing day. He has actively participated in various efforts to make the city better, busy at street intersections, residential communities, nursing homes, and many other places. He says: "The citizens have made great progress in many aspects such as environmental protection, social order, and social morality. The government has done a lot of publicity for this and has seen successful fruits."

In 2005, Rona won Magnolia Gold Award. Seven years later, he was awarded the title of "Honorary Citizen of Shanghai." He also won many other honors.

In Rona's office hangs a piece of calligraphy in a conspicuous position, which reads "Jing Shen Wen Ming Yang Lei Feng" (meaning the foreign role model in the building of a socialist society with an advanced level of culture and ideology). He says that it was written and given to him by an old Chinese man who had never met him before. "The old man read the report in People's Daily about me and knew that I was always willing to help others, so he presented this title to me," says Rona.

"I am part of Shanghai," he says.

"The CPC has much vitality"

This year marks the 100th anniversary of the founding of the Communist Party of China (CPC). Rona says: "The CPC has much vitality, and the desire and will to reform and develop itself. The decisions made are very much in line with China's social conditions and very beneficial to the Chinese people, so the CPC is supported by the people."

He says: "The way China has handled the COVID-19 pandemic is very characteristic of the CPC, showing its superiority and uniqueness, with the public supporting its various measures. The public is willing to cooperate because they believe in the party." When he says this, his eyes are filled with admiration.

Rona says: "The CPC is outstanding in its ability to organize the masses. Its influence and drive no other political parties can compare. Many foreigners are curious about how such a big country can develop so well, and it's hard to understand if you don't live in China and are not in this environment. So many foreigners can't imagine that China has developed to this level. It's a miracle, but the Chinese have made it happen."

Rona has visited a few "red" venues of Shanghai. In his opinion, foreigners often visit with a biased focus. He says: "Foreigners are looking at the architecture and are visiting with the mindset of seeing famous sites and not caring much about the rest. But I think there are quite a few events in the development of the CPC that are worth knowing and learning about."

姓　名：SONG UIJIN
中文名：宋义进
国　籍：韩国
职　位：iG 电子竞技俱乐部英雄联盟分部职业选手

宋义进：
作为一名职业电竞选手，我最爱在上海比赛

我希望在上海拿更多的冠军，并且拥有一份属于自己的事业。

"你好，我叫宋义进，来自韩国，我是一名职业电竞选手。"在上海住了 7 年，如今的宋义进能说一口流利的中文，如果不长时间交流，甚至很难相信他是一个外国人。

"美"是上海留给他的第一印象

1997 年出生的宋义进如今是 iG 战队的队长。宋义进很早就已经确定自己要走职业电竞的道路。他在韩国出道，但那时成绩不太理想，机会也不多。"我爸妈觉得男孩子可以去感受下其他国家的文化，他们鼓励孩子们去其他国家发展。"

2014 年 10 月，17 岁的宋义进决定来中国试试，背着行囊，他和朋友一起来到了上海。"美"是上海留给他的第一印象，无论是白天的街景还是晚上的夜景，都是宋义进喜欢的。"我最喜欢陆家嘴的夜景，第一次看到的时候感慨，哇！能这么好看吗？真是太美了！"

为了更好地融入这座城市，他开始学习中文。中文难学，每每遇到不懂的文字，他都会去请教别人或者查阅资料，就这样经过日积月累的学习，如今宋义进的中文水平突飞猛进。

宋义进告诉记者，在上海生活感觉非常便利，只要一部手机就可以在城市里畅通无阻，"现在，如果不住在上海会有点难受。"

宋义进：

作为一名职业电竞选手，我最爱在上海比赛

上海的电竞氛围"无敌"

作为一名职业电竞选手，宋义进最爱在上海比赛。因为，除了新的比赛场馆和优质的配套服务，粉丝也格外热情。"上海的电竞氛围'无敌'，无论是粉丝的热情还是玩家的实力。有一次我们打LPL（英雄联盟职业联赛），粉丝的欢呼声让我都不知道怎么形容，感觉是他们赢了比赛一样。"

除了热情，粉丝的实力也不容小觑。iG战队的合作伙伴会举办一些选手和粉丝们的互动比赛，宋义进感受到"粉丝们的技术也很不错"。

自2017年开始，上海出台了关于发展电竞产业的系列措施。得益于政府的支持，上海集聚了全国80%以上的电竞企业、俱乐部、战队和直播平台，超过40%的全国电竞赛事在上海举办。

《2020年1—6月中国游戏产业报告》显示：2020年1—6月，中国电子竞技游戏营销收入达719.36亿元，同比增长54.69%；1—6月中国电子竞技用户规模约为4.84亿人，同比增长9.94%。

上海给予了宋义进机遇，他从一名普通的选手成长为主力干将，现在又成为iG战队的队长。

宋义进说，希望能在上海获得更多的冠军，也希望在上海拥有一份属于自己的电竞事业。

Name: SONG UIJIN
Chinese name: 宋义进
Nationality: ROK
Position: Professional eSports Player of Invictus Gaming

SONG UIJIN:
My favorite place to play as a professional eSports player is Shanghai

I hope to win more championships in Shanghai and to have a gaming career of my own.

"Hello, my name is SONG UIJIN. I am a professional eSports player from South Korea," says SONG UIJIN who, having lived in Shanghai for seven years, now speaks Chinese so fluently that it is hard to believe he is even a foreigner without a long exchange of words.

The first impression he had of Shanghai was its beauty

Born in 1997, SONG is now the captain of iG team. SONG had already decided early on that he wanted to pursue a professional gaming career. He made his debut in Korea, but at that time the results were not too good and there were not many opportunities. "My parents felt that boys could go and experience the culture of other countries, and they encourage their kids to go to other countries," says SONG.

In October 2014, 17-year-old SONG decided to try his luck in China, and he came to Shanghai with his friends. The first impression he had of Shanghai was its beauty and he enjoyed both the daytime and nighttime street scenes very much. He says: "I like the night scene of Lujiazui the most. When I saw it for the first time, I said to myself: 'Wow! How can it look so good? It's so beautiful!'"

In order to better integrate into the city, he began to learn Chinese, which is quite difficult. Whenever he encountered words he didn't understand, he would consult other people or search for information. After years of learning, his Chinese level has improved by leaps and bounds.

SONG says that he feels it is very convenient to live in Shanghai since

SONG UIJIN:

My favorite place to play as a professional eSports player is Shanghai

people only need a smartphone to go around. "Now, if you do not live in Shanghai anymore, you will feel the life to be a bit inconvenient," he says.

The gaming atmosphere in Shanghai is "incomparable"

As a professional eSports player, SONG loves playing in Shanghai the most because, in addition to the new competition venues and quality support services, the fans are extraordinarily enthusiastic. He says: "The gaming atmosphere in Shanghai is incomparable, both in terms of the enthusiasm of the fans and the strength of the players. Once when we played LPL (League of Legends Professional League), the cheers from the fans were so loud that I didn't even know how to describe it. It was like they had won the game."

In addition to their enthusiasm, the strength of the fans should not be underestimated, either. Partners of the iG team will hold some interactive competitions between players and fans, and SONG feels that the fans' skills are also very good.

Since 2017, Shanghai has introduced a series of measures on the development of the eSports industry. Thanks to the government's support, Shanghai has gathered more than 80% of the country's eSports enterprises, clubs, teams, and live streaming platforms, and more than 40% of the national eSports events are held in Shanghai.

The China Game Industry Report from January to June 2020 shows that, during the six months, China's marketing revenue of eSports games reached 71.936 billion yuan, a year-on-year increase of 54.69%; from January to June, the number of eSports users in China was about 484 million, 9.94% up year-on-year.

Shanghai has allowed SONG to grow from an ordinary player to the main force player, and now he has become the captain of the iG team.

SONG says that he hopes to win more championships in Shanghai and to have an eSports career of his own in this city.

姓　名：Marshall Strabala
中文名：马溯
国　籍：美国
职　位：上海中心首席设计师

马溯：
我在自己设计的上海中心大厦倚窗而望，城市景象尽收眼底

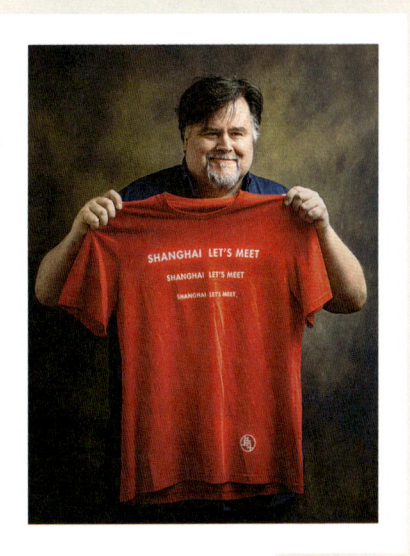

上海的公共交通，尤其是地铁越来越发达。这些四通八达的地铁网络，不仅拉近了人与人之间的距离，方便了人们的出行，还将人与建筑紧密结合在一起，赋予了建筑活力与生机。

浦东陆家嘴，上海中心大厦高耸入云，和金茂大厦、环球金融中心遥相呼应，汇成了一幅展现城市天际线的精彩画卷。身为中国第一高楼的首席设计师，马溯带领他的团队就在自己的"代表作"里办公。倚窗而望，上海美丽壮观的城市景象尽收眼底。马溯说，这栋倾注了他多年心血的"作品"，不仅让城市天际线更精彩，还见证了浦东开发开放的巨变。

中国第一高楼背后的故事

马溯是全球享有盛名的建筑大师，在上海中心之前，他就已经参与设计了迪拜塔和南京紫峰大厦这两栋世界闻名的超高层建筑。

1999年，马溯第一次来到中国。"当时我代表一家名叫SOM的设计公司来北京参加设计大赛，因为在金茂大厦有个相关会议，所以又从北京来到了上海。"马溯说，"这是我与上海的第一次见面，我下了飞机坐上出租车，和司机说要去金茂，他没有听懂，一直在问'什么路'，我只好用笔画出金茂大厦的样子，他就秒懂了，所以我学的第一句中文就是'什么路'。"

马溯：

我在自己设计的上海中心大厦倚窗而望，城市景象尽收眼底

2006年，马溯又被派往上海工作6个月，这段时间，马溯才开始真正走近上海、了解上海。"2006年，我到上海参加上海中心大厦设计竞赛，一年后又过来进行了第二次竞标，2008年6月，我们的方案被选中，自那以后，我就开始常驻上海啦！"马溯回忆。

2008年下半年，马溯和团队投入到紧张的设计环节。"我的设想是，这栋大楼要与金茂大厦及环球金融中心有所呼应。"马溯说，起初，他们为上海中心设计的高度是680米，但为了让这三栋摩天大楼之间形成完美和谐的关系，最终，他们将高度定在了632米，这在视觉上是最美的顶部上升弧线。

在马溯看来，陆家嘴这三栋最夺目的大楼之间，除了视觉上的巧妙搭配以外，还有着时间上的承接。

"金茂大厦代表着中国的过去，环球金融中心代表着中国的现在，而上海中心代表着中国的未来。"马溯自豪地说，"它们和东方明珠一起组成的天际线美轮美奂，成了世界认识上海的亮丽名片，而上海中心是其中最绿色、最环保、最能体现可持续发展理念的。"

上海是一个"可行走的城市"

中国有句古话，叫"读万卷书，不如行万里路"。行走是一种阅读，在行走中，人们才得以"翻阅"一座城市的前世今生，细品一座城市。在马溯眼里，上海就是一座经得起反复"阅读"的、可行走的城市。

"我喜欢上海很大程度上源于它的步行条件。"马溯说，他住在打浦桥的时候，总是习惯和妻子步行到徐家汇吃饭，"一来，我们都是浪漫的人，夜晚在街头漫步，欣赏霓虹灯下斑斓的城市，是一种不错的体验；二来，太太说我来上海之后胖了很多，所以总是督促我饭后多运动。但我们走着走着，就被各种餐厅的美食所吸引。我最喜欢吃的是北京烤鸭，其次是红烧肉、小笼包和扬州炒饭！"

行走是一种可持续的理念，这些年，马溯注意到上海的交通变化。"上海的公共交通，尤其是地铁越来越发达。这些四通八达的地铁网络，不仅拉近了人与人之间的距离，方便了人们的出行，还将人与建筑紧密结合在一起，赋予了建筑活力与生机。"

这些年，上海的空气越来越好，蓝天也越来越多了，马溯很享受这样的安逸与舒适。

Name: Marshall Strabala
Chinese name: 马溯
Nationality: American
Position: Chief architect to Shanghai Tower

Marshall Strabala:
Leaning against the window of Shanghai Tower I designed, I have a panoramic view of the city

The public transportation in Shanghai, especially the subway, is getting more and more developed. These well-connected subway networks not only shorten the distance between people and facilitate their travel but also bring people and buildings closer, endowing buildings with vitality.

In Lujiazui, Pudong, Shanghai Tower rears into the clouds, echoing Jinmao Tower and Shanghai World Financial Center, forming a spectacular picture of the urban skyline. Marshall Strabala, the chief designer of Shanghai Tower, China's tallest building, works with his team inside his "masterpiece." Leaning against the window and looking outside, you can have a panoramic view of Shanghai's beautiful and magnificent city scenes. Strabala says that this work on which he has made years of enormous efforts, not only enhances the urban skyline but also bears witness to the tremendous changes brought by the development and opening-up of Pudong.

The story behind China's tallest building

Strabala is a world-renowned architect. Before designing Shanghai Tower, he had participated in the design of Burj Khalifa Tower and Zifeng Tower in Nanjing, the two world-famous supertall buildings.

Strabala came to China for the first time in 1999. He says: "I got off the plane, took a taxi and told the driver that I was going to Jinmao Tower. He didn't catch my words and kept asking 'Shenmelu (Where to)'. I had to sketch Jinmao Tower with a pen and he understood it in seconds. So the first Chinese sentence

Marshall Strabala:

Leaning against the window of Shanghai Tower I designed, I have a panoramic view of the city

I learned was 'Shenmelu.'"

In 2006, Strabala was dispatched to Shanghai again for another six months, and it was during this time that he began to really get close to Shanghai and understand it. "In 2006, I came to Shanghai for the Shanghai Tower Design Competition. A year later, I came here again for the second bid," Strabala recalls. "In June 2008, our design was selected. Since then, I have settled down in Shanghai."

In the second half of 2008, Strabala and his team devoted themselves to the intense design work. "My conception is that this tall building should echo Jinmao Tower and Shanghai World Financial Center," Strabala says. The initially designed height of the Shanghai Tower was 680 meters. But in order to create a perfect harmony between the three skyscrapers, they finally set the height at 632 meters, visually displaying the most beautiful ascending arc of the three buildings.

In Strabala's view, in addition to an ingenious visual match, there is also a display of continuity in time between the three most eye-catching skyscrapers in Lujiazui.

Strabala says proudly: "Jinmao Tower represents China's past, Shanghai World Financial Center is the present and Shanghai Tower symbolizes the future. Together with the Oriental Pearl TV Tower, they form a magnificent skyline that has become a calling card for the world to know Shanghai. Among them, Shanghai Tower is the greenest, the most environmentally friendly and the best embodiment of the concept of sustainable development."

Shanghai is a city worth travelling to

"My love for Shanghai, to a large extent, originates from its walking conditions," Strabala says. When he lived in Dapuqiao, he was used to walking with his wife to Xujiahui to have dinner. He adds: "For one thing, we are both a bit romantic and it's a great experience for us to stroll on the streets at night and enjoy the colorful city life under neon lights. For another, my wife says that I have gained a lot of weight since I came to Shanghai so she always urges me to take more exercise after meals. However, we can't help but get attracted by the delicious foods in various restaurants during our walks. My favorites are Peking roast duck, followed by braised pork in brown sauce, steamed meat bun, and Yangzhou fried rice."

Walking is a concept about sustainability. Over the years, Strabala has noticed the changes in transportation in Shanghai. He says: "The public transportation in Shanghai, especially the subway, is getting more and more developed. These well-connected subway networks not only shorten the distance between people and facilitate their travel, but also bring people and buildings closer, endowing buildings with vitality."

In recent years, the air in Shanghai is getting better, and the blue skies are frequently seen. Strabala says that he enjoys this ease and comfort.

姓　名：Kamran Vossoughi
中文名：伟书杰
国　籍：法国
职　位：米其林中国区总裁兼首席执行官

伟书杰：
在上海我看到了人与自然之间的和谐发展

在上海我看到了人与自然之间的和谐发展。

带着对中国历史的喜爱以及对现代中国的向往，伟书杰来到上海，担任米其林中国区总裁兼首席执行官，并将妻子和三个孩子一起带了过来。

最爱中国古建筑

"世界上第一张纸是中国发明的，指南针也是中国发明的。中国还有一些非常重要的地标让人印象深刻，比如长城、故宫。这些都是中国文化中让我印象深刻的部分。"伟书杰说来华前，他就知道中国拥有超过五千年的深厚文化底蕴，并为之着迷。

来到上海后，伟书杰感受到这座城市不仅经济发达，人文氛围也很浓厚。"上海保留了中国文化的深厚根基。你既可以去外滩欣赏浦东的现代建筑，也可以到豫园探寻传统文化。同时，上海正在围绕绿色主题，建设绿色城市。总之，在上海我看到了人与自然之间的和谐发展。"

因为曾经是一名土木工程师，伟书杰最爱的就是中国古建筑。在伟书杰眼里，这些建筑反映了中国深厚的文化，体现了中国人的智慧，充满魅力。

一起支持碳中和

中国经济正转向高质量发展，伟书杰认为，这种高质量发展基于三大要点："第一是以科学为基础，第二是以技术为重点，第三是以创新为驱动力，而这些都与碳中和有关,高质量发展要把它与人民的生活质量和福祉联系起来。"伟书杰深信,中国关于碳中和的承诺认真且严肃,并已采取切实行动。

伟书杰介绍,米其林公司在中国的减排工作已经开展了十多年,每年都在减少碳足迹,使用更绿色的能源和运输方式,开展更绿色的生产活动。2020年,在北京米其林指南发布活动中,米其林为一家餐厅颁发了绿星奖,这是第一次在中国市场上引入米其林绿星,目的就是褒奖餐厅的环保可持续举措。

见证中国脱贫攻坚战

党的十八大以来,以习近平同志为核心的党中央团结带领全党全国各族人民,把脱贫攻坚摆在治国理政突出位置,采取了许多具有原创性、独特性的重大举措,组织实施了人类历史上规模最大、力度最强的脱贫攻坚战。

伟书杰是诸多在中国见证贫困山区改变的外国人之一。2020年底,伟书杰和同事一起去云南,从机场驱车8小时翻山越岭最终到达一个偏远的村庄小学。"途中我看到了各种道路设施和在建的工程,中国政府正努力将这些偏远的村庄与大城市连接起来。我看到了许多建成的桥梁和正在修建的道路,很多地区还在努力治理河流,让务农更加轻松。"

伟书杰感受到了中国政府解决贫困问题的决心,也感受到了发展的气息。

Name: Kamran Vossoughi
Chinese name: 伟书杰
Nationality: French
Position: President & CEO of Michelin China

Kamran Vossoughi:
I see a harmonious development between people and nature in Shanghai

I see a harmonious development between people and nature in Shanghai.

With a love for Chinese history and a desire to see modern China, Kamran Vossoughi came to Shanghai as President and CEO of Michelin China, with his wife and three children.

Ancient Chinese architecture is his favorite

Vossoughi says: "The first piece of paper in the world is invented in China, so is the compass. China also has some impressive landmarks, such as the Great Wall and the Forbidden City. These are the parts of Chinese culture that impress me very much." Vossoughi says that before he came to China, he had already known that China has a profound cultural heritage of over 5,000 years and was fascinated by it.

After coming to Shanghai, Vossoughi felt that the city is not only economically developed but also has a strong humanistic atmosphere. He says: "Shanghai has preserved the deep roots of Chinese culture. You can go to the Bund to appreciate the modern architecture in Pudong, and you can also go to Yuyuan Garden to explore the traditional culture. At the same time, Shanghai, guided by the 'Green' theme design, is aiming at building a green city. In short, I see a harmonious development between people and nature in Shanghai."

Because he was once a civil engineer, ancient Chinese architecture is Vossoughi's favorite. In his eyes, these buildings reflect China's profound culture, embody the wisdom of the Chinese people, and are full of charm.

Kamran Vossoughi:

I see a harmonious development between people and nature in Shanghai

Joint support for carbon neutrality

China's economy is shifting to high-quality development, which, Vossoughi thinks, is based on three main points. He explains: "The first is science-based, the second is technology-focused, and the third is innovation-driven, which are all related to carbon neutrality. High-quality development must be linked to the quality of life and well-being of the people." He is convinced that China's commitment to carbon neutrality is serious and earnest, and that China has taken concrete actions.

Vossoughi says that Michelin has been working to cut emissions in China for more than a decade, reducing its carbon footprint every year, using greener energy and transportation methods, and carrying out greener production activities. At the Michelin Guide launch event in Beijing in 2020, Michelin awarded a restaurant with a Green Star. It was the first time a Michelin Green Star was introduced in the Chinese market, with the aim of commending restaurants for their environmentally sustainable initiatives.

Witnessing China's fight against poverty

Since the 18th National Congress of the Communist Party of China (CPC), the CPC Central Committee with Xi Jinping as the core has united and led the whole party and the people of all nationalities, placing poverty alleviation in a prominent position in governing the country, and adopted many original and unique major measures, which is the largest and strongest fight against poverty organized and implemented in human history.

Vossoughi is one of the many foreigners who have witnessed changes in poor mountainous areas in China. At the end of 2020, he and his colleagues went to Yunnan. Driving from the airport for 8 hours across mountains, they finally reached a primary school in a remote village. He says: "Along the way, I have seen various road facilities and projects under construction, as the Chinese government is working to connect these remote villages to big cities. I have seen many bridges built and roads under construction. In many areas, great efforts have been made to harness rivers and to make farming easier."

Vossoughi is deeply impressed by the determination of the Chinese government to solve the problem of poverty and has also witnessed the country's development.

姓　名：Paul Devlin
中文名：德林
国　籍：英国
职　位：天山资本创始人

德林：
在上海看见未来，一个充满活力的现代城市的未来

曾有人说：如果你厌倦了伦敦，就等于你厌倦了生活。我认为在21世纪的现代中国，你也可以这样形容上海。

上海这座城市对英国人德林而言是不折不扣的"福地"，在这里，他遇到了妻子艾米并坠入爱河，成为了一名上海女婿，而后拥有了一个漂亮的女儿，事业也蒸蒸日上，更关键的是，他觉得拥有了未来。

上海把中国最好的一面展示出来

德林是银行家，也是私募股权投资者。早在20世纪90年代，他便在中国开展公司的业务。当时他住在新加坡，因为工作关系，常来中国。"投资方面的工作我做了将近30年，其中与中国合作超过了25年。"

20世纪90年代，说起亚洲总是离不开新加坡、中国香港或是东京，它们当时就是活力城市的代名词。而上海当时仿佛刚刚苏醒，"但你总能感受到这座城市和政府部门的美好愿景以及市民的活力。"德林回忆。

"我刚来上海的时候，它远不如现在先进。当时上海主要靠外资带动经济，但现在，上海已经成为世界上最大的金融中心城市之一。"2000年，德林正式踏足上海这片土地，然后，他遇见很多有趣美好的事情：爱情、婚姻，还有他终于有了属于自己的中文名字。

"我们之前搬回伦敦住了一段时间，伦敦也是一座伟大的城市，去年我们又搬回了上海。"德林说，在很多方面，上海把中国最好的一面展示了出来。

德林：

在上海看见未来，
一个充满活力的
现代城市的未来

"回到这里，你就能真正感受到这座城市的力量，感受到这座城市和人们的活力。"

"这是投资者的绝佳机会"

在上海工作、生活了这么多年，德林深深被这座城市的工作效率折服。"很多企业家都会来这里寻找市场，他们发现在这里做生意的节奏非常快，这种快节奏可以让企业迅速崛起，曾有人说：如果你厌倦了伦敦，就等于你厌倦了生活。我认为在21世纪的现代中国，你也可以这样形容上海。"

德林告诉记者，中国是一个巨大的市场，也是全球最大的市场之一，你会在这里看到企业家们创办公司的热情和勤奋工作的干劲。

2018年，中国为科技创新中小企业上市提供了更多支持，谈及这一点，德林说，他在中国目睹的最令人震惊的事情之一就是本土资本的急速增长，"所以我认为这是来自中国和外国的投资者的绝佳机会"。

德林常与一些外国朋友聊天，他们感到很困惑的一点是"为什么上海从来就没有什么缺点"。他深有感触地说："当你离开再回来上海，你可以看到上海依然保持了旧的美好，同时也混合了新的优点。上海有这么多上海人，这么多外国人。很多人来到这座城市，把这里当成自己生活的地方。那些来的人被称为新上海人，上海非常欢迎他们。每一个来到这座城市的人，都可以很快地成为整个城市的一部分，大家在这里享受生活，也发挥所长，回馈这座城市。"

你会在上海看到"未来"

今年是中国共产党成立100周年，德林充满钦佩。"看看现在中国的基础设施，比如地铁、高铁、机场，以及新的购物中心，再看中国共产党这一路走来的100年，真的是一个惊人的历程。中国人民如今的美好生活，我认为是来自中国共产党的大力推动，这种实质性的影响大家都能感受到。"

德林说，当你认真看待和思考，你会在上海看到"未来"，一个充满活力的现代城市的未来。"当你真正来到上海，看着天际线，你会发现上海正在孕育一个成为世界上伟大城市的蓝图。这里正在发生的事情，两年、三年或者五年的时间内，也许会在世界其他地方发生，这是非常令人兴奋的。"

Name: Paul Devlin
Chinese Name: 德林
Nationality: British
Position: Founder, Sky Mountain Capital

Paul Devlin:
Seeing the future in Shanghai, the future of a dynamic modern metropolis

It was said that "When a man is tired of London, he is tired of life." I think in the modern China of the 21st century, the same words also apply to Shanghai.

For Paul Devlin, a British citizen, Shanghai is "a blessed land." In this city, he met his wife Amy and fell in love, and became a son-in-law of Shanghai. He then had a beautiful daughter and rising business. He is convinced of a future for him in Shanghai.

Shanghai is showcasing the best part of China

Devlin is a banker and also a PE investor. In the 1990s, he came to China for business development. He was stationed in Singapore, but he frequently traveled to China for his company's business activities. He says: "I've been working in the investment industry for nearly 30 years, and I did China-related businesses for over 25 years."

In the 1990s, while talking about Asia, people would usually think about Singapore, Tokyo, or China's Hong Kong, which were typical cities full of vitality. At that time Shanghai was like just waking up, Devlin recalls that "but you could always feel the beautiful vision of the city held by the government agencies, and the energy of the residents."

He says: "When I first came to Shanghai, it was far from being a modern metropolis as it is now. At that time foreign investment was a major driving force behind Shanghai's economy, but now the city has become one of the largest financial centers in the world." In 2000, Devlin moved to Shanghai and then he met his love and got married, and finally got his Chinese name.

He says: "We moved back to London for a while. London is also a great city. Last year we moved back to Shanghai again." Devlin says that Shanghai showcases the best part of China. "While coming back, you can truly feel the

Paul Devlin:

Seeing the future in Shanghai, the future of a dynamic modern metropolis

power of the city, the energy of the city and its people," says Devlin.

"This is an outstanding opportunity for investors"

After working and living in Shanghai for so many years, Devlin was impressed by the efficiency of Shanghai. He says: "Many entrepreneurs would come here looking for market and they would discover that the rhythm of doing business here is very fast. This kind of speed enables fast growth for companies. It was said that 'When a man is tired of London, he is tired of life.' I think in the modern China of the 21st century, the same words also apply to Shanghai."

Devlin says that China is a huge market, one of the world's biggest, full of passionate and hardworking entrepreneurs.

In 2018, China gave more support to the listing of SMEs in the science and innovation industries. While talking about this, Devlin says that one of the most astonishing things that he has witnessed in China is the explosive growth of domestic capital. He says: "This is an outstanding opportunity for Chinese and foreign investors."

Devlin has had frequent conversations with some foreign friends and they share a similar myth about Shanghai which is "why the city has few flaws." Speaking from his own experience, Devlin says: "When you leave Shanghai and then come back, you would see that the old and nice things are still well preserved. While in the meantime, you can see that during your absence, new merits have been added to the city. There are so many people in Shanghai, and a large number of foreigners as well. Many people came here and chose to stay. These newcomers are called new Shanghainese and Shanghai warmly accepts them. Every newcomer can soon integrate into the community. People enjoy their lives here, and do what they can to give back to this city."

You can see the "future" in Shanghai

This year marks the 100th anniversary of the founding of the Communist Party of China (CPC), speaking of which Devlin is full of admiration. He says: "Just look at the infrastructure in China, such as the subway, high-speed trains, airports and new shopping malls, and then study the one hundred years' history of the CPC. It is really a great journey. I think the good living standard that the Chinese people enjoy today is achieved by the strong propelling force of the CPC, which has substantial evidence that everyone can see."

Devlin says that if you really look, you can see the "future" in Shanghai, the future of a dynamic modern metropolis. He says: "When you're on the ground of Shanghai, looking at the skyline, you can see Shanghai has a blueprint to become a world-level great city. What is happening here may be followed and copied in other places of the world after two, three or five years. This is really exciting."

Scan for videos

姓　名：Fabrice Megarbane
中文名：费博瑞
国　籍：法国
职　位：欧莱雅北亚总裁及中国首席执行官

费博瑞：
20多年来，欧莱雅见证中国人一步步实现"美好生活"

作为美妆行业的从业人员，我认为上海是一个极为优雅与充满魅力的都市，每天都给予我美的启迪。

将集团的北亚总部设在上海，连续三年高调亮相中国国际进口博览会，连着两年参加"五五购物节"，将多款产品的全球首发放在上海……全球知名企业欧莱雅愈发看重上海，而欧莱雅北亚总裁及中国首席执行官费博瑞也忙得不亦乐乎。

上海政府部门每年拜访企业

费博瑞告诉记者，两年多前，他刚来上海时，时任欧莱雅集团董事长兼首席执行官的安巩先生曾告诉他，每年地方政府都会过来看看，问问有什么可以为企业提供帮助的。费博瑞就任后有了切身体会，觉得这种政企关系有助于实现双赢。

作为欧莱雅集团的代表，安巩是上海市市长国际企业家咨询会议中的一员。上海每年都会举办上海市市长国际企业家咨询会议，上海市的领导们会倾听跨国企业CEO们提出的建议。咨询会结束后，政府会消化建议，并将其中一些落地实施。费博瑞非常赞赏这种举措，认为这是获得企业反馈的好方法，有助于打造优异的营商环境与推动国家发展。

2020年，安巩代表欧莱雅集团参加会议时提出一个构想，希望把上海打造成中国乃至全球"美好消费"的策源地。"这一建议今年得以实现，'五五购物节'举办得很成功。"费博瑞告诉记者，"美好消费"理念重视消费的质量，

费博瑞：

20多年来，欧莱雅
见证中国人一步步
实现"美好生活"

这不仅影响着人们的生活，还对社会和环境产生积极影响。

提及2020年，新冠肺炎疫情是绕不开的话题，费博瑞回顾："开局充满了不确定性，但随后公司得到了政府的大力支持，特别是静安区政府。各级地方政府与机构给了我们强有力的支持，帮助我们采取有效措施，保护团队的健康安全。"

随着工厂和分销中心重新开放，员工回到办公室正常上班，这些都帮助企业得以实现快速强劲的业务反弹。

中国是全球的"灵感源泉"

2020年，欧莱雅的业绩一路高走，实现全年27%的增长率。中国即将成为欧莱雅集团在全球最大的市场，蕴含着最大的增长潜力。此外，中国在北亚区"美妆黄金三角"中正发挥着越来越重要的影响力。

2021年，欧莱雅集团的全新地域架构中，中国上海升级为该集团北亚区总部。费博瑞称："作为美妆行业的从业人员，我认为上海是一个极为优雅与充满魅力的都市，每天都给予我美的启迪。我们进行全新的地域架构调整，将进一步以消费者为中心，把握消费者趋势。"

费博瑞说："中国消费者追求产品的质量、功效和安全，同时他们需要从美中得到启发和鼓舞。这就是欧莱雅一直把中国视为灵感之地的原因，我们可以为中国带来全球范围内的产品，也可以在这一过程中继续推动创新。"

进入中国20多年以来，欧莱雅见证了中国美妆产业的发展，也见证了中国人一步步实现美好生活。中国在欧莱雅集团看来，不仅是一个巨大的市场，更是启发他们不断创新的"灵感源泉"，因而，欧莱雅将越来越多的产品放在中国首发。

这家致力于美的企业将与"美好中国"继续共成长。

Name: Fabrice Megarbane
Chinese name: 费博瑞
Nationality: French
Position: President of North Asia Zone & CEO of L'Oréal China

Fabrice Megarbane:

Over the past 20 years, L'Oréal has witnessed the gradual realization of a "better life" for Chinese people

As a beauty professional, I think Shanghai is an extremely elegant and charming city, which inspires me with beauty every day.

It located its North Asia headquarters in Shanghai. It has taken part in the China International Import Expo for three consecutive years. It has participated in the "May 5th Shopping Festival" for two consecutive years, and it debuted a number of products in Shanghai.... L'Oréal, one of the world's leading companies, is increasingly focused on Shanghai, and its president of North Asia Zone and CEO of China, Fabrice Megarbane, is busy.

Regular visits from the Shanghai government

Megarbane says that when he first arrived in Shanghai two years ago, Mr. Jean-Paul Agon, then chairman and CEO of L'Oréal Group, told him that every year the local authorities would come to see what they could do to help the company. After taking up his post, Megarbane has had first-hand experience of how this relationship between government and business can help to achieve a win-win situation.

As a representative of L'Oréal Group, Agon is a member of the International Business Leaders' Advisory Council for the Mayor of Shanghai(IBLAC). Every year, Shanghai hosts the IBLAC, in which the city's leaders listen to the suggestions made by the CEOs of multinational companies. After the

Fabrice Megarbane:

Over the past 20 years, L'Oréal has witnessed the gradual realization of a "better life" for Chinese people

consultation, the government digests the suggestions and implements some of them. Megarbane appreciates this initiative as a good way to get feedback from companies and to help create an excellent business environment and promote the country's development

In 2020, Agon, on behalf of L'Oréal Group, proposed a vision at the IBLAC to make Shanghai the curator of "good consumption" in China and worldwide. Megarbane says: "This proposal was realized this year with the success of the 'May 5th Shopping Festival'. The concept of 'good consumption' places a premium on the quality of consumption, which not only affects people's lives but also has a positive impact on society and the environment."

When it comes to the year 2020, COVID-19 is an inevitable topic. Megarbane recalls: "It started with a lot of uncertainty, but then the company got huge support from the government, especially the Jing'an District government. Local governments and agencies at all levels have given us strong support, helping us take effective measures to protect the health and safety of our entire team."

The reopening of its factories and distribution centers and the return of employees to their offices helped the company achieve a quick and strong rebound in business.

China, a source of inspiration for the world

In 2020, L'Oréal's performance went all the way up, achieving an annual growth rate of 27%. China is about to become L'Oréal's largest market in the world and holds the greatest growth potential. In addition, China is playing an increasingly important role in the "Golden Triangle of Cosmetics" in North Asia.

In 2021, Shanghai, China was upgraded as the North Asia headquarters of L'Oréal Group in its new regional structure. Megarbane says: "As a beauty professional, I think Shanghai is an extremely elegant and charming city which inspires me with beauty every day. With our brand's new geographical restructuring, we will be more consumer-centric and more responsive to consumer trends."

Megarbane says: "Chinese consumers seek quality, efficacy and safety in their products, while they need to be inspired and motivated by beauty. This is why L'Oréal has always seen China as a place of inspiration, where we can bring a global reach to the country and continue to drive innovation in the process."

Since entering China for more than 20 years, L'Oréal has witnessed the development of China's beauty industry and the gradual realization of a better life for the Chinese people. China is not only a huge market for the L'Oréal Group but also a "source of inspiration" for their constant innovation, which is why L'Oréal is debuting more and more of its products in China.

This company committed to beauty will continue to grow with the "beautiful China."

Scan for videos

輔德里

中共二大會址紀念館

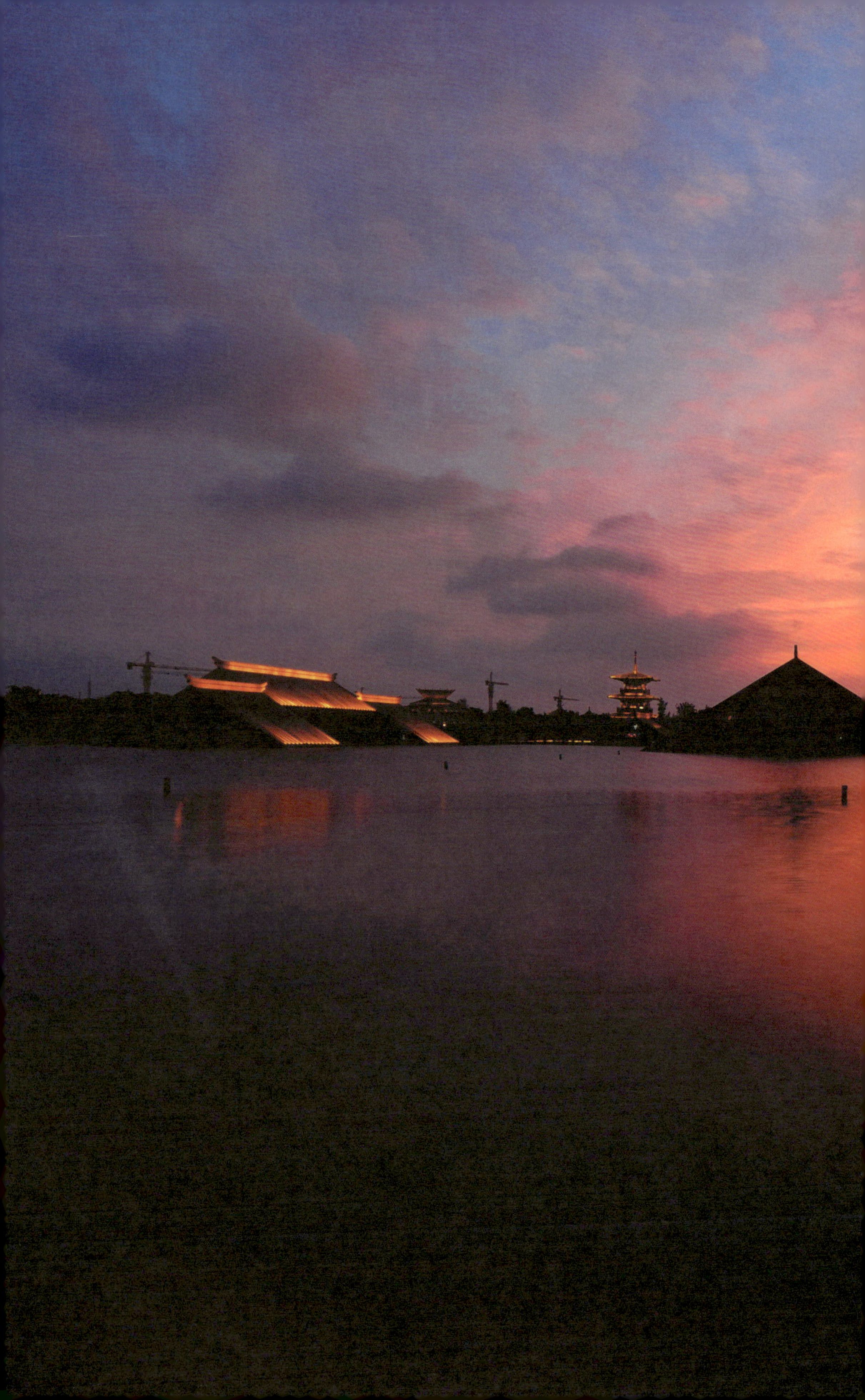

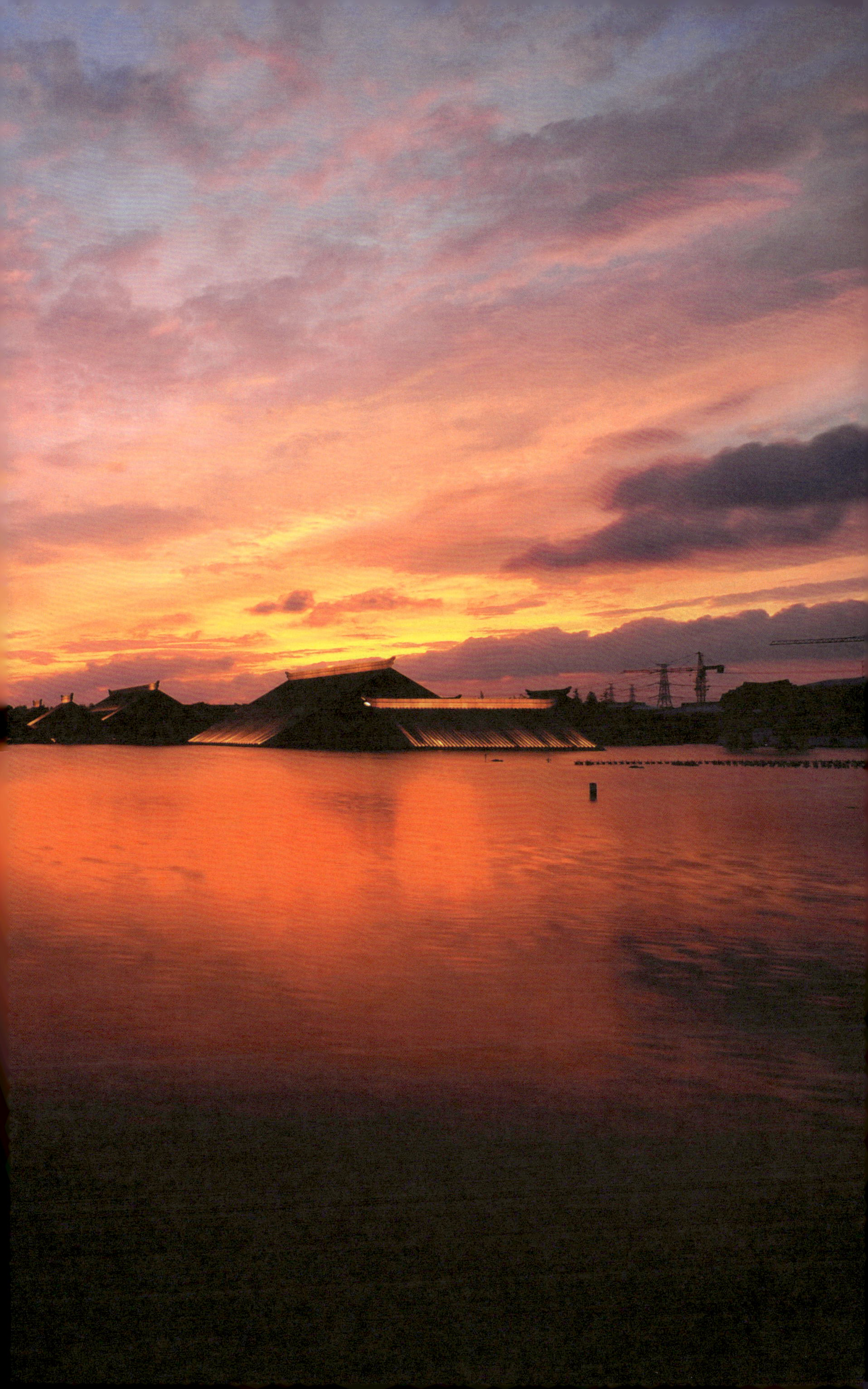

工作团队：

胡劲军　朱国顺　马笑虹　倪　珺　杜　旻　沈　良

薛慧卿　杨　江　徐轶汝　盛　盈　薛仕轩　胡彦珣

潘高峰　梅璎迪　王若弦　黄佳琪　杨　欢　屠　瑜

唐　戟　吴　健　贺　信　张　剑　萧君玮　李铭珅

孙中钦　陈炅玮　李　颖　李若楠　徐鸣慧　司徒若辰

刘力源　陶　磊　刘玉萍　郭　可　张玉双　林　岩

内容和图片、视频均由新民晚报社提供

鸣　谢：上海外国语大学翻译团队

图书在版编目（CIP）数据

百年大党：老外讲故事：汉英对照 / 上海市人民政府新闻办公室编 . -- 上海：上海文艺出版社，2021
 ISBN 978-7-5321-8040-0
 Ⅰ.①百… Ⅱ.①上… Ⅲ.①纪实文学—作品集—中国—当代—汉、英 Ⅳ.① I25
中国版本图书馆 CIP 数据核字 (2021) 第 142367 号

发 行 人：毕　胜
责任编辑：杨　婷　李　平　程方洁
摄　　影：郑宪章　邵钟瑞　袁佳青
整体设计：上海袁银昌平面设计有限公司　李　静　胡　斌

书　　名：百年大党：老外讲故事
编　　者：上海市人民政府新闻办公室
出　　版：上海世纪出版集团　上海文艺出版社
地　　址：上海市绍兴路7号　200020
发　　行：上海文艺出版社发行中心
　　　　　上海市绍兴路50号　200020　www.ewen.co
印　　刷：上海雅昌艺术印刷有限公司
开　　本：787×1092　1/16
印　　张：27.25
版　　次：2021年8月第1版
印　　次：2021年8月第1次印刷
ISBN 978-7-5321-8040-0/I.6367
定　　价：288.00元

告读者：如果发现本书有质量问题请与印刷厂质量科联系　T:021-68798999